RETRIBUTION

STARSHIP JERICHO
BOOK 4

TOBY NEIGHBORS

MYTHIC
adventure
PUBLISHING

Retribution: Starship Jericho book 4

Copyright © 2025 by Toby Neighbors

ISBN: 978-1-952260-92-6 ebook

978-1-952260-93-3 print

Mythic Adventure Publishing, LLC

Idaho, USA

CHAPTER 1

"THAT'S IT," Captain Zeke Darius said. "I can see him. Can you hear us, Master Sergeant?"

"Loud and clear, sir," Remmy replied.

"Excellent work, Ensign Stanislaus," Darius said. "Let's send for the senior officers, please."

"Aye, Captain," Alex Stanislaus said.

They were in a room with a round table. In the center, a holographic projector showed a small, highly detailed image of Master Sergeant Remmy Steel. He looked tired.

"Excellent work down there, Master Sergeant," Darius said.

He was on the *Renegade*, an alien ship that had been left abandoned in a cloud nebula for at least four hundred years. Yet, the ship was in pristine condition. The *Renegade* was bigger, faster, and more powerful than any human ship ever built. But there were some things the human engineers had to set up, like the conference call that Darius was making from orbit around the planet Casasil to the Marine still stationed on the surface.

Darius could have made the call from the Bridge, but he was about to propose something that was audacious, and he didn't want his rank to have more influence on his senior officers than normal. A captain on the Bridge of a warship was hard to say no to.

Master Sergeant Remmy Steel wasn't normally consulted by senior officers. He was only a non-commissioned officer, after all. But the crew of the *Renegade* had set off on their mission without a senior Marine officer, and Captain Darius had seen fit to let Remmy fill that role. He was the most experienced Marine and a Medal of Honor recipient to boot. In Darius' mind, that more than qualified him to weigh in on decisions.

It had been over two weeks since they left the Sol system in the *S.D.F. Jericho*. The much smaller, man-made *Jericho* had been built from plans that were furnished to the human race by GIGI, the strange alien artifact that had been hovering in the Sol system for centuries. Once the Space Defense Force built the *Jericho,* they immediately sent it to make contact with the artifact. GIGI turned out to be a sentient, non-biological device. In truth, the humans still knew very little about her. GIGI stood for Galactic Information and Guidance Instrument. She was essentially a super powerful computer with files on nearly every system in the galaxy, as well as the long history of the aliens who came from those star systems. Perhaps the most important data that GIGI carried was the Hyperspace Navigation System. GIGI had freely transferred that information to the *Jericho's* computers. She then lobbied for the crew to utilize that network to retrieve an Arodoni Power Core from a planet in a different system. The acquisition of that alien device had led them, in turn, to the nebula where they had found the *Renegade*. After spending a week exploring the alien ship, which was a marvel of design and aerospace engineering, they found themselves in the middle of a galactic war.

Going home wasn't an option. The Milky Way galaxy was firmly in the grip of the Ashi Imperium. For thousands of years, the backwater system where humanity thrived was overlooked by the powerful rulers of the Imperium. But Captain Darius was convinced that to return to the Sol system would lead the aliens straight to

Earth. It was a risk he couldn't take. But the battle in the Casa system had also convinced Darius that his small crew of just under a hundred souls, including the Special Forces platoon of Marines, couldn't continue to man the *Renegade* by themselves.

"What's it like down there?" Darius asked.

"It's busy," Remmy admitted. "There are still dozens of Ashi warriors unaccounted for."

"Enough to take over the city?" Darius asked, referring to Kipbur, the Casian capital.

"Negative sir, but the locals are terrified of the Ashi. Getting them to see that they have the upper hand isn't easy."

"I suppose not," Darius said.

The door opened to the newly appointed conference room. There were still hundreds of compartments and spaces left unused in the alien ship. None of them were small. The Arodoni had been aliens of size, and the ship had been designed in a lavish fashion to accommodate them. Darius and Ensign Stanislaus were joined by Lieutenant Vivian Ramos, the ship's Navigation specialist.

"Captain," she said, extending one of the two cups of coffee she had brought in with her.

He took a sip of the hot beverage. The warm liquid was both comforting and invigorating at the same time. One sip didn't deliver enough caffeine to affect him in a noticeable way, but his body responded to the drink from long years of experience with it. Coffee was one of the few staples that hadn't been found on the *Renegade*. She had stores of food, most of it grown or raised right on board in the long, agricultural center of the massive ship, which the crew was calling the park. It was indeed groomed like a park. There were trees, meadows, streams, walking paths, pavilions, and benches. In addition to the foliage, there were animals, too, from insects to herds of edible animals and even birds. The Arodoni had abandoned the ship for some reason. According to GIGI, it was believed they committed ritual suicide, but the humans had found no evidence of that—just an empty ship. But the *Renegade* had a host of active droids who maintained the vessel, including the park. They even harvested crops, gathered fruit and butchered animals. There were huge rooms packed with hermetically sealed pouches of food and others where meat had been packaged and frozen. It was a treasure and so well organized and maintained that nothing had gone bad. Even when the food got old, it was retrieved and processed or recycled and added to the stores of materials used to create fertilizer for the park. It was an astonishing feat. The Renegade was completely self-sufficient.

The door opened again, and two men entered who could not be more different. The first was Lieutenant Pete Best, the weapons officer. He was the youngest of the senior officers, less than thirty years old, with wavy blonde hair that he kept trimmed almost to the scalp along the sides and back of his head. With him was Lieutenant Henry Nash, the ship's chief engineer. Nash was a tall black man with broad shoulders and long limbs. He was in his early forties and had a touch of grey at his temples.

Everyone quickly found a seat. They all looked tired. No one had slept much since they entered the Casa system. It was another part of the problems plaguing the *Renegade* and exactly what Darius was hoping to remedy. But he wouldn't do it without the support of his senior officers.

"What's gone wrong now?" Pete Best asked.

"It ain't the ship," Nash said. "I just finished a complete diagnostics and everything is top-notch. I don't know how exactly, but the ship fixes itself before I can get people to the problem."

"What about the engine compartment?" Vivian asked.

"The hydrogen dioxide was vented. Don't ask me how," Nash said. "Air readings in that space come back safe."

"Wow," Pete said.

"Who ever heard of a self-correcting space vessel?" Vivian remarked.

"There's a lot to this ship we still need to discover," Darius said.

First officer, Commander Lori Lee entered the room and took a seat next to Captain Darius.

"No signs of more intruders," she announced. "The Marines just finished a fast sweep of all the major system areas. We'll need more time to search every compartment properly."

"Excellent work," Darius told her. "You've gone above and beyond, Commander."

"Damage to the flight deck has all been repaired," Nash added.

"We're lucky they didn't do worse," Lori Lee said.

Darius saw a shadow in her normally optimistic eyes. The fight against the Ashi commandos who had somehow gotten aboard the ship had left scars. It wasn't unusual for a Fleet officer to lose crew members in combat, but they didn't normally have to watch the people they were leading fight and die. Lori Lee had sought out the intruders, killing three of the aliens and wounding their leader. But she had also lost four crew members; one of them died defending her. It was the type of memory she would have to live with for the rest of her life.

"It seems we have everything in line," Darius said. "You've all performed very well."

The door swished open, and the last person they were waiting for arrived. Dr. Vinesh Lanski was a highly regarded surgeon. His presence as part of a crew their size was surprising. But everyone on the ship was battle-tested and a rising star in their own specialty. As far as Darius knew, he was the only person on the verge of retirement before being sent out to locate and acquire, if possible, the strange alien artifact deep in the Sol system.

"Doctor, how's the patient?" Darius asked.

"Alive," Dr. Lanski said. "Against all odds, he continues to breathe, and both of his hearts are beating. I have no idea what his brain activity should be, but there is activity, so I'm hopeful there will be no lasting damage."

"And Lieutenant Colt?" Darius asked, referring to the Marine officer who was brought back to the *Renegade* unconscious.

"No change," Lanski said. "He has a minor concussion and some bruising. Otherwise, he seems fine."

"Has he woken up?" Vivian asked. There was more than just casual concern in her voice. And it was no secret that she and the Marine officer were more than friends.

"Not yet," Lanski said. "I'm running a lengthy medical scan on him now. We'll figure out what's wrong eventually."

"What about Corporals Thompson and Van Winkle?" Remmy asked.

"Their wounds were treatable," Lanski said. "Thompson is patched up and recovering nicely. He'll be ready for duty in a day or two."

"And Van Winkle?"

"As you know, his arm above the elbow was shattered. I was able to fit it with an orthotic replacement and reconnect the major arteries, but the odds are high he'll have nerve damage. His recovery will take longer, several weeks maybe."

"We can't afford to lose them," Darius said. "In fact, we can't lose anyone. The battles here in the Casa system have proven that."

"Can we go back home and re-equip?" Pete Best asked.

"Any luck finding the tracking device?" Darius asked Nash.

"There are drones searching every inch of the hull, but that's a lot of real estate, sir," Nash said.

"We can't go home until we find that," Commander Lee said.

"To be honest, I don't think we can go back even after we do," Darius said softly. "That's why I've ordered this meeting. As I see it, we have two issues that need to be dealt with head-on."

"You think they can track us even without the tracking device?" Vivian asked.

"I think the risk is too great," Darius replied. "The galaxy is under the thumb of a very hostile empire. Exposing the Sol system to that threat is incredibly dangerous. But we can do something about the Imperium. This ship is more than capable of taking the fight to the Ashi."

"Except we don't have the personnel," Lori Lee pointed out.

"That's the second thing we have to deal with. What do you think about recruiting from the aliens we've met."

That brought everyone up short. For a moment, no one spoke. Then, it was Master Sergeant Remmy Steel who broke the silence.

"Captain, I think that is an excellent idea."

CHAPTER 2

THE *RETRIBUTION* WAS A NEW SHIP. The Ashi hadn't updated their technology in hundreds of years. There was simply no need. The entire known galaxy had been under their control for so long, and with no one challenging their control, there hadn't been a need to update their fleet of warships. New vessels were built, but the weapons, hyperdrive, and life support systems hadn't been updated. Still, Sheika Kahn liked being on a new ship. It was clean and spacious, not as opulent as the Emperor's flagship, but it was still comfortable.

The *Retribution* was considered a cutter, both for its speed and the simplicity of its weapons systems. The ship had one mega-laser cannon mounted right on the front of the vessel. It was a long, narrow ship, essentially a cannon mounted on the front of a hyperdrive engine, with a small crew and powerful maneuvering thrusters. A luxury cabin with a full communications suite had been installed for the Kahn, who took control of the warship and sent it to join the growing battlegroup at the Halycon system.

He sat in the master control seat. It was almost like a throne. Historically, an emperor's Kahn had very little military power. But

Sheika had never been content to simply act as a liaison between the emperor and the Prime Council. Starting first with Vang's father and then increasing his control when the young usurper murdered his parents to gain control of the Imperium, Sheika Kahn maneuvered himself into a place of power until he was second only to Emperor Vang.

"Should we proceed to the Casa system?" Shipmaster Barqus asked. He was the senior military officer in the growing battlegroup. There were nearly fifty ships gathered so far, but Kahn knew he needed more.

"No," Sheika Kahn said softly.

The other commanders were represented by holograms. They stood around the command chair where Sheika was seated. It was obvious from the looks on their faces that many thought his answer unacceptable. They imagined him weak for not rushing headlong into battle. But he had seen the Arodoni ship; they had not. He knew its incredible power. They needed a strategy to overcome it. And there were other reasons he chose to wait.

"No race in the galaxy can stand against fifty ships," another officer claimed.

"We could destroy an entire world with this fleet," Barqus announced.

"Don't be foolish," Sheika Kahn said with a wry smile. The truth was, he enjoyed putting the others in their place. "Shipmaster Krom will have seeded the hyperspace portal by now."

"So we send drones ahead of us," Basqus said. "They will clear the portal."

"And announce our arrival," Kahn pointed out. "The Arodoni would destroy half of the battlegroup the moment we dropped out of hyperspace."

"You are fearful," Basqus snarled.

Kahn leaped to his feet. It wasn't as impressive as he meant for it to be. Ulrach Sheika had served emperors and enjoyed his high station. He was no longer the young, powerful Ashi warrior he had once been. His leap was slow, his landing unimpressive as his fat rolls jiggled and his shoulders hunched. He straightened and pointed a long finger at Basqus.

"You go too far," he snapped. "I fear nothing."

"And yet you hesitate."

"We have a new enemy. It is one we have not faced for nearly a thousand years."

"Our ancestors fought the Arodoni and won!" Basqus proclaimed.

It was true, from a certain perspective. The Ashi forces had fought the Arodoni, but like much of history, the facts of those battles long ago had been skewed over time. In the archives, it was recorded that the Ashi conquered the Arodoni, but Sheika Kahn had pulled up the very oldest records of those clashes. It was true there had been battles and the Arodoni had fled, but not in defeat. Wave after wave of Ashi war ships had been sent to destroy the few Arodoni vessels. The only destruction that Sheika Kahn could find was that of the Ashi. It seemed that the Arodoni loathed fighting. Nor did the highly advanced race feel a moral obligation to help the other races, which were held firmly beneath the boot of the Ashi Imperium. Instead, they had fled, but no one knew where. The Arodoni, as powerful as they were, simply disappeared. And over time, the Ashi had changed the histories until it seemed as though they had conquered the Arodoni. Emperor Vex had declared the Arodoni extinct and made even the mention of their name a crime. But Sheika Kahn, with his access to even the most confidential of records, knew the truth.

"And our forces have fought them in recent days and lost," the Kahn said. "For now, they are contained in the Casa system. When my battle plans are ready, we will attack them. But not before we have the strength and the strategy for victory."

"Spoken like a true bureaucrat," Barqus replied.

"We have an enemy! We must fight!" Another shipmaster shouted.

"We will fight," Kahn said. "And many of you will die."

"I do not fear a glorious death," Barqus declared.

Sheika Kahn had seen ships vaporized by the Arodoni vessel. He saw no glory in that. One moment, they lived; the next, they did not. It wasn't glorious, so much as simple. And Sheika Kahn didn't want to simply throw ships full of Ashi warriors away because his commanders were impatient. With every ship lost, the Imperium was weakened. And reports were already coming in of unrest across the galaxy.

"If we are to die," Sheika Kahn said. "I wish to die in victory."

"Better to die in victory than to live with the shame of defeat," Barqus said.

It was a direct insult and aimed squarely at Sheika Kahn, who had retreated from the Casa system. There was no doubt in anyone's mind that what the Kahn had done was a calculated move. He had rushed into battle, and once Emperor Vang was engaged with the enemy, he had drawn back. It was both a cunning and diabolical quest for power. And it would have worked had the enemy murdered the emperor as the Kahn expected. Instead, they had taken Emperor Vang prisoner and that complicated matters. Sheika Kahn had failed in his first attempt to wrest control of the Imperium from Emperor Vang. Many of the commanders in the battlegroup saw that failure as a weakness. What he needed was to destroy the enemy in a spectacular fashion. And if most of his rivals were killed in the process, that was even better.

"My plan will see that the Arodoni is defeated and Emperor Vang - if he truly lives - will be liberated from their clutches," Sheika Kahn said. "There can be no victory otherwise. Rushing into battle will only endanger Emperor Vang."

"If he still lives," Barqus said.

"The Prime Council believes he does. And so we must act as though he is still alive."

No one believed that Sheika Kahn was truly loyal to Emperor Vang. But he was careful not to give them any reason to say that he wasn't.

"We have a tracker on the Arodoni ship. We will bide our time.

Let them get overconfident," Sheika Kahn said. "Then we will strike at a time and place where they cannot escape us."

It was obvious that the commanders didn't all agree with him. But Sheika Kahn was in control. The others could not challenge him while Emperor Vang lived. And once it was clear that the emperor was dead, the Kahn's agents would silence his detractors permanently. Shipmaster Basqus was at the top of that list.

CHAPTER 3

"WAIT, WHAT?" Vivian Ramos asked.

"I propose that we recruit crew members from the aliens on Casasil," Captain Darius said.

"To work the ship?" Pete Best asked.

"That's right," Darius nodded. "Look, this vessel was meant to house thousands of people. We're spread thin and overwhelmed. Even with the droids, we can't keep up with the workload of operating the *Renegade* in hostile territory."

"The Dudonus we brought on board have already volunteered to help," Commander Lori Lee said. "And they have knowledge of the Imperium that could prove vital to our survival."

"Not to mention that they are in contact with the leaders of a burgeoning rebellion," Darius continued. "I'm not proposing that we turn control of the ship over to them. But we can teach them to do the things we aren't able to do."

"And they're eager to learn," Remmy said via the holographic link. "The Casians are lining up to learn how to pilot the drones down here."

"But they're not fighters," Pete pointed out. "They said so themselves."

"That's true," Darius agreed. "They can't be Marines, but they can help us operate this ship. We haven't even begun to learn all there is to the *Renegade*. And we have more than enough resources here for many more crew members."

"I'm not sure the brass would like us sharing the technology with anyone else," Henry Nash said. "Knowledge of this ship and its technology should be proprietary."

"Under peacetime circumstances, I would agree," Darius said. "But let's face it, we didn't discover this tech. It was handed to us. We're stewards of it, not owners."

"And the Imperium has kept the galaxy in the dark," Commander Lee said. "They outlawed weapons and ships of war. These people have no way to defend themselves."

"But to what end?" Vivian Ramos said. "We're just one ship. Let's be honest. We aren't going to defeat the Imperium."

"Not without help," Darius agreed. "Which is another reason we could use their help. We need bodies and minds. We must keep the *Renegade* safe as long as possible in order to learn as much as we can from the advanced technology. And we must share it with as many other races as possible if we're to have any hope of defeating the Imperium."

"Why is that our problem?" Henry asked. "Don't get me wrong, I'm not against standing up for the weak, Captain. But, let's face it, this isn't our fight."

"That's true, but it will be eventually," Darius said. "Humanity has remained hidden in the Sol system for a long time. But every day, we work and strive to learn more with the goal of someday venturing out of our system and across the galaxy. The moment we do that, the Ashi Imperium will seek to crush us. Our people will be overwhelmed and enslaved."

"Not without a fight," Pete Best said.

"True, but you've seen what the Imperium warships are capable of. In a fair fight between the fleet back home and the Imperium, we lose."

"But we'll be more advanced by the time that happens," Vivian said. "We could take the *Renegade* home now and give humanity a boost forward."

"Again, I know you're right," Darius said. "But we can't go home without endangering humanity at the same time."

"Eventually, we will go home, though," Henry Nash said.

"Unless we die out here," Pete Best countered. "If that happens, humanity is no better off."

"But not worse off either," Darius said. "Look, I believe that we can help in the fight here. I believe we can build bonds of friendship with other intelligent races and learn from them. As soon as the tide turns in favor of liberty for the galaxy, we can go home and share what we've learned."

"In the *Renegade*?" Vivian asked.

"I don't see why not," Darius said.

"Some might argue that a ship this powerful shouldn't be in the hands of any one race," Commander Lori Lee spoke up.

"That's a consideration for another day," Darius said. "First, we have to be sure that the Ashi Imperium and their slave trade can't continue oppressing the people of the galaxy."

"That's a tall order, Captain," Henry Nash said.

"Do you disagree with it?" Darius asked.

Nash thought for a moment. "No, sir."

"Me either," Vivian spoke up. "And if bringing other races on board helps us to accomplish the mission faster, then I'm for it."

"If the volunteers agree to be under our command," Pete Best said, "I concur. But I would add one thing."

"What's that?" Darius asked.

"Everyone who comes on board should agree to come back to the Sol system with us," Pete Best said. "We can learn a lot about technology from the ship and even from GIGI, but if we're going to live with new neighbors, we should get to know them too."

"You're going to make a hell of a captain one day, Lieutenant," Darius said. "I think that's an excellent idea. Commander?"

"I say yes," Lori Lee replied.

"Then it's unanimous," Darius said. "Master Sergeant, you can begin recruiting volunteers."

"We need tech-savvy people," Henry Nash said. "And make sure they understand how to follow orders."

"Roger that," Remmy said. "From what I've seen of the people down here, that won't be a problem."

The meeting broke up, and Darius went immediately to the park and met with Ludus and Nurek. They both volunteered to help, which Darius expected would happen. He thought that once anyone was on board the *Renegade,* they would want to stay. And while Ludus seemed happy to be free, it was Nurek who had grasped the real possibilities of expanding the crew.

"Will you accept only the Dudonus and Casians aboard?" Nurek asked.

"Actually, if the rebellion you spoke of is really happening," Darius said. "We should focus on other races that could help us here."

Nurek nodded his long, conical head. "That is wise."

"Good, then you can help put together a list of the best candidates," Darius said. "Once we get enough people on board, we'll sweep the mines away from the hyperspace portal and begin recruiting."

The crew of the *Renegade* went to work preparing for the new crew members. Security protocols were put in place to keep the command section of the ship limited to Fleet personnel only. A command center was set up near the statue of the Arodoni on Epsilon deck. From there, Ensign Jacee Bertoli would be in charge of keeping track of the new recruits.

Henry Nash's engineers got busy making small lockers lined with copper and filling them with essentials in case of another EMP attack. Weapons were also distributed to key locations on the ship and secured with old-fashioned numeric combination locks.

The ship was burning through the raw materials it had on hand and Ensign Alex Stanislaus began making a list of things that would be needed for a longer cruise, from metals to rare elements. They used the gravity beam to retrieve the Ashi troop carrier that had been damaged and abandoned. With careful use of the *Renegade's* lasers, they cut the alien ship into pieces, which were brought into the Arodoni ship via the open mouth. From there, the automated industrial refining plant would break down the metals and reusable materials into specific elements. The refining plant was more sophisticated than anything humanity had built. Gases and water could be collected too. Asteroids orbiting through the star system could be hauled in and gobbled up to collect iron, nickel, cadmium, and lithium. It was a fascinating system that would take years, maybe even decades, to understand fully. But the results were simple to comprehend and put into use.

They built everything they needed using the industrial plant's three-dimensional printer. The parts were then checked over by auto-mated assembly drones and put together to make whatever was needed, from guns to tools to copper plating designed to fit perfectly inside the metal containers already on hand. They made flashlights that could be strapped onto a human's head, along with the elastic band and batteries. It was all run by the ship's computer, which was powerful enough to keep tabs on all the ship's systems and still have enough computing power to design and build whatever was needed by the crew.

With his crew busy preparing for what he thought of as the next stage of their mission, Captain Zeke Darius turned his attention to the three remaining enemy ships. They were still running for the edge of the system heliosphere. What they planned to do there was anyone's guess. As Zeke settled into his captain's chair, he asked about the enemy ships.

Pete Best was the only senior officer on duty at the moment.

Darius was glad that his officers were getting some rest. He had personally snatched a few hours here and there but never more than four hours at a time. It was difficult on him, but a steady stream of coffee kept him focused and alert.

"Sir, we're keeping tabs," Pete Best said. "Tango Six is two hundred, sixteen million kilometers away, Tango Eleven is closer to three hundred million, and Tango Two is traveling nearly half the speed of light, sir. That's around four hundred sixty million kilometers and climbing."

"What does your computer system tell you about targeting them?"

"We have straight fields of fire, although they're all in different directions, Captain."

"Let's run a test," Darius said. "Lock laser cannons in firing position."

"Aye, Captain, locking lasers into position," Pete Best said.

There were other crew members on the Bridge and in the Systems Control room, which carried an audio feed from the Bridge at all times. Darius lifted his coffee mug and sipped the scalding liquid. It felt good to his tired body and he sometimes wondered if he were to be cut open if there would be coffee running through his veins. He dismissed the idea and focused his weary mind on the task at hand.

"Target Tango Six, if you please, Lieutenant."

"Aye, Captain, targeting Tango Six."

"You said it was two hundred million kilometers distant?"

"Aye, sir, and climbing, although she's moving the slowest of the three."

"What's its speed?"

"A little over four million kilometers per hour, sir."

It was hard to gauge the speeds and distances. It had been a little over fifty-four hours since the space battle ended, and the three enemy ships started running. In that time they had managed to build massive speeds. No ship in the Earth fleet - not even the *Jericho* - could run so far, so fast.

"Can we hit it from here?"

"Yes, sir. In theory, we can, Captain."

Darius didn't care for theory when it came to a ship's capability. So far, the *Renegade* had surpassed all their wildest expectations, but he needed to know what she could really do.

"Laser capacity?" He asked.

"Cannons are fully charged, Captain. Ready to fire on your command."

"One cannon, eighty percent power," Darius said. "Nav control, can we get a better picture of the target?"

The ship had long-range telescopic cameras that would have been the envy of any astronomy program in the Sol system, but the alien ships had cut their running lights. The only visible sign of the enemy ships was the exhaust from their engines as they fled from the Arodoni vessel.

"Doing my best, Captain," a Petty Officer at the navigation station said.

The view on the high-resolution holographic display of the plot zoomed in on the alien ship until it hovered over the bridge. It looked so real Darius thought he could reach out and touch it.

"Fire at will, Lieutenant," Darius said.

"Foxtrot one, eighty percent," Pete Best said.

There was a flash of light and then, through the Bridge's canopy, Darius saw a beam streaking through space. He knew the speed of light was just under three hundred thousand kilometers per second. It would take the laser 720 seconds, or twelve minutes, to reach the enemy ship. That was enough time to alter course, maybe, if the Ashi warriors commanding the ship knew they were being fired on. Everything from scanners to radar operated within the speed of light. Which meant that the report of the laser firing might not reach the aliens any faster than the laser beam. And that wasn't factoring in the ship's progress. If its speed remained constant, it would be another eight hundred thousand kilometers distant by the time the laser reached it.

"What's the curve of energy loss?" Darius asked.

He knew the farther the laser had to travel, the less effective it would be.

"Sir, that's impossible to know," Pete Best said. "I don't think we have instruments that could read the amount of energy released when we fire the cannons."

"I guess we'll just have to see what happens," Darius said. "Let's turn and target Tango Eleven, if you please, Mister Wilkins."

The Petty Officer at the engineering station took hold of the small thruster controls and began to swing the ship around.

"Aye, Captain, bringing us around two hundred, nine degrees on a horizontal elliptic."

"Very good. Lieutenant Best, what is Tango Eleven's speed?"

"They are at five point five million kilometers per hour, sir."

They waited and watched. The distances were so vast that every-thing seemed to be happening in slow motion, which only made Darius' weariness seem even more potent. The battle had been at closer proximity and the laser had hit the targets in just a few seconds, if not almost instantly. But with their targets now literally days away from them, they would have to wait longer.

"Target acquired, Captain," Pete Best said.

"Fire at will," Darius said as he took another sip of coffee.

"Foxtrot two, eighty percent power."

He couldn't believe how casual it seemed to be fighting an enemy. They were too far away to be a threat, but the *Renegade* could still strike them down. GIGI had said the range on the Arodoni lasers would reach across a star system. So far, the alien artifact had been exactly right.

Another flash of light, and for a moment, Darius watched in drowsy fascination. The laser beams were deadly but also hypnotizing.

"Bring us to bear on the last of the ships," Darius ordered.

The ship turned, and Pete Best locked onto the final ship.

"She's really moving, sir."

"Time to target?" Darius said.

"Twenty-five minutes," Pete replied.

"Fire," the captain ordered.

"Foxtrot three, eighty percent," the weapons officer replied.

"What's the status on Tango Six?" Darius asked.

"The laser should have reached her, sir," one of the crew members said.

"It'll take another twelve minutes for the information about what happened to reach us," Pete Best said.

Twelve minutes didn't seem like a long time to wait. One of the crew members brought up timers so they would know when the information about each of their targets would be available. When the first timer reached zero, they knew the laser had impacted the alien ship. In the distance, there was a tiny flash of light and then darkness. The close-up of the alien ship that had been on the plot suddenly disappeared. There was nothing left that was big enough to be seen by the naked eye.

"Whoa!" Someone said softly.

Darius was thinking the same thing, although he managed to keep from saying it out loud.

"Total destruction, Captain," Pete Darius said. "Eighty percent power at over two hundred million kilometers distant."

"I guess now we know," Darius replied.

The damage to the second ship was just as impressive. It was nearly half an hour later when the third laser seemed to reach its target. They didn't see a flash in the distance like the other two ships. The damage to the vessel was catastrophic but not total destruction. Only half of the ship disappeared. The rest spun away as gas and debris spilled out through space.

"Still a kill shot," Pete Best said.

"Indeed. What was the total distance?" Darius asked.

"Nearly six hundred million kilometers."

"Note it all in the log," Darius ordered. "Effective range and output percentages. That could be vital information the next time we run into Imperium ships."

Captain Darius got to his feet. He had been awake too long. Everything was fuzzy. He could put his own needs off no longer.

"Lieutenant Best, you have the con," Darius said.

"Aye, Captain, I have the con."

"Wake me if anything changes," he ordered.

"Yes, Captain. Get some good rest, sir."

Darius left the Bridge and walked slowly toward his cabin, wondering how many Ashi warriors and crew members they had just killed.

CHAPTER 4

REMMY WAS A BUSY MAN. After helping the Casians attach the remote-controlled machine guns to a pair of drop ships and training them to fly them, he had immediately begun recruiting for the *Renegade*. It was a big job, not just because there were so many volunteers, but the six-legged pachyderms were so incredibly different from humans. Staff Sergeant Laila McPherson was the only other human left on Casasil, and together, they were trying to decide how to narrow down the applicants.

"How many does Captain Darius want?" Laila asked as they huddled together in the command tent near the electric-powered heater as snow fell in heavy, pink clumps outside. There was already a foot of snow on the ground and no end in sight to the storm.

"As many as we can get, I suppose," Remmy said.

"So why not take them all?"

"You and I both know what happens to people in space," Remmy said. "Homesickness, claustrophobia, physical ailments, short tempers, it's a difficult environment."

"True, but that's for Fleet ships and human transports," she pointed out. "The *Renegade* is completely different. It's spacious, luxurious even. I don't think we'll have the same problems that the Fleet has with raw recruits. And these people have a knack for remote piloting."

"I agree, but are they ready to fight?" Remmy asked. "So many of them are simply terrified of the Ashi."

"Can't blame them for that," she replied. "Conquest is all they've ever known. Can you imagine one empire lasting for thousands of years?"

"No," Steel said. "I can't."

"It's going to take some time to disabuse these people of the idea that the Ashi are unstoppable."

Remmy knew she was right. The elders of the Casian capital had reacted strongly when Remmy showed them video footage of the Ashi being defeated in battle. Thousands of the aliens had died and the humans had only six casualties: two dead, three wounded, and one mental break; still, in Remmy's mind, that was a heavy toll to pay. What had happened to Lieutenant Colt was still a mystery, and there was no guarantee that he would recover. That left the responsibility for the *Renegade's* Marine platoon squarely on Remmy's shoulders. And he feared what might happen to the ship if they recruited Casians who couldn't handle the pressures of warfare.

There were other species on Casasil that had volunteered to help on the *Renegade*. Ludus had recruited over thirty Dudonus who had been captured by slavers. Those aliens owed the humans their lives and yet Remmy didn't want volunteers who signed up out of a sense of obligation. What they needed were young beings who truly believed in the mission of the *Renegade*. Only it was hard to find them when Remmy could scarcely communicate that mission himself.

Why were the humans involved in a galactic war they had known nothing about a month ago? In his mind, it went back to GIGI. The mysterious alien artifact had manipulated them. He didn't like that term, manipulation, but it was the best way to describe what happened. GIGI had presented them with opportunities they could not turn down. What seemed like a boon to the human race had led to war … and it was no mystery what the alien artifact was doing. GIGI had admitted that her creators had sent her to the Sol system based on the fact that humans were a violent species with a long history of warfare. They were the soldiers the galaxy needed to stand against the Ashi. Only Remmy feared that there was a lot more to the alien masters of the Galactic Imperium than had been seen so far. The Ashi who reached Casasil had fought without any real strategy. They were clearly dependent on superiority in numbers and fire-power, but Remmy feared that would change. And without any hope of reinforcements, the tiny Special Forces platoon could make no mistakes in battle with their new enemy without being wiped out. Which was why he was nervous about the new alien recruits he was trying to sort through. If they picked the wrong volunteers, it could be catastrophic to the *Renegade,* which he was thinking more and more of as home.

"None of them are really suited to be Marines," Remmy said.

"Is that true or do I detect a bit of xenophobia there?" She grinned.

Remmy didn't reply immediately. In fact, he would have been angry if anyone else had accused him of being racist. But if Remmy was certain of anything, it was that Laila McPherson was on his side. He was falling in love with her. She was the most interesting, amusing and like-minded person he had ever known. Plus, she was the only other NCO left in their tiny Spec Ops platoon. She had recognized the burden of leadership that had fallen to Remmy and quickly stepped up to help him carry the load. Romantically, their time alone on Casasil had been intoxicating even if there wasn't much personal time to be shared. There were still small bands of Ashi being rounded up on the planet and once the word had gone out for volunteers, more and more aliens had arrived at Kipbur every single day, wanting to join the crew of the *Renegade.*

"Probably," Remmy finally admitted. "It's hard to imagine how they could fit in."

"They can't," she said softly. "Stop trying to make them fit into a human platoon. They'll need their own kind around them. They'll need species-specific weapons and training. If we can provide them with that, we could build an army."

"Are you serious?"

"Yeah," Laila said. "They're strong. If we designed weapons and armor for them, I think they could be effective fighters."

"And where would we get these weapons and armor?"

Laila shrugged, and Remmy felt a tug on his heart. There were moments when she did the most simple things and yet, he felt so much affection for her that it made him emotional.

"Lieutenant Colt designed a MECH on the *Renegade*. I think, with a little effort, we could create some weapons that would be ideal for the Casians. There's plenty of space on board to train them, too."

"Alright," Remmy said. "Put on your drill instructor cap and go to work. You select volunteers for the Marines; I'll select those for the ship's crew."

She agreed, and they spent the next hour creating a checklist of things to look for in every recruit, from age to aptitude, physical strength and even family support. Every volunteer needed to understand that they were going to war and that fact had to be clear in their minds. In war, there was no guarantee of going home. Remmy and Laila knew that full well.

"You ever think of what it will be like to go home?" Laila asked later that night after they had finished clearing nearly two hundred volunteers for service on the *Renegade*.

"I hope it's like this," he said

They had pushed their cots together near the heater in their large tent. The cold temperatures were pressing in, and while the city officials had volunteered to let the Marines stay in the big buildings inside the city, Remmy and Laila preferred to stay in the tent near their equipment. Where they could be alone.

"I don't mean us," Laila said. "That isn't going to change or you're going to have a problem on your hands, mister."

"The only change I see with us is perhaps making an honest woman out of you."

"Marriage?" Laila asked, then stifled a laugh. "We'll have to survive long enough."

"If we do, would you consider becoming Mrs. Remmy Steel?"

"Don't ask me that until you're really asking me to marry you," she said. "And if you're asking now, the answer is no."

"No?"

"No."

"Why not?"

"Because," she said. "I want you focused on just one thing, Master Sergeant."

"Yes, ma'am," he said, giving her a light squeeze.

They both liked to talk and joke about the future, but they were combat marines and they both knew how precious life was. There were no guarantees in war.

"I was asking about life in the Sol system," she said. "Do you think you could ever go back to a Fleet ship after being on the *Renegade*?"

"It even makes the *Jericho* seem like a dump in comparison," Remmy admitted. "Casasil, too. I don't think I've even imagined a world this beautiful."

"It isn't crowded like Earth or barely hospitable like Mars," she agreed.

"Honestly, I think it's going to be hard," Remmy said. "But I would go anywhere and do anything to be with you."

"You know how to sweet talk a woman," Laila said. "We'll probably all be court-martialed and kicked out of the Corps."

"Not everyone, just the leadership," Remmy said. "I guess that's me. There's a record of my agreement with the Captain to leave the Sol system and fight the Ashi."

"So maybe we don't go back," she said. "I mean, if the war ends, and we're still alive, maybe we just disappear."

"Plenty of space on a world like this for a couple to get lost in," Remmy admitted.

It was a pleasant fantasy. He fell asleep, imagining just the two of them on a verdant world budding with natural resources. In his mind, they built a little cabin and raised a family together, far away from the crowded conditions in the Sol system and where war was just a memory.

CHAPTER 5

"CAPTAIN ON DECK!" Commander Lori Lee announced.

Everyone rose from their seats and saluted.

"As you were," Darius told them. "What's the status from Casasil?"

"Master Sergeant Steel is on his way up with the last of the recruits," Commander Lee said. "We've got a hundred and twenty new Casian volunteers and a total of thirty-eight Dudonus. We'll be getting everyone settled and assigned for training in the next few hours."

"Lieutenant Nash, how is the ship looking?"

"We're green across the board, Captain. All systems are in optimal condition."

"What about resources for our new crew members?" Darius asked.

"I've already gotten updates," Ensign Alex Stanislaus said. "The *Renegade's* former occupants were not physically all that different from the Casians, Captain. They're able to move right into the apartments on the port side of the park, two and three to a domicile. We've got plenty of room, sir. And Nurek has made some requests for the

Dudonus, which are being implemented as we speak by the ship's autonomous maintenance droids."

"Food?" Darius asked.

"We have everything we could need," Commander Lee said. "And we'll be assigning a few of the new crew members from each species to oversee their unique culinary preferences."

"Navigation, do we have a course laid in for the hyperspace portal?"

"Aye, Captain, course is set, as is the hyperspace route to our next location, the Olotimbo system."

Olotimbo was an inhabited system with two separate planets where life was supposed to be flourishing. Of course, Darius only knew what he had read in the *Renegade's* computer logs and what Nurek had told him as the course was set for the free worlds at the edge of the galaxy. The plan was to make a run from the Casa system to the free worlds, a group of little-known, barely habitable planets with very few resources. Refugees with the means had fled from worlds laid waste by warfare and stripped by slavers to the free planets, which had managed to avoid the attention of the Imperium for many years. They were supposed to be a safe haven and perhaps a place where more volunteers could be found. But first, they had to get there ... and the trip would not be an easy one.

There was no direct route to the free worlds. The most conventional path passed through heavily populated systems where the Imperium would undoubtedly have a strong presence. In the days following the decision to recruit volunteers from Casasil, there were discussions of the best course of action for the *Renegade*. The idea of popping into populated worlds and wreaking havoc before fleeing back through hyperspace had been discussed. Earth's long, violent history was rife with examples of terrorism, from people groups who felt oppressed by those in power to zealots who sacrificed themselves in the name of their false gods. But there were very few examples of successful terrorism, and it wasn't in the best interest of the galaxy to harm the innocent. Instead, the decision had been made to run through smaller, less important systems, doing what could be done to help those worlds they passed until they could reach the free planets and regroup.

It was Darius' hope that, along the way, they could properly ascertain the true strength of the Imperium. He had no qualms about fighting, but without reliable intelligence, it seemed foolish to draw the Imperium's ire. Not that they hadn't already done that, but Darius wouldn't go looking for a fight until he knew his enemy's strength and could find the best space to fight in. Ideally, the *Renegade* could find a place and a way to draw their enemies in but still have a route of escape should the need to retreat arise. All his martial training was based on the idea of harnessing as many advantages in battle as possible. The *Renegade* and her crew were alone in their fight since the Imperium had long ago restricted weapons to the Ashi military forces. No other species had the means to wage war on the Imperium. But Darius was certain that others would join the humans in their struggle against the Ashi, and with every volunteer who was willing to risk their lives in the fight, the *Renegade* became stronger.

"As soon as we get the volunteers on board we should make for the portal," Darius ordered. "I'm going down to meet with the Marines and help ensure that we get the new crew members settled. Until I return, Lieutenant Ramos has the con."

"Aye, Captain," Vivian said. "I have the con."

Darius got to his feet and smoothed his uniform shirt. The walk from the Bridge to the armory, which had been moved from the commercial section of the ship, took a full twenty minutes. The Captain didn't rush. The long distances through the *Renegade* were unusual for a Fleet vessel, but he used the transit time to get his thoughts in order. The armory was in a storage compartment the size of a department store on Alpha deck near the gravity lift that led down to the empty hangar that had been transformed into a shooting range and training area by the Marines. By the time he arrived, Master Sergeant Steel and Staff Sergeant McPherson were back on board the ship, too.

"Glad to have you back, Master Sergeant," Darius said as they shook hands.

"Yes, sir. Glad to be back on board," Remmy replied.

"You did well recruiting new volunteers."

"That was mainly Staff Sergeant McPherson, sir. I can't really take much credit."

"You get the credit for supporting the idea," Darius told him.

"It was a good idea, Captain. And, we've had a few ideas of our own."

"Enlighten me, Master Sergeant."

"My pleasure, sir, but again, I should say that the majority of this is from Staff Sergeant McPherson. She will be better suited to explain the details."

"Give me the basics."

"Well, sir, it seems to us that the Casians aren't as helpless as it might seem, sir. They are certainly willing to join the fight. If we could design the right gear, they could become competent Marines on the battlefield."

"We need all the help we can get just manning the ship," Darius said. "How many of our new volunteers were you thinking of converting to Marines?"

"Ten or twelve, maybe," Remmy said. "We can get them into fighting shape down here. Once the weapons and armor are designed and fabricated, we'll incorporate them and see what we can do. If it works for the Casians—"

"It might work with other races," Darius interrupted. "That's not a bad idea at all. If we're going to fight the Imperium, we could use an army."

"The Casians look different, sir. It took me a while to wrap my head around things. But they have an aptitude for technology. Their trunks are very tactile and they took to flying the drones like it was second nature to them."

"That's good to hear. We'll double everyone up between ship

duty and battle stations," Darius said. "The drones increase our martial capabilities exponentially."

"Agreed," Remmy said. "They were invaluable on Casasil."

"Move ahead with the idea, but I also need your people to serve as defacto security personnel."

"You expect trouble, sir?"

"Maybe not from the volunteers, but this will be the first time most of the humans have been around aliens. Let's not assume that everyone has an open mind."

"Roger that, sir. We'll take care of it. Any word on Lieutenant Colt's condition?"

"I checked on the way down here," Darius said softly. "Dr. Lanski thinks he is in some sort of coma. There appears to be a foreign agent in his body. They picked it up on one of the scans."

"A virus?"

"No," the captain said, keeping his voice down so that no one else heard him. "We've been fortunate so far. No diseases from Casasil or the beings you all interacted with. This seems to be more like a parasite. I don't have any more details than that. I'll be getting a full debrief from the doctor soon. For now, the point I'm trying to make is that you're in charge of the Marine detail. All higher orders will come through you. I need you to keep everyone focused on the goal."

"I can do that, sir," Remmy said.

"I have no doubt about that, Master Sergeant. We'll be settling the new volunteers in and then orienting them once we make the jump into hyperspace. We're still a few hours away from that, so get your people ready, and let's keep a rotation through the park, residential, and commerce areas. We aren't going to open the R&D section yet, and the volunteers will need training before going into the engineering spaces. Also, the manufacturing and command sections are off limits to anyone but human personnel for the time being."

"Copy that. I'll have my people ready."

"Very good, Master Sergeant. I'll leave you to it."

Darius walked away and took the gravity lift up to the park. He looked across the vast expanse of agricultural space and breathed deeply. On the port side of the park, he could see the Casians moving about on the balconies of the apartments. They looked like strange elephants to Darius. Not that he had ever seen a real elephant, only pictures and videos of the endangered pachyderms. But there was something familiar about the aliens. They had wide, flappy ears, thick skin, and long trunks, just like an elephant. Darius was too far away to see their eyes. Still, he would have thought of them as animals, not an intelligent species, if not for the Marines who had interacted with them on Casasil.

It truly was a new world. He hoped that his crew was ready for it. He hoped that he was. Only time would tell.

CHAPTER 6

NUREK WAS PLEASED. He had established a cultural center for the Dudonus on board the *Renegade*. The human furnishings fit his own people well enough. There were tables, chairs, food bins, and beverage containers. The humans knew almost nothing of the other races, but the ship had detailed files on the Dudonus, including what they enjoyed eating and drinking. All he had needed to do was designate the commercial space. It was on Zeta deck, one story above the main floor, which the humans called Epsilon. In time, he planned to get some of the most notable artifacts from the ship's archives that were representative of the Dudonus culture. There were books, sculptures and paintings that could be replicated by the ship's industry devices. Connor O'Dell had spoken of it, although that section of the ship was, for the time being, restricted. It could be produced and delivered to the appropriate space with a computer command. The efficiency of the Arodoni ship was stunning.

The human crew, on the other hand, were less impressive. In many ways, they reminded Nurek of the Ashi. Their confidence and demeanor were so much like his former overlords that he had balked at the idea of helping them. But the prophecies were true, at least as much of them as he knew. Deliverance was coming through the work of the Correll, at least according to the humans. The Galactic Information and Guidance Instrument was, like certain vital parts of the Arodoni ship, off-limits to him. He bristled at the restriction, but he was a patient person. The humans were no worse than the Ashi and he could outwait them if he had to. And there was still much that could be learned from the parts of the ship that his fellow Dudonus had access to. And if he was being honest, the advanced technology of the Arodoni ship was secondary to the liberation of his people throughout the galaxy.

Once the Imperium was overthrown, Nurek would turn his attention to the human problem. If they were lucky, the humans wouldn't be a problem. Perhaps they would go back to their own star system never to be heard from again. He doubted that, but it was possible. Nurek would advocate to have the technology of the Arodoni shared throughout the galaxy. If the humans refused, it would be dealt with. They were an interesting and industrious race but incredibly limited in their range of knowledge. Outside of martial interests, they seemed to know very little. Perhaps that was due to the fact that he was only dealing with professional warriors, but he didn't think they could know much coming from an undiscovered system on the outer fringe of the galaxy.

The door to the cultural center swished open and three of Nurek's brethren entered, led by Ludus. They bowed and Nurek bowed in return.

"Brother," Ludus said, "may I present Morduc and Yolah."

"It is a pleasure," Nurek said.

"You are at work already?" Yolah said, looking around the room.

"A place for our kind to gather and take leisure," Nurek said.

"An excellent idea," Morduc said. "I have lived in isolation for many years."

"It was not safe to gather with other Dudonus," Ludus pointed out. "I hope that is changing."

"At least while we are on this ship, we may bond," Nurek said.

"What is more, there is much of our history stored in this ship's computers."

"Are we free to review it?" Yolah asked.

"Free indeed," Nurek said. "In fact, we will produce some of the artistic works from our forebears for this space. The human crew is generous with the ship's resources."

"Humans," Morduc said. "I have never heard of this race."

"No one has," Ludus replied.

"But they were known to some," Nurek said. "The Correll knew enough to send their Guidance Instrument to their star system."

"The Imperium was foolish to exterminate the Correll," Morduc said.

"Or," Nurek interjected, "maybe the Correll were foolish not to find a way to co-exist. The Imperium will not last forever. And we have found a way to endure."

"They made their choice," Yolah said. "We can only honor their courage."

Nurek wasn't sure it was courage to die rather than bend the knee. In many ways, the Correll were just as stubborn and foolish as the Ashi. Neither was willing to yield, and both would pay the price for their stubbornness.

"Where are we going?" Ludus asked.

"I am helping to guide the ship's route to the free worlds," Nurek said.

"The free worlds are a myth," Morduc said.

"Untrue, brother. They exist."

"Has anyone ever seen them?" Yolah asked.

"None who reach the free worlds have returned," Ludus said.

"Not true, I have contacts who have successfully been to the hidden systems," Nurek said. "They have been gathering resources for generations."

"For war?" Ludus asked. "They can't possibly believe they can defeat the Imperium."

"No, they will not attack. But they have defensive systems in place," Nurek said. "And contacts on hundreds of worlds. The resistance will be coordinated from the Free Worlds. Libertine, to be exact."

"And that's where we're going?" Yolah asked.

"Eventually," Nurek said. "The plan, as far as I understand it, is to meander through the galaxy, stopping in some strategic star systems and fighting the Imperium forces wherever they may be found."

The three newcomers looked at Nurek with wide eyes. It was a clear sign of fear. The Dudonus were known for avoiding dangerous situations. Fighting simply wasn't in their DNA. It was part of what made them such valued slaves. Once in captivity, they would never resist their master's rule. That, combined with their long life spans and need for very little rest, made them ideal servants.

"Do not fear," Nurek continued. "The humans will do the fighting ... and the technology on this ship is second to none."

"But it is still just one ship," Morduc pointed out.

"One ship that defeated twenty Ashi battle cruisers," Nurek pointed out.

"You were with the human warriors during the attack?" Yolah asked.

"No, we were touring the ship," Ludus said.

"The humans fared well," Nurek said. "Not perfect, but good enough to ensure success."

"And you feel confident that they can challenge the Imperium with just one ship?" Morduc asked.

"No," Nurek said. "I do not expect them to win a war. It is my hope that they can disrupt the Imperium enough that other worlds will join the rebellion. If we can cause enough chaos, it is possible that the Prime Council will fall."

"For how long?" Yolah asked. "The Ashi will never give up."

"There are weapons on this ship that can destroy entire worlds," Nurek said, leaning close and speaking quietly. "I will not rest until the Imperial Core worlds are nothing but radiated ash."

CHAPTER 7

SHEIKA KAHN WAS the new Commander In Chief of the entire Ashi military. But he was still the Emperor's Kahn, with duties that included keeping tabs on hundreds of worlds. Over the years, he had built a strong network of spies who fed him useful information so that he was rarely caught off guard. And while he waited for the rest of his battle group to assemble, he focused on the reports coming in from dozens of Imperial worlds.

There were signs of unrest throughout the galaxy. It wasn't surprising to Sheika Kahn. He was a plotter who had spent most of his adult life pulling strings behind the scenes to get the outcomes he desired. It didn't matter what faction of the Prime Council claimed the credit as long as the Kahn got his way. In most matters, he had worked to ensure that the Emperor remained the most powerful sovereign in the galaxy, but at times, he also tweaked events that were in his own favor. From amassing a fortune, to propelling his career until he was ready to step into the Emperor's boots himself, Ulrech Sheika Kahn had manipulated and maneuvered himself through the vacillating halls of power until he was at the pentacle of success. He wasn't about to let a few dustups on backwater planets keep him from taking the throne.

An urgent message from Hurz, one of the Prime planets, popped up on his screen. It was marked with the highest level of importance and secrecy. With a gesture, the message opened. It was a video projected by a hologram unit built into the ceiling directly in front of his command chair. The image of Bul'Gasy, an insectile being with a broad back and tiny, round eyes, appeared. At the same time, walls rose up around the Kahn, ensuring his protection and privacy before the Top Secret message could be played.

"My Lord," the Hurzian said, bowing his stiff, rotund body as if he were really in front of Sheika Kahn instead of across the galaxy on a core world with billions of other Hurzians, "there is vital news you must know. Nic'Tal, illustrious representative to the Prime Council, has been assassinated. The news has not broken wide yet but my source within her palace has confirmed the death. Nic'Tal was murdered in her sleep. Someone drove a ceremonial dagger into her carapace. It is believed that her Dudonus slave was involved. He cannot be found, but there is no proof. The Council do not have surveillance in their private quarters. The weapon was cleaned of any residual forensic evidence that would prove guilt beyond all doubt.

"I assume my Lord knows that there have been demonstrations on all the core planets. On Hurz, those protests have become violent at times. Nic'Tal's staff believe news of her death would only make things worse. They will keep the assassination a secret for now, but your presence will be requested soon. Without the Emperor, no new representative can be appointed, as you are already aware."

The hologram stopped, and the image of the Hurzian vanished, but Sheika Kahn did not immediately press the button that would lower the privacy walls. He needed time to think. There were protests and outright rebellions on more worlds than he could keep track of. News of Emperor Vang's capture had emboldened the enemies of the Imperium. Sheika Kahn did not blame them. While many might preach for reform, even succession from the Empire, what the leaders of these squabbles really wanted was more influence, riches and advancement within the Imperium's bloated bureaucracy. It was what he would have done in their place. A good politician knew how to take advantage of every opportunity.

But outright rebellion was something else. Assassination of a sitting representative of the Prime Council was unheard of. Not that the rich and powerful on all five core worlds didn't fight over the appointment, which could only be made by the Emperor. Yet murdering a representative, especially at a time when the Imperium faced its first true threat in hundreds of years, could not be a coincidence. Nor was it simply a quest for power. Someone, somewhere, was encouraging Imperium worlds to shake off the shackles that had bound them for millennia. And it was up to Sheika Kahn to root out that source and bring them to justice.

Normally, he would send an armada of warships to frighten the unruly back into line. But military vessels were restricted from entering the galactic core. And Sheika Kahn needed every ship he could muster. The Arodoni vessel was without equal in battle. He was an Ashi warlord from a long line of powerful warriors, and yet he had never seen or heard of such a ship as the Arodoni vessel. He would not engage the aliens without overwhelming firepower, not just on his personal ship, *the Retribution,* but with a host of battleships. There must be no chance of the alien vessel out-fighting his forces. They would soon be assembled. Then, they could track down and destroy the Arodoni. If Emperor Vang died with the aliens, Sheika Kahn thought, so much the better.

Another report pinged in his message queue. It was from a minor planet called Hismania. Rioters there had slaughtered the government outpost in one city and set the buildings on fire. Other government officials were requesting immediate evacuation. There were eight government employees killed and nearly sixty locals dead as protests turned violent. Hismania had only a token military presence, and according to the report many of the local law enforcement personnel had joined in the growing revolt. But it was of little concern to Sheika Kahn. Planets like Hismania served a purpose and would be brought to heel easily enough. One division of Ashi warriors would cow the protests and any protesters that turned violent would be publicly executed. They would lose some government officials but every herd needed culling from time to time. Sheika Kahn thought of the bureaucrats as little more than cattle. They had a purpose, yet they were easily replaced.

The priority wasn't quelling unrest across the galaxy. One didn't chase the symptoms of a problem but rather searched out the root cause. Sheika Kahn had no doubt that the root cause of his problems was the alien warship. He would track it down and destroy it. Once news spread of the military's great victory, the unrest across the galaxy would settle back down. And he would be the Emperor. The people would tremble in his presence. Armies would bow before him. Nothing would ever be denied him. He would produce a suitable male heir and begin a dynasty that would last forever. Of that, he was certain. But first, he had to chase down the alien ship and destroy it.

He rose to his feet, stretched his back, and adjusted the ornamental armor he wore as a sign of his authority to command the Ashi military forces. It was a bit tight, but he was getting used to it. The galaxy would get used to seeing him in it. Soon, they would bow to the ground in his presence, when Ulrech Sheika was the sole ruler of the entire galaxy.

CHAPTER 8

INSIDE THE NEW ARMORY, there were a dozen recliners fresh from the ship's production plant and delivered to the large room by droids. Their lockers had been moved, too, and while the armory had racks for their weapons and shelves of neatly arranged ammo, it was mostly empty. They could have used a space a third of the size, but like most things on the *Renegade,* the new armory was big. The Marines settled into one corner of the space.

Most of them were seated. Remmy tried not to think about the empty chairs and who would never be coming back. Since leaving the Sol system, three Marines had been killed: Corporal Wendy Downs on Lawash, Sergeant Jay Thorne, and Corporal Jack Fortnoy on Casasil. Three more were wounded, including Lieutenant Colt. And Gunny Rand had experienced a mental breakdown during the fighting on Casasil. That left six Marines other than the Master Sergeant, seven abled-bodied Marines, to fight a war. It wasn't nearly enough.

"Alright, I'm sure you've heard," Remmy said softly. "Captain Darius wants us to patrol the ship."

"Rent-a-cop duty," Hugo McManus said with a sneer.

"Someone needs to keep the wrench spinners in line," Izzy Berry said with a smile.

Remmy shook his head. "Officers and NCOs will be making sure Fleet personnel stay in line, but it doesn't hurt to remind them what they're up against if they don't."

"We're also going to be training a group of Casians to fight," Staff Sergeant Laila McPherson added. "That includes PT, sim training and weapons design."

Hugo raised a hand, and Remmy nodded for him to speak.

"I'm all for it," he said. "Tex and I will move the sim gear from the *Jericho*. But how are we going to arm the Casians."

"Can they use their trunks to fire weapons, maybe?" Corporal Leigh Ann Poh asked.

"That's what we need to find out," Laila replied. "They're strong. I was thinking we could mount two belt-fed machine guns onto their back that would swing up into the firing position. Like I said, we'll need to design it for them."

"They can't design it themselves?" Izzy asked.

"I'm sure they can help," Laila said.

"The problem isn't the anatomy," Remmy explained. "And they are very intelligent. But weapons have been illegal in the Imperium for centuries."

"The Casians have the capability, just not the experience," Laila said.

"Are we doing the same for the Dudonus?" Leigh Ann asked.

"No," Remmy said. "They are too fragile for fighting and don't have the physical strength to be much good in battle."

"What if we suited them up?" Hugo said. "I mean, assuming we could produce more MECH armor like the Lieutenant, the suit would protect their fragile bodies and give them the strength needed to fight."

"That's not a bad idea," Laila said.

"Agreed," Remmy said. "I'll talk to them, see if any of the

Dudonus have the desire to pilot a MECH in combat. If so, we'll start training them right away."

"Training them where?" Tex asked.

"Charlie Hangar has been designated Marine Country for now," Remmy said. "We'll start there. Our initial goals will be physical fitness and team coordination. Once we have weapons designed for them, we'll run simulations and have them moving in full armor. We're all starting from scratch here. We need to get to know these people."

"Aliens, you mean," Hugo said.

"They are a different species, but they are intelligent and capable," Laila said. "I think it's best if we think of them as people."

"Who would have dreamed we'd be on a ship like this," Izzy spoke up, "training aliens for war."

"It's a trip, that's for sure," Leigh Ann said.

"We can do it," Sergeant Dirk Oliver said. "If we're going to be risking our lives, the people who live here should be doing the same."

"And they are," Remmy said. "Everyone on this ship is going to be working toward the same goals. We all have a stake in the well-being of this enterprise."

"I know we're asking a lot of you," Laila added. "We're all combat vets and your experience will be vital in helping to prepare the Casians for whatever we might face in the days ahead. You need to set the example, and if you have any ideas for weapons and armor design, don't hesitate to come forward."

"The Casians won't be the only aliens joining the ship and becoming Marines," Remmy continued. "As we travel through the galaxy, we will continue to recruit more volunteers. That means more training, more weapon and armor design, as well as strategy and tactics innovations. We aren't just training and equipping these people to fight; we'll be leading them into battle, if that becomes necessary."

"So, we're officers now?" Hugo asked. "When do I get a bump in pay?"

"I know that's right," Tex said.

"We are foregoing promotions for now," Remmy said. "But you'll all be acting as NCOs. Once Lieutenant Colt is back, we'll see about making the changes official."

"For now, we're splitting up into three groups," Laila said. "Izzy is with me, Leigh Ann is with Hugo, and Tex is with Dirk. We'll operate in four-hour shifts, making patrols through the ship focused on the Park and the Commerce sections of the ship. Focus on being seen. This is deterrence; we're not hunting down criminals here."

"Make sure you have a translation device and stun batons, no lethal weapons. Light armor, no helmets, and keep your comlinks on at all times."

Izzy raised a hand, "Master Sergeant, the alie... I mean, the Casians are moving into the apartments by the park. Is there any way we could do the same?"

"I've already reserved units for each of you on Kappa Deck, starboard side," Remmy said. "That will put you closer to Marine Country than hiking all the way to the Command section of the ship."

"Nice," Leigh Ann said.

"Kappa, that's all the way at the top," Hugo said.

"Enlistment has it's privileges," Tex said. It was a standard Marine joke and usually referred to duties that no one wanted to do, but occasionally it was used for good assignments. It got a laugh from the other Marines.

"Have you checked in on our people in the med bay?" Laila asked.

"Captain said they're on the mend. No change in the LT; he's still unconscious. I'm heading there now if anyone wants to go along," Remmy said.

They all got up. No one liked going to the medical bay, but the platoon was close. They were all hurting from the loss of Sergeant Thorne and Corporal Fortnoy. It didn't seem possible that they were gone. Remmy expected to see them coming around the corner at any moment. But he knew they wouldn't. Life was precious. No one could outwit death. As Remmy led the way out of the armory and toward the nearby gravity lift, he thought the human life span was too short, especially when there were so many wonders in the universe to see. A person could spend their life traveling from system to system and still not see all there was to see in the galaxy.

They drifted up the gravity lift to Epsilon deck, which was more often called the main deck since it was the same level as the Park and the open concourse through the Commerce section of the ship. They hurried along the trails and through the arching entry to the wide corridor that reminded Remmy of a shopping mall. Other than the occasional bridge, the main concourse was open all the way to the upper hull of the ship. It was five stories high and made him feel like he was in an extravagant resort rather than a military vessel.

They passed the Dudonus lounge and the magnificent fountain with the towering Arodoni statue. On the other side, not far from the gravity ring that separated the Commerce section of the ship from the Command decks, they reached the medical bay. It was directly across from the newly set up Admin Center. Remmy saw Commander Lee giving orders to a group of spacemen who were getting the Admin space all set up. Soon, everyone but Command staff would get their orders from the Admin Center, or AC.

"Hey, who let the riff-raff in," Corporal Ricky Thompson said as the group of Marines converged just inside the wide sliding doors.

"Doc, he still needs surgery," Tex said. "You forgot to stitch his mouth closed."

Thompson was sitting in a chair but got to his feet. He had a brace around his leg. He hobbled toward his friends.

"Man, it's good to see you guys," Ricky said.

"How are you, Corporal?" Remmy asked.

"On the mend, Master Sergeant. I'll be good to go any day now."

"He's not been cleared for duty yet," the surgeon, Dr. Lanski said as he came around from his desk that was covered with video screens on upright displays.

The medical bay was stocked with human equipment brought over to the *Renegade* from the *Jericho*. It included the medical scanners, which displayed information on several high-resolution screens. There was no office available in the new medical bay, which was one large, open space. The doctor had a desk moved in and used the large video screens as a partition to give himself some privacy while he worked.

"How is his injury?" Laila asked.

"The wound is healing, but there was tissue and nerve damage," Lanski said. "The brace will be necessary until he regains full strength of the quadriceps muscle."

"He's got me doing exercises three times a day," Ricky complained.

"We'll keep him on communications duty for a while," Remmy said. "Keep him off his feet."

Hugo grunted, "Polishing a seat with his—"

"Sergeant," Laila snapped, cutting McManus off in midsentence.

"Two more days," Dr. Lanski said. "Maybe three."

"I'm fine, really I am," Ricky complained.

"You do what the doctor says," Remmy ordered. "How's Corporal Van Winkle?"

"Still in recovery," Dr. Lanski said. "We repaired the bones in his arm using medical grade plastic and stainless steel, but it's vital to his recovery that the arm not be moved. It takes time for the muscles and tendons to bond to the artificial materials. Given time, he should recover full use of his arm, but..."

Remmy stepped closer to the doctor, who spoke quietly. "He'll probably always suffer pain in that arm."

"We can deal with pain," Remmy said. "Just take good care of him."

The master sergeant gave the platoon several minutes with Ricky Thompson, then sent them off to prepare for peacekeeping duties. When they were gone, Remmy asked the doctor about Lieutenant Colt.

"He's alive," Lanski said. "In fact, according to my scans, he's in good health. You heard about the parasite?"

"The Captain mentioned it."

"Come, take a look for yourself," Dr. Lanski said.

He led the way over to his desk and brought up images from Lieutenant Micky Colt's medical scans.

"We missed it at first," the doctor said, pointing at a screen that showed the Lieutenant's upper spine and skull. "Here, you see that line?"

"Yeah," Remmy said.

"And now?" Laski said, tapping a few keys on his computer's control pad.

The image changed, and the line, which looked no thicker than a human hair, could be seen laying diagonally across several of the officer's vertebrae.

"It's growing," Remmy said.

"Exactly," Lanski confirmed. "It's wrapped around his spine and moving up the brainstem. I've run tests on Lieutenant Colt's brainwaves. They're normal. He should be awake, but he's not."

"What's your best guess as to why?"

"It's complete conjecture, I'm afraid," Dr. Lanski said. "I did scan the other Marines for signs of the parasite. I'll need to run tests on you and Staff Sergeant McPherson, but I doubt you've been infected."

"Why's that?" Remmy asked.

"Because you're still conscious," the doctor explained. "My theory, and mind you that's all it is, just a theory, is that the Lieutenant is undergoing some type of metamorphosis."

"Like a caterpillar becoming a butterfly?"

"Something similar, yes," Lanski said. "In his comatose state, all his strength is being used by the parasite to grow. And while I have no way of knowing short of cutting him open and poking around, I believe the parasite is embedding itself into the spinal column. My guess is that among the bundles of nerves that run down our spine, the parasite is growing a web like appendage that is tapping into all the major nerves. It could even be feeding off the electrical impulses or drawing energy; I really have no way of knowing."

"What's that mean?"

"I don't know. He could wake up at any moment. Or he could never wake up again. If he does wake up, I expect there will be symptoms, perhaps loss of sensation or even paralysis. It's also possible that there is nothing noticeable at all. It could be no different than the bacteria in our digestive tract, a perfectly symbiotic relationship. Only time will tell."

Remmy felt a cold lump in his stomach. Fear didn't often get the best of the master sergeant. He had stared into the abyss, and it stared back, but Remmy Steel didn't blink. Still, the thought of an alien parasite burrowing into him and leaving him comatose was unnerving.

"Can you remove it?"

"That is doubtful and dangerous," the doctor said. "If it hasn't burrowed into his spinal column, it's still lying against it. I doubt it would come free in one long sliver. And whenever you're dealing with the spine there are great risks. Even if the surgical bot carried out the procedure, he could be paralyzed or killed."

"So we leave it," Remmy said. "And if he wakes up?"

"We keep a close watch on him. Run tests and try to deal with any associated symptoms, but that's all we can do."

"Alright, thank you, doctor," Remmy said, feeling helpless.

"I'll send word if anything changes," Lanski said.

"Please do. I've got my comlink on day and night."

They shook hands. Dr. Lanski was a high-ranking Fleet surgeon, but on a battleship at war, they were just two men with jobs to do.

Remmy left the med bay, promising to return soon for his own scans. But there was still so much to do and so little time to do it. Even back on the *Renegade* and with his platoon, Remmy knew that the enemy could return at any time. There was no safety on the ship and no rest for the weary.

CHAPTER 9

IS THERE any way to bring one safely on board?" Darius asked.

"I don't think so," Henry replied.

"As soon as the magnetic field picks up a metallic object, the explosive is activated," Pete Best said. "Even if we could get it safely inside the ship, we couldn't let it touch the deck without it blowing up."

"Not worth the risk, Captain," Henry said.

"Alright, so how do we move them?" Darius asked.

"We could use the gravity beam," Vivian said, "but they would still be dangerous."

"Hurl them into the sun?" Pete Best asked.

"If we're just going to destroy them," Henry pointed out. "Might as well do it here and now. We've got plenty of raw metal from the alien transport we picked up for the manufacturing plant."

"Send out the trash," Captain Darius said with a nod. "Add some scrap metal to activate the magnetic controls and detonate the mines."

"That's a pretty good solution," Pete Best said. "Another would be to just vaporize them with the laser cannons."

"No debris," Vivian Ramos said. "That would be the safest way to clear the portal."

"I doubt debris would harm the *Renegade*," Henry Nash said.

"But it might damage another ship," Vivian pointed out.

"Safe, fast, it seems using the laser cannons is the best option," Darius said. "Lieutenant Best, begin your targeting algorithms."

"Aye, Captain," Pete Best said.

They were still a hundred thousand kilometers from the portal. The *Renegade* was building speed, preparing for the transition into hyperspace. It didn't take long for the ship's targeting computer to prepare for the volley of shots needed to wipe out the mines around the portal. They were static objects with no stealth features. Using radar it was a simple matter to identify each of the mines and then calculate the shots needed to vaporize them.

"Targets acquired, Captain," Pete Best said.

"Lock the lasers in attack position," Darius said.

"Cannons extended, Captain," Pete replied. "We are ready to fire, sir."

"Fire," Darius said.

There were four huge laser cannons on the *Renegade*. Each one fired in rapid succession, using only a tiny fraction of the available power. The flashes of light ripped across empty space, with additional flashes as the mines detonated. Without oxygen, an explosion produced almost no fire, but the sudden release of energy was brighter than the dark void beyond. It was a beautiful sight that Zeke Darius could appreciate. It helped to know that no one had been hurt or killed. It wasn't like firing on an enemy ship which could weigh heavy on the captain's conscience.

"That was fast," Henry said.

"All mines are detonated," Vivian Ramos announced. "I don't read anything on radar."

"Nothing but space dust," Pete said with a chuckle.

"Alright, retract the cannons," Darius ordered. "Accelerate to speed for the hyperspace jump. And let's send word to Casasil that the portal is clear."

"Do you think the Imperium will come back here?" Vivian asked. "Will they harm the Casians?"

"Maybe," Darius said. "Although I'm guessing they didn't mine the portal on a whim."

"They were ordered to do it?" Pete Best asked.

"If they operate like we do, that order had to come from somewhere," Darius said.

"That's one way to motivate people to fight," Henry Nash said. "They were locked into the system with us."

"That's a hell of an order. Win or die," Pete Best said, "no other alternatives."

"But the Imperium will think it's sealed off," Darius said. "At least until they discover that we're no longer in the Casa system."

"It's too bad we couldn't set them up with a defensive weapon system," Pete said.

"We did what we could," Darius replied. "Now it's up to them. Let's have a system check and let the crew know we'll be jumping into hyperspace."

The work of a military vessel in space never stopped. Fortunately, most of the work done on the *Renegade* was carried out by the automated systems. The crew didn't have to spend hours cleaning or maintaining the machinery on board that kept everyone alive. But there was still plenty to do, especially with over a hundred and fifty new volunteers.

The trip through hyperspace was scheduled to take just over three standard days. That would give the crew time to orient and begin training the new recruits. Darius was a believer in delegation. He trusted the chain of command, as well as the members of his crew, to carry out what needed to be done. And to everyone's relief, things seemed to go well. The Casians were eager to jump into their new roles and had a real aptitude for the work. It was only in the physical engineering that they struggled, and only because their large bodies didn't fit the narrow maintenance corridors as well as the humans.

The Dudonus were eager, too, and helped set up what became known as Flight Control, which was really the drone flight control center. No one knew how the Arodoni had flown the drones. No control stations could be found. But GIGI designed remote control flight consoles, which were set up in a big room. Everything was built, installed, and ready for testing just before the ship dropped out of hyperspace.

And it wasn't a perfect utopia on the ship either. Working with different races took adjustments from all of them. Darius enjoyed walking through the ship, seeing the aliens pitching in, or enjoying recreation in the park. The Dudonus set up their communal center with large paintings, music, and even sculptures. They printed books in their native language and spent most of their free time together.

Likewise, the Casians and humans worked together but spent their free time apart. The Casians preferred to do everything in the park, even eating. They didn't graze like the herds of animals kept by the ship's agri-droids, but they consumed large amounts of harvested vegetables, which were served in wide troughs. There was an attitude of wonder and excitement among all the crew, which Darius hoped would continue once they engaged in battle with the Imperial forces.

After three busy but productive days traveling safely through hyperspace, Darius found himself back on the Bridge with his senior officers as they prepared to enter the Olotimbo system.

"All stations report?" Darius said as he settled into his captain's chair with a view of the entire Bridge.

"Engineering and Life Support systems are functioning at optimal levels, Captain," Henry Nash said. "My people are in place."

"Navigation and Radar systems are ready for normal space, Captain," Vivian Ramos said.

"Outstanding," Darius replied. "Weapons?"

"Standing by, Captain," Pete Best responded.

"Communications?"

"All divisions are standing by for instructions, Captain," Ensign Bertoli said.

Darius pressed a button that connected his comlink to the Systems Control room. "Ensign Stanislaus, how are we looking?"

"All systems are in the green, Captain. Standing by for ship-wide diagnostics once you give the word, sir."

"Power?" He asked.

"I've completed both visual and computer-driven inspections, sir," Stanislaus replied. "The power core in the *Jericho* is in good shape, and energy levels are optimal."

"Thank you, Alex," Darius replied before pushing a button that connected him to the new Admin Center. "Commander Lee, report."

"Aye, Captain, all crew are accounted for. We are standing by for the transition to normal space."

"Very good. I want battle stations; sound the red alert, Commander."

"Aye, Red Alert, all hands to battle stations," Lori Lee replied.

Darius waited as the call went out across the ship-wide comlink, first in English, then in Casian, and finally in Dudonus. Unlike human-built vessels, the *Renegade* had no ship-wide communication system. There were no flashing red lights or voices booming from hidden speakers. They relied instead on basic comlinks, which every member of the crew was required to carry at all times.

"Five minutes until transition, Captain," Vivian Ramos said.

"Thank you, Lieutenant," Darius replied as he pressed a button that connected his comlink to the Marines down in grunt country.

"Master Sergeant," Darius said. "What's your Sit Rep?"

"Marines are in full battle rattle and at their stations," Remmy replied. "All flight decks are locked down tight, sir."

"Very good, Master Sergeant. And your volunteers?"

"They are here with me in reserve, Captain. For now, they will move essential supplies wherever they are needed in the ship, sir."

"Outstanding. Keep up the good work, Master Sergeant. Darius out."

There was nothing left to do but wait. And on everyone's mind were the mines that had lined the hyperspace portal in the Casa system. Would the *Renegade* come out of hyperspace only to run directly into space mines that would rip them apart? A quick glance at the other officers told Darius he wasn't the only person wondering about the answer to that question.

A timer floated in the air where the holographic projection of the ship's plot and surrounding space would appear the moment they dropped out of hyperspace. They watched it slowly descend.

"One minute until transition," Vivian said.

It wasn't necessary, but it was protocol. Under different circumstances, they might not have time to watch the countdown. It was her job to make sure everyone on the Bridge knew what was coming. And there were more than just the senior officers in the wide space used to control the ship. Fourteen enlisted officers were there as well, everyone backing up the others in case of an emergency. Darius knew he had a fine crew, but he could tell they were all concerned with what they would find in the Olotimbo system.

"Fifteen seconds," Vivian said.

"Let's all relax," Darius ordered. "No matter what is waiting for us, we're ready."

It was true; the *Renegade* was a ship unlike any other.

"Ten seconds," Vivian said.

"Weapons, standing by to project sonic shielding," Darius said.

"Aye, Captain, standing by with sonic shielding," Pete Best replied.

"Five, four, three, two…"

Darius held his breath. The mottle glow of hyperspace so clearly visible through the Bridge's overhead canopy disappeared. In its place, stars shown in the deep black of space.

"We are in regular space," Vivian announced. "Radar is active."

"Shields!" Darius said softly.

"Up, sir. We have sonic shields in place, Captain."

"I'm getting some traffic behind us, Captain," Vivian said.

"Henry, activate thrusters and move us away from the portal," Darius said. "And spin us around. I want to bring our weapons to bear."

They knew the hyperspace portal was seventeen billion kilometers away from the system star at the edge of the system's heliosphere. It would take the radar time to reach all the way into the system and reveal the activity around the system's primary world. But there was only one reason for ships to be on the backside of the hyperspace portal. Darius felt his stomach clench in fear.

"Sir, we have no headway," Henry said. "Thrusters are responding, but we aren't moving."

"Energy readings from our stern, Captain," Vivian Ramos said. "I'm picking up five different sources."

"They've got us pinned with artificial gravity," Darius said.

The image of the ship on their holographic plot began to shrink as the radar gave them a view of space around them. Five ships were behind them. They were frightening-looking vessels with sharp, pointed spines sticking out in all directions.

"Slavers," Darius said.

"We can't move," Captain," Henry said. "What do we do?"

It was an excellent question. If the *Renegade* had a weakness, it was that all her weapons were pointed forward. From behind, she was helpless.

Darius pressed the comlink and said, "Master Sergeant, we have five ships behind us. They have us locked together with gravity beams. I need you to shake us loose."

"Copy that, sir. We'll make it happen."

"Make it happen fast, Sergeant. We're sitting ducks here."

"We're on the move now, sir. Steel out."

Darius sat back, cursing the fact that, once again, all he could do was sit and wait. It seemed at every turn, he was getting caught off guard by the enemy. That would have to stop.

CHAPTER 10

REMMY HAD SPENT the last three days working with the new recruits. There were twenty Casians who were busy learning to prepare for war but were still far from ready. Laila and Alex Stanislaus had designed a prototype weapon system, but it had yet to be tested and would almost certainly need refinements.

As the ship prepared to drop out of hyperspace, the alien pachyderms were ready to help if the ship was attacked, but there wasn't much they could do other than move materials. They were incredibly strong but still needed human help getting the heavy loads onto their broad backs. He was waiting with the Casian reserve when the Captain's call came in. Remmy, like the rest of his Marines, were all in full space armor. He heard the Captain's request via his battle helmet and immediately relayed the danger to his platoon.

"You heard the man," Remmy said over his comlink. "Alpha, Bravo, and Charlie teams prepare for Exfil with heavy weapons."

"Copy that, Master Sergeant," Laila said.

"Rocket's not rifles, understood," Hugo said.

Remmy turned to Corporal Thompson, who had been cleared for light duty but not combat.

"Corporal, you're in charge of the reserve," Remmy said. "Start moving rocket-mounted munitions to all three flight decks."

"Yes, Master Sergeant!" Ricky shouted. Unlike the rest of the platoon, he was in light armor and piloting a cargo lift that could be used to get heavy equipment onto the backs of the Casians. "You heard him, let's move. Go! Go! Go!"

Remmy didn't wait to see what was happening. The Casians knew where the weapons were. There were crates with long-range missiles that could be fired from big shoulder cannons. After the battle in the Casa system the flight decks on the *Renegade* had been outfitted with a variety of weapons and supplies. There were just two Marines in each of the three teams, but it was enough to deal with the ships who had latched onto the *Renegade* with artificial gravity beams.

Hurrying out onto the converted flight deck where the Marines did their training, Remmy caught up with Laila and Corporal Izzy Berry just inside the airlock.

"Master Sergeant," Laila said.

"Both of you take cannons," Remmy said. "I'll carry the reloads."

"Copy that, Sergeant. Activate your magnetic boots, Corporal," Laila said.

They both hefted the big, tube-shaped weapons as the airlock cycled open. Remmy grabbed the crate, which had missiles packed into dense foam that had been cut in the exact shape of the missiles. He undid the latches as the airlock closed behind him.

"Master Sergeant, I'm downloading targeting information to your battle helmets," Lieutenant Pete Best said over the comlink.

"Yes, sir. Thank you," Remmy replied.

He pulled a missile out of the foam and, at the same time, began assigning the targets on his helmet's HUD to the Marines in his platoon. Bravo team would take two targets, while Alpha and Charlie teams each took one.

"Any idea what we're shooting at, Master Sergeant?"

"No clue," Remmy replied, as he pulled the arming pin from the missile and shoved it inside Laila's cannon.

The airlock's outer door slid open and the trio stepped out onto the hull of the ship. They were suddenly outside the *Renegade's* artificial gravity and would have floated away if not for the electromagnets inside the soles of their combat boots.

"That thing's a nightmare," Izzy said as Remmy loaded her cannon.

"Looks like a slave ship," he replied.

"That's nothing like what we boarded," Izzy argued. "It's more like something from a horror movie."

"So kill it," Laila said. "Clear?"

"You are clear to fire," Remmy said, kneeling down just inside the airlock, which caused his stomach to flip as he passed back through the invisible barrier of gravity.

Laila's missile shot out of the tube, pushed by a carbon fiber plunger built onto metal hydrogen rails that had almost no friction. The rail sent the missile flying out of the tube like a bullet. Once the missile was well away from the weapon, its own fuel system ignited, and the rocket flashed off toward the spiny slave ship.

"Target located," Izzy said.

"Fire away," Remmy told her.

She repeated the process. Both rockets zoomed through space toward their targets. They were simple weapons, just a high-yield explosive inside a depleted uranium cone that was attached to the front end of a rocket with small extendable stabilizers, which were only needed in atmospheric flight. Laila's rocket burned through its fuel but kept right on flying until it entered the slave ship's gravity beam. Then it dropped down and came out on the other side. It was still armed and ready to explode on impact, but its trajectory had been altered by the gravity beam. The rocket flew away harmlessly on the underneath side of the ship.

Izzy's had more success and reached the target, but only impacted on the end of one of the long spiny protrusions.

"No luck," Izzy said

"Hit them again," Remmy said.

He quickly reloaded their rockets, and each of them fired again. Izzy's second missile made solid contact and blew a hole in the front of the slave ship she was targeting. It spewed gas and began to drift in a slow turn.

Laila had to aim at the rear of the other slave ship. Her missile reached the vessel and shattered the spines along one side.

"Two beams down," Pete Best said over the Marine comlink.

"Three to go," Remmy said.

"We need to get a better angle," Izzy replied.

Remmy rammed a fresh missile into her cannon and then pulled the last one from the crate.

"We need to move up the hull," Izzy said, pointing around the side of the ship.

"Permission to advance our position?" Laila asked.

"Granted," Remmy said. "But connect your safety tethers to one another."

"Copy that," Laila said.

"I'm going back for more missiles," he said. "Watch yourself, Staff Sergeant."

"We will," Laila said.

Remmy stepped back into the airlock and hit the cycle control switch as Laila and Izzy moved slowly away. They could walk on the outside the ship with their boots but it was slow going, and one wrong move could send them drifting off into space. Remmy didn't like taking a command role in the battle. He preferred to be leading the charge, but he had to do things differently as long as he was the ranking officer. Until Lieutenant Colt was back, Remmy would need to give the orders, not carry them out.

The airlock seemed to take forever to cycle. The chamber he was in filled with air, not that Remmy needed it in his space armor. But the airlock had to pressurize or he could be hurt trying to move back into the hanger.

When the door finally opened he ducked under it, pulling the empty munitions crate and sliding it across the deck. He hurried over to where more of the missiles had been stacked and pulled a crate down. He flipped the latches and opened the crate just to ensure it was filled with the proper type of missiles. He had been in the Marines long enough to know better than just to trust what was printed on the outside of a shipping crate.

There were missiles inside the box, packed in foam, just like the crate he had emptied. He closed the lid and hauled the container back across the floor in a rush. He didn't want to waste a second, not while his people were outside the ship, putting their safety on the line. He might have to hold back while he was in command, but he didn't have to like it.

CHAPTER 11

"THAT'S THREE SHIPS DOWN, CAPTAIN," Vivian called out.

"Can we break free?" Darius asked.

"Not yet," Henry replied. "We're still in two gravity beams. They're holding us from opposite angles. We're stuck until they're gone."

Darius could see the three compromised slave ships. Two were damaged but still operational even though they had dropped their hold on the *Renegade* and were limping from the fight. The third had taken a more drastic hit. It was in a slow spin, with gas and debris spewing from a gaping hold in the side of its hull.

"Keep trying," Darius said.

He had a terrible feeling about the fight. There was nothing worse for a ship commander whose vessel couldn't maneuver ... and for all the wonderful things about the Arodoni ship, it needed some new weapons installed to protect its blindside.

"Why the hell are the slavers attacking us?" Darius said. "Are they working with the Imperium?"

A computerized voice answered from the speaker built into his

Captain's Chair. "The slave ships engaging us are unregistered, Captain," GIGI said. "They have no authority or connection to the Imperium military."

"So what's happening?"

"It appears they were waiting for prey," GIGI said. "It is not an uncommon practice. They might have thought we were a freighter or passenger vessel."

"Meaning, they want to enslave us?" Henry said with a shake of his head.

"They would enslave the crew and break up the ship to add to their own vessels," GIGI said. "It is how they operate."

"Who are they?" Darius asked. "What race are these slavers?"

"In most instances, they would be crewed by beings from different star systems," GIGI continued. "It is likely they were criminals before joining the crew of the slave ships."

"And are there slaves on board their ships?"

"That is impossible to know," GIGI said. "Registered slavers operate within certain boundaries that define who they may capture and how the slaves should be treated. But these unauthorized slave ships have no such oversight. Attacking space vessels, for instance, is prohibited by Imperium law and could result in the death of innocents and races that are not authorized to be enslaved."

"Sir, we have to do something," Henry said. "If there are slaves on those ships..."

"I hear you, Lieutenant. First, we need to break free."

"And watch for more EMPs," Pete Best said. "Remember the slave ship we ran across before."

"I won't forget," Darius said, his eyes blazing. "Is there any chance that Nurek sent us here to be captured?"

"The odds of such a betrayal are slim, Captain," GIGI said. "Even if the Dudonus was in contact with outlaws, it is doubtful they would work with slavers. Their race has been a primary target for slavers since before I was constructed."

"Maybe they want control of the ship," Darius said. "It was Nurek's idea to come to this system."

"They haven't shown any interest in testing our boundaries," Vivian said. "It's got to be a coincidence that we're under attack."

"The Olotimbo system is neither rich in resources nor populated by a vital race," GIGI said. "It is what your people would call a 'back-water system'. The odds of Olotimbo having an Imperial military presence is only two point seven six percent."

"Maybe it's known to not have Imperium ships," Pete Best said. "That's why the outlaws are congregating here."

"Keep scanning for EMPs," Darius ordered before pressing a button to open a comlink channel. "Commander Lee, how is the crew performing?"

"No reports of problems, Captain," Lori Lee said. "Everyone is at battle stations, and every group has reported in."

"That's good, Commander, but don't let your guard down," Darius told her. "Be on the alert for threats within and without."

"Aye, Captain. We will remain vigilant."

He closed the channel to the Admin Center, and opened another to Master Sergeant Steel.

"What's the sit rep, Master Sergeant?"

"Three targets down, two remain," Remmy replied, his voice calm over the comlink despite the fact that they were fighting to save the ship. "Alpha and Beta teams are moving along the hull, sir. We can't get a clear line of fire from down here, Captain."

"As soon as we get free, I want all your people back inside," Darius said. "Remain on alert until further notice."

"Copy that, sir. Marines on heightened alert until further notice."

Darius looked up. He wanted to do more, but there was precious little that could be done. They still had drones that could be launched against the slavers, but his crew wasn't ready to deploy them yet. And letting GIGI do all their fighting for them seemed wrong somehow, too.

"That's a hit!" Pete Best said. "Tango four is off our back."

"Are we free?"

"We can move, sir," Henry said. "But the fifth ship is locked onto us. We can't turn and fire on it as long as that gravity beam is intact."

"What about the others?" Darius said.

"Bringing them into laser range," Henry said. "But, sir, there could be innocent people on board."

"Agreed, but I don't want them going anywhere," Darius said. "What's the status of our artificial gravity weapon?"

"It's active and ready to go," Pete Best said. "We'll have to turn the ship toward the target, though. It only shoots straight out of the *Renegade's* mouth."

Darius understood what his weapons officer was saying. The Arodoni ship was built almost like a giant fish. Its body was long, with massive engines and enormous laser cannons that were built onto the after section of the ship. Near to the front was the round, collar-shaped gravity ring that led to what looked like the head of a fish with an open mouth. The upper section of the V shaped bow was the Command decks, while the lower portion was the Industrial section. The ship's artificial gravity beam was used to pull in resources that could be broken down into useful, recycled materials, which were stored until needed by the advance three-dimensional printer that could make everything from a microchip to shuttles large enough to carry an entire Marine platoon into battle.

"Good enough," Darius said. "We'll draw them in, search for captives, then blast those ships into atoms."

"What about the crew?" Vivian asked.

"We've got no space for prisoners," Henry said.

It was less of a warning and more of a suggestion. Slavery as a concept struck the crew in different fashions. No one liked it. The institution of slavery had been outlawed and decried on Earth for centuries. But in the vast reaches of the Sol system, especially in those places with little or no law enforcement, people were some-times trafficked. It was a harsh reality but a fact that had followed the human race through the centuries. Despicable people still did despicable things, including holding people against their will and forcing them to do things they didn't want to do.

But to some people, slavery was an affront to their identity. While every ethnicity among the human race had been slaves at some time or other in the history of Earth, those of African descent seemed to feel the sting of the abominable practice the strongest. There was no doubt in Darius' mind what Lieutenant Henry Nash wanted to do with the slavers.

"Can we turn them over to the authorities on Olo Prime?" Darius asked.

"It makes sense," Vivian said.

"It's better than they deserve," Pete Best added.

When GIGI spoke up, it quickly became clear that they had a difficult decision ahead of them.

"There are law enforcement facilities on Olo Prime, but they are not suited for outside races," the alien artifact said. "The Oltims are a type of Mollusks, mostly closely identified with what humans would call slugs. They are larger in size than most invertebrates found on Earth. The average size is one meter long by half a meter tall. Unlike most other species in the galaxy, Oltims can remain stationary for exceedingly long periods of time. Hence, their detainment facilities most closely resemble hives of what you might think of as cocoons."

"So, the locals can't handle slavers," Henry said. "And if we leave them in their ships, they'll just go back to their evil ways."

"We could disable their ships," Pete Best said.

"And leave them stranded in space?" Vivian said. "Talk about cruel and unusual punishment."

"Look at those vessels," Henry said with a shake of his head. "They're cobbled together from other vessels they've attacked. I wouldn't think that leaving them in possession of their ships, even if we disabled their engines, would stop them for long."

"It's not our place to judge the galaxy," Darius said.

"They attacked us," Henry said. "Seems to me they deserve what they get."

Darius found the entire group of senior officers looking at him, waiting for his judgment. It was an awkward place to be.

"Let's search their ships," Darius finally decided. "If we find slaves on board, we'll let them decide what to do with their abductors."

CHAPTER 12

THERE WAS nothing quite as exciting as being outside a spaceship in the middle of a battle. Laila McPherson wasn't crazy. She was relieved that the slave ships weren't firing lasers or missiles back at the *Renegade*. But it took a certain amount of bravery to leave the safety of the ship and rely solely on a person's equipment to survive. That danger pumped adrenaline into her bloodstream and filled her with an awareness of her life that she never felt at any other time than when she was in extreme situations.

"This is taking too long," Izzy remarked.

"We can't fire until we have a good shot," Laila remarked as they crept up the port side of the ship.

Thrusters began to fire around them, turning the ship. Laila froze, wondering if the last slave ship had already been disabled.

"Master Sergeant? Are we a go?" Laila asked over the platoon comlink.

"Roger that, Bravo team," Remmy replied. "Take that slaver out of commission. The other four are down. Tango five is all yours."

"Moving into position now," Laila said.

It was difficult to move quickly. There was no resistance in space,

no feeling of weight, which, surprisingly enough, made every movement consequential. Just tightening a muscle could send a person's
body moving in a direction they didn't expect. And the pair of space
Marines had to keep one foot on the ship at all times. The magnets in
their boots went on and off. When the sole of the boot touched the
firm hull of the ship, the electromagnets powered on. When she tried
to lift her foot, they switched off. It was a bit like walking on an
extremely sticky surface. And she had to be careful to always keep
one foot connected. If both boots released at the same time, she
would float away from the ship with no way to return. There hadn't
been time to load up the compressed air thrusting canisters to their
space suits. She had enough oxygen to breathe but no air to correct
her course if she flew away from the ship, which was why she was
tethered to Corporal Izzy Berry. It was a redundancy just in case one
of them slipped up in an environment that was deadly.

They could see the final slave ship. It was almost directly behind
the *Renegade*. But to take it down, they needed to get an angle that
would allow their missiles to impact that slave ship without crossing
into its gravity beam. Suddenly, the alien ship turned.

"Master Sergeant, the last slaver is turning," Laila announced.

There was a slight hesitation, and then Remmy's voice sounded
in her ears. "It dropped the gravity beam. They're going to make a
run for it."

"Should we—"

"Affirmative. Take out the engines if you can," Remmy ordered.
"There could be slaves on that ship. Captain Darius wants it out of
commission but not destroyed."

Laila didn't think the missiles she and Izzy had on their rocket
launchers could destroy the slave ships. They were only a fraction of
the size of the *Renegade,* yet they were fearsome-looking vessels.

"Take the first shot," Laila ordered Izzy, "just as soon as the
engines are visible."

"Got it," Izzy said.

They were both excellent shooters, but Laila wanted to see if the slave ship had some sort of defense system that might hinder her attack. The two women spread out nearly as far as their five-meter retractable tether would allow them to go. Izzy steadied the missile launcher on her shoulder and fired. The rocket flew from the tube and then streaked away from the ship, leaving a contrail of exhaust as the missile burned through the solid fuel that propelled it.

"Come on, baby," Izzy said.

There was a flare of light as the slave ship increased the power of its engines. The spiny ship had two large exhaust ports that glowed red in the darkness of space. Laila brought her rocket to her shoulder and activated the targeting app on her space helmet's HUD. Her right hand held the launcher's controls. With a flick of her thumb, she deactivated the weapon's safety and laid her index finger lightly on the trigger. She rested the aiming reticle on the tail of Izzy's missile. The spiky ship had simply turned tail and run.

Laila took a breath, released half of it slowly, then locked every muscle in her core and shoulders. Without gravity to interfere, the missile would fly straight and true. She held her breath while she squeezed the trigger. The missile shot forward, and Laila relaxed. They had done all they could.

A few seconds later, the first missile flew straight into the exhaust port. There was a flash but no sound, no spectacular explosion. The only sign that anything had happened was the red glow from the exhaust port growing duller.

"Was that a hit?" Izzy asked.

"Looks like it to me," Laila confirmed.

The slave ship, which had been running straight away from the *Renegade*, slowly began to turn. Thrusters fired on the port side in an effort to keep the ship on its heading. Then Laila's missile hit the dark exhaust port. Without the engine fire, the projectile penetrated deeper into the engine. There was no flash, but after a moment, gas and debris began to trail out of the ship. And even more importantly, the other engine died.

"Looks like we stopped it," Izzy said.

"Nice work, Bravo team," Remmy said. "Now hustle back inside. We're boarding the slave ships."

"Wonderful," Laila replied, remembering their misadventure in the Casa system when they boarded a slave vessel.

"At least we know what to expect this time," Izzy said as the pair of Marines started back around the hull of the ship.

"Last time, we boarded an authorized slave ship," Laila said. "And we got lucky they were using stun weapons."

"You think they might up the ante?"

"They're outlaws fighting for their lives," Laila said. "They won't pull their punches."

They hurried back to the airlock. Even moving fast, the rest of the platoon was already gathered by the time they got into the hangar. Gravity felt intense after being weightless. Her boots didn't stick to the deck, but Laila's entire body felt as if it weighed five hundred pounds.

"Welcome back, Bravo team," Master Sergeant Remmy said. "Ditch the missile launchers."

"I've got them," Izzy said, taking Laila's weapon, which was suddenly heavy and cumbersome.

"Thanks, Izz," Laila said. "What's the plan?"

"Captain Darius has one slave ship in tow," Remmy told her. "Using the artificial gravity beam, we'll haul it in. From there, you will lead a boarding part inside to search for prisoners."

"What's our rules of engagement?" Laila asked.

"Do we even know what we're up against in those ships?" Hugo McManus asked.

"No clue," Remmy admitted.

"There could be a hundred aliens waiting for us," Sergeant Dirk Oliver said.

"Or maybe just a few," Tex argued.

"What are the odds there are slaves on board?" Leigh Ann Poh asked.

"Nurek is on his way to give us some intel," Remmy said. "But ultimately, the slavers on these ships are outlaws. We aren't going to take any chances. You see a bad guy you put them down."

"We could damage their ship if we go in hot," Tex pointed out.

"The Captain doesn't care what happens to their ship," Remmy said. "He's willing to give the slavers over to the captives or at least let them decide the fate of the outlaws who abducted them. But we aren't taking prisoners, and I don't want a single casualty."

"Finally, it's about time we got taken off the leash," Hugo said.

They made their way up through the ship and met Nurek just outside the new Admin Center, where the tall, frail-looking alien was putting his skills and experience serving the royal family to good use. Nurek bowed in front of Remmy, who looked uncomfortable. Laila stepped up beside him. She was not the kind of person who craved control. It had never been her ambition to lead a platoon. Not that she couldn't be decisive or make command decisions, but she preferred a supporting role, which was what she was attempting to do with Master Sergeant Steel.

"How may I be of assistance, Master Sergeant?" Nurek asked

"What can you tell us about the slavers we're likely to face on these ships?" Remmy replied.

"Unauthorized slavery is a savage practice, but one that is rarely seen as a problem in the Imperium," Nurek explained. "Laws are made by the ruling class and carried out by high officials on Imperium worlds where there is a hierarchy of importance among the citizens. Certain races are considered to be elite and, therefore, suited for political office. There is a strong upper-echelon class consisting of wealthy individuals with higher education from the right institutions, which make up most of the Imperium bureaucracy, corporate leadership, and manufacturing higher management. These individuals are all considered untouchable by the slavers and, in fact, make up a majority of their customer base. That still leaves thousands of worlds, some are wealthy enough to pay the Imperium to keep their citizens off limits to the slavers. But many more cannot pay and become targets for the authorized slave trade."

"That's a fascinating lesson, but we're talking about outlaw slavers," Remmy pointed out.

"Outlaw may be too strong a word," Nurek said. "On worlds in good standing, crime is harshly punished by the Imperium. On worlds with less resources, opportunities are rare. If one hopes to get to space it can be accomplished by joining a crew."

"If you're trying to tell us that beings who kidnap others and sell them into slavery aren't ruffians, I would beg to differ."

"That is not my point. They can be brutal, but they are not soldiers. And most ships run with a small crew. Desertion is high. They often fight among themselves. They are, in general, a disillusioned, bitter lot."

"That helps," Remmy said. "Any chance you know about their weapons?"

"No," Nurek said. "Guns are illegal in the Imperium, but there is a thriving black market trade of older firearms. Most will be laser weapons with adjustable power modes cobbled together from old parts."

"Thank you," Remmy said.

Nurek bowed. And Remmy waved the platoon of Marines forward. At the gravity ring they went down to the big space where ships and other materials could be taken on board to be processed by the recycling facilities. There was already a big chunk of what had once been a troop carrier laying in pieces and being processed by the *Renegade's* industrial bots. It was a noisy place that appeared to be open to space. Looking up Laila could see what appeared to be the inside of the fish's mouth. There were running lights all along the inside of the big V-shaped opening of the ship. Laila didn't know if it was because of her space armor or if the ship had some sort of invisible way of holding back the hard vacuum of space, but they had no problems on the open deck. Nearby was the slot the *Jericho* had flown into. It was sealed up with a massive door, but she knew inside the cylindrical corridor, the corkscrew-shaped ship was turning and producing power for the entire alien vessel.

"Here it comes," Remmy said, pointing toward the opening.

"Crazy," Izzy said.

"They can just pull ships right inside," Leigh Ann Poh said.

"What can't this ship do?" Dirk responded.

"I'm not sure I want to know the answer to that one," Tex said. "It might be a little too smart if you ask me."

"Once it's inside on the deck, Alpha team will breach," Remmy said. "Bravo will back them up. I want a full sweep, no surprises."

"Yes, Master Sergeant," the group said in unison.

"I'll join Charlie team, and we'll start moving out the captives. Ricky Thompson is bringing our new recruits to help get the slaves settled," Remmy continued. "We've got five ships to search, so don't waste time."

"And if the crew surrenders?" Hugo McManus asked.

"The goal is to leave them on the ship," Remmy replied. "Lock them up in a small compartment until the slaves are offloaded, then we send their ship back out."

"We're letting the slavers go free?" Tex asked.

"We're not making that call," Remmy said. "Captain Darius is letting the captives decide. But don't take any chances. You engage with the enemy, you shoot to kill."

"Hell yeah," Hugo said.

"No mercy?" Leigh Ann Poh asked.

"Does it look like they practice mercy?" Tex asked as the ship loomed before them.

Laila couldn't argue the point. The ship was frightening from a distance. Up close, it was horrific. She understood the psychological impact of making a slave ship so terrifying. Hundreds of years prior, back on Earth, pirate ships had done the same thing. And a millennia before that, Norse raiders had done it too, carving dragon heads to mount on their ships as they went viking.

"Hard to imagine what it must be like to be enslaved," Laila said.

"Maybe it's like us," Dirk Oliver remarked. "We were taken from our home system without consultation. And we don't have any say over where we're going or what we're doing."

"It ain't the same," Hugo said.

"Not even in the same galaxy," Tex said.

"We're Marines," Laila said. "Every single one of us signed up for this."

"If you need to be excused, Sergeant," Remmy spoke up. "You can do so now. No judgment."

"I just don't think it's worth risking our lives for people we don't even know," Dirk said.

"Fair enough," Remmy replied calmly. "But on that ship, there could be innocent victims abducted from their homes and forced into slavery. We can't even imagine what they must be going through or what horrors they have to look forward to. I, for one, think that helping them is worth fighting for."

"Well said," Laila replied.

"Sign me up, too," Hugo said. "If this is where I punch my ticket, I can't imagine a better cause."

"It sure beats fighting cartels and rebels back in the Sol system," Izzy said.

"I'm good," Sergeant Dirk Oliver said. "Just venting a little."

"Understandable," Remmy said. "We're all in uncharted waters here. If anyone feels like they need a break, all you have to do is say the word."

"We don't need another mental breakdown," Laila agreed.

"Until we get back home," Remmy continued. "It's up to us to watch each other's backs. That includes the mental strain that comes with the territory. We've all seen it get to good Marines back home. But out here, things are different. So, let's make sure we're all good and we all lean into the platoon when things get tough."

"Here, here," Leigh Ann Poh said.

"Sounds good to me," Tex said.

The alien ship settled onto the deck with a loud clank and grinding noise. The Marines all checked their weapons. Laila was carrying a Sterner M88 Classic. It wasn't fancy, but it did have a piston stock that nullified nearly ninety percent of the weapon's recoil. It also had a barrel suppressor that minimized the report of the rifle and redirected the outgassing so that it didn't blow straight back onto the shooter. The barrel-shaped magazine held eighty-eight rounds of standard .223 ammunition. Her's was loaded with soft alloy bullets that maximized impact as the bullets smashed into a target.

"We're clear," Remmy said. "Alpha, Bravo, move in."

CHAPTER 13

THEY APPROACHED THE SHIP CAUTIOUSLY. There were big seams in the hull and patches, too. She saw rough welds with sloppy beads and lots of repaired surfaces. What she didn't see was a way in.

"What a piece of junk," Izzy said.

"Any idea how we're supposed to get inside?" Leigh Ann Poh asked.

"We'll blow a hole in it if necessary," Hugo said.

Laila was used to human spacecraft. Every ship made by man had emergency hatches that could be opened from the outside. Likewise, the *Renegade* and even the slave ship they had boarded in the Casa system had easily recognized hatches and ways to get in. The cobbled-together slave vessel, what spacers back in the Sol system would call a 'Franken-ship', had no discernible features other than the spikes that stuck out at all angles.

"Who makes a ship like that?" Izzy asked. "I wouldn't trust it to stay together."

"I suppose they have to build them off the grid," Laila said. "They're unauthorized slavers."

"But why not just steal a regular ship?" Leigh Ann wondered.

"Regular ship can be tracked. It's the same reason gangs steal hovercars and then disassemble them," Hugo pointed out. "Chop shops do it all the time. Take a hood from this car, the doors from that one, it makes the vehicle harder to track."

"My dad used to build racers back when I was a kid," Laila said. "He was always getting new parts and fabricating things to make his hovercar faster."

"There," Hugo said, pointing up. "Bet that's a hatch. We get it open it probably lowers right down."

"Start climbing, Sergeant," Laila ordered.

Alpha team consisted of Sergeant Hugo McManus and Leigh Ann Poh. They used the ship's spikes to climb up the side of the ship. When they reached the hatch, they found a manual release. The atmosphere from inside the vessel hissed out as the hatch slowly descended.

"Stay alert," Laila ordered. "Bravo team will cover the hatch while you climb back down, Alpha team."

"Copy that," Leigh Ann replied.

A minute later, the hatch had lowered to the deck of the *Renegade,* and Alpha team went inside first, followed closely by Laila and Izzy. The slave ship was not like the vessel they had boarded in the Casa system. It was one big, open space on the inside. There were a lot of structural supports and gears but no compartments to separate one space from another. All around the big ramp were cages. Most were empty, but Laila counted twenty-three small beings huddled in some of the cages. They looked like mythological creatures. They had sleek bodies that reminded her of felines, but their feet were more like horses' hooves, and their heads were feathered. They had big, sad eyes and long curved beaks. They had wings, too, but the feathers had been plucked and many of the wings drooped from broken bones.

"Fascinating," Hugo said as he approached one cage.

"We aren't here for them," Laila said. "Stay sharp, head on a swivel."

It was difficult to see in the gloomy ship. The interior was open but crowded with gear. There were empty cages on the deck and giant hoses hanging from the ceiling. Lalia saw pincer arms and what had to be extendable boarding tubes. What she didn't see was the crew of the slave ship.

"Master Sergeant, we've got prisoners here," Laila said.

"Copy that," Remmy replied.

"Alpha and Bravo team are continuing our sweep."

"We'll go forward," Hugo suggested. "You go aft."

"Sounds like a plan," Laila agreed.

Hugo and Leigh Ann Poh turned to their right around the row of cages filled with the strange beings. Laila and Izzy went to their left. It took effort not to get lost in conjecture about the captives. Laila's empathy was high. She couldn't imagine what it must be like to have the ability to fly taken from her. She hoped the aliens could heal, but there were no guarantees. She had to shake her head to clear the depressing thoughts that crowded her mind.

"You good, Staff Sergeant?" Izzy asked.

"Tiptop," Laila replied.

They moved slowly, their guns held ready. The sweep took several minutes, but eventually, they came to a section of the ship with old gear that formed a sort of barricade. There was movement behind the wall of debris. As they approached it, a voice barked out at them. It was part growl, part yipping. To her ears, it was complete gibberish, but a translation came across her HUD.

Don't shoot! We surrender.

"I've got slavers wanting to surrender," Laila radioed in.

"Activate your translation app," Remmy replied via the comlink. "Order them to lay down their weapons and get on the ground. Face down if possible."

"Copy that," she said. "Lay down your weapons. We're coming in."

Hugo pulled back a section of the materials the crew was hiding behind. Inside were six beings. They were all the same race of average height bipeds with dark skin, narrow eyes, and sloping foreheads. The biggest difference between them and the humans was in the number of limbs. The aliens had four arms. They didn't wear much clothing, and they looked smudged and smeared with dirt.

"Glad we can't smell them," Leigh Ann Poh said.

"I don't think their weapons are even functional," Tex said. "I sure wouldn't want to shoot one."

"Junk, just like everything else in this heap," Hugo said.

They did a full sweep through the ship. It was dark and dirty, with piles of trash and debris that, in places, was taller than Laila. There were no more slaves on board. From a Marine perspective, the operation was anti-climatic. The weapons were taken, but the slaver crew was left on the ship. The artificial gravity beam lifted the terrible-looking craft from the deck and sent it racing away from the *Renegade*.

"Just another day in the service," Hugo said as they waited for the next slave ship to arrive.

"We saved some people, though," Izzy pointed out. "I feel pretty good about that."

"People?" Hugo asked. "They looked like magic creatures from a storybook. I don't think I'll ever get used to that."

"Does it make you think that maybe the idea that aliens visited Earth long, long ago could have been right?" Leigh Ann asked.

"Hard to say," Laila commented. "There's a reason the Imperium doesn't know about us."

"If that's really the case," Hugo said. "We don't really know that. Maybe they just realized we're too dangerous to mess with and moved on."

"He's got a point," Tex said.

"With all our advancements through the years, we're still pretty violent," Izzy said. "It's in our nature to wage war."

Remmy and Dirk Oliver returned from taking the refugees onto the ship, where a group of Dudonus were waiting for them.

"How are the survivors?" Laila asked.

"Good as can be," Remmy said.

"Happy, I think," Dirk added. "Glad to be free."

"What were they?" Leigh Ann asked.

"Nurek called them Gildons," Remmy said. "They were communicating. I'm pretty sure that was just one family of them."

"At least they're together then," Hugo said. "And safe now."

"That makes all the difference," Izzy added.

"Did they say anything about the crew of the slave ship?" Leigh Ann asked.

Remmy shook his head. "Not to me. And we didn't stick around long enough to ask. The Captain can make that call."

The next three ships had no slaves on board. The crews were all different. Each one was manned by beings of the same race, and none put up any resistance. Their ships were all dirty and seemed on the verge of falling apart. From each one, the Marines collected laser weapons. They were designed to fit the slavers, most of whom were smaller than the humans. But there was no flair in the designs, and the weapons were mostly junk.

"I don't think they even work," Leigh Ann had pointed out.

"They probably don't need them to," Hugo said.

"It's all about fear," Tex agreed. "Besides, they don't want to damage their captives. That would cut into their profits."

"It's hard to imagine these people making any money," Izzy said. "The slavers look just as bad off as the slaves."

"Let's not get lax in our attentiveness," Remmy said. "Just because the other ships weren't violent doesn't mean this last one won't be."

It was good advice and almost prophetic. Once it was pulled into the *Renegade,* the teams went to work. They were accustomed to the slave ships and knew just what to do after hours of searching the franken-ships. But they noticed that the fifth and final slave ship was different. When the hatch opened the first thing they noticed were lights on inside the vessel.

"I got artificial lighting," Hugo said. "And voices."

"They surrendering already?" Dirk asked.

"Negative," Hugo said. "It's slaves. Lots of 'em."

"We go in slow," Laila said from the bottom of the ramp. "Alternate positions. Head on a swivel."

"Copy that," Leigh Ann Poh said. "There must be a hundred slaves up here."

"Some of them seem to be in bad shape," Hugo added.

"Hold that position," Remmy ordered. "We'll secure the captives before sweeping the ship for the crew."

"Alpha Team is in position," Hugo said.

"Bravo Team in position," Laila spoke up. "This ship is different, Master Sergeant. The slaves seem to be held in an enclosed compartment."

"There's refuse everywhere," Izzy added. "They've been locked up a while."

"I got eyes on the entrance," Hugo said. "It's a big steel door. Looks secured from this side."

"Charlie team is on-site," Sergeant Dirk said. "It may take a bit to cut open all these cages."

"McManus was right," Tex said. "We're gonna need some type of gurneys for a bunch of these creatures. There are injuries, and what I'm guessing are infirmities from being locked in the cages. I've never seen anything like it."

"I'll call it in. Alpha team covers the main door. Bravo, sweep the compartment for any other exits," Remmy ordered. "And watch for traps, too. There could be anything on that ship."

"Roger that, Master Sergeant," Laila said. "We're on it."

She and Izzy Berry moved slowly down the center aisle. There were cages stacked nearly to the ceiling with all sorts of alien creatures inside. There was no doubt about the mistreatment. She saw open wounds, swollen limbs, glassy eyes, and everywhere there was filth. The captives were obviously not removed from their cages once they were locked inside. Those on the deck had the worst of it. She could see dark sludge oozing around the bottoms of the cages.

"It's more than just these," Izzy said as they reached a gap in the stacked cages. "There's another row."

Laila could see two more rows of cages beyond the ones on the central aisle. She could also see that some of the captives were dead. They were all aliens. Some looked like animals, and others were strange, distant cousins to the human race. It reminded her of a movie she had seen about traveling groups in the distant past called Freak Shows. The poor, malformed individuals had been exploited and abused until they eventually turned on the vile men who were running the circus. But most of the captives were too weak to fight against the slavers. And despite their alien appearance, Laila recognized the dull stare of dead eyes from some of the cages.

What they didn't find were any other entrances or exits from the cargo area. The walls and ceiling were made from metal with thick, shoddy-looking welds. There were lights in the ceiling and what appeared to be hoses on two of the side walls. She could only imagine how the space was used once it was time to unload the cargo of beings unfortunate enough to be captured by the slavers. They found what appeared to be a type of cargo lift but nothing else.

"I think we're clear, Master Sergeant," Laila reported. "No other way in or out of this section. No traps or danger either, just a lot of unfortunate souls."

"Corporal Thompson is on his way with the new recruits," Remmy reported. "Medical personnel are standing by. Have your team support Alpha team, Staff Sergeant. We'll get the captives off that ship before proceeding."

"Bravo team is standing by," Laila said as she moved up behind Hugo McManus.

"This is the worst thing I've ever seen," he said. "War, murder, natural disasters, nothing comes close to this, Staff Sergeant. I thought I understood slavery. I didn't."

"I agree," Laila said, forcing her eyes to remain on the steel door. "How anyone can do this is beyond the pale."

"And beyond forgiveness in my book."

Laila nodded. She wondered if, when she came face to face with the aliens who could do such heinous deeds, she could keep herself from gunning them down. It would be no less than they deserved ... or maybe it would be better to lock them in their own cages and send them on their way. At least then, they would know what it was like to be prisoners with no hope. To make them suffer as they had made so many others suffer seemed more like justice to her than a quick death.

CHAPTER 14

"HOW MANY?" Captain Zeke Darius asked from the Bridge of the *Renegade*. "Do we have a number?"

"Nearly three hundred," Dr. Lanski replied. "About half of those will require medical treatment."

"Can we provide it?" Darius asked.

"No, Captain, unfortunately, we can only do the most basic first aid. But Nurek is certain that there are facilities on Olo Prime that can do more. We've set up an area to treat the wounded and house the rest until we reach orbit."

"Very good," Darius said. "Are any of the captives in good enough shape to give us an account of where they came from?"

"I think so," Dr. Lanski said. "Nurek and his companions are seeing to the aliens. Once the Marines get them all off the slave ship, we'll make a report, sir. But I must also inform you that not all the aliens are alive."

"Some are dead?"

"Aye, Captain," Dr. Lanski said sadly. "I've visually examined a few of the captives. They have injuries that can only come from extended periods of time locked in their cages. Some couldn't even move around inside the metal cages. It's abhorrent, sir."

"I've no doubt," Darius said. "Do what you can for them, Doctor. Once we've dealt with the ships, we'll proceed directly to orbit at speed."

Darius looked around the Bridge. No one was talking. It felt like there was a general sense of grief. Darius knew it wasn't the first time a military force had found innocents in such heinous conditions. And after conversations with Nurek and some of the Casians, Darius was aware that slavery, both authorized and unauthorized, was rampant in the Imperium. For every free race, there was a species designated as slave-eligible. And some races could only be slaves with no rights of their own on any planet.

"Captain, you have a message from the Admin Center," Ensign Bertoli said. "It's Commander Lee."

"Put her through," Darius replied.

Through the transparent canopy over the Bridge, Darius could see the four slave ships they had already caught and released. They were all damaged, although it appeared that the cobbled-together vessels were designed for space flight even with damage to their hulls. Two were still operational and were making what appeared to be wide arcs that would take them to the hyperspace portal. The other two were drifting ahead of the *Renegade,* clearly helpless to escape.

"Captain," Commander Lori Lee said. "We have four spaces designated for refugees. The Dudonus are taking the lead, but some of our people are helping out. These poor refugees need a lot of help."

"Medical or something else?"

"Just to get cleaned up, they need facilities," Lori Lee said. "Their clothing is ruined, and many will need some type of help just to get around. They've been locked in cages for who knows how long, sir. I would guess that only a fraction are unharmed in some way."

"Doesn't make much sense, does it?" Darius replied. "Why mistreat the beings you hope to sell?"

"That's just it, sir. Lutus believes these were the slaves they couldn't sell."

"What were they doing with them?"

"Unknown, Captain. Authorized slave traders are responsible for the health and well-being of all their slaves, even those they cannot sell. But we're dealing with outlaws, sir. They could be doing anything with them."

"See if you can find out," Darius said. "We need to make a decision on these slave ships. Two could possibly escape if we don't act soon."

"Yes, Captain. I'll see what I can learn. They're moving some of the healthy refugees into the compartments off the main concourse on Epsilon deck now. I'll be in touch."

Darius turned and looked at Lieutenant Peter Best. "Do you have a firing solution on those ships?"

"Aye, Captain. We'll need to adjust our position to get all four, but it won't take us long," Pete Best said.

"Excellent, Lieutenant. Nav, what's our best speed to orbit?"

"Six hours, thirty-one minutes," Vivian Ramos replied.

"Any word from the planet?" Darius asked.

"Not yet, sir. We're still on the fringe of the system," Ensign Bertoli replied. "It will take some time for the signals to reach the planet."

"Very good. Get me, Master Sergeant Steel, please."

"Aye, Captain, Master Sergeant Steel is standing by," Jacee Bertoli said.

"Master Sergeant, how do things look on that slave ship?" Darius asked.

"Not great, Captain," Remmy replied. "We're still moving refugees out. There are a lot of them, sir."

"What about the ship's crew?"

"No sign of them. This ship is built different from the others, sir. The slaves are in a sealed compartment."

"Will we have any problems getting into the ship?"

"No, sir, we have the tools to breach their defenses."

"I'm getting word that we're dealing with the worst of the worst," Darius said. "At this stage, I think we're better off dealing with the slavers on a permanent basis."

"Sir, if you're saying we should kill every one of the filthy animals responsible for this, then I say 'Oorah', sir."

"We'll take care of the other ships," Darius said. "Have your people take out that crew ASAP. We need to get these people help and we're still nearly seven hours out from orbit."

"Copy that, sir. We'll take care of things down here."

"Keep me in the loop, Master Sergeant. I want to know when we can jettison that ship."

"Yes, sir," Remmy replied.

Darius leaned back in his chair. It weighed on him to give an order that would lead to the death of the people on the slave ships. But they weren't innocents. They chose to abduct people and sell them into slavery. Darius could think of very few things worse than that.

"Lieutenant Best, fire on the slave ships," Zeke Darius said. "Let's make sure there's nothing left to recover."

CHAPTER 15

"WE'RE ALL SET, MASTER SERGEANT," Hugo McManus said as the last of the caged refugees were taken out of the huge, hangar-like collection bay at the front of the *Renegade.*

Remmy Steel turned and looked up the ramp into the slave ship. There was a weight on his shoulders that he wasn't used to. It wasn't there physically. His space armor was bulky, but not uncomfortable, and he was used to the weight of it. But there was a sensation of weight, perhaps from the responsibility of the platoon. He was making the decisions with Lieutenant Colt still in a coma. Or maybe it had settled in after seeing the refugees. There were hundreds of aliens that had been locked in cages for who knew how long. They were covered in filth. Their bodies injured. Their skin covered in sores from the unrelenting steel of the cages. Most looked half-starved and traumatized by their captors. And it was up to Remmy to make things right.

"Alright, let's do it," Remmy said, waving a hand toward Hugo McManus, who had extruded a thick line of thermite paste along the locking side of the steel door.

McManus ignited the thermite with his laser pistol. The paste glowed red, then bright yellow. Smoke billowed from the door as the chemical burned through the metal locking mechanism. In the cargo area where the slaves had been held, seven space Marines stood ready for whatever was waiting for them on the other side of the doorway.

The smoke stopped once the thermite had burned up. The edge of the door had been transformed into a jagged line of scorched metal.

"Alright, platoon," Remmy said. "Weapons hot. Hugo, pull that door open. If it moves, it dies."

"Copy that," Tex replied.

"Bravo Team is ready," Staff Sergeant Laila McPherson said.

Hugo reached out and pulled the door open. It swung on rusty hinges that squealed under the weight of the heavy door. Beyond it, the corridor was dark.

"Night vision," Remmy said. "Let's move people. Two by two. Alpha Team, you take point."

"Yes, Master Sergeant," Leigh Ann Poh said as she and Hugo moved quickly into the dark space.

Bravo Team was Laila and Izzy. They followed. Alpha team stayed to the right side of the corridor, and Bravo Team moved against the left side. Charlie team was Sergeant Dirk Oliver, and Corporal "Tex" Fry, who waited at the entryway with Remmy.

"Looks like crew quarters," Leigh Ann announced as they passed a doorway.

"Weird," Hugo added.

"What's weird?" Remmy asked.

"Don't know, Sarge. Seems familiar somehow," McManus replied

"I've got crew quarters too," Laila said. "There's a stairway up ahead."

"Any sign of the crew?" Remmy asked.

"Negative. The compartments are small. There's no place to hide inside."

"Hold up at the stairs," Remmy ordered. "Charlie Team with me."

They moved into the dark corridor. The night vision on their battle helmets made everything either green or black, but they could see. As they passed the first compartment, Remmy looked inside. It reminded him of a bedroom occupied by children. There were two unmade bunks, the blankets and sheets rumpled and discarded. There was a tiny table and two stools. Trash covered the table and was overflowing from what appeared to be a wastebasket. Likewise, clothes were littered about. Remmy got the same strange sensation as Hugo as if he had seen the compartment before.

"The clothes look almost human," Dirk pointed out. "Two arms, two legs."

"Don't mean they're human," Tex said. "Lots of folks walking upright these days."

They reached the stairs which were made of bare metal with no handrail. It stood out to Remmy only because the *Renegade* had no stairs. The Arodoni who built the advanced ship used ramps, not stairs. Likewise, on Casasil, the natives used ramps instead of stairways going into their large, barn-style homes and up into the loft areas. The slave ship was the first vessel he had seen with stairs. Even the slave ship they had boarded in the Casasil system used a completely different system for transitioning between the levels.

"Let's continue forward one team at a time," Remmy ordered. "Leapfrog positions. Call out if you see anyone."

Hugo led the way up the stairs. They were wide enough for two people, but not two Marines in full space armor with weapons. Leigh Ann Poh followed Hugo but stayed a few steps behind him.

"Second level is living space," Hugo said. "Looks like a galley and some—"

The sound of laser fire was heard—a high-pitched whining sound as the batteries refilled the laser's power reservoir between shots. There was no thump of bullets, just the sizzle of laser blasts on metal. The laser blasts were followed quickly by weapon fire from projectiles. Remmy felt a wave of relief as he recognized the report of two different types of weapons, which told him that Hugo and Leigh Ann were still alive.

Added to the weapons fire was the sound of boots pounding up the stairs. Laila led the charge, and Remmy brought up the rear. Then he heard a scream. It was strange and made the hair on the back of Remmy's neck stand straight out.

"I got one," Hugo said.

More shooting erupted, and then, just as suddenly, it stopped. The strange, haunting wail continued.

"Clear!" Leigh Ann shouted.

"Clear," Hugo said.

Remmy bounded up the steps and found Hugo on his knees with a black scorch mark on his shoulder.

"Are you hurt?" Remmy asked as the rest of the platoon moved toward a cluster of furniture where the crew had been hiding.

"No, the armor held," Hugo said. "Some minor burns, that's all."

"Master Sergeant!" Laila called out. "You need to see this."

Remmy pulled Hugo to his feet, and together, they crossed the room. What the others had discovered made Remmy's blood run cold. He immediately toggled his comlink to the command channel.

"Captain Darius, sir," he said. "I have something you need to see."

Using his battle helmet's controls, he activated the video feed so that it would transfer to the Bridge.

"Master Sergeant," Darius replied, his voice strained. "Is that what I think it is?"

"I think so," Remmy said, panning his camera around so it could take in the four dead crew members as well as the wounded one.

"Humans?" Darius asked.

"Looks like it, sir. We haven't cleared the ship, but I'll leave a team here to scan the bodies. Our trauma kits don't do much more than assess tissue damage, but it'll be a start. We can move the bodies to the med bay and get DNA profiles. That should give us the information we need."

"Agreed," Darius said. "Excellent, Master Sergeant. Let us know if you run into anything else unusual down there. Darius out."

Remmy looked at Izzy, who had sprayed foam into the wound on the injured man's shoulder. He looked human. His skin was light brown, his greasy hair darker, and he had a tangled beard too. He moaned loudly in pain, mumbling in a language that Remmy didn't recognize. Nor did the translation app in his helmet's computer.

"This can't be happening," Dirk said as he scanned the wounded man with a trauma wand.

"Hard to believe, that's for certain," Tex agreed.

"Is he really human?" Leigh Ann Poh asked.

"All the systems read like he is," Dirk replied. "Organs are all in the right place."

"How bad's he hit?" Remmy asked.

"There's structural damage to the shoulder," Dirk said. "He needs surgery. The blood loss is significant, too. It's fifty-fifty he'll survive."

"This changes everything," Laila said. "We can't let him die."

"You take him back," Remmy ordered. "Hugo, too. I'll take Leigh Ann with Charlie team and we'll finish the sweep."

"I can't believe a human would be involved in this," Dirk said. "No way."

"Maybe they didn't have a choice," Hugo said.

"We'll find out," Remmy replied. "As long as this guy doesn't shuffle off into the sunset. Get him to Doc Lanski as quickly as you can. The surgical robots can patch him up, but he'll need plasma, maybe even a blood transfusion if he's really human."

Izzy pulled the man into a sitting position, then onto her shoulder. Hugo helped and steadied Izzy as she got to her feet.

"I can do that," he said to her.

The man was thin and only about her height. Izzy, like most

special forces commandos, was strong enough to carry a fellow Marine off the battlefield in an emergency.

"I got him," she said.

Laila picked up Izzy's rifle and led the way back toward the stairs. Hugo went down first, and Izzy steadied herself on the way down with a hand on the big man's good shoulder. Remmy turned to the three Marines waiting for his orders.

"There's gotta be more to this ship," he said. "Let's find it."

There was another stairwell, this one spiraling up. The third deck of the alien ship was smaller. Narrow corridors led to rooms that were filled with machinery, from life support to the engine compartments and even a strange device that was probably the slave ship's gravity beam generator, although Remmy couldn't be sure. They searched every compartment. The small group of Marines was quiet, but Remmy knew what they were thinking. Humans on an alien slave ship didn't make sense. Yet the proof seemed undeniable and left only two possibilities: either the crew of the *Jericho* wasn't the first people to leave the Sol system, or humans weren't exclusive to Earth.

The second option seemed to be the most likely scenario, and yet it opened up a host of questions. Remmy had always been a simple person. He didn't feel the need to exhaust the philosophical demands of life's biggest questions. Where did mankind come from? Why were they created, and by whom? And, of course, were they alone in the universe?

The last question had been answered. Humans were not alone. Mankind had believed that to be the case for centuries. Not simply because the universe was so big but because, for thousands of years, people had reported encounters with the supernatural. But coming face to face with a human being who was not from the Sol system was a shock, even to Remmy, who prided himself on being steady in the most difficult of circumstances.

"Found something," Tex reported.

"Wait for us," Remmy told him.

The rest of the group found Tex looking at what appeared to be a hatch but a strange set of controls. Most of the ship was simple, almost old-fashioned in Remmy's mind. But the control panel by the hatch was more advanced.

"Looks like a touchpad," Dirk Oliver said.

"Small though," Leigh Ann added, holding her empty hand up, fingers spread apart.

The control pad was smaller than her hand.

"Touch it," Remmy ordered. "Let's see what we're dealing with."

Leigh Ann touched the control pad. A red light appeared. It pulsed for a few seconds, and then the control pad went dark again.

"Not gonna figure that out any time soon," Tex said.

Dirk Oliver rapped on the hatch with a knuckle. It sounded hollow or thin.

"We can burn through it," Dirk said.

"Do it, but let's take up defensive positions," Remmy said. "Whatever's in there doesn't want us to find it."

Remmy moved past the hatch with Tex, while Leigh Ann Poh stayed on the other side of the corridor with Dirk. Tex pulled his laser pistol, transferred it to his left hand, and started cutting down the right-hand side of the hatch. From the far side, Dirk joined in. They burned long, vertical cuts along the edges of the hatch, then turned and cut in toward each other at the bottom. Once that was done, they cut another line along the top until the entire center of the hatch was free. It fell inward, and immediately, a series of laser blasts flashed out. Someone was inside the compartment shooting at them.

"Anyone got eyes?" Remmy asked.

"Negative," Tex said.

"I saw something," Dirk said. "Not human. But it's dark in there."

The Marines all had urban warfare weapons as part of their regular supplies. Remmy reached back and pulled a flash-bang grenade from a loop in his belt. It was a small device, non-lethal, that emitted a very bright flash and loud bang meant to stun humans without protective gear. There was no way to know if it would have any effect on the being inside the compartment. But Remmy pulled the pin and tossed the grenade into the room. It went off with a loud report and a flash. They heard a cry of pain, and Remmy, forgetting that he was the platoon leader, spun out from his place in the corridor and charged through the opening his Marines had cut in the door.

He found himself inside a dark room with strange furnishings. An odd, reptilian creature, tall and thick through the body, raced through a doorway at the far end of the dark compartment.

"I got one bogey," Remmy said as the other Marines filed into the room behind him.

They lit their helmet lights and looked around the dark space.

"Hot and wet in here," Dirk said, touching a wall that was dripping with condensation.

"I've got something," Leigh Ann said. "It's a tank with some kind of animal inside. A lot of them."

Remmy joined her. The creatures in the tank were hopping around and making odd chirping noises.

"It's food," Remmy said.

"What?" Leigh Ann said. "Food? Are you serious?"

"I think so," Remmy said.

"So, we aren't dealing with another human," Dirk pointed out.

It was obvious as Remmy looked around the dark space. There was what looked like an infrared heater built into the ceiling. And instead of couches or chairs, there were round, flat-topped rocks. Next to the tank full of fist-sized bugs, there was a waterfall of sorts. Water came out of a pipe and flowed down between rocks that were mounted into the bulkhead before pooling at the bottom.

"A reptile," Remmy said as he moved to the doorway he had seen the creature escape through. "At least, a reptilian creature. It stood upright, but it looked like it had a lizard head and tail."

"Great," Tex said. "Everything about this ship makes my skin crawl."

"Yeah, I'm gonna need a very long, very hot shower after this is over," Leigh Ann said.

Remmy stepped up to the doorway. There was no hatch to

remove or cut through. Just a short corridor with a doorway to the side and another directly ahead. They moved slowly, and Remmy kept his Nelson LTX rifle pulled tight against his shoulder with the barrel up and ready to fire. The side room was clearly another living space. It was almost a replica of the room they had come through. At the end of the hallway, they came to a vertical tunnel. Remmy looked up but couldn't see anything.

"This has to lead to the control center," Tex said.

"But there's no way up," Leigh Ann said.

"No easy way," Remmy corrected her. "The lizard people obviously have no problem climbing the walls."

"I bet we can, too," Dirk said as he reached out and touched the wall of the vertical shaft.

"It'll be slow going," Tex pointed out. And we'll have our hands tied up at the top. They can pick us off as our heads pop up."

"We can't just let them go," Leigh Ann argued.

"We won't," Remmy said.

He was already using his mental link with GIGI to activate a small, armed drone. GIGI did the real work. The alien artifact had enough computing power to control hundreds of drones at the same time. But Remmy only needed one.

"You three stay here," he ordered. "I'll go up."

"It's too dangerous, Master Sergeant," Tex said.

"He's right," Dirk spoke up. "You can't take that risk."

"I'm not," Remmy said. "GIGI is sending in a drone. I won't take any chances."

"Unless you're halfway up the shaft, and they decide to take a potshot at you," Tex said.

"So cover me," Remmy said.

He started climbing while the other three Marines watched for any signs of the last remaining crew members. Remmy was halfway up the shaft when the drone appeared below him. It was bigger than he expected, disk-shaped with a built-in propeller and a pair of small guns mounted on top. It flew up past him, hovering for a moment as

Remmy's helmet synced with the drone. He didn't control it, but the video feed it recorded showed on his HUD. He waited and watched as it continued upward.

Just before it breached the top of the tunnel, the aliens fired on it. Laser beams scorched the heat-resistant plate armor. The drone rotated quickly and fired a series of shots at one alien. The small, dart-like flechettes ripped through their clothing and sank deep into the reptilian flesh. The aliens looked like a mashup of humans and lizards. They stood upright with short arms and legs. A long tail stood out horizontally behind them, but they wore boots and tunics with belts around their middle. They also held strange-looking laser pistols. The one the drone shot went down with a hiss. The device immediately rotated back around, targeting the second creature. The alien threw down its weapon and held up its short arms. Remmy could see four fingers but no thumb. Each finger ended in a claw. It appeared to be surrendering. Then, without warning, it spun around and lashed out at the drone with its powerful tail.

The drone fired at the same time. The tail hit the drone and sent it crashing into a bank of controls. The lizard man was screeching and Remmy climbed upward until he could get his head above the opening in the floor of the ship's control center. One alien was on the ground, bleeding to death. The other was wounded but still on its feet. Remmy drew his pistol, a Yagger HC. The lizard alien started to spin again, lashing out with its tail, but Remmy fired first. The pistol was loaded with shotgun-type shells that were loaded with Buzzers. They were small, disc shaped blades, which were only effective at close range. The Buzzers hit the alien as it was turning, ripping through the flesh in its shoulder and neck. Blood sprayed out in a fine mist of brilliant blue, and the alien was knocked off its feet. It lay on the deck, twitching as Remmy climbed up the rest of the way.

"Everything okay?" Sergeant Dirk Oliver asked.

"Roger that," Remmy said. "This is the Bridge up here, from the looks of things."

"What about the bad guys?" Leigh Ann Poh asked.

"Dead," Remmy said. "They managed to get the drone, though. Looks like our work here is done."

Remmy made a video record, then climbed back down the shaft.

"The reptiles were calling the shots," Tex said as they moved back through the habitats where the lizard creatures lived.

"Looks that way," Remmy replied.

"And the humans, if they really are human," Leigh Ann interjected, "were just muscle?"

"Maybe even slaves themselves," Dirk suggested.

They stopped on the second level and looked again at the dead humans lying where they had been killed. They had weapons that looked old and patched together from a variety of parts. Their laser rifles were nothing like the sleek weapons of the aliens on the upper levels.

"Damn shame," Tex said, looking at the bodies.

Their wounds still oozed red blood.

"We came thousands of light years across the galaxy," Dirk said, "just to end up killing our own."

"We don't know that," Leigh Ann argued. "They may not be human at all."

"Genetic cousins, though," Tex said. "Has to be. Just look at 'em. Eyes, ears, nose, mouth, it's all the same."

"The med staff will be able to tell us more," Remmy said. "And the brass can decide what to make of it. But don't forget they fired on us first."

"Maybe because they had to," Dirk suggested.

Remmy nodded. "Maybe, but maybe not. It wouldn't be the first time humans traded in slaves, you know."

"They were probably just as surprised to see us as we were to see them," Dirk added. "They may not have even realized we were humans in our space armor."

"You think they might not have fought back if they had?" Leigh Ann asked.

"Maybe," Dirk said.

"Let's stand down," Remmy said. "We've been at it a long time today. Go back to the armory. See to your weapons and armor. As soon as I know more, I'll let you know."

"You need rest too, Sarge," Tex pointed out.

"And I'll get some, but until the LT is back on his feet, I've got his job to do. I'll make the report, check in with the Captain, then I'll meet you all back in grunt country."

The three Marines filed off the alien ship in front of Remmy. He was proud of them, proud of what they had accomplished. Walking back into the ship, he passed several of the new Casian recruits helping the recently freed aliens. Some were walking beside the big, six-legged pachyderms. Others were actually on the backs of the Casians, who didn't seem to mind at all. In fact, if Remmy was reading their alien body language correctly, they seemed thrilled. He could only guess that they felt good about freeing slaves or maybe it was just being useful that they liked. Unlike the Marine Commandos, the Casians weren't burdened by the knowledge that their own kind could be involved in such a horrific activity as slave trading. Remmy didn't know what the future held, but he knew the discovery of the humans on the slave ship had radically changed everything for the crew of the *Renegade*.

CHAPTER 16

"HE'S HUMAN?" Captain Darius asked.

He was gathered with his senior staff and Master Sergeant Steel in what had become their wardroom. They had invited Connor O'Dell as well, and everyone had questions for Doctor Vivik Lanski.

"Yes," the doctor replied. "Medical scans show them to be like us in every way. I even ran a DNA test. They are human. I've sent for the bodies of the others. We can run tests and autopsies to get a better idea of what their physiology can tell us."

"But how?" Peter Best asked. "We're the first humans to leave the Sol system."

"That we know of," Henry Nash said. "There's plenty of black ops that no one knows about 'cept the top brass. Am I right, Master Sergeant?"

Remmy nodded but didn't speak.

"Let's not get carried away with conspiracy theories," Captain Darius said.

"I doubt it was the government," Connor spoke up. "We've been trying to find a way to manage deep space travel for a long time to no avail."

"If not us, then how?" Vivian Ramos asked.

"I do have a theory," Connor said. "We know that aliens have visited our home world in the past."

"I thought we weren't going in for conspiracy theories," Pete Best said.

Connor shook his head. "It's fact. GIGI is proof of that. I believe there are answers she's not telling us."

"And you think these visitors," Darius spoke up, "took people?"

"I think it's a strong possibility," Connor said. "GIGI is proof that we were visited; perhaps studied was a better word. Also, we know that abducting individuals for slavery is common in the galaxy. Those two facts alone point to an obvious conclusion."

"But no one knows about the Sol system but us," Pete Best said.

"Actually," Vivian interjected, "what GIGI said was that the Imperium doesn't know about the Sol system."

"But obviously, some space-faring people did," Nash added. "There are reports of UAPs going back centuries, as well as abduction stories and people who just vanish for no reason."

"They were taken as slaves?" Pete Best asked.

"Slaves, subjects for investigation, perhaps even experimentation," Connor O'Dell said. "And, if I'm being honest here, it seems like a lot of these aliens have familiar animal characteristics from Earth fauna."

"What are you suggesting?" Darius asked.

"I've spent my entire life in the sciences," Connor said. "Mankind has been experimenting for centuries with gene editing. There have been cases of cross-species genetic hybrids ... and studies made by serious academics on the alien abduction phenomenon point to the same conclusion. The so-called aliens were harvesting human genetic materials and carrying out their own experiments."

"You're saying that genetic material from animals was used to create alien races?" Darius asked.

"I'm saying it's possible," Connor argued.

"But they've been around a lot longer than we have," Vivian

pointed out. "Humanity has only been in the space age for a few centuries. The Imperium has been in power much longer than that."

"An old theory for the origins of the human race was called Panspermia," Connor said.

"Pan what?" Nash asked.

"Panspermia, it's from the Greek. Pan meaning *all*, and spermia meaning *seed*," the scientist explained. "Essentially, it proposes that life on earth arose from sources outside the Sol system. Some argued that genetic material was carried on space debris, asteroids, comets, even space dust. Others made the case that advanced civilizations brought the genetic materials and launched life on Earth as a kind of experiment."

Darius felt a chill. He didn't like the idea of being someone's test case. Science didn't have a good answer for why humanity had arisen on Earth. He had always been a believer in God, even if his career made it impossible for him to practice his religion in an organized way. Circumstances were looking more and more as though aliens, not God, were responsible for the human race.

"If that's true," Vivian replied. "Then Earth isn't where mankind began."

"Possibly," Connor O'Dell said. "The theory of evolution was dismissed because no one could explain how the information in our DNA arose strictly through natural processes. But if it was planted on Earth by an outside source..."

He let the thought hang in the air for a moment. Darius didn't like it, but he couldn't deny that there were humans on his ship that didn't come from Earth. Or, at least, they were different in some way. The answers lay with the wounded slaver.

"Will the prisoner live?" Darius asked.

"Yes," Doctor Lanski said. "We stopped the bleeding and started a full spectrum of antibiotics to combat the threat of infection, along with IV fluids that should aid in rebuilding his blood supply over time. He'll need surgery on his shoulder, but I didn't think making him whole again was the top priority at the moment."

"We need to question him," Darius said.

"That might not be easy," Remmy said, speaking up for the first time. "He was talking after the fight, but it didn't register with our communication app."

"No translation?" Connor asked.

"No," Remmy replied. "And he wasn't speaking any language I ever heard before."

"Did you try to engage with him?" Darius asked.

"Negative, sir."

"If he was taken from Earth within his lifetime, he might recognize our language, even if we don't recognize his," Darius said. "As soon as he's able to talk, I want Commander Lee to interrogate him."

"Aye, Captain," Lori Lee said.

"In the meantime, we'll continue on to Olo Prime," Darius continued. "Once we're in orbit, we'll move down the refugees."

"If the locals will take them," Pete Best said.

Vivian shook her head, "Are you suggesting they won't?"

"Wouldn't be the first time refugees weren't wanted," Pete replied.

"We didn't take them from the Imperium or even from authorized slave traders," Darius pointed out. "For all we know, they were abducted from Olo Prime."

"That I highly doubt," the doctor said. "Their wounds suggest the refugees were captive for a long time. Months, most likely."

"Either the people on Olo Prime will help or they won't," Darius said. "Our plan was to move from system to system, recruiting help along the way until we reached the free worlds. As things stand, we may need to change that plan."

"How so?" Henry Nash said.

"If there are humans in the galaxy, our first priority would be to find them," Darius said. "Especially if they're being held against their will. Plus, the reality of our system being hidden might not be as secure as we thought. If anyone recognizes us as humans and reports that back to the Imperium, they could find our home and launch an invasion."

"So what are you suggesting we do, Captain?" Lori Lee asked.

"I think we have to find out what we can from the humans on that slave ship," Darius said. "If there are more in need, we help them. If they have a presence in the Imperium, we have to go home."

That phrase hung heavy in the air. It would have been cause for rejoicing just a few hours earlier. But the only reason for the *Renegade* to go to the Sol system would be to defend it.

"I've been arguing for that very thing since we left," Connor O'Dell said. "It's not our place to wage war across the galaxy. Our duty must be to humanity and that duty must come first."

"In this ship, we've got a fighting chance," Pete Best said. "No matter what the Imperium sends after us."

"I disagree," Darius said. "We defeated their last attack."

"Which they made with twenty ships," Pete pointed out.

"But we made mistakes," Darius said. "One that nearly cost us this ship. If they had gotten more of their commandos on board, there's no telling what kind of damage they might have done. In every war, there are novel strategies and tactics that must be learned. I would prefer to learn them far from home."

"But if we have to go back..." Nash said.

"Then we will," Darius replied.

"We still have one ace up our sleeve," Remmy suggested.

Everyone turned and looked at the NCO. He was the lowest-ranking individual apart from their civilian observer, but he was also the most experienced in combat.

"We have their Emperor," Remmy continued. "If he's still alive."

"He is," Doctor Lanski said. "We're keeping him sedated, but he's healing fast."

"Having their leader might not be as big of a benefit as we hope," Darius pointed out. "According to Nurek, there are plenty of people who would be happy to see the Emperor dead."

"But can they disregard the fact that he's our prisoner?" Vivian

Ramos asked. "It might even be possible to negotiate a peace with him and send him back."

"Possibly, but highly unlikely," Commander Lee said. "I don't think peace is what they're after."

"He was important enough to send commandos after him, though," Pete Best said. "Right?"

"Maybe," Darius said. "We didn't get the chance to interrogate the Ashi. We don't know what their orders were. Finding the Emperor on our ship might have been a happy accident."

"We have the edge in technology," Remmy said. "They have numbers. It would be a good idea to find out how many ships they have and how quickly they can get more into space."

"There's no way we fight them alone and succeed," Henry Nash said.

"But we're not alone," Lori Lee pointed out. "According to the Dudonus, there's a rebellion underway."

"Which gives us a clear goal," Darius added. "Our task is to disrupt the Imperium and buy time for the freedom fighters to get organized and take the fight to their overlords. We'll continue to do that as much as we can, but I think we need to know more about the humans outside the Sol system. Until we know where they are and how they got there, we can't go home."

"What happens if we're too late?" Pete Best said. "For all we know, the Imperium already knows where we came from."

"Nurek was the Emperor's slave. He knows quite a bit about the Imperium," Darius said. "Yet, he didn't know what we were. He had never heard of the human race. That fact, plus what GIGI has told us leads me to believe the Sol system is still safe for now."

"But it's only a matter of time before we're found out," Pete Best said. "It seems to me like we should go home before something bad happens."

"Returning to the Sol system may not be the last thing this ship does," Connor O'Dell pointed out. "But it would give us the chance to utilize the advanced Arodoni technology to better prepare our defenses."

"What about the tracking device?" Darius asked.

"We found one," Henry said. "The drones did, at any rate."

"And removed it?" Lori Lee asked.

"Correct," Henry replied. "It's still in the Casa system."

"They probably think we're still there," Connor O'Dell suggested.

"That is what we hope for," Darius replied, "but we must plan as if they know our every move."

"But how could they?" Connor asked.

"Spies," Darius said.

"On this ship?" Connor was aghast at the very idea of it.

"Again, we hope not, but we must prepare for the worst-case scenario. If the rebellion has agents on every planet, then the Imperium must also have agents who are all too willing to send word to their overlords. Our task, therefore, is to prepare as if they might attack at any moment."

"And along the way, find out all we can about the humans outside the Sol system," Vivian Ramos said.

Captain Darius nodded. "Alright then, we have our plans, back to duty stations. Let's make sure that everything is as ready for the unknown as we can make it.

CHAPTER 17

NUREK WALKED into the medical ward. He was a common sight on Epsilon deck, spending long hours everyday in the admin center helping to direct the new recruits in their duties. The Casians were eager to carry out their new jobs and were enthusiastic in their training, but it helped to have someone guiding them. And the dudonus were known to be calm, reliable beings. That made them natural administrators.

The chief medical officer, Doctor Lanski, was out of the medical ward. None of the technicians thought anything odd about seeing Nurek there. Hundreds of refugees had been taken onboard and were being treated for a variety of wounds that were a result of being locked in cages. It made Nurek's blood boil and he knew exactly who was responsible for it. Not just the freed refugees but the entire institution of slavery.

Behind a set of screens in the back of the room designated as the new medical ward was a flatbed cargo lift. On it was a pair of round mattresses that had been cut and sewn to fit the rectangle device. And strapped across the mattresses was a huge, green behemoth.

Nurek had only seen him from a distance since coming aboard the *Renegade*, but he knew exactly who the hulking Ashi warrior was.

"You are awake," Nurek said as he approached the patient.

"You are a traitor," Emperor Vang growled as he struggled to break free of the cargo straps that held him fast.

"How the mighty have fallen," Nurek said before pressing down on the wound where Vang had been shot. "Does it hurt?"

The alien grunted in pain but didn't cry out. Nurek didn't smile. He didn't laugh at his former master's misery. If it were up to him, Nurek would have exterminated the Ashi in one simple moment. He had seen too much pain, too much torturous agony - both physical and mental - to ever wish it on anyone. It was better if the Ashi were simply gone and the galaxy could choose for itself how to be ruled. But Nurek didn't have that power. He couldn't wish the Ashi away. But there was one Ashi that was under his control.

"You must know that the empire has fallen," Nurek said.

"Liar," Vang growled.

"Sheika Kahn will have already replaced you," Nurek said. "The Prime Council will expect him to stop this ship."

"Even an old Ashi warrior is more than a match for the pathetic Arodoni," Vang said. "The fools keep me alive. I will make them pay for their stupidity."

"It is compassion, not stupidity, but I agree: it must be corrected."

Vang stared at Nurek, who didn't blink. Slowly, what his former slave was implying dawned on the Emperor.

"Release me, and I will free you," Vang said.

"No."

"Release me now, slave! I command you."

"You command no one any longer," Nurek said. "Not even yourself."

"If you raise your hand against me, I will see to it that every Dudonus slave on every world in the galaxy is killed."

"You no longer have the power to accomplish that," Nurek said.

"You are no longer an Emperor. You are a forgotten, unwanted, powerless thing that will never hurt anyone ever again."

"You are a coward," Vang growled. "If you want to kill me, slave, then set me free. We shall settle this honorably."

"No," Nurek said simply.

He lifted a tiny vial that he had picked up in the research laboratories in the stern of the vast ship. There had been ample opportunity. Since the new recruits had come on board, Nurek had gone through the vessel on an almost daily basis, checking to make sure everything was where it was needed. One of the classrooms had been converted into a training area. Every day, groups of Casians filed in and out to learn about their assigned duties. Getting the vial of poison had been easy enough. The Arodoni had vast stores of various chemicals, each one labeled in their own language. Nurek, along with several other members of the *Renegade's* crew, had scanners that could translate the Arodoni script into any language. Nurek had found the deadly chemical agent and taken it without any qualms about his actions.

"You could have set things right," Nurek said softly. "You had the power to end the corruption and free the slaves across the galaxy. Instead, you chose to indulge yourself, turning a blind eye to those who mistreat and abuse the masses they govern. You choose to continue a savage institution that is a plague on the galaxy. And now it is time that you paid for your crimes."

"You cannot," Vang snapped. "I forbid it."

"You and your kind are passing away," Nurek said. "On a thousand worlds, uprisings are stripping the Imperium of control."

"The Imperial Navy will rain down death and destruction on those worlds."

"They could, but they won't," Nurek said calmly as he began to screw the vial into Vang's IV port. "You see, like your war-mongering forebears, Sheika Kahn will spend all his efforts chasing this ship. There will be no concerted effort to put down the rebellion, which I promise you will spread and grow. Every victory will inspire more people to resist, and eventually, the Imperium will collapse entirely. When that happens, your kind will be hunted to extinction."

"We conquered the galaxy once," Vang snarled. "We will do it again."

"Not this time," Nurek said, pressing the plunger that pumped the poison into Vang's bloodstream. "This time, we are ready for you. The Ashi will soon be a blight that has been removed and forgotten. Think on this as you die, Emperor. You will be the first, but not the last."

Vang roared in fury and fear. Nurek could see it in the Emperor's eyes. But his growls and shouts grew weak. And there was no one to hear him. The medical bay had a few refugees in it, but they were all unconscious. There were a few of the humans, too, but they were used to hearing Vang's loud protests. They ignored the Ashi ruler, completely unaware that he was being murdered by his former slave.

Vang struggled, but that only made his heart beat faster, which sent the poison rushing through his veins and into his twin hearts. The first stopped. Nurek saw the pain on his former master's face. His lips pulled back over the sharp teeth and his eyes rolled back until only the whites showed through the narrowed lids. His struggles turned to spasms. His body stiffened and his muscles twitched. White foam gurgled up from his throat as he died. Nurek watched. He was neither happy nor sad. There was no affection for the Emperor. There was no fear of death as he watched him die. Nurek felt as though he had switched off a light in a room where it was not needed. Satisfied that the task was complete, the Dudonus alien turned on his narrow heel and walked calmly away.

CHAPTER 18

SHIEKA KAHN WAS PACING across the open Bridge of the *Retribution*. The distances between star systems made travel and communications slow. Good leadership required patience and the Kahn was accustomed to how bureaucracies worked. Nothing ever happened quickly. His armada, one hundred ships strong, was finally in place, but they needed to know where the enemy was lurking. It would do no good to go racing around the galaxy hoping to catch the Arodoni ship. Not only would that be a waste of resources, but it would make him look overly anxious and weak. An Emperor should be strong and in full control at all times.

Unfortunately, as they waited for word from the Casa system, there were reports of minor rebellions and uprisings against the Imperium from across the galaxy. None were a real threat to the existing order. They were localized and unconnected, yet they were in some way coordinated. News of Emperor Vang's failure in the Casa system was widespread. Perhaps that was enough to inspire fringe groups to resist Imperium rule. Or maybe it was news of the Arodoni ship. The Ashi's old nemesis had returned, bringing with it a sense that maybe the Imperium was in trouble. That could certainly have given the cowardly rebels enough false courage to rise up against their Imperial rulers.

Sheika tried to cast the bad news away and focus on the only task that mattered — crushing the Arodoni ship. In fact, he shouldn't be pacing. He was well aware that the crew of the *Retribution* could see him. They would take his impatience for weakness, but he didn't care. Nervous energy was coursing through him. To stand still would be torture; to sit still was impossible. Even eating, normally the most delightful part of his day, seemed like a burden.

He was still pacing the deck when the ship master approached.

"We have word from the Casa system."

Sheika Kahn was older than the ship master. He was fat, his tusks dull, his shoulders stooped, but he was still in command. The ship master bowed low, showing his respect. It felt off, as if he were just pretending. It was all a big practical joke, and yet, when Kahn looked out the ship's viewports, he could see the armada gathering around his vessel. This was his time; it had finally come. He had always believed that it would, although it felt wrong somehow. There was no sense of power or pride, only the crushing weight of responsibility.

"Speak," Sheika growled.

"The mines have been cleared from the portal," the ship master explained. "The Arodoni ship is gone. As are our own vessels."

"What of the report from our people on the ground?"

"There is none," the ship master said, carefully ensuring as he paced with Sheika Kahn that he remained just out of reach.

"What?"

"There was no signal from Casasil, Lord. The planet was silent."

"Did the drone send word to our forces?"

"It was programmed to signal the planet but got no response before it returned."

"How long was it in system?"

"Six hours," the ship master explained. "Radar showed no ships in the system. Not even the wreckage of damaged vessels, Lord.

There may have been some further out. As you know, the Casa system portal is not that far from the planet."

"Six hours... that's too long for our ships to hide."

"I would agree," the ship master said. "If the Arodoni ship is still in the system, it remained hidden. The tracking device was in open space. They must have found and removed it."

"And run," Sheika Kahn said. "They fear us."

"As they should, Lord. What are your orders?"

"We wait," the Kahn said, even though the words were bitter in his mouth. "If the Arodoni are wise, they will avoid the major trade routes and stick to back channels, perhaps even systems sympathetic to their cause."

"They are cowards, Lord."

"But not fools," Sheika Kahn said. "Do not forget that. Our enemy is formidable. When we act it must be decisive, but also strategic. The utter destruction of twenty Imperial ships is not easily accomplished."

"Perhaps they were destroyed in the fighting?"

"If that were true, the tracking device would have been destroyed as well."

It was another eight hours before a message was patched through from the Olotimbo system. It had bounced between six other systems and then left waiting in the galactic core before someone finally forwarded it to the armada. Sheika Kahn had taken to his bed. The interim emperor tossed and turned, struggling to sleep. The communication officer was a big Ashi warrior with scars on his chest and neck. Waking the Emperor was not without risks. Of course, Sheika was still the Kahn, not actually the Emperor, but he knew it was only a matter of time.

"Lord, there is word from the Olotimbo system," he said.

Sheika Kahn sat up. "Speak."

"An unknown ship entered the system and dispatched five unauthorized slavers."

Sheika grunted. "Slavers have no weapons."

"Indeed, Lord, but the other ship did. Four ships were destroyed. One was captured."

"And this intelligence is reliable?"

"It is from the Imperium offices on Olo Prime. There are protests there, but the governor is still in his palace."

"It is the Arodoni ship we seek," Sheika Kahn said, flinging back the silky sheets. "Prepare the armada. We leave at once."

CHAPTER 19

CAPTAIN DARIUS WAS STARTING to feel like the *Renegade* was more of a diplomatic ship than a vessel of war. They had reached orbit without further incident, thanks to the ship's powerful engines. Darius still marveled at the incredible speed of the enormous ship and its almost magical energy converter. How so much power could be generated from the mysterious dark energy, which humans couldn't see or even pick up on their primitive scanners, was astounding. Yet the results were undeniable. He knew that even just the understanding of that one advanced technology would radically alter the human race. And yet, he also knew he couldn't return home while the Imperium continued to threaten them and the other helpless worlds in the galaxy.

The refugees were being transported down to the surface of Olo Prime for medical treatment. The planet itself was in the midst of a revolution of sorts. According to Nurek and GIGI, the Imperium only kept a few small outposts on Olo Prime. There were few natural resources on Olo Prime. The Oloans were rotund beings with short appendages that couldn't really be classified as arms or legs. They weren't considered valuable on the slave trade market, and with the system several hundred light years off the major trade routes, they were mostly an afterthought to the Imperium. But that didn't stop the Oloans from rising up against the Imperium officials. It wasn't a violent affair, but the government officials were confined to their embassy offices while the Oloans began to meet and make plans to throw off Imperium rule.

To that end, the Oloan officials had requested to meet with Darius. He had boarded a shuttle, along with Master Sergeant Steel and Nurek, who was acting as a cultural ambassador to the aliens both on the ship and on the planet. What Darius wanted was to get back to his ship. He would have gladly delegated the duty of meeting with the Oloans, but there were no threats in the system and the aliens had made a special request to meet him. It left him with no other alternative than to fly down to the surface.

The trio sat close together on the shuttle which GIGI was piloting from the *Renegade*. It was flanked by a squad of surveillance drones that were feeding real-time intelligence to the alien artifact and the *Renegade*. Olo Prime was an interesting world. There were no oceans, but water flowed through deep rivers that crisscrossed the surface, serving as a network of roads. The result was a very green world, and the Oloans, while intelligent and capable of building ships that would traverse outer space, traveled across their planet mostly in simple boats that utilized the river currents rather than any motorized conveyance.

"What should we expect?" Darius asked Nurek.

"The Oloans are a curious people," Nurek replied. "I suspect they want to take advantage of the opportunity to study your race."

"We aren't Arodoni," Darius pointed out. "Is that going to be a problem?"

"I don't think so," Nurek said. "You are courageous fighters. You have proven that. The tales of what you did in the Casa system are being spread far and wide."

"I hope we aren't a disappointment," Darius said.

The ship settled on a landing pad surrounded by domes. The

Oloans built structures that reminded Darius of the colonies on Mars. But the air was fresh and clean as the trio stepped out of the ship. The sky was a brilliant blue with dazzling white clouds. The temperature was just slightly warmer than what Darius was accustomed to and there was a refreshing breeze that gave the starship captain a sudden longing for Earth.

"It's too bad you're in full armor, Master Sergeant," Darius said. "You should take that helmet off."

"Yes, sir," Remmy replied.

He flipped the latches that sealed his helmet to the space armor and pulled it off his head. The Marine NCO took a deep breath and his normally stoic expression shifted into the most subtle smile that Darius had ever seen.

From the nearest dome, a procession of individuals came trundling toward Captain Darius. It felt almost surreal to watch the Oloans. They seemed more like characters from a children's program than real people. Once they were within a few yards of Darius, the group spread out and formed a semi-circle around him. One spoke in a cooing, hooting language. Fortunately, the translation program did its job. With one ear, Darius heard the Oloans in their native tongue; in his other, the comlink translated the words into English.

"We are honored by your presence," the lead alien said. "Welcome to Olo Prime."

"It's an honor to be here," Darius said.

"I am Louvee," the alien said, "Chief Caretaker of Hooso City. These are our elders."

Darius listened as each of the aliens said their names. When they finished, Darius introduced the small party from the *Renegade*.

"I am Captain Zeke Darius, commander of the *Renegade*. This is Master Sergeant Remmy Steel and our volunteer liaison and adviser, Nurek Dudonus."

"You were the Emperor's slave?" Louvee asked.

Nurek bowed, his narrow body bending deeply at the waist. "I was. Captain Darius and his crew freed me."

"We have heard stories," Louvee asked. "But they are surely exaggerations. The people say your ship defeated the Imperium."

"That is not completely true," Darius said. "We defeated a small squadron of Imperial ships."

Nurek raised his hands. "The Captain is being modest. The *Renegade* - his ship -defeated an armada of Imperial warships. And a small group of ground fighters defeated an invasion force on Casasil."

"The circumstances were in our favor," Darius said. "The *Renegade* has many advantages. But we are just one ship."

"No one has defeated the Ashi in battle for over a thousand years," Louvee said. "It is a great privilege to have you here at the dawn of this new age. Come, we have refreshments for you."

"We can't stay long," Darius said. "There is still a lot to do and once we have transferred the refugees to your care, we will be leaving the system."

"What if the Imperium sends ships to fight us?" Louvee said. "Would you leave us helpless to defend our planet and our people?"

Darius felt a stab of guilt. Leaving was exactly what he planned to do. The *Renegade* had picked a fight and it would be the innocent who paid the price.

"We cannot stay," Darius said.

"Your people must rise up," Nurek said. "There are protests and rebellions on hundreds of worlds. If we act together, we can throw off the yoke of the Imperium."

"Our people have isolated the Imperium officials inside their compounds, but we are not prepared to wage a battle against Ashi ships of war."

"The Imperium will pursue us," Darius said. "Once we leave your system, the planet should be safe."

"Until you have been destroyed," Louvee argued. "And then every planet that has offered you succor will be punished."

"We already live in constant fear of the Imperium," Nurek said. "My people are enslaved; your planet is disregarded and left isolated from the rest of the galaxy while being forced to pay taxes to the core worlds. The Imperium is a plague that must be resisted. Now is our best chance to break free of the bonds they have held us in for so long."

"We cannot tell you how to lead your people," Darius said. "But we will fight the Imperium's forces wherever we find them. That is my promise to you."

The Oloans had naturally cheerful expressions but Darius could tell that they were unhappy. He couldn't blame them, either. The *Renegade* might be capable of fighting and defeating the Imperium warships, but the Oloans were not. And as much as he wished things could be different, Darius couldn't keep the ship in the Olotimbo system. He had to press on, keep moving and hopefully discover more about the humans they had fought on the slave ship.

"We are grateful for the people you have rescued from the slavers," Louvee said. "But we must also warn you that Olo Prime cannot aid you in the battle against the Imperium. It is not in our ability to wage war."

"We understand that," Darius said. "Please know that we will do all we can. But for now, we must return to our ship."

There were bows and pledges of friendship. Given more time, the Oloans might have even volunteered to serve on the *Renegade*, but Darius would leave that up to Nurek. The flight back up into space was quiet. Darius was reflecting on what he had learned. It was not unexpected. GIGI had explained how most of the intelligent species across the galaxy were not suited for war. The Oloans were slow-moving and physically incapable of fighting the way humans were. Darius couldn't help but wonder if he had made a terrible mistake. Perhaps fighting the Imperium was right in principle, but it was looking more and more as if it was a terrible mistake in practical terms. The Oloans wouldn't be useful in manning the *Renegade*. They couldn't contribute to the war effort, which left Darius wondering how many planets were the same way. The Oloans hadn't even imprisoned the Imperium officials. Darius could only speculate that they were in their compounds planning to crush the Oloan resistance the moment that the *Renegade* left the system.

"You are not wrong to fight the injustice of the Imperium," Nurek said, breaking the silence.

"Are you a mind reader, Nurek?" Darius asked.

The alien gave a soft chuckle. "My people have served others for so long that we have learned to observe many non-vocal cues. I would be a poor servant if I had to be told what to do all the time."

"You aren't a servant anymore," Remmy said.

"I am no longer a slave, but I serve my people and the rebellion against the Imperium," Nurek countered. "It is a service that I gladly perform. And, if you will grant me the right to say what I think, Captain Darius, I would encourage you to keep up the fight."

"No one is thinking about throwing in the towel," Darius said.

"I am unfamiliar with that turn of phrase," Nurek said.

"It means to give up the fight," Remmy said.

"Ah, good. I was afraid the Oloans had changed your mind."

"No," Darius confirmed. "That hasn't happened. But I feel responsible. We kicked the hornet's nest and there are worlds with no way to defend themselves."

"That is true, but that is a failure on their part, not yours. We each must decide how to live. I was a slave with few choices over my own life, and yet, I fostered the opportunities before me. My position in the Imperial household gave me access to beings on many worlds. I could not fight to free myself, but I was ready to resist when the opportunity arose. The Oloans must do the same. If they do not prepare - or have not prepared - to defend their planet, then they must accept whatever fate another has in store for them."

"Doesn't mean we can't do something," Remmy said.

"We can't stay," Darius pointed out.

"Yes, sir, I understand that," Remmy said. "But we gave the Casians equipment and training. Maybe there is something we can give to the Oloans, too?"

"Like what?" Darius asked, his curiosity peaked.

"Technology, sir," Remmy said. "They don't have defenses, but it doesn't mean they can't make them, right?"

"The Oloans have manufacturing capabilities," Nurek said.

"They could build weapon platforms to defend themselves from orbital threats," Remmy said. "If they're capable, they might build orbital defense measures that would keep an enemy at bay before it reached the planet."

"Surely they've already done all that," Darius said.

"Actually," Nurek interjected, "many races have no understanding of weapons. The Oloans did not fight one another as their society developed over time. I doubt they know the first thing about building the weapons Master Sergeant Steel is suggesting."

"But they could get the plans to build them, right?" Darius asked. "Surely, there are companies they could purchase weapons from."

"Weapons are outlawed by the Imperium," Nurek said. "Even the plans for building them are a closely guarded secret. And the rebellion has not been able to secure them."

"That's how they keep these planets in line," Remmy said. "They take away their ability to fight."

"But given enough time, surely they could develop weapons technology," Darius said.

"And risk slavery?" Nurek said. "The Dodonus was named a slave race for helping the Correll develop arms against the Imperium. Few planets would be willing to risk such a fate."

"So, if we give them access to weapons technology, won't they be too frightened to use it?" Darius asked.

"Under normal conditions, I would agree," Nurek pressed his case. "But with the arrival of the *Renegade* and the defeat of the armada in the Casa system, there are liberation movements on nearly every world outside the galactic core. Now is the time for people like the Oloans to implement a strategy of planetary defense."

"It wouldn't take much to transfer plans for a variety of weapons," Remmy said.

"And with that knowledge, they could develop their own ideas,"

Darius said, warming to the plan. "When the Imperium shows up, they'll be in for a surprise. Alright, we'll do it."

Darius started issuing orders as they escaped the planet's gravity and headed for the *Renegade*. It came none too soon, either. The moment the shuttle landed inside the massive Arodoni ship's hangar, they were hit with a flurry of news.

"Sir," Ensign Bertoli said as the hatch lowered and Darius walked out. "Commander Lee sent me."

"Why?" Darius asked.

"Sir, the alien leader is dead."

"What?"

"He was found dead just a short time ago," Jacee explained.

Darius felt lightheaded suddenly. He had thought it was just the changes in gravity, but he reached out a hand for Master Sergeant Steel.

"You okay, sir?" Remmy asked.

"Yes," Darius said. "Thank you, Sergeant. How did the Emperor die?"

"Doctor Lanski isn't sure."

"I thought he was recovering?"

"So did the doc, but..." Ensign Bertoli shrugged her shoulders. "He was in with Lieutenant Colt. There's some good news, Captain. Lieutenant Colt is waking up."

"Thank God," Darius said. "At least he's going to live. Thank you for the update, Ensign. Notify the Commander that you gave me the update and have her meet me in the Medical Bay."

"Aye, Captain, notifying Commander Lee, now."

Darius turned to Remmy. "Walk with me, Master Sergeant."

They made straight for the gravity lift. Both men were silent. Remmy checked his weapons and slung the rifle over one shoulder before activating his suit's magnetic clamps to hold the gun steady against his back. They drifted up through the shaft that had no artificial gravity and Darius once more marveled at the technology the Arodoni had mastered. Humanity was still faking gravity with spinning ships that used centrifugal force to hold things onto the deck.

Then they stepped out into the agricultural section of the ship. The park was paradise. Warm air flowed over Darius's skin and the scent of flowers mingled with rich soil. Silence was replaced by the buzz of insects and the gurgle of water flowing over rocks in a nearby stream. Despite everything going on, when Darius stepped into the park, he felt a sense of peace that he had never experienced on a spaceship before.

"Do you ever feel like you've come home, here?" Darius asked.

Remmy had his helmet under his arm. He nodded in response. "Odd, isn't it, sir?"

"It is. There is nothing about this park that is earth-like. The flora and fauna are all alien. The architecture and the technology, too. Yet, it feels like where I belong. Or maybe it's just that I never want to leave."

"I feel that way too, sir. I've wondered if the scent of some of the flowers is psychotropic."

"In a bad way?"

"No sir, a good way. Like caffeine, maybe."

"The way a cup of coffee can make you feel better no matter what your circumstances?"

"Exactly, sir. Do you think that's possible?"

"It must be," Darius said. "I never thought it possible for mankind to feel comfortable among the stars. All my career, I chalked it up to survival instincts."

"Space will kill you, that's for certain," Remmy said.

"It has to be respected," Darius continued. "And in a Fleet ship, you're always aware of that. But here? In this place, you forget all of that. It's like its own little world."

"I suspect they built it that way on purpose, sir."

"Yes, they probably did. Paradise among the stars."

"Indeed it is, sir," Remmy said. "It'll be hard to go back to anything else."

They were approaching the arched opening to the commerce section of the ship. Darius looked at Remmy.

"I just realized that I set foot on an alien planet today," the Captain remarked. "I nearly let the enormity of that fact slip past me."

"It was a beautiful planet," Remmy said. "Casasil was too."

"Not like Earth," Darius said.

"Different, but good."

"Yes, that's what I was thinking. I'll be honest with you, Master Sergeant. When I'm on this ship, I don't miss Earth. Is that wrong, you think?"

"Not everyone feels that way, sir."

"No, they don't. I'm sure most of the crew would like to return home."

"They think they would, sir. I doubt it would live up to their expectations after this."

"We've seen things, experienced things, that would make it hard to face never leaving the Sol system again. I couldn't live on Mars after this. Or a space station, either. I'll have to be careful not to let my personal feelings affect my judgment for the ship and crew."

"If anyone can do it, sir, it's you."

"Thank you for that vote of confidence, Remmy. But between you and me, if you catch me slipping, I hope you'll say something."

"Doubt I'll need to, sir. But yes, I would let you know."

"Thank you, Master Sergeant," Darius said as they approached the medical bay. "Now, let's find out what happened to Lieutenant Colt."

CHAPTER 20

"YOU LOOK LIKE HELL, LIEUTENANT," Remmy said as they approached the bed where Micky Colt was reclining.

"Captain Darius, I apologize for my..." Colt began.

Darius waved the apology away. "No one is blaming you, Lieutenant. Why don't you tell us what happened."

"I don't know, sir," he replied.

Remmy reached out a hand and put it on his Lieutenant's shoulder. Micky Colt was trembling slightly. Steel knew him to be a lot of things but frightened wasn't one of them. Perhaps it was possible that Lieutenant Colt was trembling as a result of the coma he had just come out of, but Remmy had his doubts. Something was different about the Lieutenant.

"Try and think," Darius ordered. "You were on Casasil."

"Yes, sir," Micky said. "I remember that I waited on the enemy. They eventually came out of the woods. I hit them pretty hard, sir. Killed at least half their number in a missile strike. The rest retreated into the forest, and I followed."

"And after that?" Remmy asked.

"I don't recall. It's like a dream. I know something happened, but I don't remember it."

Doctor Lanski approached, and Remmy took a step back.

"How's the patient, doctor?" Darius asked.

"Improving rapidly," Lanski said. "It seems the alien bug's life-span ended, or maybe the lieutenant's natural defenses dealt with it. Time was all that was needed."

"And his scans?" Darius asked.

"Clear," Lanski said.

He sounded happy, and Captain Darius seemed satisfied, but Remmy had his doubts. Lieutenant Micky Colt was a confident officer. He had been proud, opinionated, what some would call a hard charger. The man in the medical bed seemed more frightened than anything else. But it was Remmy's job to help the Lieutenant, not to judge him.

"Is he cleared for duty?" Darius asked.

"He will be in a few more hours," Lanski said. "We've used transcutaneous electrical nerve stimulation to keep his muscles from atrophy during the coma, but he won't be back to full strength for a bit. I'd like to keep him long enough to observe his normal routines, eating, sleeping, that sort of thing. He'll get up and move around the medical ward before being released to active duty."

"Good enough," Darius said, turning back to Micky. "There have been some developments. I'll leave it to Master Sergeant Steel to get you up to date, Lieutenant. We're glad you're back."

"Yes, sir, thank you. It's good to be back."

"Now, doctor, talk to me about our prisoner."

The two officers walked away and Micky watched them go. There was a look that reminded Remmy of regret in the Lieutenant's eyes.

"Help me out of this bed, Master Sergeant," Micky said as he swung his bare legs out from under the thin blanket. "I'm not sure what they did to me, but I feel jittery all over."

"Meds can do that to a person, sir," Remmy said, moving closer and letting Lieutenant Colt put a hand on his armored shoulder.

"Why are you in battle rattle, Remmy? What did I miss?"

"A lot, sir. We took care of the enemy on Casasil, but there was a breach on the *Renegade*."

"They got inside our ship?"

"They hit us with EMPs and knocked out the power," Remmy explained. "Commandos in space armor got to the ship and made their way inside."

"How many?"

"Just five," Remmy said. "They're all dead now. They were trying to sabotage the ship. And nearly got away with their leader, but the crew rallied. We lost a few people, though."

"Crew or Marines?"

"Crew, sir. But our platoon isn't at full strength either. We lost Sergeant Thorne and Corporal Fortnoy on Casasil."

"I remember that," Micky said as they began to slowly walk down the deserted medical ward. "Gunnery Sergeant Rand was incapacitated."

"Still is, sir. He's had a mental breakdown."

"Damn, we need him."

"Yes, sir, but I don't think he'll be much use to us. We've been back on board a while now, sir, and he's no better. Stays in his quarters mostly. Just getting him to eat has been difficult."

"We can't give up on him."

"No sir, we would never do that," Remmy said. "Corporal Van Winkle took a round in his arm that has required surgery and physical therapy. He's on the mend but not on active duty, yet."

"Anyone else?" Micky asked.

"Corporal Thompson was wounded, but it was minor, sir. He's back on restricted duty now."

"It's like a nightmare, Master Sergeant. You have no idea. I woke up and half my platoon is gone."

"We're still here, sir. Still taking the fight to the enemy."

"You've been in combat? That's why you're wearing armor?"

"Fortunately, no," Remmy said. "I was escorting the captain on a diplomatic run. We left the Casa system, sir. We're in the Olotimbo system now and were immediately hit by a group of slave ships. We took them out, no issues there, and rescued a little over three hundred refugees. They needed more care than we could give them. Most were taken down to the planet. It's called Olo Prime, sir. A beautiful world."

"The slavers just surrendered?"

"Most did, yes sir," Remmy said. "But not all. In fact, we had to fight it out with a group of humans."

"What?" Micky asked.

He stopped walking and turned to look at Remmy.

"Yes, sir. We've run tests. They're human—five in all. Four were KIA, and one survived. He's being looked after. The Captain is planning to question him as soon as the doctor gives the green light."

"You fought humans on a slave ship?"

"Yes, sir. They attacked us, we fought back, it was over quick. You can review the action from our helmet cams, sir. It was all by the book. Sergeant McManus took a laser shot to the shoulder, but his armor held."

Micky Colt took a deep breath. "I think I need to sit back down." They turned and moved slowly back toward the bed. "How were there humans on a slave ship?"

"That's a good question, sir. Everyone is anxious to find out."

"I thought we were the first to leave the Sol system. Don't tell me there's been some strange time warp something or other. I can't take that, Master Sergeant."

Remmy knew that Micky wasn't joking. He had a hand on his commanding officer's arm to help steady the man. Lieutenant Colt was trembling more than ever. Remmy wasn't sure how much was fatigue and how much was fear, but the quaking increased as he talked about moving through time.

"No sir, nothing like that," Remmy assured him. "I believe we were the first people to willingly leave the Sol system."

"Willingly?" Micky said as he settled back onto his bed.

"Yes, sir. They were on a slave ship. I think the most likely explanation is that they were abducted from Earth. Maybe by the slavers and put to work on that ship."

"I thought no one knew of our star system."

"The Imperium government doesn't know, but the Correll who built GIGI knew about us. It stands to reason that maybe others do, too. The slave ships were unauthorized vessels, sir. They utilize back channels, rarely traveled space lanes and the like. Whatever the source, we should know soon enough, sir."

"Humans..." he said as he wrestled with the new information.

A med tech appeared with a tray of food. Micky Colt settled onto his bed and poked at the options with a fork. He didn't appear very interested.

"Eat up, sir. We need you," Remmy urged. "I'll let you eat and get some rest."

"Thank you for the update, Master Sergeant."

Remmy gave a nod, then headed out of the medical bay. He saw Rip in a side room doing some exercises with a dumbbell. The scars on his arm were still vivid but he seemed capable enough. The arm moved through the exercise and Rip showed no signs of being in pain. Remmy hoped that meant he would be back on duty soon.

As he headed back toward the park, his stomach growled. He needed to get some food and rest himself. Being in charge sounded good, but in reality, it was a lot of work. And not the type of duty that Remmy enjoyed. He'd rather be shooting a rifle than typing reports or escorting flag officers. But Remmy was a man of duty. It didn't even cross his mind to shirk the tasks that had fallen to him since Lieutenant Colt's injury. Soon, the officer would be back in charge, but Remmy wasn't sure that was a good thing, either. As he made his way along the idyllic path between a row of flowering bushes and a narrow stream, he thought about his motivations.

Remmy liked being able to decide his own fate. If he was going to fight there was something to be said for making the command decisions. But Remmy didn't think his foreboding about Lieutenant Colt was merely a desire to stay in charge. In fact, Remmy had plenty of opportunities to shift over to the officer track. He could have been a Captain by that point of his career if he had so chosen. But Remmy was a fighting man and the idea of holding back while others did the dangerous work didn't appeal to him. He would rather lead a platoon into battle himself. It was what he loved and what he was good at.

Yet when he thought about Micky Colt returning to command, there was something that made Remmy uneasy. The Lieutenant had seemed like himself. The only real difference was his shock at the news of what he had missed. Plus, the trembling. It was strange, Remmy thought. He would have to keep his eye on the LT once Micky Colt was cleared for duty.

Remmy drifted down the gravity shaft and went straight to the armory. He wanted to eat and sleep, but he would see to his weapons and armor first. That discipline had been drilled into him from his very first days as a Marine. And it wasn't surprising to him when he found Staff Sergeant Laila McPherson in the armory.

"Imagine meeting you here, Staff Sergeant," Remmy said.

"Just trying to stay busy," she replied with a smile.

"And here I thought you were waiting on me."

"Don't flatter yourself, Master Sergeant. I have better things to do than wait around on you all day."

Remmy removed his weapon and released the magazine. He caught the component as it dropped out of the slot on his Nelson XTL and stored it in his locker. Next, he cleared the breach using the charging lever on the weapon. The bullet in the firing chamber popped out and he caught it mid-air. It wasn't a fancy trick. Marines used their weapons on an almost daily basis and one of the first things they were taught was to clear a rifle for storage and transport. Remmy dropped the bullet into a little box in his locker and secured the rifle into a rack. When he turned around, he discovered that Laila had moved up right behind him.

"You move like a shadow," he said. "Silent and stealthy."

"Just the way you want it, right, Master Sergeant," she said in a playful tone.

He glanced around. They were alone in the armory, but the door was open and it was a common area for the Marine platoon on board the *Renegade*. Not that he was ashamed of their romance; in fact, he was falling in love with Laila McPherson. But fraternization between members of the same platoon was frowned upon. That didn't mean it never happened, but as the senior NCOs of the platoon, Remmy and Laila didn't want to send the wrong message.

She reached up and started flipping the tension clips that held his space armor in place.

"Thank you," he said.

"Any time," Laila replied. "What's the word from upstairs?"

"LT Colt is awake," Remmy said.

"Really?"

He nodded. "Doesn't remember what happened to him. He seems okay."

"Seems okay, or *is* okay?"

"Too soon to say," Remmy said. "He's weak. The man's been asleep for days."

"I wouldn't complain about getting to sleep for a few days," Laila replied. "I've been on a lot of missions, Master Sergeant. I've never felt pressure like I do now."

"Copy that," Remmy said. "We've got a lot on our plates."

She helped him with the Velcro-covered zippers that held the insulated undersuits closed. Once the under-armor was unfastened, Remmy had to open the clasps at his waist that held the suit together and created a vacuum-tight seal. He bent over and Laila pulled the shirt portion of the suit off.

"That feels better," he said.

"Why do I get the impression you're making a pass at me," she teased.

"What? Can't a man get undressed without it meaning something?"

They both chuckled. Remmy wasn't naked. He wore compression fatigues under his armor. After getting out of the pants and thick-soled boots, he went to work cleaning the armor. The inside of a space suit could get dirty from sweat and body oils. It was best to keep everything clean and in good order, so that the gear was ready at a moment's notice.

"What about the ship?" Laila asked. "Where are we going next?"

"I think that depends on what we find out from the prisoner," Remmy said. "But everything is on the table."

"Including going home?"

"Yes," Remmy said. "Even that. Is it what you're hoping for?"

Laila shrugged. "I feel homesick," she admitted. "But if we go home, we'll be sidelined for who knows how long. I want to go home and I'm afraid the moment we get there, I'll wish I was back out here."

"Does the ship feel like home to you?" Remmy asked.

"Not yet," she said. "I like it. But I'm not used to having so much space."

"Odd how we get used to close quarters."

"Speaking of close quarters," she said. "Why not meet me in mine unless you've got something better to do?"

"I have to check in with Thompson and see what he's got the recruits doing."

"I think they're off duty," she said. "Once they helped move the refugees to the shuttles, he sent them to their quarters."

"And the rest of the platoon?"

"Same," Laila said. "Are you trying to ditch me, Master Sergeant?"

"I just don't want to feel guilty for being with you."

"We aren't the only couple in the platoon," she told him. "You know that, right?"

"Tex and Izzy?"

Laila nodded. "I think Poh and Sergeant Oliver are too. At least they have chemistry. I'm not sure they've acted on it."

"We're all a bunch of rule breakers," Remmy said, pulling her close.

"None of us have ever been on an assignment this long," she said.

That wasn't exactly true, but there was a big difference between life on the *Renegade* and being assigned to a post on Mars or a duty station on the *Ares* space station. Most Marines were assigned to a ship that spent three-quarters of its time in dock, which meant that the Marines moved back and forth from the space station to the ship. When they went on cruises they were usually back within a couple of weeks. More time than that in a standard Fleet ship could make a person stir crazy.

Remmy was about to suggest that they head back to her apartment. His quarters were officially in the command section of the ship. As one of the two senior leaders of the Marine platoon, he was required to be available to Captain Darius at all times. He could have taken one of the apartments overlooking the park but it felt overly extravagant. His berth in the Command section was larger than any he had ever had before. And the truth was, just like Laila, the extra space felt strange. He had so few personal items. His clothing, toiletries and personal items all fit in one rucksack. Weapons were kept in the armory, so all that was in his berth were clothes, his razor, toothbrush and personal hygiene supplies. Remmy kept books and movies on his data pad. It was easier than carrying physical books around and, most of the time, he could pull movies, television shows and sporting events off the data cloud. But they had no access to the Fleet Information Network outside the Solar system. He couldn't send emails or make video calls. Which meant time alone in his large berth seemed strange to him. At least in the apartments overlooking the park, they could sit on the balcony and feel like they weren't trapped on a spaceship millions of light years from home.

But before he could make the suggestion, she kissed him. It was fast, just a brush of the lips. They couldn't take the chance that they might get caught by someone walking by the armory.

"There's more of that if you'll meet me in my apartment," she suggested.

"Wild horses couldn't—"

His comlink chirped, and then he heard Commander Lee's voice in his ear.

"Senior staff, please report to the Medical Bay. I repeat, all senior staff are to report to the Medical Bay."

Remmy groaned. Laila tried not to look disappointed but Remmy saw it in her eyes. Still, they were Marines first and lovers second. Duty was always the priority.

"You were saying?"

"There's nothing I would rather do, Laila," he said softly. "I hope you know that."

"I do," she said. "Go, I'll be waiting for you when you're finished."

They kissed again, lingering close for just a moment as they savored the intensity of their feelings for one another. Then Remmy grabbed his belt from his locker and slung it around his hips. It had a thigh holster, which he fastened before dropping his Yagger HC pistol into it.

"You planning on doing battle with the Captain?" Laila asked.

"Not planning on it, but not dismissing the idea either," Remmy said with a grin.

Leaving her wasn't easy, but he forced himself to turn on his heel and head for the door. He stopped just before leaving the armory and turned back. She gave him a smile that nearly made his heart stop. When he continued on his way he felt as if he was walking on air.

CHAPTER 21

REMMY WAS SHOCKED when he reached the Med Bay. Commander Lori Lee had Nurek's narrow wrists bound behind his back. The tall, thin alien's cone-shaped head was bowed as the Commander escorted him away from the Med Bay.

"Everything okay here, Commander?" Remmy asked.

"I suppose," Lori Lee said. "It seems our guest here murdered the Emperor."

"I will not deny it," Nurek said.

Remmy was stunned. The Dudonus were calm, rational beings. Nurek was not only their leader but a leader in the rebellion that was taking place across the galaxy. And he had proven himself to be a hard worker as part of the ship's new administration group.

"Why?" Remmy asked.

"For crimes against the galaxy," Nurek said.

"He should have been tried for that," Lori Lee said.

"By who? He is feared on a thousand worlds," Nurek said, still calm and seemingly rational. "He was a danger and a drain on our resources."

"Then it was a call for the Captain to make, not you," Lori Lee said. "The others are waiting for us. Let me get him secured, and I'll join you."

Lori Lee led the alien across the broad hallway and into the Admin Center. They had no brig on the *Renegade*. But a few rowdy crew members had been detained by clipping the plastic restraints to a group of chairs that were bolted to the floor.

Remmy turned to the Med Bay and went into where Lieutenant Colt was resting. He wasn't asleep but had returned to his bed.

"Everything okay out there, Master Sergeant?" Micky asked.

"A-Okay, sir. Just a little housekeeping. How do you feel?"

"Tired."

"Get some rest then, sir. I'll keep you informed of anything you need to know."

"Will you?" Lieutenant Colt asked.

Remmy didn't respond immediately. He was shocked by the look in his commanding officer's eyes. The two men had their differences in the past, but Remmy always took them to be misunderstandings. The Lieutenant had been a little insecure about his command of the platoon, with Remmy being a war hero and winner of the Medal of Honor. But Remmy had no ambitions to take the Lieutenant's place. For a moment, as the two men stared at one another, Remmy felt sure the animosity was back and stronger than ever.

"Yes, sir," Remmy said.

"You had better," Micky said, sounding like a child.

Remmy nodded and moved on. Perhaps it was the ailment. Remmy had been wounded in action before. It was hard to see your fellow Marines moving on while you were held back, but Remmy feared the Lieutenant was going a little overboard. It was a fact that Remmy had been in charge while the Lieutenant was medically compromised but that was due to the chain of command. Remmy had no say in the matter. He hadn't sought the command nor shirked the duty that was his. In his report of the action the Marines had taken since entering the Olotimbo system, Remmy had noted Lieutenant Colt's authority and physical condition as the reason why he had taken command of the platoon. Everything was above board.

The space that had been converted to the Medical Bay was what Remmy thought of as a standard storefront with a storage space in the back. The technicians who had moved the supplies from the *Jericho* to the *Renegade* had used the small storage space to arrange racks of medical supplies, from IV bags to bandages. Once the prisoner from the slave ship began to wake up, he was moved into the storage room to be questioned.

The small space was crowded. Captain Darius was there, along with Vivian Ramos and Henry Nash.

"Sorry to have to send for you again, Master Sergeant," Darius said. "But I need you for this."

"Happy to be here, sir," Remmy said.

"Can you access GIGI?" Darius continued. "I think we'll need her help to work out a translation."

"Yes, sir," Remmy said. "That won't be a problem."

A few moments later, Lori Lee returned with Lutus. He looked sad, although Remmy wasn't sure how well he could read the alien's features.

"Crewman Lutus, we are hoping that you might be able to help us identify the language that this prisoner is speaking," Darius said. "Are you willing to help us?"

"Of course, Captain, although I doubt I'll be much help. The honorable Nurek would be a much better choice."

"Maybe so, but as of now, that's not an option."

Remmy saw the alien look up with what he could only guess was fear in his eyes. The officers of the *Renegade* were careful in how they spoke to the former slaves on board the ship. Direct orders were avoided whenever necessary. Remmy thought the crew was doing a good job of cultivating an atmosphere of teamwork, but Lutus was clearly anxious. Perhaps he had seen his friend being detained. That would certainly dampen anyone's spirits.

"Alright, let's rouse him," Darius ordered.

The prisoner was a pale-skinned man in his twenties with a shaggy head of hair that had been poorly cut and traces of a wispy beard along his jaw. He was thin. Remmy could see the bones in his shoulders and collar. His arms were bare and the elbows stuck out as if the joints were too big. An IV was taped to his left forearm, and there were belt restraints around his wrists. Bandages covered his left shoulder where he had taken a bullet in the fighting.

Commander Lori Lee reached out and gently shook his unwounded shoulder. The man's eyes fluttered open. He seemed confused at first. Darius held up a translation device and spoke.

"Do you understand me?" The Captain asked.

There was no recognition in the prisoner's eyes. The translation device played back the Captain's question in a variety of languages, but the prisoner didn't understand any of them.

"If he could speak," Lutus said, "perhaps we might discover what language he is using."

Darius reached his hand up to his mouth and mimicked talking then pointed at the prisoner. The man spoke, but Remmy couldn't understand what he was saying. The prisoner's voice was weak.

Any chance you understood that? Remmy thought, addressing GIGI, who was in a different section of the ship. Since discovering the alien artifact just beyond the orbit of Saturn in the Sol system, Remmy had shared a mental link with the device. It could hear his thoughts, and he could hear its replies in his head, even from a great distance.

Negative, Master Sergeant. That language is not in my data banks.

"GIGI doesn't recognize the language," Remmy said.

"I feared as much," Darius replied.

"So what do we do?" Vivian asked. "We have to know this man's story."

"Teach him," Henry said. "Teach him our language."

"That would take weeks," Darius said, "if not longer."

"It's possible the ship's computer could learn his tongue faster," Commander Lori Lee said.

"Lutus?" Darius asked.

"I'm afraid I'm no help at all, Captain," the Dudonus said.

They all stood silent for a moment. It was a frustrating situation. To find a human being outside the Sol system was a monumental discovery but only if they could learn from one another. That didn't seem possible with the language barrier they faced.

The meeting might have ended in frustration if Laila hadn't sent Remmy a text message. His datapad was in the cargo pocket of his fatigue pants. He felt it vibrate and with that movement, an idea occurred to him. He pulled the pad out and slid the small stylus he rarely used from the sheath that was built into the device's anti-shock casing.

"Sir, maybe this might help," Remmy suggested.

He opened a drawing app and wrote: ***can you write?***

"Excellent idea, Sergeant," Darius said, taking the data pad and holding it up in front of the prisoner.

They watched the man focus on the words. He shook his head a tiny bit from side to side. Remmy wasn't sure if he was communicating or trying to clear the cobwebs. With his good hand, he reached up. Darius gave him the stylus. The man wrote a few strange looking symbols, then gave the stylus back to the captain.

"It's no good," Darius said, turning the data pad around and looking at what was written. "It's gibberish."

"May I?" Remmy asked. "Perhaps GIGI can make sense of it."

Darius handed Remmy the data pad. He looked at the markings. They were triangular shapes, not like letters or even pictures. Remmy felt a sense of frustration and was about to shut the device off when GIGI spoke inside his head. It was like hearing someone else's thoughts.

Cuneiform.

For a moment, Remmy was stunned. The information didn't

compute to him. He had heard the word as if it was spoken, but he didn't understand it.

It is an ancient Earth language GIGI explained. *Most scholars attribute it to the ancient Sumerians.*

Remmy was not a history buff. He had read about military history going back as far as the ancient Greeks, but neither *Cuneiform* nor *Sumerians* meant anything to him.

"Captain, GIGI has information about this," he said, holding out the pad so that the others could see it.

"What?" Darius asked.

"She identified the writing as something called Cuneiform. It's Sumerian."

"What's Sumerian?" Vivian Ramos asked.

"Old," Henry said. "Very old. One of the earliest human civilizations that has been positively confirmed to have existed."

"What does it say, Sergeant?" Darius asked.

"GIGI translated it to mean, *who are you?*"

"If GIGI can read it, why not understand the spoken language?" Commander Lori Lee asked.

"It hasn't been a spoken language for thousands of years," Henry Nash said. "But their writing influenced the written language that came after it."

"You know a lot about this," Darius said.

"Not really, sir. I don't think anyone knows much about the Sumerians. It's ancient, sir."

"So what does that mean?" Lori Lee said. "This man was taken from Earth thousands of years ago?"

"That's impossible," Vivian said. "He could be an ancestor of the Sumerians, I suppose."

"Languages change over time," Darius said. "I don't think this writing means he was Sumerian or that his forebears were."

"It could be that his people started life on Earth," Vivian said. "That's always been a possibility, right? If the Sumerians were the first civilization, maybe it's because they were the first people on the planet."

"Maybe," Darius said. "But that would mean they came from an advanced, intergalactic society. How would that be possible if no one recognizes us as one of them?"

"He's got a point," Lori Lee said. "Humans aren't in the Imperium files as a known species, according to Nurek. We've had a few late-night conversations about that."

"It doesn't make any sense," Vivian decided. "How does this guy know an ancient language from Earth?"

"Perhaps time will tell," Darius said. "The good news is that if we can communicate, then we can get answers to our questions."

"It'll be slow going if we have to write everything down," Henry said.

"Slow is better than nothing," Darius said. "We'll have GIGI write out a list of questions. Once the prisoner is able, he can write out his answers."

"What if he doesn't know the answers?" Henry asked.

Before anyone could reply, their comlinks chimed. Lieutenant Peter Best's voice came through clear enough that they heard the fear in it.

"Captain! We have contacts on the board. Enemy ships are entering the system!"

"We're on our way to you, Lieutenant," Darius said. "Master Sergeant, you're with us, but send the alert to your platoon."

"Yes, sir," Remmy replied.

There was a flurry of activity as they hurried from the storeroom. Doctor Lanski looked up from the bank of monitors on his desk.

"Doctor, please secure the prisoner and prepare for battle stations," Darius ordered as they hurried past.

"Battle stations?" Lieutenant Colt said, sitting up on his bed. "What's happening?"

"Enemy ships just entered the system," Darius said. "Stay here, lieutenant. But keep your comlink on."

For a split second, there was a defiant expression on the lieutenant's face. But then he nodded. From the other side of the room, Corporal Rip Van Winkle hurried to Remmy's side.

"Master Sergeant, I can help. What are my orders?"

"Are you cleared for active duty?" Remmy asked.

"Sir, I can do whatever you need," he said, sounding desperate.

Remmy nodded. The Naval officers were all ahead of him, and he didn't want to waste time.

"Head to the armory, Corporal. Help everyone get into full armor and prepare for battle stations."

"Yes, Master Sergeant!" Rip nearly shouted.

They were at the concourse and Rip sprinted away down the gleaming corridor. Remmy understood the younger man's enthusiasm. The best way to deal with battle trauma sometimes was to fight another engagement. Remmy headed straight for the gravity ring and followed the ship's senior officers up to the Command Section.

"I want everyone suited up," Darius ordered as he strode onto the Bridge. "No exceptions."

"Captain!" Pete Best declared. "There's over a hundred enemy ships."

Remmy hesitated for a second just inside the door to the Bridge. He could see out through the canopy. The *Renegade* was in orbit around Olo Prime. They seemed to be turning past the planet. Beyond that was dark space. No enemy ships were visible. It felt like a false alarm.

But down past the Captain's chair was a lower section of the deck. There, a hologram of the system was visible. Remmy saw the planets and the *Renegade*. He could also see an armada of ships way out at the edge of the system.

"Are the targets marked?" Darius said.

"Tangos one through one hundred and twelve, Captain," Pete Best said. "Distance is nearly four billion kilometers. They've been in the system for a couple of hours, sir."

"Understood," Darius said. "Get suited up, Lieutenant, and good job."

Remmy turned to the lockers along the back wall of the Bridge. They were new. Henry Nash had them fabricated from copper. Inside were emergency space suits with oxygen canisters and computer-interfacing helmets. There was one for him, too. It was sleeker than his space armor and all one piece. He removed his belt and thigh holster, then stepped into the flight suit. He zipped it up and covered that with a pair of opposite facing velcro flaps to hermetically seal the suit. It wasn't made for hard vacuum, just a lack of oxygen or the presence of smoke, perhaps even toxic gas.

When he finished and turned around, he saw Lori Lee taking the captain an emergency suit. She was already in hers, including the helmet. Remmy slipped his on and activated the comlink. He switched it to the platoon channel before speaking.

"Staff Sergeant, are we geared up?"

"We're on our way, Master Sergeant," Laila said. "What's the danger?"

Remmy looked up. On the holographic plot he could see that Captain Darius had zoomed in on the enemy ships. Remmy realized it wasn't an armada; it was an entire fleet of Imperium vessels.

"Suffice it to say we're way up the creek and there is no paddle in sight, Staff Sergeant," Remmy said. "Get everyone suited up and armed for combat. The Captain will be calling everyone to battle stations soon."

"And where will you be?" Laila asked.

"Looks like I'm stuck up here," Remmy told her.

"Well, at least you'll have a front-row seat to all the action. Keep us informed, Master Sergeant. We want all the gory details."

Remmy understood what she meant. Grunts on a Fleet warship rarely had any idea what was happening. They certainly had no warning if an enemy was about to blast their ship and kill everyone on board. It was an ongoing complaint among the enlisted Marines whose lives were on the line but who had no control over the situation.

"Will do," Remmy said. "Take care of yourself, McPherson."

"You do the same, Master Sergeant."

Remmy turned to face the Bridge. He spread his feet apart and wrapped his belt back around his waist, securing his thigh holster and checking the pistol's safety before pressing it back down where it belonged. It was a futile gesture in the face of an entire fleet of enemy battleships, but if they were going into battle, he felt a little better knowing he was armed.

CHAPTER 22

"DO YOU WANT TO LEAVE ORBIT?" Henry Nash asked.

Darius thought about the question for a few seconds. He had already done the math in his head. The enemy was four billion kilometers away. That was a very long distance. In fact, it was taking the radar tracking system moving at the speed of light, which was approximately three hundred thousand kilometers a second, three and half hours to reach the alien ships. And, of course, another three and half hours to return to the *Renegade*. Which meant the Imperium vessels were seven hours beyond what he was seeing on the plot.

Normally, in a regular Space Defense Fleet vessel, a ship that far out wouldn't even register on their radar. It would have to close to within a few hundred thousand kilometers to be in range of standard weapons. At least those standard to the human race. Of course, the *Renegade* had very advanced weapons. They had hit targets of more than four billion kilometers, but it was only because those ships were moving in a straight line.

"Negative," Darius said. "Let's stay by the planet. Someone get me Nurek up here. I need more information on those ships."

"Aye, Captain," Lori Lee said. "I'll bring him up."

She left the Bridge and Darius knew he was crossing a line. He saw the other officers glancing his way, but he felt justified in his orders. There were more than one hundred ships between them and the only way out of the Olotimbo system. He felt a deep sense of dread welling up inside him.

"Alright, people, we're in for it now," Darius said.

"How the hell did they find us here?" Henry Nash wondered aloud.

"That's secondary," Darius said. "They are here now, and we need a battle plan."

"I can begin tracking targets," Pete Best said. "That's a long shot, but we've bulls-eyed targets at that range before, Captain."

"Begin preparing your targeting solutions," Darius said. "But if they're smart, they won't keep traveling in a straight line."

"Neither should we," Henry spoke up.

"We won't for long but we're in a good position here. The planet may be hiding us," Darius said. "Besides, I don't think they have anything that can target us at this distance."

It was all conjecture. He simply didn't have enough intelligence on the enemy's capabilities.

"GIGI, are you monitoring our developments?" Darius asked using the comlink.

"Yes, Captain. I am aware of all the data coming into the *Renegade*."

"What do you know of those Imperium ships? We need all the information we can get."

"There are several classes of Imperium warships: Carriers, Interdictors, Sentries, and Battleships," GIGI replied. "My information on those ships may not be up to date depending on the amount of technological development within the Imperium."

"Alright, very good," Darius said. "I want you to bring up the information on those ships to console seven. Can you do that?"

"Of course, Captain."

"Excellent. Please stand by for more instructions, GIGI."

Darius turned in his chair just as Commander Lori Lee stepped onto the Bridge with Nurek in tow. He was still in restraints but looked around the Bridge with a keen eye.

"I cannot condone what you did," Darius replied.

Nurek glanced at Master Sergeant Steel, who was the only armed personnel on the Bridge. Darius wondered if the alien was calculating the odds of being able to seize control of the *Renegade*.

"I do not expect you to," Nurek said.

"He was a captive and completely unable to defend himself," Darius said, referring to Emperor Vang.

"Does your species allow the condemned to fight to the death?"

"No," the Captain explained. "But we have laws against executing prisoners of war without a trial."

"The Imperium has no such laws," Nurek said via the translator device he still wore on the front of his tunic. "And while I respect that you have command of this ship, which gives you a say in everything that goes on inside it, I also had a stake in the outcome of the Emperor. I was enslaved to his father and grandfather before him. I was a witness to the horrors they inflicted on thousands of innocent beings, as well as the abuses of their slaves."

"He could have been useful in negotiations with the Ashi," Darius said.

"There can be no negotiations," Nurek said. "I have tried to communicate that fact to you, Captain. They know only aggression, not surrender, not mercy. They will fight until either you are dead or they are. To let them live is tantamount to admitting defeat. They will never stop trying to kill you."

"We won't pretend to understand your motivations," Darius said. "But now I need your expertise. There is a fleet of Ashi warships in the system now."

"How many?" Nurek asked.

"One hundred and twelve," Darius said.

The former slave's eyes opened wide in fear. "Are we doomed?"

"Not yet," Darius said. "But I need to know everything about the ships we're fighting."

Nurek nodded his long, conical head.

"Captain, I have a firing solution on four of the largest ships," Pete Best said.

"Activate the cannons," Darius ordered. "Lock them into firing positions. Helm, prepare to bring us around point seven degrees."

"Aye, point seven degrees," Henry called out.

"Cannons are activated and locked in firing positions, Captain," Best said.

"Navigation, we can't continue moving in a straight line. Please plot out a course toward the largest of Olo Prime's moons. Include evasive actions every five minutes, if you please."

"Aye, Captain, plotting a course for Alpha Moon," Vivian said.

"Commander Lee, show our guest to console seven," Darius said. "Mr. Nurek, I need to know the capability of the Ashi ships. GIGI will have loaded the vessel classes onto the computer. Whatever you can share with us will help."

"Yes, Captain, I will do my best," Nurek said.

"Commander Lee, bring us to yellow alert status."

"Aye, Captain, yellow alert status."

"Check in with every division. I want people ready to man battle stations on my command," Darius said. "We've got the biggest test of our lives ahead of us people. I want every single one of us at our very best."

It didn't take long for the ship to alter course or for the enemy ships to be in their line of fire. Darius knew it was likely a wasted effort, but he needed to do something. His mind was still reeling at the number of ships. His rational mind was telling him to escape. One vessel, even the powerful *Renegade*, was no match for an entire fleet. Better to live and fight another day when the odds were in his favor. But, as far as he understood it, the galaxy didn't work that way. He couldn't just leave the system or make the jump into hyperspace anytime he wanted to.

They needed to pass through a portal into a hyperspace lane. He was sure the reality of inter-dimensional travel was much more complex, but that was how he thought of it. And the alien fleet was between his ship and the only known way out of the system.

"GIGI," Darius said, calling on the ancient artifact. "Are there any other portals out of the Olotimbo system?"

"There is only one known hyperspace transition point," GIGI replied. "Although the planet Timbo does move in and out of the system. Its movements have never been mapped. Nor has it been discovered how the planet makes the transition. It is a rogue planet that has been observed moving through hyper-dimensions."

Darius was fascinated but also disappointed. The rogue planet wasn't the help he needed at the moment, no matter how interesting it might be.

"Sir, we have brought our cannons to bear on the enemy positions," Lieutenant Best said.

"Very well," Darius replied. "Fire at will."

"Fox one!" Pete Best declared before pulling the trigger on the firing mechanism. There was a flash of light. For one moment, Darius could see the bolt of energy racing through the space.

"Time to impact?" Darius asked.

"Roughly three and half hours, sir," Pete Best said. "Fox two!"

Another flash. Darius thought it silly to be shooting at an enemy so far away. It wasn't like targeting a planet or a space station. The targeting computer would calculate the enemy ship's position, speed, and trajectory, then fire at where it expected the ship to be when the laser reached it. It was all they could do, but of course, if the targeted ships made even one-course correction, if they sped up or slowed down, the shot would miss. If the *Renegade* used conventional methods to power its cannons Darius wouldn't have wasted the energy. But since they had a practically endless supply of power, it seemed foolish not to at least try.

"They'll know we're shooting at them," Henry Nash said.

"Not until the laser reaches them," Vivian pointed out. "Their radar can't move any faster than the laser beam."

"But once they know, they'll outmaneuver us," Henry said. "They'd have to be fools to hold their course."

"And shoot back," Commander Lori Lee pointed out. "Don't forget that."

"It won't matter," Darius said.

"Fox three!"

"We're going to take shelter behind the big moon. I want to see what they do next."

"Fox Four!" Pete Best said.

"Begin your evasive maneuvers," Darius said. "Raise the shields."

"Aye, Captain, sonic shielding is at full power," Pete Best said.

"Beginning our run to Alpha Moon," Henry said.

"GIGI, what's their best speed into the system?"

"At full power, they will reach Olo Prime in twelve point two-five hours, Captain," the computerized voice replied.

"Mr. Nurek, what can you tell us about those ships?"

"Traditionally, only Dreadnoughts carried mega cannons. They were used for destroying a planet's defensive capabilities from a distance, usually several billion kilometers. Once the defensive systems were down, the smaller, more agile vessels would lead the charge toward a planet and engage enemy ships. The assault carriers would then move into orbit and land thousands of Ashi warriors who would subdue the planet. If these tactics didn't work, or the Emperor wished to make an example of a defiant world, Orbital bombers would move into place and drop various types of mass destruction warheads onto the population centers."

"Yes, we've seen what they can do to a world," Darius said, thinking of Lawash. "Do we have any idea how many Dreadnoughts they have in their fleet?"

"I show fourteen, Captain," Vivian Ramos said.

"I concur," Nurek added. "I don't believe they will fire for some time yet, Captain."

"Why?" Darius asked.

"Because of the energy expenditure," Nurek said. "The Dreadnoughts are massive ships with thick armor for the greatest protection. Their mass makes them slow and difficult to maneuver, but it's necessary because the amount of fuel used to power the mega cannons is prodigious."

"How many times can they fire without needing to refuel?" Pete Best asked.

"Four times," Nurek said. "Although my console shows that there are eight refueling tugs in the fleet."

Darius was beginning to get an idea of what he was up against and what his enemy would probably do. The Dreadnaughts were the long-range artillery meant to cover the approach of the smaller, faster vessels as they moved into range. The fleet also had supply ships, which were necessary to refuel or repair damaged vessels without the need to return to port somewhere else. He could work with that. But he still needed to draw the fleet in, get them in close enough range that they couldn't out maneuver his laser barrages.

"They'll try to box us in, Captain," Nash said. "Use their numbers against us, but the real threat is the long-range ships."

"We can't be predictable," Pete Best said.

"There's time," Darius said. "Send the crew to eat. We might not have another chance."

"Aye, Captain, sending word to all divisions," Lori Lee said.

"In the meantime, we need stats on those ships," Darius continued. "Speed, maneuverability, everything we can find."

"Most of that information is not readily available," Nurek confessed. "I know a little about the Ashi Fleet, but not specifics."

"We can have the ship's computer match the ships in the enemy fleet with those we fought in the Casa system," Lori Lee said. "That'll give us some idea of their capabilities."

"Excellent idea, Commander. Inform Ensign Stanislaus to start the comparisons," Darius ordered. "Once we're behind the big moon, we'll launch surveillance craft to keep tabs on that fleet. I want to know every move they make. In the meantime, we'll take half-hour breaks so that everyone can get chow and use the facilities. Why don't you start, Lieutenant Best."

"Aye, Captain," Pete said.

"All we can do now is wait and see what the enemy will do," Darius said, more to himself than to his officers. He turned around and focused on Master Sergeant Remmy Steel. "Why don't you go down and check on your Marines," he said. "Once the shooting starts, there won't be time to do it, and I'd like to know they're armed and ready if the enemy gets people on board our ship again."

"Yes, sir," Remmy replied.

"Get yourself some food, too, then return to the Bridge. We might need you."

"Copy that," the Master Sergeant said.

Darius turned back around and looked out through space. He couldn't see the enemy, but he knew they were there. Over a hundred enemy ships were flying silently through the void. He was moving his own ship to meet them in battle. His mouth suddenly felt dry. He wondered briefly if he would be remembered as the fool who tried to fight an entire fleet. Then, he pushed all doubts from his mind and focused on the battle to come.

CHAPTER 23

OVER THE NEXT SIX HOURS, the Ashi fleet moved into the system. Just as Darius had expected, they avoided the initial shots fired at them and immediately began to spread wide to avoid overlapping.

Darius had napped in his Captain's chair. Leaving the Bridge wasn't an option and he couldn't really sleep, but waiting was tiresome, so he dozed off and on for a few hours. Eventually, he ordered himself a cup of coffee and stepped into a nearby head to splash water onto his face. He rubbed the back of his neck with a damp towel and thought about the two hundred souls on board the *Renegade*. He owed them his very best. The ship was powerful, fast, even nimble, but she was still just one vessel. If they were going to stay and fight, it needed to be on his terms, not the enemy's.

"Status?" He asked as he walked back onto the Bridge and took a tall travel mug full of coffee from an enlisted crew member. "Thank you."

The culinary specialist smiled and hurried away.

"Captain," Lori Lee said. "We have a total of seventy-seven ships moving to engage. They've spread wide in a long arch. Over fifty are the standard battleship class vessels. There are twelve Dreadnoughts, eight bombers, and the rest appear to be support class ships."

"Any carriers?" Darius asked.

"According to Nurek, they all contain squadrons of fighters," the Commander continued. "Cannon range is just about five hundred thousand kilometers. They're approaching at speed."

"How fast?"

It was Vivian Ramos who answered. "Almost half the speed of light, Captain. Five hundred million kilometers per hour and holding."

"What's their current distance from us?"

"Just under a billion kilometers from the closest ship," Commander Lee said.

"They're using thrusters to alter their course every half hour," Vivian added. "Just enough to throw off our targeting algorithms."

"Is there any way to anticipate their moves?" Darius said as he studied the holographic plot.

"Negative, Captain," Pete Best said. "I've run computer simulations. There's no way to know what direction they'll move or how much."

"Alright, well, it looks like we'll just have to wait a bit longer," Darius said. "In the meantime, let's move to red alert status. All hands to quarters. I want everyone in emergency gear."

"Aye, Captain. Red Alert Status," Commander Lee said before turning to his console and giving the order to the rest of the ship via her comlink.

"Let's have a system check," Darius said. "Engineering?"

"We're good to go, Captain," Henry Nash said. "Main engines are active and ready. Thrusters have all been tested in the last half hour. The *Jericho* and our energy converter are functioning at optimal levels, sir. We're ready for whatever you need."

"Excellent," Darius said. "Weapons?"

"All laser cannons are in firing position," Lieutenant Best said. "In addition, we have about six hundred space-ready drones with ship-to-ship missiles. And our Casian crew members will be piloting torpedo drones. They're essentially guided missiles, Captain. Their range is only a few hundred thousand kilometers, but they should do the trick to cover our backside."

"What about the Marines?" Darius asked as he turned in his chair.

Behind him, Master Sergeant Remmy stood at attention.

"Sir, we are ready. I have units on all three hangar decks, sir. And the new Casian Marines are standing ready in reserve however you need them."

"Outstanding, Master Sergeant. Any word from Sick Bay?"

"Lieutenant Colt is recovering quickly, sir. But Doctor Lanski wanted to keep him there for the duration of this fight."

"Probably for the best. And our guest?"

"I have Corporal Van Winkle with him, sir," Remmy explained. "They are working together to answer the questions the computer translated into Sumerian, but it's slow going. I don't think the young man is a scholar if you take my meaning, sir. And he's still pretty weak. Rip reports that he's moving in and out of consciousness pretty quickly."

"Good enough," Darius said. "Navigation, are we ready?"

"Aye, Captain. The plot is set and engaged. Once you give the order, we will come up from behind Alpha Moon and proceed in reverse back over the planet."

"Do we have eyes and ears in position?"

"GIGI has twelve drones in space, another four in atmosphere," Vivian continued. "There's no reason that we won't be able to keep the entire system on the plot at all times."

Darius looked at the plot. The alien ships were visible in a wide line. It was obvious that the holographic projector was enlarging the alien vessels to make them visible. They were also labeled in red, T-1 through T-118. Their strategy seemed clear. They would try and flank him on both the port and starboard sides. Darius didn't intend to let them get away with that. But he was outgunned. He had the advantage in distance. His laser cannons were more powerful than anything the Ashi fleet could bring to bear. Plus, he had an almost unlimited supply of power. But the enemy had an advantage in numbers and speed. The *Renegade* was just as fast as the enemy ships, but getting up to speed would take time. The enemy would, if given the chance, race past him, firing as they went. If they could get ships to either side of the *Renegade*, they could cut off his line of retreat and make hiding behind the planet useless.

"We have to time this just right," Darius said. "Priority one is taking out the Dreadnoughts. Do we have them targeted?"

"Aye, Captain, I've already got them selected in the targeting computer," Pete Best said. "The problem is they're slower than the other ships."

"How far out are they?"

"Closer to one point, two billion kilometers," Vivian replied.

"And they're spread wide across the line ships," Pete continued. "We'll have to swing our bow around to target them."

"Understood," Darius said. "How close are their battleships now?"

"Seven hundred eighty-three million kilometers from their lead ship," Vivian said.

Time ticked by slowly. Darius reviewed his plan twice while they waited for the Ashi to close the distance. Finally, after over an hour of waiting, the enemy ships were just one hundred million kilometers away.

"It's time," Darius said. "Bring us up, Lieutenant Nash."

"Aye, Captain, firing thrusters. Bringing us over the moon's horizon in fifteen seconds."

"Lieutenant Best, I want you to fire all four lasers at top speed. Is that clear?"

"Aye, Captain."

"You have your targets selected?"

"Affirmative. Fox One and Three will fire on Tango eighty-four and Tango sixty-seven at full power. Fox Two and Four will only fire at half power at the closer ships."

"I want six fast shots, then we push back down," Darius said. "All hands prepare to fire."

"Aye, Captain," Lori Lee said. "All hands are ready."

The ship drifted up. It was tense for a moment. The ships still weren't visible to the human eye.

"Firing!" Pete announced.

The cannons went off in quick succession. The flashes created a strobing effect and lit up the gray surface of Olo Prime's biggest moon.

"Take us down!" Darius said.

"Thrusters engaged," Henry replied.

The big ship was like a mythical sea creature. It had come to the surface for only a few seconds before disappearing back down. Only the *Renegade* wasn't in the water but in the shadow of the big moon.

There was silence on the Bridge as they watched the plot. The laser beams didn't show on the hologram, but the enemy ships targeted were lit in yellow. Darius knew it would take the lasers nearly a minute to reach their targets. He counted down silently in his mind. He was just about at zero when Tango eighty-four disappeared.

"That's a hit!" Pete shouted.

They were all hits. The first four lasers vaporized their targets. The last two ships had just enough time to realize what was happening and call for evasive action, but they weren't nearly fast enough. One lost its entire back half. The remaining front section went spinning to the side. Darius couldn't help but wish the ships were closer together where they might crash into one another. But that didn't happen. The sixth ship took a glancing blow. The laser tore a hole in the hull of the enemy vessel. It spewed gas in a cloud, and the ship's running lights blinked off.

"Six down," Henry said. "Good shootin', Pete."

"The computer did all the work," Pete Best admitted.

"There are still over a hundred ships in the fleet," Darius said. "Let's stay focused. What's the power status on those cannons."

"Recharging, sir," Pete said. "Ten more seconds, and all four will be ready to fire."

"Alright, get ready to engage again," Darius ordered. "Alter our course, Nav. Let's slip out to the side a bit."

The second barrage was not as successful. The aliens were still too far out and moving erratically. It was impossible to track them all. Two more battleships were hit, but the Dreadnoughts, with their mega cannons, were not.

The *Renegade* made two more firing runs before the final move. In that time, fourteen ships were either destroyed or out of commission, including four Dreadnoughts. The enemy fleet still had plenty of firepower. And they were closing in fast.

"This is our big move, people. Let's stay frosty. Nash, bring us up and standby on reverse thrusters."

"Aye, Captain, increasing altitude, standing by on reverse thrusters.

"Pete, quick shots with the cannons. Target the closest ships. One-third laser power," Darius explained. "Have drones standing by."

"Aye, Captain, weapons are hot. One-third of laser power is set. Drones are ready to launch."

It all happened quickly. The enemy ships were close in military terms. The nearest had closed to within fifty million kilometers, which meant most of their lasers could hit the Ashi vessels in just under thirty seconds from when they were fired. But the enemy wasn't flying in a straight line. They were rushing forward at nearly one hundred and forty thousand kilometers per second but also bobbing up and down, side to side, like a prize fighter stalking down his opponent in a boxing match.

The *Renegade* cleared the horizon of the moon and immediately began to fire. At the same time Darius gave the order to fire the reverse thrusters. The Arodoni ship was still out of reach of the

Imperium vessel's laser cannons, but they knew it wouldn't last long. And so it seemed that the enemy knew the moment was upon them as well. Just as the *Renegade* began to fire, the ships directly ahead of her slowed while those wide to either side sped up and began moving toward one another. It was a perfect pincer maneuver. Both sides of the enemy line were swooping in toward the *Regengade*. But Darius had planned his maneuver, too. The ship slipped back over the northern pole of Olo Prime and then began to drift down, turning as she went to target the enemy ships along the enemy's starboard line.

The entire maneuver took two and a half minutes. In that short span, Pete Best fired the ship's cannons forty-eight times. Thirty of those shots were hits. Twenty-eight enemy vessels were knocked out of the fight, but there were still over fifty in the battle line and another twenty-nine farther back.

The *Renegade* slipped down, turning as she went like a diver in a practiced jump from the high platform. Using the planet's gravity, they gained speed. But the enemy was thundering ahead, racing through space at almost half the speed of light. It was a dazzling aerial display. The enemy ships were closing in second by second. They spread apart, some running around the planet, others diving under it.

The timing had to be perfect. It was not unlike ancient naval warfare when two ships sailed straight at one another. They would slip past the other, firing their cannons in the hope of doing catastrophic damage to the other's ability to sail and control their ship before they raced out of range again. The enemy closed in and hoped to catch the *Renegade* off guard. She was a powerful ship, but one with limits. All four of her massive laser cannons could only face forward and had a limited range of movement. Her rear was vulnerable. The Ashi ship masters knew that. They expected to sweep past and hit her from the side and rear, but Darius had taken his surroundings into consideration. After sliding around Olo Prime, the Arodoni ship moved between the planet and a small moon. There, it stayed as the Imperium fleet raced past. None of the enemy vessels could get a shot at the *Renegade*.

It was a superb plan and the crew of the ship executed it perfectly. They had, in a very short time, won a statistical victory, as any historian looking back would have to admit. One ship had destroyed a third of the opposing fleet. But the battle wasn't over. And while the opening gambit had seemed neat and clean, everything dissolved into a fog of war as the *Renegade* reappeared from behind the small moon.

Fortunately, most of the enemy ships were already out of range. The closest fired at the *Renegade*, but only two blasts came close to the Arodoni ship. And with the sonic shield up at full power, the laser energy was easily deflected. The real threat came from the dreadnoughts with their mega cannons. Two fired at the *Renegade*, but the human-led vessel was moving too fast. A human ship the size of the *Renegade*, which was over seven kilometers long from stern to bow, would have been slow and cumbersome. But with her powerful engines and thrusters, the *Renegade* moved more like a fighter than a ship-of-the-line.

They raced out from behind the little moon, still flying backward and utilizing the gravity of Olo Prime to sling-shot themselves back up into the path of the Imperium fleet.

"Target the dreadnoughts!" Darius ordered.

"Aye, Captain, targeting the dreadnoughts. Calculating firing solutions now."

"Distance?" Darius asked.

"Five hundred million kilometers and closing," Vivian Ramos answered.

Darius had to do the math in his head, but it was second nature. The laser blasts, traveling at the speed of light, which was roughly three hundred thousand kilometers per second, would need just under half an hour to reach the target. It would take less time for the *Renegade* to circle the planet, which Darius was planning to do.

"Target's locked in," Pete Best said. "Ready to fire."

"Do it," Darius said.

Four bright flashes followed. Pete Best began targeting the other ships, and Darius checked their position. They had just passed the equator on Olo Prime.

"Keep up the evasive maneuvers," Darius said. "They'll be firing back at us."

It was odd fighting such a huge force and doing it across such vast distances. In many ways, it reminded him of the old game of Battleship, where a player has no idea where their opponent has placed their ships on the board. They must simply guess until they get lucky. In the same way, it was useless to take aim at a ship when one's ordinance would not reach that vessel for over twenty-five minutes. In that time, it could do just about anything. And one had to calculate for every possibility except that it would continue straight on its course.

"Lasers are ready to fire again, Captain," Henry Nash called out.

"Weapons?"

"Almost," Pete Best said.

"Make it count, Lieutenant. We only get one more try at those dreadnoughts on this pass."

"Captain, the fleet battleships are slowing down," Vivian called out.

"Good, that will make them easier targets when we circle around the planet again," Darius said. "Begin your calculations for an evacuation run. I want us to swing wide of the enemy and press on toward the portal."

"Aye, Captain," Vivian said. "Plotting an escape vector now."

"We'll come all the way around the planet," Darius said. "Building up our speed and taking another shot at those dreadnoughts, then we arch around what forces remain to reach the portal."

Darius was thinking out loud. It wasn't uncommon. It gave Darius the clarity he needed to formulate his plans but also allowed his crew to know what he was thinking at the same time.

"Target's set," Pete Best said. "Permission to fire."

"Granted," Darius said.

Four flashes followed as the *Renegade* neared the polar region of the planet below them. Darius couldn't help but feel a thrill. Battle was tense, dangerous, and frightening. The Arodoni ship was also exhilarating.

"Alright, Lieutenant Nash, flip us around," Darius ordered. "Once we cross the horizon line, we can begin firing on the fleet battleships."

"Aye, Captain, engaging thrusters to turn us about."

The ship turned without slowing or changing directions. It was still moving at speed, only it had gone from flying backward to forward. It was the type of maneuver only a ship in zero gravity could perform. They had been using the planet's gravity to build their speed but Darius would add the Renegade's powerful engines as well. They would soon be moving too fast and in the opposite direction of the fleet, which would have no chance of catching up to them. The best they could hope for was to shoot the *Renegade* down, but Darius didn't plan to give them that chance either.

"Captain!" Vivian Ramos' voice cared a note of near panic in it. He knew her well enough to recognize the tone, and he knew instantly that he had missed something. "Enemy fighters! Thousands of them!"

"Where?" Darius said, his voice had gone from excited enthusiasm to lethal seriousness.

"Everywhere," Vivian said. "They're converging on the planet!"

"How is that possible?" Pete Best said.

"Nash, engage engines," Darius ordered. "Take us out of orbit now."

"But we're on the wrong side of the planet," Henry said.

"We won't make another revolution," Darius said. "Not with that many fighters coming in. We're almost in their range now. Get us out of here, Lieutenant!"

"Aye, Captain. Engaging thrusters."

"Commander Lee, launch all remaining drones," Darius said.

"They won't do much good," Lori Lee said. "There's too many enemy fighters."

"I don't need the drones to stop the fighters; just slow them down," Darius said.

Everything about the battle had suddenly shifted. Darius thought it was like when he played chess with his father and the old man would bring his queen out suddenly. Darius was often forced to move players he didn't want to move and to recalculate every move he had been anticipating.

"What's our vector, Navigation?"

"We're traveling at almost one hundred thousand kilometers per hour on a heading of two-two-niner above the system orbital plane, sir."

"Calculate a long turn," Darius said. "We should still be able to outrun them."

"Drones launching, Captain," Lori Lee said.

"Very good, Commander," Darius said as he settled back into his captain's chair. "We'll reassess our plans once the enemy has their fleet back under control."

"Continue evasive maneuvers?" Vivian asked.

"Affirmative. We're still in range of those dreadnought cannons."

"That will slow us down," Henry Nash said.

"We can't risk taking a direct hit," Darius said. "We have no way of knowing if the shield will hold up. And if we lose an engine now, we're done for."

"Sir, we took out a third of their ships," Pete Best said. "They're down to nine dreadnoughts, forty-seven battleships, and thirteen support vessels."

"And who knows how many fighters," Vivian pointed out.

"They can't catch us now," Nash said.

"Doesn't look like they're even trying to," Commander Lee said. "They're focused on the drones."

The ship was facing away from the planet. Darius couldn't see the fighting behind them, but the plot showed tiny flashes as the drones and fighters engaged in battle. He thought about trying to increase their number of drones, but it wouldn't do any good. They would all be destroyed. And as fast as the production area on the ship was, it couldn't replenish the drones and weapons fast enough to help them in their current struggle.

Darius knew that every plan required adjustments when the fighting started. In war, anything was possible. He had been jubilant that his plan had worked, at least to a point. He had used the planet and her moons to even the odds a little, but he wasn't sure it was enough. Sixty-nine enemy ships were still more than enough to destroy the *Renegade*. And they were no longer in proximity to the planet, which had given them cover. The other worlds in the system were not aligned with the hyperspace portal. He couldn't effectively use them on his way out of the system. Speed was his only real asset left and he planned to use it to the fullest extent possible.

CHAPTER 24

SHEIKA KAHN GRUMBLED as he watched the Arodoni ship slip out of his trap. The enemy commander was brilliant. Sheika Kahn would have preferred to dominate his adversary, but he was still an Ashi. Perhaps his warrior days were behind him. He would admit that his position of power had led to some excesses. He could no longer see his feet without bending forward, and that effort made him huff and puff. Still, he admired a skilled opponent whether he was fighting on the battlefield or in the boardroom. Politics, Sheika Kahn knew, could be just as thrilling and sometimes as deadly as the battle-field. Only the strategies and tactics were much more difficult to master. The Kahn was no longer a threat in physical combat, but he was more than a match in the political arena.

Commanding a battleship was not that different from warring at the highest levels of politics. From his ship, the *Retribution,* he could direct his forces and react to his enemy. He had watched with rapt fascination as the enemy ship made its first moves. As it slipped around the planet, using Olo Prime to shield it from the majority of the Imperium fleet, Sheika Kahn had marveled. His adversary was canny and would need a reason to move out into the open.

He had immediately seen that the ship would hide between the planet and one of her moons at exactly the moment when she would have been the most vulnerable to the fleet's concentrated firepower. So Kahn had changed his strategy and ordered half of his battleships to launch their fighters. The fleet was still moving too fast to stop and engage or chase the alien ship. Sheika Kahn didn't need a tactician to tell him that the enemy vessel would continue around the planet, using it to shield it as it fired at the dreadnoughts and bombers who were still on the far side of Olo Prime. But the fighters would have an advantage the battleships couldn't match. They would launch in the opposite direction of the fleet. Nothing could be done about their momentum, but being much smaller craft with less mass and having powerful engines built for speed instead of hyperspace travel, they would be able to close on the planet quickly, perhaps even catch the enemy vessel by surprise.

"Lord Kahn, we have lost over forty vessels," the ship master said. "Perhaps it would be better to—"

"No," Kahn interrupted. "The battle isn't over."

"Mighty Kahn, I would not dare to argue, Lord, but the truth is, we cannot match their speed in time to stop them from reaching the hyperspace portal."

"Agreed," Kahn said.

He was not a ship master, but he was a very learned being. It was one of the reasons Vang's father had appointed him as Kahn. He had always been able to recall information quickly, such as the capabilities of fleet ships and the practical physics of bodies moving in space. Chasing after the alien ship would only result in the loss of more Imperium vessels. What Kahn needed was a way to draw the Arodoni back into battle.

"Have our ships converge on the planet," Kahn said.

"My Lord?" The ship master asked.

"I want our remaining dreadnoughts behind those moons," Kahn said, pointing to the hologram of Olo Timbo and her moons. "Have them ready to move out and fire on my command."

The ship master bowed. "Of course, Lord Kahn."

"And bring the bombers into orbit. Have them target the major cities with their kinetic warheads. If Olo Prime thinks it can aid our enemies, then we will show them what the Imperium does to traitors."

"Lord, it is my duty to inform you that kinetic bombing often results in heavy metal poisoning."

"I am aware," Sheika Kahn said. "Let us see if the aliens are. Perhaps they do not care about the Oloans, but I suspect they do."

"Yes, Lord Kahn," the ship master said as he hurried away.

Ulrech Sheika was starting to feel like an Emperor. He held the fate of an entire planet in his hands. No one would ever oppose him again once word got out about the Oloans and how they had been abandoned to die, slowly choking to death on the toxic fallout from the kinetic bombardment.

And maybe, just maybe, his enemy would come back in a futile effort to save the pathetic world. Olo Prime offered so very little to the Imperium. Sheika Kahn knew that no one in the core would care about its loss. But the aliens might care ... and if they did, it would be their turn to come through open space to attack his fleet. Then, all of the advantages would be with the Imperium. Kahn would use them to crush his enemy and secure his place as emperor of the galaxy.

CHAPTER 25

"THEY AREN'T FOLLOWING, CAPTAIN," Vivian Ramos said. "Trajectory of fleet ships shows them moving to Olo Prime."

"That's good, right?" Pete said. "We don't want them coming after us."

"Show me," Darius ordered. He had a growing sense of dread. The Imperium fleet wasn't predictable. They had surprised him in every engagement. Fortunately, the *Renegade* had survived the unexpected strategies of the Imperium forces, but he had a bad feeling about what he was seeing.

The ship was on a long, arcing course back to the portal. If the Imperium fleet could have simply turned around and gone straight back to the portal they would have cut the *Renegade* off. But the physics of space flight required that their momentum first be halted. They had to either flip around and do a retrograde burn to slow them and reverse course, or they had to used thrusters to make a curving turn like the *Renegade* was doing. In either case, they were too far out of position to stop the Arodoni ship from getting away. Not that they couldn't follow. The Imperium had shown time and again that they were able to keep tabs on the alien vessel. But it was clear that following them wasn't the priority of the Imperium fleet.

"They're going back to the planet," Darius said. He pointed to a group of rotund ships in a cluster. "What are these ships again?"

"Those are the bombers, sir," Commander Lee said. "Orbital bombing vessels."

"Why am I not surprised," Darius said. "Lieutenant Nash, will you stop your engines, please?"

"Aye Captain, disengaging main engine thrust," Henry replied.

"Why are we slowing down?" Pete Best asked.

It wasn't an accurate question. The *Renegade* didn't slow down, she just stopped accelerating.

"They aren't coming after us because they're going to bomb the planet," Darius said.

"What? Why?" Best asked. "We don't have any people down there."

"I think they know that," Vivian said. "And I don't think they care."

"Dirty bas—"

"Lieutenant Nash," Darius said, cutting his friend off. "Let's try to stay focused on what we can do."

"Target the bombers," Pete Best said. "If we swing around, we can hit them before they reach the planet."

"Distance to target?" Darius asked.

"We're nine hundred thousand kilometers from Olo Prime," Vivian replied. "The plot shows us about twelve million kilometers from the bombers, and another sixteen million from the dread-noughts."

"We're in their range," Best said. "Why don't they shoot?"

"Conserving their energy would be my guess. We don't have that constraint," Darius said.

He was watching the enemy move into position around the planet. It reminded him of studying military history. There was a time when armies needed to form themselves into battle lines. Fleets still made similar maneuvers as they closed in on one another in space, but the *Renegade* wasn't a fleet. The enemy had them outnumbered, but the Arodoni ship had the advantage in range and power. She was faster too. So, why were the Imperium ships acting like they were preparing for a long, drawn-out engagement?

"Prepare to fire on the bombers," Darius said. "Lieutenant Nash, bring us about. Thrusters only."

"Aye, Captain, bringing us about," Henry Nash said.

"Can we predict their trajectory, Lieutenant Ramos?"

"Aye, Captain, showing each ship's projected course."

From every ship on the plot a green line appeared. Those from the bombers showed them closing in on the planet and making orbit.

"How close would they need to be to fire on Olo Prime, Commander?" Darius asked.

Lori Lee shook her head. "I have no idea, Captain. Let me see if Nurek knows anything more."

The rogue alien had been helpful, but his knowledge of the warships was limited. After sharing all he could, Commander Lee had him escorted back to the Admin Center, but with access to his comlink.

"You can't really tell on the plot, but the bombers are making evasive maneuvers every few minutes," Vivian Ramos said.

"And the dreadnoughts?"

She nodded. "Them too. Firing at this range won't be easy."

They were still far enough out that a laser blast would take nearly a minute to reach the target. Which also meant that the radar returns were two minutes behind the actual position of the enemy ships.

"I want to take a shot anyway," Darius said. "Maybe we can slow them down."

"Even if we take out the bombers, we can't save the planet," Commander Lee pointed out. "The Imperium has too many ships in the system."

"We have to try," Darius told her. "It could be that they're only attacking Olo Prime to force us to try and help."

"All the more reason to keep going and leave the system," Lori Lee said.

"And let the innocent die in our stead?" Vivian Ramos asked.

"If the Imperium would attack the innocent that's on them," Lori Lee said.

"But the people on Olo Prime didn't ask for us to come to their system," Nash pointed out. "They didn't request our help. We needed them to help with the refugees we rescued."

"But they are taking part in the rebellion," Lee said. "They have to know there will be consequences."

"So, we should just leave them defenseless?" Ramos asked.

"No, they should see to their own defense. I know there are laws about that sort of thing, but it isn't our responsibility. I don't like the idea that we're playing right into the enemy's hands."

"That's a chance I'm willing to take," Darius said. "It might not be in our best interest to stay and fight, but I can't just turn my back on the planet."

"I have firing solutions locked in, Captain," Pete Best said.

"Very good, Lieutenant. Fire at will."

"Fox one," Pete announced.

He fired four shots in quick succession. Darius and the other officers watched the laser beams flash away from the *Renegade*, then their focus shifted to the plot.

"Time to impact?" Darius asked.

"Thirty-two seconds, Captain," Best said.

"Sir, I'm picking up some—"

There was a flash of light and sirens sounded on the Bridge of the *Renegade*. A split second later two more flashes of laser light raced past them.

"Sir! The shield is down," Pete Best shouted.

"Evasive actions," Darius ordered. "Engage main engines."

"Aye, Captain, engaging main engines," Henry Nash said.

"Damage report?" Darius asked.

"The sonic shield deflected most of the laser blast," Commander Lori Lee said. "Looks like we have some minor hull damage on the port side. Nothing catastrophic."

"The Dreadnoughts are heading for Alpha Moon," Vivian said.

"Do you have a firing solution, Lieutenant Best?"

"Not on the dreadnoughts, sir. Laser Cannons are at sixty-seven percent power."

"Make your shots on the bombers, then target the Dread-noughts."

"Incoming!" Vivian said.

Fortunately, the next volley of laser blasts flew wide of the Renegade. On the plot two of the bombers disappeared, and a third was hit with a glancing blow that sent it spinning out of control.

"Three hits, Captain," Pete Best said. "Fox four was a miss."

"If they get close enough to the planet, we won't be able to target them directly," Vivian Ramos said. "Not without risking our shots hitting the surface."

"What about our shield?" Darius asked.

"There was a power surge when we were hit," Henry Nash explained. "It burned out some of the circuits. My people are over-seeing the repairs now, Captain."

"How long until we have that shield back in business?"

"Fifteen minutes, maybe more," Nash said. "The drones are involved, sir."

"Fox one," Pete Best said, firing another blast from the laser cannons. "Fox two!"

He continued until all four cannons had fired. The ship thruster began to turn her again in an evasive maneuver to avoid the enemy counterattack. But the move came a second too late. A laser blast hit the Renegade on her stern, setting off more warning sirens.

"We're hit," Nash declared in a loud voice. "Engines are down. I repeat, the engines are offline."

"What's that mean?" Best asked.

"It means we're sitting ducks," Darius said, fighting the wave of cold fear welling up inside him. "Commander Lee, sound the ship alarms. Prepare for impact."

CHAPTER 26

"DAMAGE REPORT ON THOSE ENGINES, Lieutenant Nash," Darius ordered.

"It's mostly the exhaust system sir," Henry replied. "We lost forty percent of the heat shield. Those are made of interlocking panels, Captain. The drones are already replacing them. Another group is replacing the energy converting mechanism is the secondary engine. Once that's done, we'll have thrust again, sir."

"How long?" Darius asked.

"A few minutes," Nash said. "My engineers are rerouting power from the main drive to the secondary."

"I want human personnel not involved in ship repairs moving toward the *Jericho*," Darius continued giving instructions. "Emergency suits on, including helmets."

"Are we going to abandon the *Renegade*?" Vivian asked.

"We might have to," Darius said.

Another series of flashes tore through space around them. Darius felt a slight tremor through the deck and in his Captain's seat.

"Are we hit?"

"Affirmative," Nash said. "Hangar One is compromised, sir, but it was empty anyway and already sealed off."

"Can we seal anything else off?"

"Captain, the ship has emergency settings," Lori Lee replied. "Essentially everything gets sealed down, every section, every deck, even the individual rooms in most cases."

"We should do it," Darius said. "The next volley could compromise the hull."

"Captain," Ramos spoke up. "I can't be certain, but it appears that the dreadnoughts are preparing to refuel."

"That could buy us some time to make our repairs," Henry Nash said.

"Initiate the emergency measures anyway," Darius ordered. "We can't risk losing the entire ship if we're wrong about those dreadnoughts."

In the back of the Bridge, forgotten about by Captain Darius and his crew of officers, Remmy Steel activated his comlink to the platoon-only channel.

"Marines, move toward the *Jericho*," he ordered. "I repeat, all Marines move toward the *Jericho* ASAP."

"You want us to abandon our posts, Master Sergeant?"

"The hangers are vulnerable," Remmy said. "And the ship is about to go on lockdown. Get as close to the center of the vessel as possible."

"That's going to be a problem," Laila said.

Remmy felt a stab of fear in his gut. It was so powerful he actually doubled over in pain.

"Staff Sergeant, what is your status?"

"Corporal Berry and I are on station in Hangar One," she said. "I think the ship got hit."

"Affirmative. We are taking fire. Can you get out of there?"

"No, Master Sergeant. We're locked in. The hatch controls aren't working."

"What's your status?"

"We're fine. There does appear to be an air leak of some kind, but we're in full armor. We're good to go for at least an hour."

"Move to the interior as far as you can," Remmy said. "The engines are down, and the shields are out. Things don't look good up here."

"Master Sergeant," Dirk Oliver spoke up. "The gravity lifts aren't working."

"Compartments are sealed off, too," Ricky Thompson said. "The reserves and I are trapped in the armory."

"You aren't trapped," Remmy said, although he knew that description was close to the truth. "The entire ship is being locked down for safety. Everyone needs to get as deep into the ship as possible."

"What about the *Jericho*?" McManus asked.

"I guess that's off the table. Everything's happening fast here. Standby for more information," Remmy said as the stood up straight and looked toward Captain Darius.

"Captain, emergency measures are activated," Commander Lori Lee called out. "Everything is sealed up tight. We have eight crew members on the Jericho, including Ensign Stanislaus and Ensign Bertoli. The rest are maintenance and culinary specialists, sir."

"At least they'll be able to escape if things get worse," Darius said. "Lieutenant Best, target the refueling ships."

"Aye, Captain, targeting the refueling ships now, sir."

"Are we in a position to fire?"

"Negative," Henry Nash said. "That last shot left us spinning. We can't course correct until the thrusters are back online."

"Sir, I'm getting a hail from the Imperium ships," Vivian Ramos said. "It's a direct beam message, Captain, from Tango nineteen."

"That must be the flagship," Darius said.

"It's hovering just above the planet," Vivian said.

"Ready to run and hide once the shooting starts again," Henry Nash said.

"Put it through," Darius ordered.

A hologram of a huge Ashi head appeared. The jaw was wide, and the cheeks were flabby. There were wrinkles across the wide forehead and around the eyes, which were bloodshot and hooded with drooping eyelids. The tusks that stuck out of its mouth were gray with age. Darius realized he was not dealing with a young warrior like Emperor Vang had been.

"Arodoni vessel, this is Sheika Kahn, commander of the Ashi fleet, and representative of the illustrious Emperor Vang of the Galactic Imperium. You have been defeated. It was inevitable, but your demise need not be. Surrender your ship and crew. We will, this one time, extend mercy to your people. If you refuse, we will destroy you utterly. Of that, you can be sure. Respond quickly or face the consequences of my wrath."

Darius realized the huge face belonged to the same alien who had spoken to him in the Casa system. Nurek had supposed that the Kahn, who Darius remembered was second in command of the empire, had purposefully left Vang to die so that he could become the new ruler of the galaxy.

"Should we respond?" Ramos asked.

"And surrender?" Henry Nash replied. "No way."

"They'll kill everyone on board," Commander Lee said. "Or worse, put us in slave camps."

"We aren't going to surrender," Darius said, standing up from his chair. "Did you notice that he didn't say he was the new emperor."

"I guess I missed that," Henry admitted.

"Didn't Nurek say he abandoned the emperor so that he could take over?" Vivian asked.

"Exactly. But for some reason he hasn't."

"Maybe they think the emperor is still alive," Pete suggested.

"And we've got him," Henry said.

"Bingo," Darius agreed. "That's our ace in the hole."

"What do you mean?" Vivian asked.

"I mean, it's possible they won't destroy the ship. It could buy us some time. Put me through to him, Lieutenant. Let's try and keep them talking. Nash, get us moving. I don't care what it takes, we cannot remain as we are."

"Aye, Captain. My people are on it."

Of course, Darius knew the truth. The engineers from the *Jericho,* as talented as they were, knew very little about the *Renegade*. It was far more advanced than any human vessel. Mostly, they had lingered in the engineering spaces, watching and trying to learn what they could. The maintenance droids did the real work. Darius hoped they were working quickly now.

"Sheika Kahn, this is Captain Zeke Darius. We spoke before, in the Casa system, just before you fled the battlefield. I'm sure you're aware that Emperor Vang is our guest aboard the *Renegade*. Your threats fall short, sir. Do not think that we will hesitate to kill your emperor. Take your fleet out of the system, and we will release the emperor to the people of Olo Prime."

Darius turned to Vivian Ramos. "Send that," he ordered.

"It'll take a full minute to reach his ship," Vivian said.

They waited for the reply, which did not come. Instead, a group of over thirty battleships altered course and headed straight for the portal.

"Looks like your threat had some effect," Henry Nash pointed out. "They're moving to cut us off."

"Can we outrun them?" Darius asked.

"Negative, Captain. We'll have the secondary engine back online soon, but it won't give us the same amount of thrust as the primary, and we're out of position."

"What do we do, then?" Pete Best asked. "If those ships get ahead of us, we could be taking fire from two directions."

"We'll be in real trouble," Darius said. "We need a way to escape."

"There is no other way out of the system," Vivian said. "We're trapped."

"Could we make hyperspace with just the secondary engine operable?"

"It's possible," Engineer Nash said. "But with just one engine engaged, we won't have the same maneuverability. Usually, the secondary engines power the thrusters, while the main engine propels the ship. To make the jump to hyperspace, we'll need all the thrust from the secondary engine moving the ship forward."

"It's all for nothing if we can't outpace those battleships," Vivian said. "Our second barrage was a success. The fleet is down to just two bombers, but they've got plenty of dreadnoughts. And we're still in their range."

"For now," Darius said. "We're still moving away from them. One hundred thousand kilometers per hour isn't slow."

"May not be fast enough though," Nash said. "Once those dread-noughts have refueled and gotten their lasers back to full charge."

Darius knew the plan, what was left of it, wasn't good enough. They could get the ship moving again, but not like before. Evasive maneuvering would be limited. The Ashi fleet still had enough dreadnoughts to calculate their moves. Eventually, they would be disabled and most likely, destroyed. They needed another way out of the system. But running away was futile. They could escape the system and live out the rest of their lives on the Arodoni ship, but Darius wondered what kind of life it would be. The ship was lavish and almost completely self-sustaining, but his crew would be greatly discouraged by the prospect of being trapped between star systems.

"What's the next closest system to Olotimbo?" Darius asked.

"Exeter Three Nineteen," Vivian said. "No life is registered in that system, Captain. None of the planets are habitable."

"Is there a portal to the hyperspace network?"

"Negative," she replied.

"How far is it to the closest inhabited system or hyperspace portal?" Darius asked.

"Eighty-eight light years," Vivian said.

"Damn," the captain muttered.

"Sir, may I ask a question?" Remmy said.

Darius turned in chair. He had completely forgotten the Master Sergeant was even on the Bridge.

"You have something to add, Master Sergeant?"

"I'm not sure, sir," Remmy said. "But our navigation of the hyperspace lanes comes from GIGI, correct?"

Darius nodded.

"So, it's possible that her information isn't up to date," Remmy said.

"That's possible, but I don't see how it's relevant, Master Sergeant."

"Well, sir, I was just thinking. We've still got the slave ship. Maybe it has more data in its navigation system than we have."

Darius just looked at Remmy for a moment. He felt a glimmer of hope but clamped down hard on it. Instead, he turned toward Vivian.

"What do you think?" He asked her.

She shrugged her shoulders. "Anything is possible," she replied. "GIGI would have to uplink to their navigation computer and see if anything else gives us a better chance at survival."

"Can she do that with the ship on lock down?" Darius asked, turning his attention back to Remmy.

The Master Sergeant was quiet a moment, then nodded. "She's on it, sir."

GIGI, the alien Galactic Information and Guidance Instrument was in the Systems Control room, which had been abandoned when Darius gave the order for all human personnel to return to the *Jericho*. GIGI, Remmy realized, would not have gone. Losing her would be a blow to the human race. He needed to do a better job of including the alien artifact in his orders for the crew.

How the living computer could access another system that was down in a different section of the ship was a mystery to Darius. But the master sergeant felt his spark of hope growing warm within him. If there was another way out of the system, it would change everything.

"Sir, we're almost ready to activate the secondary engines," Henry Nash said. "We just need a couple more minutes."

"Very good, Lieutenant. Let's have an update on all systems, please."

"Power supply and life support are both in the green," answered Henry Nash. "Propulsion is down. Hull integrity is still at ninety-eight percent sir. Maintenance droids are activated."

"What about those battleships, Lieutenant Ramos?"

"They're gaining speed, Captain," she said. "Even with full power I don't think we could beat them back to the portal."

"We don't need to beat them," Pete Best said. "We can blow them out of the system."

"Not while we're still under the guns from those Dreadnoughts," Darius said. "If we even start moving in the direction of the portal, they'll target us."

"So, we target them," Best said. "We have more firepower than they do."

"But they have all the advantages," Darius said. "They pushed us away from Olo Prime and now they have cover ... and we don't."

"Doesn't mean we can't beat 'em," Pete Best said. "There's still a chance."

"My guess is if we make a move toward the portal, they'll be coming out shooting," Darius said. "And if we fire at them, they'll immediately fire back."

"So, what options does that leave us?" Vivian asked.

"One, we can't let them know we have full control of our ship," Darius said. "Once they know that they'll hit us again."

"We can fly like we're trying to compensate for problems," Nash said. "Fool 'em into thinking we're worse off than we really are."

"But fly where?" Best asked. "There's nowhere else to go."

Remmy got the word from GIGI the instant she found it. He held up a hand.

"That might not be the case," Remmy said. "GIGI found something."

"What is it?" Vivian asked, her hands flying over the controls on her console.

"GIGI is forwarding it to the nav computer now. It's a portal to hyperspace," Remmy said.

Henry Nash clapped his hands, "Then we can get out of here. Where should we go next?"

"Actually, that's the issue," Remmy said. "The portal doesn't connect to the network."

"Where does it go?" Darius asked.

Remmy shrugged his shoulders and it was Vivian Ramos reading her computer screen that answered. "The Mot system," she said. "But there's no information about it. I can't even find it in the ship's computer."

"An unknown system," Darius said. "Like Sol."

"It could be anything," Pete Best said. "Just because we don't know about it, doesn't mean the Imperium doesn't."

"Maybe there's something about it that is bad," Vivian said. "And that's why they aren't worried about it. Maybe no one in their right mind would go there."

"I don't think we have a choice," Darius said. "How long will it take to repair the main engine, Lieutenant Nash?"

"Unknown," Henry replied. "Most of the electrical was fried in the blast. It'll have to be rebuilt. The maintenance drones can do it, Captain. I just don't know how long it'll take."

"Then we make for the new portal," Darius said. "Can you plot the course, Lieutenant Ramos."

"Aye, Captain, setting a course for the hyperspace portal to Mot."

"What's the status on the secondary engine, Lieutenant Nash?"

"Coming online now, sir," Henry said.

"Fire your thrusters randomly. We can't look too competent without drawing fire. What about the sonic shielding?"

"Still under repairs, sir," Pete Best said. "We have weapons but no defenses."

"Distance to the portal?"

"It's close, Captain," Vivian said. "We have just enough space to get up to speed."

"Keep us in this tumble, Henry. Let's make them think we're out of control but get us moving toward the hyperspace transition point. Can we do that?"

"Aye, Captain. It'll take some effort with the thrusters, but we can do this."

"Good, let's make it happen people," Darius said, turning to face Remmy. "Was tapping into the slave ship's computer your idea or GIGI's?"

"Hard to say, sir."

"Well, it was an excellent suggestion, Master Sergeant. And we're lucky to have you on this mission."

"Thank you, sir," Remmy said, looking uncomfortable.

"Let's just hope we aren't jumping from the frying pan into the fire."

CHAPTER 27

THE MESSAGE HAD INFURIATED Sheika Kahn. The pale, puny alien was grotesque to him. Hairless, small through the shoulders and chest. It was impossible to ascertain height since the recorded message showed Captain Zeke Darius from the chest up. He appeared old to Sheika Kahn, weak and desperate. It was obvious he was trying to sound strong, but the alien failed to pull it off. Perhaps it was his voice, quiet and squeaking.

"Have you finished your language analysis?" Kahn asked the shipmaster.

"It is not a known language. Perhaps the Arodoni language has evolved over the past five hundred years."

"It is of no concern," Sheika Kahn thought.

In reality, he was bothered that the message came to him already translated. The aliens knew his language, but he did not know theirs. It was, to his mind, a weakness that needed to be rectified. But the last thing Sheika Kahn wanted was for others to hear the alien's message. It contained two very troubling statements. The first was that Emperor Vang lived. It was no surprise to anyone that Sheika Kahn had tried to take the throne for himself. In the Ashi culture, ambition was a prized character trait. In fact, Sheika Kahn knew that the moment he was installed as the new Emperor several of the Fleet commanders would challenge his rule. That was why he ordered them to the forefront of the attack. The Arodoni had already killed most of the veteran warriors who stood ready to attack his reign as Emperor. But Sheika Kahn could not be seen neglecting to try and save Emperor Vang. It was one thing to challenge a ruler to his face, it was quite another to turn one's back on him in the face of the enemy.

But it wasn't Vang that bothered Sheika Kahn the most. It was the direct challenge to Sheika's courage on the battlefield. The Ashi were proud warriors with reputations to uphold, and yet, it wasn't his reputation that worried him. It was the truth that he had, in fact, fled the battle in the Casa system. He had told himself he was in control. He had actually planned to leave Emperor Vang vulnerable in the hopes that the sovereign ruler would be killed in battle, saving the Kahn from having to kill Vang himself. But deep down inside, Sheika Kahn knew the truth. He was afraid. Risk was part of life and one could never truly get ahead without some risk. Kahn had taken political risks many times, but the Arodoni ship terrified him. From its first shot in the battle of Casa, when it completely vaporized an Ashi warship, he had trembled with fear. Hundreds of strong warriors had been on that spaceship. They had all died in a split second. The Arodoni weapons were simply too powerful not to respect. Only Sheika Kahn's feelings were deeper, more potent than mere respect. He was afraid.

"They are bluffing," he said, happy that he had spent years training his voice so that it did not reveal his feelings. Such small details made all the difference in the political realm where everything was recorded and every last nuance of what a person said was analyzed by one's enemies.

"Perhaps," the shipmaster said. "We could pull back to the portal and see if the enemy will release his Majesty."

The word made the Kahn furious. He spun around lashing out with one hand. His knuckles struck the shipmaster's cheek and sent him staggering backward two steps. The shipmaster growled angrily as he reached up and felt the cut on his jowl.

"We will not leave the field of battle until we have gained possession of that ship," the Kahn snarled. "That was the emperor's final order, and we will carry it out. Besides, we have taken the upper hand. We hold the planet. It is the only cover they could hide behind. In the open, they are vulnerable."

"But they might kill him," the shipmaster said, wisely staying just out of reach as he spoke.

"We have no proof that he is still alive," Sheika Kahn argued. "But if Emperor Vang lives, then we will free him. Prepare two fighter squadrons. Arm them with EMP weapons."

"What about their drone fighters?"

"If they have any left, it won't be enough to stop us. Besides, the EMPs will knock them out as well."

"Lord, Kahn, their ship is still moving at great speed. We will lose hundreds of fighters and pilots with no guarantee that we can even get on board the alien ship."

Sheika Kahn turned suddenly. He was bigger and heavier than the shipmaster. Life on board an interstellar warship did not have the same luxuries as those found in palaces and planets. The Kahn used his bulk to his advantage, moving close, and leaning forward in a menacing fashion.

"We have always attacked enemy ships in this manner, Shipmaster," Kahn growled. "I do not care how many die. I want that ship and I want it now!"

The shipmaster grimaced in either anger or disgust at Sheika's lack of concern about the loss of life, he couldn't be sure which. It didn't matter. The entire Imperium could hate him, but they would obey him. Better yet, he would make them fear him.

"Do it or are you unwilling to carry out your duties, Shipmaster?"

"I will give the order," the shipmaster said, although without adding the respectful title that Sheika Kahn was due.

He was just about to correct his underling when one of the offi-cers nearby called out, "The enemy ship has regained propulsion."

Kahn snarled as he spun back around to view the holographic plot. The enemy ship was too far away to be seen. The *Retribution* was hovering just on the far side of the planet from the Arodoni ship. There was no sense in leaving themselves open to attack. The Kahn ignored the shutter of fear that flashed through him as he thought of the alien's ship's spectacular power and watched as it continued to spin.

"Its thrusters aren't operational," came a call from the pit where the ship's crew operated her many systems. "They can't control it."

"It could be a ruse," the shipmaster suggested.

"Or perhaps they are damaged beyond repair," Sheika Kahn argued. "Launch the fighters."

"They're moving," came another call. "The ship is still malfunc-tioning, but they have restored engine power."

"They are running in fear," Sheika Kahn said. "They cannot outrun our battleships. We control the system. There is nowhere for the cowards to go."

"It could be a ruse to draw us out," the shipmaster said. "Many creatures feign injury to lure their prey out of hiding."

"They are not the predators, and we are not hiding!" Sheika Kahn screamed. "Get out of my sight or I'll have your head removed from your shoulders!"

The shipmaster hurried back to the pit. Kahn was breathing heavy. Everything taxed his fat body. Once the Arodoni ship was captured, he would never be in anything but a leisure position. He reached out a hand and squeezed the holographic image of the Arodoni ship. Soon, it would really be in his grasp ... and so would the entire galaxy.

CHAPTER 28

"STATUS?" Captain Zeke Darius asked.

"On course," Lee said. "We're still an hour away from the portal."

"Weapons?"

"Laser cannons are fully charged, Captain," Pete Best said. "Sonic shielding is still inoperable."

Chief Engineer Henry Nash spoke up from his station. "Hull damage to hangar one has been repaired, Captain. The main engines are still out of commission. We're at least a few hours away from getting it back online."

Remmy Steel in the back of the Bridge activated his comlink on a private channel to Staff Sergeant Laila McPherson.

"Your hangar is repaired," he said. "They should be pumping air into it now."

"What about getting us out?" Laila asked.

"The ship is still on lockdown. I don't see that changing until we're out of the system. Maybe an hour or so from the sounds of things."

"What are the enemy ships doing?" She asked.

"Nothing so far," Remmy said. "It's all quiet now. Half the fleet is converging on Olo Prime. Half is moving back toward the portal."

"How are we getting out of the system?"

"Secret transition point," Remmy said. "GIGI pulled it from the slave ship's navigation computer."

Tension was high, but Remmy could hear the woman he loved relaxing a little bit. He thought that was good and was just about to tell her that, when Pete Best at the weapons control station spoke up.

"Sir, our current spin will bring the last two bombers into range momentarily."

"What about the dreadnoughts?" Darius asked.

"We can fire on them too," Pete Best explained.

"Range?"

"We're twenty million kilometers out," Ramos said.

"Alright, Lieutenant Best, take the shot," Darius ordered. "As soon as he does, I want the ship moving in a fast evasion. Utilize all engine power to the thrusters. Most of their dreadnoughts are out of position behind the moon. If we can keep it between them and us, we stand a chance."

Remmy knew everything had to happen in a symphony of coordinated events. He was no mathematician, but they were far enough away from the enemy that he knew it would take some time for their shots to reach the fleet. And they were still an hour away from the transition point. That meant using the orbit of Olo Prime's primary moon to help shield the ship from return fire. How the officers kept up with the planetary motion and made the massive *Renegade* a difficult target was a mystery to Remmy. But he was glad to be on the Bridge instead of deep inside the ship with no clue was to what was happening.

"Remmy, what's happening?" Laila asked. "You've been quiet too long."

Pete Best's voice seemed loud to Remmy. The emergency suit wasn't like space armor. It didn't cover his ears or keep outside sounds muted. Remmy had his comlink in one ear, but his other was uncovered as the weapons officer announced the laser fire. Through the transparent ceiling of the Bridge, Remmy saw the flashes of light.

"We're firing on them," Remmy said.

"Still fighting then," Laila said. "Which means they'll be shooting back."

"We're out of range of most of their fleet," Remmy told her. "And the captain knows his business."

"I wish I was up there with you instead of down here in the dark," Laila confessed. "I prefer to see the enemy coming."

"We all do," Remmy said, thinking of the Marines he had known. Most were dead and few had actually seen the bullet that killed them coming.

"Did our shots land?"

"Too soon to tell," Remmy reported. "We're far enough away that the lasers take over a minute to reach the target."

"That's terrible," she said. "It feels like we're walking on thin ice and I can hear it cracking."

"Maybe," Remmy said. "Main engines are still down. The secondary is running, but by itself it isn't as fast."

"That cabin on Casasil is looking pretty good right now," Laila said. "Tell me again why we didn't just stay there?"

"I can't quite remember," Remmy said, although it wasn't true. Neither of them would have turned their back on their duty. Perhaps if the galaxy had been at peace, they could have made a go of it. But not while their ship was under threat and their fellow Marines needed them.

"I keep thinking about that pink sky. I've never seen anything like that," she said. "It would have been a nice place to make a life. Maybe have a family."

"Hard to see you as the domestic type," Remmy said.

"I could be," she responded. "There's a lot about me you don't know, Master Sergeant."

"There's a lot of you I'm looking forward to discovering, Staff Sergeant."

They could flirt on the private comlink while the rest of the ship was busy fighting to escape the Olotimbo system. It seemed both trivial and incredibly valuable to Remmy. He was a man of duty, but having someone he cared about to fight for was a much more powerful motivation.

"Hang on," he said. "Reports are coming in."

"That's a hit," Pete Best said. "Both bombers are out of commission, Captain."

"Outstanding," Darius said. "What about the Dreadnoughts?"

They were too far away to see anything happening around the planet, but the plot showed them everything they needed to know. One refueling ship had been hit a glancing blow. It spun slowly between the two dreadnoughts with the best chance of returning fire on the *Renegade*. Suddenly it exploded and damaged both of the big alien vessels.

"Two down," Best declared. "Maybe not for long but they're out of the fight."

"Lieutenant Nash, take us down twenty-seven degrees," Darius ordered.

"Aye, Captain, moving down to point two-seven," Henry echoed.

"Sir, the fourth shot hit the moon," Pete Best said.

"Damage?"

"Nothing substantial," Pete explained, but it did kick up a dust cloud.

Remmy stepped sideways for a better view of the plot. He didn't want to do anything that would interfere with the work that the senior officers were carrying out on the Bridge, but he did want to see what was happening.

Captain Darius zoomed in on Alpha Moon. The Oloan name for the moon was too difficult to pronounce so the crew had labeled the moons with standard military designations. The laser blast from the *Renegade* unleashed a massive amount of energy even from twenty million kilometers away. A huge cloud of moon dust had been kicked up into the very thin gravity of the lunar body high enough to envelop one of the dreadnoughts in low orbit around it.

"We got them," Remmy said. "The bombers are all destroyed."

"At least the planet is a little safer now," Laila said.

It wasn't as though they didn't recognize the threat that still existed for the Oloans, but they both felt better knowing they wouldn't be bombed from orbit just for being hospitable to the humans on the *Renegade*.

"They are, we aren't," Remmy said. "We're still in range of the dreadnoughts."

For the next half hour, the enemy ships slipped around the moon and fired at the *Renegade*. It was tense, but their evasion tactics worked to keep them safe. But all that changed in an instant.

"Incoming," Pete Best said.

He had made the announcement many times, and in each instance the laser blasts flew wide of the *Renegade*. But their luck ran out halfway to the hidden hyperspace portal. There was a violent shake, and the sound of metal bending. Sirens went off on the Bridge again and Remmy felt a lump form in his stomach.

"We're hit!" Henry Nash called out. "Laser cannon three took the brunt of it, sir. But we have hull damage too, and electrical issues."

"Cannons are offline," Best called out. "I don't know what's happening."

"That's it," Captain Darius said. "Full power to the engines. Get us to the portal as fast as you can, Henry. Evasive movement every three minutes."

"Aye, Captain, engaging the secondary engine. Full power, evasive maneuvers every three minutes."

"How far are we from that portal?" Darius asked.

"Still fifty thousand kilometers, sir," Vivian Ramos said.

"Commander Lee?"

"Everyone is reporting in," Lori Lee said. "So far, no casualties."

"Maintenance system is down," Henry called out. "I'm trying to reroute power now, but we couldn't have been hit in worse place."

"How bad is it?" Darius asked.

"Bringing up the ship schematic, Captain," Henry said.

The plot hologram shifted to a view of the *Renegade*. One entire side was black. Her laser cannons were still extended. One had been snapped in two with only a few metal girders still connecting the two halves. The part that broke off had smashed into the side of ship gouging a huge dent in the hull.

"Are we compromised?" Darius asked.

"Unclear," Henry Nash replied. "There's a lot of damage. Hull integrity is down to sixty percent, sir. But we aren't venting atmo. Looks more like crush damage. I think we can make the jump to hyperspace."

"You think?" Pete Best asked.

"Best guess," Henry replied.

"We can't stay here," Darius added. "The outcome is certain if we try that. Better to take our chances in hyperspace."

"If we can get there," Ramos said.

"Remmy, what happened?" Laila asked. "Don't tell me nothing, because we felt it down here and it was something."

"Another hit," Remmy said softly. "Cannons are down. One was hit directly and tore into the side of the ship."

"Are we..."

"Not yet," Remmy told her. "So far, she's holding together."

"Incoming!" Pete Best shouted.

Fortunately, the laser barrage missed.

"Captain, I think dreadnoughts are out of fuel again," Vivian Ramos said. "I've got refueling ships moving toward Alpha Moon."

"It's about damn time," Darius said. "Bring the plot back up, Lieutenant Nash."

"Aye, Captain," Henry said.

The hologram of the ship changed back to the Olotimbo system. Remmy could see the bright star at the center, and the planets. Small dots showed the Imperium fleet vessels, and another showed the *Renegade.*

"Give us a trajectory to the hyperspace portal," Darius ordered. "And keep track of the dreadnoughts. I want to know the second they come out from behind the moon."

"Continue with evasive maneuvers, Captain?" Henry asked.

"Do we save much time without them?" Darius asked Vivian Ramos.

"Negative," Ramos replied. "We're on track to make the jump in twenty-seven minutes, Captain. Without the evasions, we only gain about ninety-seconds."

"Keep them up, then," Darius said. "Any idea how long it will take to get the maintenance system back up and running?"

"Negative sir," Henry admitted. "We'll have to do the work ourselves and for now with the ship on lockdown my people can't even get to that section of the ship."

"What about the laser cannon? Is it going to cause more damage the way it is? Do we need to cut it off?"

"Again, I'm not sure we could, sir," Henry replied. "Fortunately, it seems to be wedged between the hydraulic extenders and the hull on that side, Captain. I think we can go ahead and make the jump to hyperspace just like we are."

"Who has systems oversight?" Darius asked.

"That would be GIGI with our people on the *Jericho*, Captain," Lori Lee said.

Darius hit the transmit button on his chair's comlink. "GIGI, can you give me a status report on the ship's systems?"

"Affirmative, Captain," came the computerized voice. "Life support systems are functioning at optimal levels across the ship. Artificial gravity is utilizing the back-up generators but functioning at an acceptable level. The ship's power grid is damaged. Only thirty percent of the power is available until the circuits can be reset and damaged areas restored. Maintenance system is off-line. Weapons systems are off-line. Manufacturing and refining systems are off-line."

"It's worse than I thought," Darius said. "But we'll make it to the portal as is. I don't want to open up more compartments until we're sure the hull won't break open."

Remmy relayed the bad news to Laila.

"Twenty minutes," she said. "That seems like an eternity."

"The dreadnoughts don't have our power capability," Remmy assured her. "They can't keep up the same rate of fire."

"It only takes one hit," Laila said.

Remmy felt a chill run down his spine. He couldn't help but wonder what the laser blast might have done if it had hit the hull directly instead of the laser cannon. They might all be dead if that had happened.

"We're still whole," Remmy said. He sounded more confident than he felt. "We'll make it."

"We better. You're not getting away from me that easily, mister."

"Copy that."

They both chuckled, then focused on the timer counting down to their jump into hyperspace. Remmy had to admit it was nothing short of a miracle that they had survived the attack at all. One spaceship against an entire fleet of enemy warcraft. Remmy wouldn't have given them any hope at all, if they were in any other vessel. But somehow the *Renegade* had survived and was still able to get them to safety. Remmy only hoped they could repair her quickly and with half the beauty and style she had before the fight. He was thinking of the ship as his home. It was certainly their safe haven as they made their way through the hostile forces spread across the galaxy. He didn't like to think of her as anything other than the pristine vessel Remmy and Laila had first explored together.

CHAPTER 29

THE REPORT on the enemy dreadnoughts had been right. Whether it was because they were refueling, or just conserving whatever power they had left, no more shots were fired at the *Renegade*. As they approached the hyperspace portal, Captain Darius' worries shifted from the attack to the transition through inter-dimensional space. It was entirely plausible that the stresses on the ship would rip her to pieces. At least, Darius thought, if that happened, it would be quick.

"Approaching transition point," Ramos announced.

"Very good. Alert all hands."

"Aye, Captain, alerting all hands," Commander Lee responded.

"Are we at the right speed?" Darius asked.

"Affirmative, Captain. Everything is as it should be."

Except the ship. Darius felt her damage the way a person might feel an injured limb. He couldn't get the image of the broken ship out of his mind. He had been reckless and negligent. Under normal circumstances his actions would be reviewed by his superiors during an after-action reporting. Ships inevitably took damage during battles, but he was the captain of a ship of incalculable value, not just to humanity, but to the galaxy at large. Every planet was affected by the advance of technology. Some worlds were in competition with others to gain a technological advantage, but as that tech was assimilated every world in the Empire would benefit. For many, the tech on the *Renegade* would be a huge leap forward. No one understood that more than Darius. The reality was both theory and a practical application for him as he spent time on the ship. Anything he wanted was produced for him on board by a squad of robotic fabricators. The ship had a source of power that was collected from the very space they traveled through. Any materials they lacked could be hauled in using the artificial gravity beam and refined in the ship's processing plant.

Food was grown on board. Animals were raised and butchered by the agri-bots who also kept the park in pristine condition. The plants produced enough oxygen for the entire ship and filtered the carbon dioxide humans exhaled, so that the air was always clean. Nothing humanity had ever built could come close to the engineering marvel that was the *Renegade*.

Darius didn't know if he had the right to put the incredible vessel at risk, but he also didn't think he could hide it away when it seemed alone capable of challenging the Imperium. He had to keep all his emotions and conflicting thoughts about the ship to himself. It was the burden of command. Not only did the entire crew weigh on him, but so did every decision that kept the treasure trove of technology away from his fellow man.

"Transition in three... two... one..." Vivian Ramos called out.

The ship didn't vanish but it did break through into a hyper dimension that took it far from the reach of the enemy fleet. If they were monitoring the *Renegade* closely, they might have a fix on the transition point. For all Darius knew, the fleet ships could recognize the portals which were invisible to the naked eye. Without the data from GIGI, humanity would still be bound to the Sol system because of their own lack of technological understanding. Darius made a mental note to ask GIGI how the portals to hyperspace were discovered.

"We're safe," Darius said. "Open the ship back up. Let's get Engineering on the move. All personnel, including yourself, Lieutenant Nash."

"Of course, Captain," Henry said as he got up from his console.

"How long until we come out of hyperspace?" Darius asked.

"Twelve hours, sir," Ramos replied.

"Alright, we can't see to anything else until the power is back up," Darius said. "I want everyone to work in six to eight hours of sleep sometime before we transition back to real space. Is that understood?"

"Aye, Captain," the senior officers all replied.

"That goes for the crew as well ... and for the Marines. Master Sergeant, please go and make sure all your people are rested and ready when we drop back out of hyperspace."

"Yes, sir!" Remmy said with a salute. He turned on his heel and headed out of the Bridge.

Darius stood up as well. "Lieutenant Ramos, you have the con. I'm going down to the Med Bay to question our prisoner."

"You think he knows about the Mot system?" Ramos asked.

"Yes," Darius said. "I think he must. Lieutenant Best, you should get some rest now. I'll be back up as soon as I can."

It felt good to walk. Darius hadn't realized how tense he had gotten during the battle. It was an understandable result of combat. He felt a sense of relief as his legs stretched the muscles in his quads and calves.

Doctor Lanski met him at the entrance to the Medical Bay. He was clearly frightened.

"We've survived the battle," he said, his eyes blinking rapidly.

"Are you okay, Doctor?" Darius asked.

"Yes, just a nervous habit. You should have seen me in medical school. Anyway, it sounded bad down here. Is everything okay with the ship?"

"We took damage," Darius said. "The electrical system is down to just thirty or forty percent. Our engineers are working to fix it."

"Oh," Lanski said, still blinking. "And I suppose it can be repaired?"

"Yes," Darius said. "It will take some time, but once we get the electrical system back online, the maintenance drones will do the rest. There's nothing that we need that the ship can't fabricate, including parts that were damaged."

"Good," Lanski said with a sigh. "That's very good."

"I want to see the prisoner now."

The doctor nodded and led Darius to the storeroom where the prisoner had been placed. He was still on the medical bed but propped up in a sitting position. One arm was in a sling that was also strapped to his body so that it couldn't move even by accident. The arm was slowly marking out a reply to some of the questions that Darius had left for him. Beside the bed Marine Corporal Rip Van Winkle was sitting. He was slowly flexing his recently wounded arm. Darius could see the dark red scars from the surgical incisions and felt a chill at the thought of taking such damage. But the wound hadn't seemed to have affected the Corporal's sense of humor. Rip stood up, saluted with his good hand, then rested it on the grip of his pistol that was strapped to his hip.

"How's it going down here?" Darius asked.

"He's productive when he's awake," Rip replied. "I got a name out of him. Calls himself Hazi."

"Thank you, Corporal," Darius said. "Hazi, may I see what you've gotten done?"

Darius reached out for the datapad that Hazi was writing on. The wounded man hesitated for a second, then handed the device to Darius. None of it meant anything to him. The language didn't look familiar in any way. There were markings all over the screen, but he couldn't even tell what the questions were he had wanted the man to answer and what Hazi had written. Fortunately, the datapad had a translator with the Sumerian Cuneiform programmed in. With the tap of a few icons the unfamiliar markings transformed into text he could read.

The questions were numbered. The first was *Where are you from?* The answer surprised Darius. *The domain of the God of the dead.*

"This is fine," Darius said. "I'll go over it in detail later. I'll have more questions, but for now, you should get some rest."

"Agreed," Doctor Lanski said.

"Corporal, please stay with the patient."

"Sir, yes sir!" Rip said, saluting again.

Darius left the storeroom and headed for the exit.

"Is everything okay, Captain?" Lanski asked.

"Of course. Thank you, Doctor."

A few minutes later Darius was in the Admin Center with Commander Lori Lee, Nurek who was still in restraints and Connor O'Dell. He showed the answer to the first question.

"Wow!" Commander Lee said. "That's ominous."

"Perhaps not as terrible as it seems," Connor argued. "What was the name of the place we're going?"

"The Mot system," Darius said.

"If I'm not mistake," Connor continued. "Mot was the name of the God of Death in ancient cultures. Perhaps what he is saying is that he's from this system we are calling Mot."

"That makes a sense, I guess," Lori Lee said.

"Do you know anything about this?" Darius asked Nurek.

The alien shook his long, conical head. "I know nothing of this system, or this language."

Darius looked at the screen and scrolled to the second question: *How did you come to serve on the slave ship?* The answer to the second question was more straight forward. *I was taken.*

Question three was the one Darius was most interested in: *Are there more people like you?* The answer was simple, *Yes.*

The final question was open ended: *What was your life like before you served on the slave ship.* The answer was only half finished but shed some light on the man's past. *I was a servant to the mechanism in the offal pits. Duri taught us the talking symbols before she died. Everything before was darkness and pain.*

Darius read the questions and answers out loud. The others listened in silent until he finished.

"Is that all?" Commander Lee asked.

"Apparently the prisoner has been in and out of consciousness," Darius said.

"I doubt he's a fast writer in any condition," Connor said. "That sounds like something a slave would write. Serving in an offal pit? Everything was darkness and pain?"

"It could be metaphorical," Lori Lee suggested.

"Undoubtedly, but I don't think the prisoner is that well-reasoned," Darius said. "He simply knows no other way to describe his life. And the point is, he wasn't taken from our world. He must have been born outside our star system."

"Perhaps there is a planet in the Mot system," Connor suggested.

"Doesn't sound like nice place," Lori Lee said.

"All the more reason why we need to find out if there are any other people there," Darius said. "They might need our help."

CHAPTER 30

CAPTAIN DARIUS WAS TIRED. His eyes burned with dryness and fatigue. His back ached and his mind felt sluggish and unable to focus.

"Hi-stim coffee, Captain," Lori Lee said, handing him a cup of the bitter brew. "With sugar, I figured you needed all the pep you could get."

"Thank you, Commander, that is very kind," Darius said, taking the warm cup in both hands.

Unlike the rest of his senior officers, Darius had not gone to his quarters for a six-to-eight-hour rest. He had returned to the Bridge and at times dozed while he waited on updates from the engineers and technicians. The repairs were taking longer than he wanted them to but that was a result of a crew that was too small and a ship that was so advanced that most of them didn't know how to do their jobs.

Darius sipped his coffee. It wasn't something he relished. The sugar helped, and the warm liquid was nice. It seemed as though a hot beverage was somehow easier on his body than a cold one. And then the caffeine hit his system. It drove the fog from his mind and even though his body still felt weary, he wasn't sleepy anymore.

"Captain," Henry Nash said as he walked onto the bridge. "We have power restored."

"That's the best news I've heard in hours," Darius said.

"It took a while to find the circuits. The old ones weren't just tripped, sir, they were melted. Some had to be cut out but we got it fixed."

"So, we have full power to all systems?"

"That's correct. The maintenance droids have taken over the repairs. They know the ship better than we do, so I've ordered my people to get out of their way."

"Very good, Lieutenant. We'll be coming out of hyperspace in a few minutes. Please return to your station."

Nash nodded and walked quickly to his console. He sat down wearily and Darius made a note to send the Chief Engineer to his quarters as soon as they could spare him. But coming out of hyperspace into an unknown system was not the time.

"Lieutenant Best, what is the status on our laser cannons?" Darius asked.

"Still down, sir. I've been looking through the information on the ship's computers. As you know, there aren't any manuals or guidebooks. It's like the builders of the ships just expected the crew to know everything."

"Maybe they did," Commander Lee said.

"But it seems like with one laser cannon down they're all down. I'm not sure why," Pete explained. "They're connected and it might be due to the huge amount of power they discharge."

"If a laser cannon failed in mid operation, it could blow up the entire ship," Henry pointed out.

"So, we're out of options in regard to the lasers," Darius said. "There's no telling how long it will take the droids to repair it. What about the engines?"

"Secondary engines are in the green, Captain," Nash reported. "The droids are working on the primary engine. I don't have a solid timeline for you, sir, but it shouldn't be too long. They were moving repair parts to the engineering compartments and there are several dozen droids all working on the problem."

"Very well," Darius replied. "Keep me updated on their progress. Commander Lee, what about the crew?"

"Everyone's rested, fed and ready for whatever we find in the Mot System, Captain. We have people ready in all the primary sections of the ship, sir. Including the *Jericho*. If all else were to fail, sir, she could launch from the *Renegade* and return home. I've moved GIGI on board and updated the logs, as well as the *Jericho's* computer systems, with all the information about the *Renegade*. If our mission were to fail, the *Jericho* could get the vital technology back home."

"Excellent. As you all know," Darius said, "the enemy is learning what we're capable of. That's both good and bad. So far, we've held our own, but the odds are high that we can't keep it up much longer. The last go round in the Olotimbo system proved that. We need to be more selective in when and where we fight. But we also need to be ready for whatever the Imperium might throw at us. So, let's repair the ship and make sure we're taking care of ourselves. Nothing is more vital than the people crewing this ship."

"We're ready, Captain," Pete Best said.

"He's right," Vivian Ramos said. "You can count on us, Captain."

Darius couldn't help but smile. He had started the cruise with genuine respect for his officers but over time that respect had grown to admiration and eventually to love. He knew them, cared about them and believed in them. It seemed; the feeling was mutual.

"What's the status on our shields?" Darius asked.

"Ready to deploy sonic shielding, Captain," Best replied.

"Radar?"

"Ready, Captain," Vivian replied.

Darius turned in his seat. It wasn't surprising to find Master Sergeant Remmy Steel standing in the back of the Bridge. The NCO had gone to check on the Marines during the voyage through hyperspace, but he was back at his post without any sort of fanfare. It occurred to Darius that if the master sergeant wanted to take his Captain out, that Darius would never hear the man coming.

"What about the Marines, Master Sergeant?"

"Deployed to their duty stations, sir," Remmy replied. "Lieutenant Colt is in command from the armory. Corporal Van Winkle is still in the Medical Bay per your orders, sir."

Darius noticed that the Master Sergeant had opted to report to the Bridge in his Space armor. But after the near disaster in the Olotimbo system, Darius couldn't blame the man.

"Are the Marines prepared for extra-vehicular combat in the event we come under attack again, Master Sergeant?"

"Yes, sir! They are all in full space armor with shoulder mounted rockets and high caliber machine guns. That's the best we could do, sir, although if he's needed Lieutenant Colt can mount up in his space armor. He has the capacity to launch warheads with greater yield."

"Let's hope it isn't necessary," Darius said. "I appreciate your professionalism and the platoon's willingness to step up while the lasers are down."

"Happy to do it, sir."

Darius spun back around to face forward again. "Okay, what's the ETA on the Mot system."

"Just under two minutes, Captain," Vivian Ramos replied.

"Very good. Commander Lee, please inform the crew of our imminent transition."

"Aye, Captain, alerting the crew," Lori Lee said.

"Stand by on that shield, Lieutenant Best."

"Aye, Captain, standing by."

"Lieutenant Ramos, I want radar up the second we hit real space."

"Aye, Captain, radar is ready, sir."

"Very good. Lieutenant Nash, let's prime the thrusters. We might need to move quick depending on what we find."

"Any idea what that might be, Captain?" Lori Lee asked.

"None," Darius said. "The prisoner was questioned, but he doesn't know much. He was taken from someplace he calls the Offal Pits straight on board the slave ship. They had no access to what was taking place in the system. But my guess is they were on some type of space station. According to him, they left one area and ended up on board the slave ship. There was no shuttle or transition from a planet."

"I guess we'll find out for ourselves," Lori Lee said.

The seconds counted down and suddenly the view through the transparent canopy over the Bridge changed. They were back in real space. In the distance was a huge, red sun. It was dim but cast a red light across a massive space station with an enormous, triangular solar sails that looked like they were from an old Dutch windmill. All around the station were spaceships, most had been long abandoned, their useful parts clearly cannibalized. It reminded Darius of the salvage yards on Mars.

"Shields up," Pete Best announced.

"Radar is pinging a lot of ships, sir," Vivian Ramos said. "Hundreds, maybe more."

"Ghost ships," Commander Lee said. "Just look at all of them."

There were ships everywhere. The star system was unlike anything Darius had ever seen before. Some of the vessels were obviously slave ships, the unauthorized kind that were covered in huge spikes. Most were what Darius thought of as regular ships, although there were vessels of every shape, size, and description.

"Look," Henry said pointing. "They're cutting that one up."

It was true. They were too far out to see who or what was doing the cutting, but there was a shower of sparks that were undeniable, even from a distance.

"How far out are we?" Darius asked.

"Ninety thousand kilometers from the debris field," Vivian said. "About three hundred thousand from that space station."

"Are any of the ships moving toward us?" Darius asked.

"The computer is tracking them," Vivian said. "None have triggered an alert."

"What is that?" Pete Best said, pointing to what looked like a glassy ring that encompassed everything in the system, even the star. The ring looked like the one that encircled Saturn back in the Sol system.

"Must be asteroids," Lori Lee said. "That star is a red giant. It's possible that when it expanded it destroyed the planets that were closest to it."

"Incredible," Henry Nash said.

"Are there any other planets in the system?" Darius asked.

"Negative Captain, unless they're on the far side of the star. Radar and visual scans show no planetary bodies in the system."

"Unless you count that space station," Pete Best said.

It was a massive complex of cobbled together components. Just like the slave ships, the space station had been expanded many times. Parts of it resembled the ships that had been used to build the station. There were pipes and tubes covering the entire structure. Some of it looked old and worn down, other parts seemed to have just been added on recently.

"Lieutenant Nash, turn us so that the damaged laser is facing that space station," Darius ordered. "Shut down the engine and the running lights. I want it dark on this ship, even in the park. Let's look like one more drifting hull amid the countless others."

"Aye Captain, turning us now," Nash said. "Running lights are off. Sealing the overhead skylights above the park. We should be dark now, sir."

"Very good. Let's keep the radar operating and the sonic shields up at full power," Darius said. "I want to know the moment anyone takes notice of us."

It was tempting to just watch the massive space station and the surrounding field of old ships, but Darius needed to stay focused on their mission. The top priorities were repairing the *Renegade* and discovering if more humans were on the space station. He swiveled around in his chair.

"Master Sergeant, do we have a shuttle left in the primary hangar?"

"A few were held back in case the crew needed to be taken off the ship, Captain," Remmy said.

"Excellent. I want you to meet with your platoon and give me a reasonable idea of what it might take to infiltrate that space station."

That statement caused the other officers and crew on the Bridge to turn and look at Remmy. Fortunately for him, with his battle helmet on, no one could see his face. They had no idea what he thought of Darius' plan.

"Unless you need me up here, sir," Remmy said. "I'll go right now."

"I don't think we're in immediate danger here," Darius said. "We'll drift at the edge of the debris field while repairs are underway. Be sure you plan for a blind launch from the *Renegade*, Master Sergeant. Stay in our lee until you're far enough out to circle around without drawing attention to the ship."

"Yes, sir," Remmy said.

He saluted, spun on his heel and marched out of the Bridge.

"Is that the best plan?" Lori Lee asked.

"Maybe not," Darius said. "Time will tell."

"They don't seem to be monitoring the portal," Vivian said. "I can't find any sort of defensive measures."

"It's like a pirate town," Pete Best said. "A safe haven for the slavers to come and spend their money."

"And make repairs," Henry said. "Ships like those we've encountered would require heavy maintenance."

"So, they capture people and haul the ships back here where they can be cut up and refit onto their slave ships," Vivian said.

"That does seem to be the M-O," Darius said. "They use a gravity beam to haul in all sorts of ships. The passengers and crew are sold off. Every ship needs to resupply. Maybe this is where they do it."

"Seems like a savage way to make a living," Vivian said. "Surely there are better ways to get ahead."

"I doubt they want to get ahead," the chief engineer said. "They aren't in the slave trade to get rich."

"Some people just want the freedom to do whatever they want," Best said. "It's too bad they won't join us in fighting the Imperium."

"None of the slave ships have had weapons other than the EMP we were hit with early on. My guess is they would run from a real fight," Darius said. "That's always the way with this type of person. It takes a certain kind of coldness in a person's soul to kidnap the innocent and sell them into a life of misery."

"And the cowards hid behind the slaves they capture," Nash said. "So, you don't even feel like you can go hard at them."

"The Marines will figure it out," Darius assured them. "Infiltration, reconnaissance and disruption are their specialties. If there are more humans on that space station, we need to find them. Someone knows where they came from. We can't call our mission complete until we know there aren't more humans suffering somewhere in the galaxy."

CHAPTER 31

"HE WANTS US TO DO WHAT?" Laila asked.

They were in the armory. Remmy had activated the holographic projector with the ship's plot displayed. They could see the massive spread of old derelict space vessels, the solar powered space station and the massive red star beyond it.

"There's a possibility that there are more humans on that space station," Remmy explained. "The captain wants a plan for getting in, finding them and getting out again."

"How can we do that if don't know anything about that place?" Sergeant Dirk Oliver asked. "He's asking the impossible."

"They could be locked in cages anywhere on that station," Hugo McManus said. "We wouldn't even know where to start."

"Or how to get in and get started," Tex pointed out. "It don't look like the kinda place that welcomes visitors."

So far, Lieutenant Colt had remained silent. When he spoke up, it was in a quiet voice. "The prisoner knows."

"What was that, Lieutenant?" Laila asked.

"The prisoner you captured," Micky Colt said. "He's from here. I heard that from one of the officers. He would know where there are more humans, maybe even the layout of the entire station."

"The way I see it," Remmy said. "We take a shuttle to the station, get inside, put down any resistance and recover any humans staying there."

"Without getting killed," Laila said.

"That would be my preference," Izzy spoke up.

"Easier said than done," Dirk Oliver said.

"But it's what we do," Remmy reminded them. "If we go in hot, the leaders of that place will lock themselves behind closed doors and pray we leave."

"You're assuming they're like the slavers we encountered," Laila said.

"It's all I've got to go on," Remmy said. "Staff Sergeant McPherson, why don't you take Sergeant Oliver and go find out everything you can from the prisoner. He's slow, and there's a language barrier, but see if you can get us some intel. Sergeant McManus you're in charge of weapons. I want to hit that place with shock and awe. Urban combat, plenty of flash bangs and tear gas. I'll get a full complement of medical supplies in case the people on that space station need it."

"What if they don't wanna leave?" Tex asked. "They might be happy as pigs in a sty on that station."

"Or just too afraid to leave," Leigh Ann Poh suggested.

"We won't force anyone," Remmy said. "And keep in mind we're just putting together a plan for the captain. He may not send us on this op after all's said and done."

"Do you have plans for me, Master Sergeant?" Lieutenant Colt asked.

The group fell silent. Remmy kicked himself for taking too strong a role in giving orders. He should have simply turned it all over to the LT, but Micky Colt didn't seem ready to take the lead. Of course, that didn't really matter in military matters. The chain of command was incontrovertible. Micky Colt was the officer in charge. Remmy was at his disposal, not the other way around.

"Sorry, sir," Remmy said. "I didn't mean to overstep my bounds."

Micky raised a hand in a placating gesture. "I'm still getting my bearings, Master Sergeant. You've done nothing wrong. I appreciate your willingness to step up and take command in my absence."

"Well sir, I figured we would divide and conquer so to speak. Everyone could bring their part of the plan back to you here, and you could formulate the whole. Not to mention pitching it to the captain, sir."

"You and Captain Darius have a rapport, Master Sergeant. I think the plan should come from you. Besides, I'm not yet strong enough to go with you on this mission. And I doubt my MECH armor would even fit inside that space station. It's probably better that I stay behind with the shuttle and serve as a rear guard in case there's trouble."

"Are you sure, Lieutenant?" Remmy asked.

"Positive, Master Sergeant. I'll stay with Corporal Thompson and the new recruits while the rest of you plan the operation."

"Very well, sir," Remmy said. "You all have your assignments. Let's get this done, Marines."

A few minutes later Remmy found himself walking down a corridor with Laila beside him. They were still in their space armor. The entire ship was on yellow alert with the threat of attack from the slave ships in the system, but it seemed like overkill. Still, Remmy was glad to be able to talk to her privately, even if he would have preferred to see her face, maybe even touch her hand.

"Why do you think the captain wants to send us into that station?" She asked.

"What choice does he have?"

"Couldn't he just contact them and tell them to send over the humans?"

"Maybe," Remmy said as he considered the question. "But we're a Fleet ship, not a diplomatic vessel. Besides, the *Renegade* can't use its laser cannons right now. For now, we only have defensive capabilities on the ship. I would have thought you would jump at the chance to mix things up."

"There could be ten thousand aliens on that space station, Remmy. It could have automated defenses we've never dreamed of. I don't mind a good fight, but I don't relish seeing our people slaughtered."

"So... what? Do we just leave the humans there?"

"First, we don't know that they are humans, at least not Earthlings. And second, we don't know that they're captives there."

"The odds are pretty good," Remmy said.

"Not good enough to lose someone else," Laila argued.

Remmy wanted to say they wouldn't lose anyone, but he knew that anything was possible in a combat situation. He could die, she could die, they could be wiped out to the last Marine. Her point was valid. They didn't know what to expect. They were going in blind and based on the word of one prisoner who couldn't speak a language anyone understood.

"Maybe we won't have to go," Remmy said. "Hope for the best, plan for the worst, right?"

"I suppose," she said. "Don't listen to me, Remmy. I'm just frustrated. We haven't had a moment's peace since coming back to the ship."

"Yeah, this command thing isn't much fun," he admitted. "I'm sorry."

"It's not your fault," she said. "I'm proud of you."

That caught him by surprise. They were both Marines. Their jobs were practically identical, except that circumstances had thrust Remmy into a command role. It was one he wasn't comfortable with, but he would do his best. It was flattering to have someone he respected as much as Laila say she was proud of him. He felt his face blush inside his battle helmet.

"You have no idea how much that means to me," he admitted.

"Well, it's true," Laila pressed on. "You got us through every engagement so far. I'd follow you, *sir*."

She was teasing him. NCOs weren't called sir, only officers. He would have corrected her if she hadn't been joking.

"The LT is back," he insisted.

"Sort of."

"He will be in charge soon," Remmy said. "Then things can go back to normal."

"I wouldn't complain about having more time alone," she said softly.

"Me either," Remmy said.

They walked together all the way to the Medical Bay. While Remmy gathered supplies for their mission, Laila and Sergeant Dirk Oliver tried to talk to the freed human prisoner, Hazi. It was a tedious process and not just because of the language barrier. The prisoner simply didn't know much about the station.

"He must been have isolated to one area," Laila said when they all met back up in the armory. "He doesn't know much about the entire station."

"It's a rough place," Sergeant Oliver said. "He's terrified of going back."

"What did you learn?" Remmy asked.

"The only thing we know for sure is that there are about thirty humans on the lower level," Laila explained. "They work in the sewage treatment facility."

"Wonderful," McManus said.

"Are they captives?" Leigh Ann Poh asked.

"That's still unclear," Dirk replied. "They don't have access to the rest of the station. And from what we could make out they don't have any real say over their lives. But it could be that they're being controlled by another human."

"A little dictator?" Izzy asked.

"It's possible," Laila said. "And convincing them to come with us might be difficult either way."

"I'm working on that," Remmy said. "Or, at least, GIGI is."

"First we have to get to them," Hugo McManus said. "After cataloguing the weapons we've got, a raid isn't ideal. We don't have a lot of urban warfare gear. A dozen flash-bang grenades, no tear gas or concussion weapons. Everything is potentially lethal and potentially catastrophic on a space station."

"It's tough to know what to use when you don't know who or what you'll be fighting," Tex added.

"From what we've seen on the slave ships, they don't have the best gear," Remmy said.

"Doesn't mean they won't have better equipment on the space station," Hugo McManus said. "But Tex and I have an idea."

"What's that?" Remmy asked, glancing over at Lieutenant Colt who hadn't said a word since the platoon returned from their assignments.

"Oh, you're going to love this, Master Sergeant," Tex said.

Hugo nodded. "It's truly inspired."

"Inspired by what?" Laila asked.

"Hey, even a blind squirrel finds a nut every once in a while," Tex said.

Hugo chuckled. "And this is a good one. Trust me."

CHAPTER 32

"YOU WANT TO DO WHAT?" Captain Darius asked.

"We'll use the slave ship, sir," Remmy explained. "Staff Sergeant McPherson, Sergeant McManus, Corporal Fry and I will take the slave ship to the station and pose as slavers."

"Is that even possible?" Darius asked.

They were back in the Wardroom with the senior officers. Captain Darius looked around but the others weren't meeting his gaze.

"It might work," Commander Lori Lee said. "How will you fly the ship, Master Sergeant?"

"We won't," Remmy said. "GIGI can pilot it remotely as long as she's in range. If worse comes to worse, she can direct me. There were only two of the aliens in the ship's command center. I think we'll be alright there. We're just going straight to the space station. We'll recon and if we're lucky, free the humans there. If not, at least we'll have workable intel."

"You could get killed," Darius said.

"That's always a possibility, sir," Remmy replied.

"We don't have weapons to back them up," Lieutenant Best said. "The laser cannons are still down."

"He's right. We're making progress on the engine repairs, Captain," Henry Nash added. "My guess is we'll be flying with both engines in twenty-four to thirty-six hours. But repairs on the laser cannons won't even begin until they finish with the engines."

"The rest of the platoon will serve as our backup," Remmy said.

"The Casians?"

"No, sir," Remmy explained. "They're not ready, and their weapons aren't finished yet. Sergeant Dirk Oliver will keep a team consisting of himself, Corporals Berry, Poh, and Thompson, in a drone shuttle. If we run into trouble, they'll come to our aid. Lieutenant Colt isn't quite ready for active duty, but in a pinch, he'll join us in his MECH armor, sir. If you want us to infiltrate that space station, this is the best plan we have."

"Why wouldn't they just kill you the moment you step out of the slave ship?" Lieutenant Ramos asked.

"Good question, sir," Remmy replied. "I can't guarantee they won't, but our experience has been that every ship is crewed by a different species. We know humans are involved with these outlaws, so it stands to reason that we won't be suspect. We'll dress accordingly, not in standard space armor. We'll take small arms hidden in our clothing. It's a risk but a minimal one. If something happens to us, you'll still have some Marines on board."

"I don't like it," Darius said. "Send someone else, Master Sergeant. You're too valuable to risk on a mission like this."

"Sir, Lieutenant Colt is our C.O. My place is with the platoon. I wouldn't feel comfortable sending someone in my place, sir. I hope you can understand that."

"I understand the feeling, Master Sergeant, but I do not agree with it."

"None of us are looking for a fight," Remmy explained. "McManus, Staff Sergeant McPherson and I have the most combat experience. Corporal Fry is the best marksman. The four of us give this mission the best chance for success, sir."

"If we want to rescue the humans on board that space station," Henry Nash said softly. "I think this is the only way to do it."

"I concur," Vivian Ramos said.

"Me too," Pete Best added.

Darius looked at Lori Lee. She was his executive officer. Her job was to ensure that everything on the ship functioned the way he wanted it to. And he trusted her opinion. She didn't speak, but just nodded.

"Alright," Darius said. "So far, we haven't drawn any unwanted attention. But it's possible we're being tracked by the other ships in the system and whoever is aboard that space station. Which means, you could run straight into a hostile force, Master Sergeant. Your mission priorities are as follows: one, locate any humans on the space station, two, gather as much intelligence about the facility and crew as possible, and three, rescue any humans being held there. If that involves combat, my preference is that you return to the *Renegade* first. It might be that things will have changed and a better course of action should be taken. At the very least, you can go in fully prepared with the entire platoon if you have to fight. But remember, above all else, your main responsibility is to get everyone back to the ship alive and without injury. If you can't do that, then I expect you to abort this mission."

"He's right," Commander Lee said. "If we can't get the humans off that space station without losing some of our people, then it will have to wait until we can return with superior numbers."

"Marines don't leave people behind, Commander," Remmy said.

"Then I'll order you stand down," Darius said. "I don't want to lose anyone else. Every member of this crew has gone above and beyond what we were tasked with. I have half a mind to turn this ship around and go home."

"We won't take unnecessary chances, sir," Remmy said. "I promise that."

"What about comms?" Vivian asked. "Is there any way to stay in touch while you're on that ship?"

"That's another reason I have to go," Remmy said. "My link with GIGI will be vital to our success, but also, it will enable you to stay in contact with our team the entire time."

"Very good," Darius said. "Alright, you have my permission to move forward with your plan, Master Sergeant. Gear up. Lieutenant Nash will ensure that we are facing away from the space station when you're ready to launch. Please check your communication through GIGI before leaving the *Renegade*. And good luck, Master Sergeant Steel."

"Thank you, sir," Remmy said.

He stood to attention and saluted. Captain Darius returned the salute and watched Remmy leave the room. No one else moved.

"You have to admit, they're fearless in the face of mortal danger," Commander Lori Lee said.

"Yeah, I'm glad he's on our side," Pete Best added.

"Until the covert ops team returns, I want everyone at their stations," Darius said. "We'll continue repairs, but I want us ready to act if they run into trouble."

"Aye, Captain," the others said in unison.

"And Commander Lee, let's get Nurek back on the Bridge," Darius said. "He might have some insights that could be useful to this operation."

"I'll bring him up myself," Lori Lee said.

An hour later they were all on the Bridge when Commander Lee escorted Nurek to the console he had used before. Darius noticed that the Dudonus alien's hands were no longer restrained, but that Commander Lee was wearing a laser pistol and utility belt with a variety of tools normally reserved for military police.

"Welcome back, Nurek," Darius said. "Have you been informed about our plans?"

"Commander Lee was kind enough to fill me in," Nurek said. "I appreciate your willingness to let me contribute, Captain. That is all I ever wanted."

"We can discuss what you've done, and how your actions should be judged, another time. For now, we need all the help we can get."

"I stand ready to assist in any way I can," Nurek said with a bow.

Darius felt uneasy. He didn't like sending his people into danger, but that was part of a Captain's job. He had to make the hard decisions and had to live with the consequences of them.

"GIGI, can you hear me?" Darius asked.

Vivian Ramos and Ensign Bertoli had set up an open comms channel between the Bridge of the *Renegade* and the Systems Control room where GIGI was currently set up.

"I can, Captain Darius," the computer-generated voice said. "Master Sergeant Steel reports that his team is nearly ready to board the alien ship."

"Very well," Darius said. "Let's hope that his team is successful."

It was the right thing to say, but he couldn't shake the feeling of anxiety that was plaguing him. Perhaps it was because of the friendship he had developed with Remmy Steel. The Master Sergeant was the kind of man that Captain Darius admired greatly. In their time together on the *Renegade*, Darius had come to depend on the master sergeant, not just for leadership with the Marines on board, but in deciding the course for the ship too. Remmy Steel had a keen mind. He was a man of duty, and yet, he could think independently and wasn't afraid to speak his mind when he felt it necessary. It didn't hurt that he and Zeke Darius had similar opinions and often came to the same conclusions. Under different circumstances they might not have had the chance to become friends and the captain of a fleet ship had to keep everyone at arm's length. Yet he felt a bond with the master sergeant that was rare for Darius. The thought that something could happen to Remmy made the captain uncomfortable.

"Do we have a video feed from the capture hangar?" Darius asked.

"Aye, Captain," Lori Lee said. "I'll bring it up now."

The ship was so big that it was necessary to have a video system installed. The engineers had been working on it between combat engagements. The *Renegade* didn't have video screens, but the holographic projects worked with the cameras to display the video feed. The Bridge had several projectors. The main hologram of the ship's plot in the Mot system remained, while a smaller second hologram showed the slave ship in the bow hanger near the refining equipment from a high perspective.

The slave ship was terrible to behold. It was covered with spikes and the hull was fashioned from a hundred different ships to make it seem like a patchwork vessel crafted by an evil force. And, considering its purpose, Darius supposed it had been built by evil beings.

On the deck near the ramp leading up into the alien ship, Darius could see four people. They didn't look like Marines. Their clothing looked like it had been made from old blankets that were ripped, mended, patched, and dirty. Darius hoped it was enough to convince whoever was on that space station that they belonged. He whispered a silent prayer and waited to see what would happen.

CHAPTER 33

LAILA THOUGHT Remmy looked rather roguish in his patchwork clothing. It hadn't taken long to adhere the strips of cloth to their compression fatigues. Remmy wore a thick coat with a wide collar. His disguise was just a little nicer than the others so that he looked like their leader.

They all had a pair of pistols under their coats. Laila had a Yagger HC in a shoulder holster tucked under her left arm. And a laser pistol with extra batteries tucked inside her belt at the small of her back.

Next to Remmy stood Hugo McManus. He was thickly muscled through his shoulders and arms, so he wore a ragged vest instead of a full coat. And behind Hugo, Tex wore what looked almost like a duster. His coat was long, hanging to his knees, and he wore a wide brimmed hat as well. He looked like the love child from a cowboy and a homeless person.

Laila's coat was shorter than the others, but long enough to hide her weapons. She also had a combat knife tucked into each boot and she wore fingerless gloves with hard lumps of metal over each knuckle.

They traded their usual in-ear comlinks for translation devices that were pinned to their coat. It was the bare minimum of what she thought of as protective gear, but it also wasn't the first op she had carried out in less-than-ideal conditions. Part of her special forces training had been deception and stealth insertion behind enemy lines. She would have liked to have been in full armor with serious weapons, but the circumstances of their current situation called for a different approach.

"Here, everyone take a weapon," Remmy ordered.

They had collected some of the cobbled together laser guns from the slave ships. They were all different sizes and shapes. Hugo took the biggest, Laila took the smallest. Once they all had their weapons they filed onto the ship.

"I hate this," Hugo said.

"Not a fan of special operations?" Tex asked.

"Nah, it's not the op that bothers me, it's this stinking ship," Hugo complained. "It's like being in a haunted house or something."

"It is foul," Tex agreed.

They hadn't bothered to clean the filth from the cargo area. And without their sealed battle helmets, they could smell the refuse and body odor from the prisoners who had been locked into cages on the slave ship. Those cages had been returned. They stood as a stark reminder of the nefarious purpose of the vessel.

"Let's get moving," Remmy said. "I don't expect you'll feel any better about that space station."

"Wonderful," Hugo said.

They took the stairs to the upper levels of the ship. It still reeked, but not as strongly as the cargo area. The entire ship had been searched for information about the humans on board, and the reptilian masters who commanded the vessel. There wasn't much to learn. The humans had almost nothing. They subsisted on the same vat grown protein and fat that their captives were fed. Other than the furnishings, which had all been damaged in the firefight, there were very little possessions. The human crew slept on pallets of whatever they could scrounge together. There was nothing to entertain them, no trinkets or personal items to show that they had been to exotic worlds throughout the galaxy. There were some markings gouged into the common room wall where they had slept. It was more of the strange, ancient language they used, which was itself a mystery.

"GIGI, we're ready," Remmy said, after climbing up into the command deck.

Laila had followed. Tex and Hugo stayed down on the deck where the human crew had fought and died. No one had bothered to clean the blood and gore from the deck, which only added to the smell.

"I've been in some real hell holes," Laila said. "But this bucket of bolts takes the cake."

"Hard to imagine living on this tub," Remmy replied.

They felt the ship lift off the deck and fly out of the big open-mouthed shape on the front of the Arodoni ship. The gravity on the slave ship was weaker. Still, Laila was glad they weren't floating around. If they had to fight, she preferred to have her feet on the ground.

"What do you think we're going to find in that station?" She asked.

"Could be anything," Remmy said. "I really don't know."

"Can't be good though," Laila said. "It takes a certain kind of evil to kidnap people and sell them."

"You really think so?" Remmy asked. "I've been pondering that. Maybe if you're taking aliens who are nothing like you, it doesn't seem so bad. We used to capture monkeys and use them for medical experimentation. Was that evil?"

Laila thought about the question. Experimenting on animals had been banned in the Sol system. But she knew that humanity had a long history of exploiting all sorts of animals ... and human beings, too.

"I think we're better than that now," she said.

"I like to think so too," Remmy said. "And I don't disagree with Hugo; this entire ship seems evil to me."

They looked out through the view ports. The slave ship was moving steadily through the maze of derelict vessels. Ahead, the space station was growing larger every second. They could see the patchwork nature of it. Bad welds had left black scorch marks on the bland, gray metal. There were sections that seemed to have been torn off and just left with jagged edges. Everywhere on the surface of the station there were conduits, pipes, and vents. Occasionally, gas vented from a stained exhaust duct. In several places slave ships were docked close into the station. They looked like burrs that had stuck to the space station by their spiny hulls.

"And evil has a home," Laila said. "Just look at that place. Is it too late to abort this mission."

"'Fraid so," Remmy said with a chuckle.

"Of all the places to die," she said, thinking about what potentially could be waiting for them on the space station.

"Better to die fighting than to become a slave," Remmy said. "Keep that in mind. These beings, whoever they are, make their living by condemning the innocent to a fate worse than death."

Laila agreed.

It wasn't long until the station took notice of them.

"We're in a gravity beam," Remmy said. "Looks like they're pulling us in for docking."

"We should warn the others," Laila said.

"You tell them. I'll join you soon."

"Roger that," she replied.

Getting down from the command deck required a climb down the scabby wall. Laila didn't have any trouble with the climb, but it felt like an odd thing to do in a spaceship. She left the domicile of the reptilian creatures who had commanded the slave ship. Their bloated, stinking bodies were up on the command deck with Remmy. She made her way to where Hugo and Tex sat at a rough table that was made of some type of polymer. It was rough, the tabletop uneven and the gun fight hadn't helped it any.

"We're docking," Laila told her companions. "It's time to see who's waiting for us in that station."

"Good," Hugo said. "Let's get it over with."

A few minutes later Remmy joined them. A tube was extended from the station to an airlock on the crew level where they were waiting. Remmy was the first through the door. The airlock was only big enough for two people at a time. Hugo went with him, and Laila waited with Tex. When it was their turn, her heart pounded in her chest while the airlock cycled. They had breathing tanks with face masks tucked into the floppy pockets of their coats, in case the air on the station wasn't safe to breathe.

Laila led the way through the tunnel. There was no gravity. Her stomach flipped as she stepped out into the tunnel and propelled herself through the corridor. When she reached the far side, she grabbed a handle and pulled herself into the space station's airlock. It was much larger. She turned around to help Tex, who probably didn't need any help, but he took her hand anyway. She pulled him into the airlock and they hit the switch to cycle the chamber.

"So far so good," Tex said.

"At least we haven't had to kill anyone," Laila said.

The inner door swooshed open. Laila hadn't known what to expect, but an empty passageway wasn't it. In front of her Remmy and Hugo stood looking around.

"Glad you could make it," Hugo said with a grin.

"We're not too popular," Tex said.

"No welcoming committee," Remmy said. "Maybe that's a good thing."

"So, what now?" Laila asked.

"Let's stay together," Remmy said. "It might be better to guard the ship, but I'm not so worried about that."

"Agreed," Laila said. "Let's find out what this place is all about."

It didn't take them long. The corridor from the docking berth led straight in a big, open chamber. It was a massive space, bigger even than the park on the *Renegade*. But it was nothing like that agricultural park on the Arodoni ship. Instead, the massive chamber in the space station was more like a black market. There were aliens everywhere. Some moved around freely, others were tied or chained to their masters. Laila saw beings of every shape, color, size and description. Some walked upright on two feet, others had multiple legs and moved more like animals. A few even slithered around like insects or snakes. Most had no breathing apparatus, yet a few did. Some lingered near pools of murky water. There were sections that were clearly hotter than others. Big heat vents stuck up from the floor like metallic mushrooms. The heat vents were surrounded by all sorts of aliens. Some even lounged on top of the vent domes.

There were stalls too, with aliens hawking wares. Nothing looked new or sanitary. But there were engine and generator parts, tools, weapons, clothing, and goods that Laila didn't recognize. Foods of all types were being cooked over electric griddles and grills. The smells mingled with the odor from the masses. Mostly, there was drinking. Dozens of stalls were selling beverages that were clearly intended to intoxicate.

"Some party," Hugo said.

"Your kind of place?" Tex asked.

"Nah, but I've been to a few of these markets. Nothing good to be found here. Drugs, contraband, stolen goods mostly."

"No humans," Remmy said. "Our guy said they worked the offal pits."

"Which were on the lower levels," Laila said. "He remembers being taken up before boarding the slave ship."

"So, we need to go down," Hugo said.

"Awesome," Tex said. "Let's get moving. I feel like I'm picking up some exotic disease just being here."

They moved slowly around the open space avoiding the other aliens who paid them no attention at all. Remmy seemed almost mesmerized by the crowds. Laila was glad she was there. She felt protective of him and didn't like the looks of most of the aliens in the bizarre market.

"There," Tex said with a discrete nod of his head. "That hatch."

Laila saw a spiraling ramp through the open hatch.

"Looks promising," Remmy said.

"Time to see what lies beneath," Hugo said.

Laila frowned. "It can't be anything good."

"Never is," Tex agreed. "Never is."

CHAPTER 34

REMMY WAS in constant communication with GIGI. The alien device was recognizing the various alien species. How GIGI could see and hear what he saw and heard was a mystery to Remmy. It seemed that the more time that passed, the more access the alien device had to him.

In the moment he didn't mind so much. GIGI was a living computer, or at least, that's how he thought of the alien device. It was sentient, as in capable of independent thought. But it wasn't a personality. It wasn't like Remmy had another person in his head all the time. Maybe GIGI was recording everything he saw and thought, but the device made no comment on it. He didn't carry on conversations with the artifact as if it were a friend or peer. Remmy was accustomed to having a comlink in his ear that kept him connected with people that were often far away from the front lines where he normally operated. GIGI seemed no different than that, and maybe even less than that because when he communicated with the alien device, it was usually to exchange information, which made Remmy think of GIGI as a device, not a person. It was sort of like having a calculator in his brain. He could access it when needed, but he rarely needed to.

GIGI was simultaneously communicating with him, storing information on the *Renegade's* computer and updating Captain Darius. The artifact's ability to multitask was astounding. Remmy knew it could fly nearly a thousand drones at the same time. He often had trouble doing more than any one thing at a time.

We've reached a passage that winds downward, he thought.

GIGI didn't respond, just recorded the information and relayed the news to the ship's crew. Remmy followed Hugo who had taken point as they descended. They all had their cobbled together laser weapons. And Remmy had seen weapons on almost all the aliens in the big, open-air market. Even the vendors were armed. There was no doubt they were in a dangerous place taking risks that could cost them their lives. But Remmy wasn't afraid. To him, the aliens above and the unknown below were just factors. It was like a puzzle and he was simply separating and identifying the pieces. Once he had them arranged in his mind, he could solve the problem.

"We have to be getting close," Hugo said. "Can the rest of you smell that?"

"Smells like—"

"We all know what it smells like, Tex," Laila interrupted.

"Keep going," Remmy urged.

They ended up in a room with a low ceiling. The walls were lined with small doors. The group approached one. There was a small window. Looking in, they could see a group of short, thin bodied aliens huddled together on a dirty floor. One looked toward them. It had large, dark. Almond shaped eyes.

"Are they children?" Laila asked.

"Who knows?" Hugo said.

"They're not human," Remmy said. "Our priority is to find where there are humans on this station."

"I'm getting sick to my stomach of the slave trade," Tex said, as he glanced into another window in the door on the opposite side of the hallway. "There's more aliens over here."

"Holding cells," Remmy said.

"Has to be," Hugo agreed.

Tex reached out and tried the handle on the door. "Locked," he said.

"No surprise there," Remmy said. "Keep moving."

He glanced in through every window. It only took a second for GIGI to recognize and record the species being held. The information popped into Remmy's head. It wasn't like a voice, more like recognition. He saw the aliens, knew what species they were and that was all. GIGI shared the information, which was somehow stored onto Remmy's brain. He didn't know how he knew he would never forget the information, but he did.

Some of the prisoners made noise when they saw the humans. Most huddled back in fear, but a few shouted for help. Again, Remmy didn't know how, but the understanding of the various languages passed into his brain even faster than the translation apparatus pinned to his coat could process and translate the information.

At the end of the hall was another spiral ramp, this one narrower and steeper than the other. They took it. That ramp ended on a similar floor, but one without holding cells. Instead, there were pallets and small crates piled with cooking instruments and stuffed with goods that a person might collect over time. Some were empty. In other hovels aliens loitered. They looked sad, tired, and more than anything else, afraid. Some appeared to be sick or injured.

"Stay here," Remmy ordered.

He stepped close to a hovel where a spidery looking creature was sitting on a filthy, tattered blanket and stirring a tiny pot with one leg. The creature made a chattering sound: *what do you want?*

"Information," Remmy said. "Have you seen beings that look like us on this station?"

What if I have, the spider alien asked. *What's it worth to you?*

"What do you want?" Remmy asked.

What everyone down here wants, the creature said, *off this cursed station.*

That struck Remmy as odd, but the pieces of the puzzle were coming together. The beings in the market were crew from the slave ships. Some had captives in the cells, either for trade or being looked after while the crews were busy getting drunk or stoned and fulfilling their alien fantasies above. Below that was where the refugees lingered. Those beings who weren't slaves, but for one reason or another had lost their ship, or their place on a ship. They scraped by, hoping for a way off the space station.

"You tell me all about this place, and where you've seen more beings like me, and I'll get you off this station," Remmy promised.

The spidery alien stopped stirring. It raised itself up on tall, thin legs. The alien had four round, bulbous eyes that were all black. Remmy felt nervous being so close to the creature. He couldn't see a mouth, or a weapon of any kind, but he felt a sense of danger.

"How can I trust you?" The alien said.

"You tell me," Remmy replied. "Are there more people like me?"

The spidery creature bobbed up and down.

"Where?" Remmy asked.

"Down below, in the deep dark."

"You know the layout of this place?"

"I must," the creature said. "How else can we survive?"

"Gather your things," Remmy told the spidery alien. "You can come back to our ship with us."

The alien looked around, then bobbed again. Remmy walked back to the group.

"Is this a good idea?" Laila asked.

Remmy shrugged. "We're flying blind. Maybe this being can help us."

"Or kill us," Hugo said. "I'm just saying, it could go either way."

"Fifty - fifty," Tex said with a smile.

"So, keep your guns close," Remmy said. "Let's go."

The trek back up to the market level of the space station was slower. There was a growing sense of danger. Remmy led the way, followed by the spider alien. The other three members of the team walked behind them. The alien creature was weak. That much was soon obvious. It skittered along, keeping pace with Remmy at first, but halfway up the first spiraling ramp it slowed. By the time they reached the holding cells the alien was wheezing. Its legs trembled and its body was held low to the ground.

"What's your name?" Remmy asked the alien.

It chittered in response, "Klicka-tac"

"Are you okay?"

"Tired," it huffed.

"We can stop and rest."

"No," he said with a sense of urgency.

The walk up the wider ramp was even slower and they did have to stop twice before reaching the top. Remmy could tell that his companions were nervous. There was something about partnering with the spider creature. Maybe because it was so different. Or maybe because it reminded them of an arachnid. Remmy also felt a sense of danger building. They had contacted and in essence partnered with a being who had been, and might still be, a slaver. That alone felt wrong and things only got worse when they reached the market level.

Remmy once more followed the wall, doing his best to avoid the aliens who were carousing throughout the massive chamber. But they were only halfway back to the corridor that led to their ship when a reptilian creature approached.

"Klicka-tac!" The newcomer shouted. "How dare you show you face here!"

Remmy marveled at the knowledge in his mind. The reptilian alien was a Shartal. His hissing, guttural language was odd, yet familiar somehow. GIGI was in many ways enhancing his intelligence.

"I have a place," Klicka-tac replied.

"Your place is in the compost pit," the reptilian alien snarled.

It darted toward the spidery alien, moving fast on all four feet. It looked to Remmy like a Komodo dragon, but with a look of intelligence on its leathery face. Remmy intervened, kicking the reptilian with a powerful front kick. His boot smacked the alien in the neck and pushed it away from the new member of Remmy's team.

"He's with us," Remmy said.

"He's a traitor and full of lies," the alien hissed.

"Remmy!" Laila said, getting his attention.

Remmy glanced around. Well over a hundred aliens had fallen silent. They were watching the conflict with interest. And the reptilian wasn't alone. There were five other beings like him moving closer through the crowd.

"You misunderstood," Klicka-tac said.

"Lies!" The alien shouted.

Suddenly everything around him was in motion. The reptilian darted forward again. Klicka-tac tried to jump away but was too weak. Remmy had no idea what his cobbled together laser rifle would do. He pointed the weapon and pulled the trigger just as the alien snapped its jaws onto Klicka-tac's leg. The laser burned through the alien's skull and turned his brain into liquid. At nearly the same moment the other reptilians charged into the fray.

Three more weapons fired. Three aliens dropped, but the other three attacked. Remmy had to duck as a powerful tail was lashed at his head. He pointed his laser weapon and fired at the creature, but nothing happened. The reptilian spun around and dove toward Remmy. Without even thinking about what he was doing, Remmy dove over the creature, landing on its back and rolling over to land on his feet. The creature lashed out with its tail again but Remmy was closer to its hind feet and the tail didn't have as much force at the base as it did at the tip. Remmy grabbed on with two hands. The creature screamed and tried to pull the tail away, but Remmy wouldn't let go. The alien lashed out with its hind feet which had short claws on the toes. Remmy felt a searing heat on his thigh and he yanked backward. The reptilian flopped onto its side and Remmy spun around, raising one boot and slamming it down on the right rear leg of the creature. He heard the bone snap and the alien wailed in pain, but Remmy wasn't finished. He dove toward the alien's head and rammed his elbow into the wide jaw. It snarled and the teeth snapped at him, but Remmy pulled away. His left hand drew a combat knife from his boot and one quick slash opened the alien's throat. Orange blood surged out as Remmy moved back. The blood splashed onto the dirty floor. The creature shook and shuddered, then lay still.

When Remmy glanced around the other two aliens were dead with smoke rising from the laser blasts in their bodies. He looked over at his people, who were calmly watching the crowd for any more threats. Remmy looked to Klicka-tac.

"Are you okay?"

"Broken leg," the alien chittered.

"Can you walk?"

"I can."

"Good," Remmy said. "Let's get out of here."

The crowd by that point was busy drinking and talking again. Hugo pushed past Remmy.

"Not bad, Sarge," the big man said.

Remmy hadn't been thinking about the fight or what he should do. Years of fighting had honed his mind and body to react to a threat. It all came back to him in that moment, as if the fight had been a dream. He could remember it better than when he was doing it.

Klicka-tac hobbled after Hugo and Tex followed. Laila approached Remmy and glanced at his leg.

"You okay?" She asked.

"Sure," Remmy said, even though his leg felt like it was on fire.

"How about we get you some antiseptic and clean that wound."

"Good idea," he told her.

They followed the others back to the ship.

CHAPTER 35

BY THE TIME they made it back to the slave ship their guide was exhausted. Klicka-tac dropped to the deck, curling up his long, spindly legs.

"This doesn't look good," Laila said.

"He's still breathing," Hugo pointed out.

The spidery alien was wheezing and sounded sick. Remmy was beginning to doubt his plan.

"You think them lizard people got friends?" Tex asked.

"Doubtful," Laila said.

"No one seemed to mind when we killed 'em," Hugo said.

Remmy retrieved the first aid supplies. He had to take off his pants and spray medicines onto the wound. The cuts, there were three of them, weren't deep. He wrapped a bandage around them to help stanch the bleeding and carefully pulled his pants back on.

"How bad is it?" Laila asked.

"Barely skin deep," Remmy said. "I'll live."

"We need to be more careful," she said. "The next time you might not be so lucky."

"I'd say he wasn't lucky this time," Hugo said. "What happened to your weapon, Master Sergeant?"

"It ran out of power I think," Remmy replied, handing the rifle to Hugo. "Let's see if we can get a new battery in it."

"Roger that," the big man said.

Remmy got a data tablet and stylus from his supplies and began sketching the floor plans of the space station. He could only do the small sections they had been in, but he hoped that it would help him get the rest from Klicka-tac. While Hugo worked on the rifle, and Tex ate from a meal pouch, Remmy and Laila questioned their new ally.

"How many levels down to where the beings like us are?" Remmy asked.

"Three," the spidery alien huffed.

"Straight down?" Laila asked.

"No," Klicka-tac replied.

"Can you show us?" Remmy said. "Can you draw it out, so we know how to get there?"

"Need... rest," the alien said in a weak voice.

"You can rest when we have the information we need," Laila said. "We did our part and got you off that space station. You failed to mention you were hiding in fear of your life."

"How could I know you would be attacked," Klicka-tac replied, sounding a little stronger than before.

"How could you not warn us it was a possibility?" Laila said. "We could have been killed."

"How's your leg by the way?" Remmy asked.

"Broken."

"Will it heal?" Laila asked.

"Eventually."

"Sketch out the floor plan," Remmy ordered. "Show us the quickest way in and out."

"And anything we need to know," Laila said. "Who runs this station?"

"Dyka clan," Klicka-tac said. "But different factions are always fighting for control."

"Who are the Dyka clan?" Remmy asked.

"You know nothing," the spidery alien grumbled. "You're not even slavers, are you?"

"No, and neither are you. Not anymore," Remmy told him.

That made the alien laugh, a barking sound that wasn't pleasant.

"The Mot station has been here for a thousand star cycles," he replied. "It will continue for a thousand more."

"Slavery is cruel and barbaric," Laila began, but halted as Remmy held up a hand.

"It is the way of the galaxy. No one can stop it," Klicka-tac argued.

"We aren't here to stop it," Remmy said. "We don't care about this space station or the people on it. We only want to free our kind and be away."

"The darkness below is not a kind place," the alien said. "It is savage. You would be better off to leave now."

"That's not an option," Laila said.

"Show us the way," Remmy said. "We'll do the rest."

It took the alien half an hour to sketch out the plans. It wasn't because his articulated legs weren't dexterous enough, but he turned out to be a bit of a perfectionist. The sketch was rough, but detailed. While he drew, he talked about the Dyka clan.

"They're big," he explained. "Large enough to challenge the Ashi if they had a mind to."

"Describe them," Remmy ordered.

"Tall, thick bodied bipeds. Long hair from their heads and shoulders. Two sets of arms. You can't miss them. They all carry laser rifles. Not the junk you have, but military grade weapons."

"What do they get from running this place?" Laila asked.

"Riches," Klicka-tac said. "A cut from all slaves passing through. A percentage of the money spent in the market, the taverns, the brothels and narcotic emporiums. It all flows through the Dyka clan."

"Will they be after us for killing the aliens who attacked you?" Remmy asked.

"There are fights all the time," the spidery alien grunted. "They'll be harvested, their bones sent to the compost pits."

"That's where our people are?" Remmy pressed.

"Yes, the deep pits. They work the renewables and recycle all biologics to feed the protein vats. It's hard work in a dark place. You're just as likely to get killed in the down deep."

"We'll take our chances," Laila said.

"It's your neck on the line," the spidery creature growled. "It matters not to me."

"Our people deserve better," Remmy said. "We're not leaving without them."

"Will the Dyka fight us for them?" Laila asked.

Klicka-tac bobbed up and down. "They won't let you steal their slaves without a fight."

Remmy sat back. He had known the humans were slaves and yet hearing someone from a different species say it out loud hit him hard.

"If they want a fight, we'll give them one," Remmy said. "Laila, get the others ready. We're going in."

She nodded and got to her feet.

GIGI inform Captain Darius that there are humans on the station and we're preparing to bring them out, he thought.

Message delivered Master Sergeant. Captain Darius approves and wants to know how they can help.

Have the rest of the platoon mount up. We may have to fight our way out of the space station. If that happens, I want them close.

Captain Darius approves and is giving the order to Lieutenant Colt. He wishes you God speed, Master Sergeant.

Remmy could feel his heart rate speed up. It was one thing to go into an unknown situation hoping to learn something useful. But he had proof that humans were on the space station. He even knew where they were and how to get to them. He also knew who to look for that might give them trouble. As the other three Marines approached Remmy had an idea.

"Let's break those weapons down," he ordered. "Hugo, grab us some bonding gel. We're going to take our weapons into the station."

"Why didn't I think of that," Hugo said as he opened a crate which had their rifles inside.

"You think they'll pass for the same type of third-rate laser rifles?" Laila asked as she started taking her laser weapon apart.

"No one is checking them," Remmy said. "So yeah, at a glance, I don't think they'll stand out as anything special once we camouflage them."

"We've got headlamps and flashlights too," Tex said. "If it's dark in the lower levels, we'll need them."

He passed out the gear. It only took a few minutes for the Marines to disassemble the laser weapons, which were made from second and third hand components. Some they even cut apart with a rotary tool, before gluing them onto their regular weapons. Under their coats they stuffed their belts with ammo refills.

"We all need flash-bangs," Remmy said. "There are plenty of enclosed spaces down there that will enhance the effects."

"You want us carrying regular ammo, correct?" Laila asked.

"That's right. If we have to fight, and Klicka-tac is right, the Dyka clan are big. We need to be able to put them down fast."

"And permanent," Hugo said. "We can't afford to have them coming at us more than once."

"Agreed," Tex said.

"We don't have radio comlinks, so we stay close. Once we have our people, we get out as fast as we can."

"Doesn't mean they won't come after us," Laila said. "What then?"

"Then we let Captain Darius worry about it," Remmy said. "Everyone ready?"

"What do we do with him?" Hugo asked, pointing at the spidery alien who appeared to be sleeping on the floor near the hatch that led into the space station.

"Leave him," Remmy said. "I don't think he can do much harm. Let's go."

They left the ship two at a time. For several minutes nothing happened inside the slave ship. Then slowly Klicka-tac got up. He stopped wheezing. The broken leg snapped back together as if it had never been injured. The alien skittered around the deck, then dashed up the stairs. Klicka-tac had no trouble climbing the wall and the vertical shaft that led up to the command deck. It checked the bodies of the dead slavers, then turned its attention to the controls, before hurrying back down to the main deck.

Without slowing down it opened the airlock and passed through the docking tube. Once back inside the space station it hurried to a terminal just outside the marketplace in the massive central chamber. With one spindly leg it lifted a communication device and chittered into it for a moment. His message delivered; Klicka-tac stepped into the market. Half a dozen spidery creatures were waiting for his signal. They came hurrying toward him.

Klicka-tac led the way back to the slave ship. They rushed in through the docking tunnel and quickly hurried up to the Bridge. A signal was sent to the station and the docking clamps were released. The docking tunnel was retracted, and the ship moved slowly away from the space station.

CHAPTER 36

"CAPTAIN, THE DRONE SHUTTLE HAS LAUNCHED," Ensign Bertoli said. "ETA to the space station is fifty-seven minutes."

"Very good," Darius said. "What's the update on our engines."

"Maintenance system shows seventy percent completion on repairs, Captain," Henry Nash replied. "The drones are making quick work of it, sir. My people are overseeing the rebuilds. It's complicated work, but we should have main engines back online in the next few hours."

"Outstanding," Darius said.

He loved it when things went smoothly. And everything seemed to be happening without incident. The power was back up, which meant the manufacturing facilities were able to fabricate replacement parts for the engine. Soon, Darius hoped, they would be able to do the same thing for the laser cannons. Ship repairs were part of any naval operation, but they rarely went so smoothly, and almost never got done ahead of schedule.

"Captain, I'm picking something up that's a little strange," Vivian Ramos said.

"What is it?" Darius asked.

"The slave ship," she said. "The one that Master Sergeant Steel's team took to the station. It's leaving."

"What?"

"It's undocked and moving away from the station."

"GIGI check with the Master Sergeant. We need to know if the plan has changed."

"Yes, Captain," the computerized voice replied.

"Let's keep tabs on that ship, please," Darius said.

"Aye, Captain, tracking the slave ship," Ramos called out.

"Captain," GIGI responded. "Master Sergeant Steel and his team are in the space station. They have no knowledge of the slave ship leaving the dock."

"Wonderful," Darius said. "Looks like it's getting stolen."

"Not surprising," the chief engineer said. "This is not what I would call a good neighborhood."

"You think it's that alien they brought on board?" Pete Best asked.

"That would be a good guess, Lieutenant," Darius replied. "GIGI, is it possible to fly that ship with just a single person on board?"

"Negative, Captain Darius," GIGI replied. "Analogue controls on the slave ship require at least two beings, depending on the species."

"So, the alien recruited some help," Vivian said. "It must have happened the moment our people left."

"We trusted the wrong person," Darius said. "Any chance you can override their controls, GIGI, perhaps lock them out?"

"Affirmative Captain, I am still synced to the slave ship's computer controls."

"Well, I guess they didn't count on that," Darius said. "I want that ship back in the same berth they took it from, but we can't let the thieves back onto the space station. They'll make trouble for our Marines."

"Shut down the life support system," Henry Nash said. "And vent the atmo. Can we do that?"

"Affirmative, Lieutenant Nash. Is that the order you would like to give, Captain Darius?"

Zeke Darius thought about it for a moment. Stealing a person's means of transportation was a serious crime. In many cultures it was a capital crime. Darius didn't think it rose to that level, but he wasn't dealing with a group of teenagers taking someone's hovercraft out for a joy ride. These were slave traders who stole an intergalactic ship, probably with the intent of using it to waylay other vessels.

"Do it," Darius said. "Can that species survive without air?"

"Negative, Captain," GIGI said. "Everyone on board the ship will be dead within five minutes, unless they find some way to circumvent the lack of oxygen on board."

"Very well," Darius said. "Lock them out of the ship's controls too and start it back toward the space station."

"You ride with outlaws, you die with outlaws," Henry Nash said. "Frontier justice."

"It seems a bit harsh," Ramos said.

"You disagree with the consequences" Nash asked.

"Not in this case," Vivian said. "And not with these people. But still, I like to think we're a species that can have mercy when it's called for."

Darius didn't join in the conversation. He had made his decision; he wouldn't question it or second guess it. Instead, he focused on what remained.

"GIGI, inform the Master Sergeant of what has transpired with the slave ship. Assure him it will be back in the same berth as before, when he needs it."

"Sending your message now, Captain Darius."

"And tell him to watch his back. They can't trust anyone on that station."

Darius turned and looked at the plot. The high-resolution hologram showed most of the system by that point. The radar expanded from the *Renegade* in all directions at the speed of light. But like most of outer space, the Mot System was almost entirely empty. What they could see was the space station. It was completely surrounded on all sides, above and below, by thousands of derelict spacecrafts, or parts of old ships. There were so many ships that Darius wondered how the dull, red light from the star even reached the solar sails, but they were turning, and he supposed they were capturing enough energy to run the station. Beyond the field of junked space craft was the ring of asteroids. They had already picked up several small tugs pulling the rocky chunks from the ring. They carried them to a refining ship, which melted the ice from the asteroids and spewed the chunks of dry rock back into space. There were transport vessels that went from the space station to the refining ships and back again. Darius assumed whoever was running the space station was utilizing the liquid water for both air and hydration. If they had the technology, he knew it was possible to capture the energy released when the hydrogen and oxygen atoms were split. Perhaps they had that sort of technological sophistication, but looking at the hodgepodge space facility, he doubted it.

"Lieutenant Ramos," Darius said. "Do we have the navigation from the slave ship in our computers now?"

"Aye, Captain, we do," she said.

"What does it show as a way out of here?" Darius asked. "There must be more than one portal through hyperspace. This many ships couldn't have moved through the Olotimbo system without the portal being discovered."

"You're correct, Captain," Vivian said. "In fact, there are hundreds of portals here, sir. It looks like this is a hub of some kind."

"Do the portals show in our normal navigation system?"

"Negative, Captain. Apart from the information from the slave ship, we wouldn't know about these."

Darius leaned back in his seat. It made sense. Not every hyperspace lane and portal would be reported to the Imperium. That secret knowledge gave the unauthorized slavers a way to move in and out of Imperial systems without being followed by the military or law enforcement.

"Mr. Nurek, would you be so kind as to go through that information. We may need to leave the Mot system quickly, once Master Sergeant Steel has completed his mission. We need to move quickly to another system, preferably one with multiple hyperspace portals."

"I will do my best, Captain," Nurek said with a bow.

Darius glanced wryly at Commander Lori Lee, who raised her eyebrows. He turned back and looked through the big transparent canopy. There was nothing more to be done until the Marines returned. He hoped there would be no more surprises, but he had commanded enough missions to know that there were always surprises no matter how well prepared they might be. He would just have to be ready for whatever was waiting and hope that he was up to the challenge.

CHAPTER 37

REMMY STOPPED the group of Marines he was leading at the boom of the second spiral ramp, just outside where they had met Klacka-tac.

"You're not going to believe this," he said.

"What?" Laila asked as the Marines gathered close.

"The alien just stole our ship," Remmy said.

"You're kidding, right?" Laila said.

"I knew it!" Tex said.

"I'll kill this spidery bastard," Hugo snapped.

"I'm afraid so," Remmy said. "But Captain Darius is taking care of it. Plus, the rest of the platoon is in-bound."

"So, we're supposed to just keep going?" Laila asked.

"That's exactly what we're going to do."

Remmy moved off through the open, low-ceiling room that was crowded with homeless aliens. They got strange looks, but none of the pathetic looking aliens tried to stop them. For that, Remmy was grateful. He wouldn't let anyone interfere with the mission, but he didn't want to kill the aliens or draw more resistance by shooting their projectile weapons in the space station.

"There's the stairs," Laila said, pointing to Remmy's right.

"Good eye," he said. "Tex, how are we looking?"

"No one is following us yet," Corporal Fry said.

"Alright, down we go," Remmy said, leading the way down another narrow ramp that spiraled from one level to the next. The lights from the level above weren't very bright to begin with and there were no overhead lights on the lower levels, just an occasional utility light. They were in an engineering space. Remmy pulled out the headband that had an LED light attached. He put it on and clicked the light on. A strong beam showed him what was on the engineering level.

"Someone needs to clean this place up," Hugo said.

There were big machines humming around them. Oil and grease dripped from the mechanisms and a thick layer of dust covered everything. Only a small walkway led between the heating units and electrical converters.

"Not us," Laila said. "Keep moving."

They did, each one following one another in a single file line. It was hot amid the big machines. They soon started to notice blankets and narrow pads in the filthy corners between the machines.

"People are sleeping here," Tex pointed out.

"More riffraff from upstairs?" Hugo asked.

"No," Laila responded. "I think humans are taking refuge here."

Remmy felt like he might be sick. The air in the engineering space was hot and damp. They hadn't gone far when a nasty stench wafted into their nostrils.

"Oh, no, that's rank," Hugo said.

"Sewage," Tex replied. "We must be getting close."

"Sewage and other things," Remmy said. "I can smell rotting flesh."

They found a spiraling ramp and went down to a long room that was filled with barrels attached to the floor and ceiling. There were lights on the barrels, dull little LEDs that showed the units were powered on but didn't give very much light to the space.

"What is this?" Laila asked.

"Food processing would be my guess," Remmy said.

"Nah, this place ain't sanitary at all," Hugo said. "They wouldn't grow food here."

"I don't think they care about sanitation," Remmy said. "They're feeding these tanks with whatever protein they can get. It ferments as it breaks down and reforms into a solid chunk."

"Is this what we eat?" Tex asked, aghast at the very idea.

"Negative," Laila said. "Our protein is mostly synthetic."

"And clean," Hugo said.

"My guess is the lizards we killed up top will be butchered," Remmy explained. "What isn't immediately edible will be ground up and put in these vats."

They were halfway down the long aisle between the rows of vats when they heard a sound. It was loud, like the sound of a brake squealing. Remmy held up a fist and dropped to one knee. He shut off his head lamp and the others followed. With his rifle to his shoulder, he could activate the night vision scope. The room became visible around him and between the vats he could see a large hatch. Then the sound of feet. Not human feet or even boots on the steel deck, but more like hooves.

The Marines didn't move. They stayed down and kept watching. Soon, the sound of footsteps, if they could be called that, got close enough that the group could see a pair of strange looking aliens. They had four thick legs that ended in large hooves. Their upper bodies were shaped like a triangle with what looked like tentacles waving in the air. The aliens opened the industrial looking hatch and pulled out a big crate. They set it on the floor and pulled large cutting instruments from a hatch in the wall.

"What are they doing?" Laila whispered.

Before anyone could answer the aliens shoved their tools into the crate. A loud grinding sound was heard. Remmy could see bits of something flying up from the crate. It was fascinating in a macabre kind of way, but the tools made more than enough noise to mask the movements of the Marines.

"Let's move out," Remmy whispered.

He got to his feet and moved swiftly toward the far end of the room. They had to pass through a perpendicular hallway. The room directly across from the one filled with vats was busy. There were tubs and tables. More of the strange, squid headed aliens were mixing and moving some sort of substance through a process of different chemicals. Remmy guessed it was the final stage of the recycling process. Whatever couldn't be used directly in food production, things like skin, cartilage, and bone, could still be processed. They would refine whatever could be of use. Humans had done the same thing to make animal feed until they realized that animals eating their own kind was unhealthy.

Remmy didn't think the Dyka Clan cared about the health or well-being of the people on their space station. He had seen how their slaves were treated, and it was not good.

He turned right and hurried down the hallway. They passed several closed doors. Whenever a hatch was open Remmy stopped and checked inside. The rooms were all dark. He decided the night vision on his scope was safer than the headlamp. The other Marines followed his example. None of the other rooms were occupied. They were filled with equipment that Remmy didn't recognize. The deck was metal, as were the walls and doors. It reminded Remmy of old S.D.F. ships. They were built for utility - not aesthetics - and had a prison vibe. The lower levels of the Mot space station were the same.

When they finally reached another spiraling ramp leading down into pitch blackness, Remmy felt a bit better. He kept his rifle to his shoulder so he could look through the night vision aiming reticule. He was fortunate that his scope wasn't telescopic, just a square aiming device mounted on the rail that ran along the top of his Nelson LTX rifle. Not that there was much to see. The spiral went down a long way, then opened into a massive chamber with round pits. There was no light, but as Remmy swept his rifle from side to side, he spotted three humans. They were pulling garbage from chutes and separating things into piles.

"How do they know what is what?" Hugo asked in a whisper.

"Feel, I suppose," Laila said.

"What do we do now?" Tex asked.

"You and Sergeant McManus hold this position. I want to know if anyone comes down that ramp."

"Copy that, Master Sergeant," Hugo said.

"Laila and I will make contact," Remmy went on. "Stay close, Staff Sergeant."

"You'll get no argument from me," Laila said.

They went slowly toward the first of the open pits. It was much deeper than Remmy had thought. He could hear a mechanical grinding sound from down in the pit, but there was no sign of movement. At another pit raw sewage and water was raining down from an overhead chute. It fell into the pit with drips and the occasional splash.

When they were closer to the three humans, with a clear walkway between them, Remmy switched on his head lamp. The three humans froze. One turned, looking into the light.

"My name is Remmy Steel. I'm with the Space Defense Force. We're here to rescue you."

His words seemed to echo in the big chamber. The slaves didn't react at first, but then the translator app transmitted Remmy's message into the ancient language the prisoner they had captured from the slave ship spoke. It was a very rough translation. The written language had a history of translation. Humans had found clay tablets and stone monuments with ancient Cuneiform written on them. That allowed the language to be studied and eventually translated. But GIGI had very little to go on to recreate the spoken language. Everything the prisoner on the *Renegade* said was recorded for GIGI and the ship's computer to create a rough translation.

The slaves didn't look at one another. Their heads didn't move.

They were focused completely on the light from Remmy's head lamp. But they reached out and linked hands together.

"We are like you," Laila said. She switched on her headlamp and held it in one hand, pointing the beam of light back on herself and Remmy. Then she took a flashlight from her pocket, switched it on, and held it out. "Here," she said. "Take it."

The translation app was obviously close enough to their language that they understood the offer. One of the slaves reached out with a trembling hand and took the flashlight. It was a girl, although gender was hard to discern since they were all skinny, with long, dirty hair, and baggy clothes that had been mended and patched many times. The girl flicked the switch that turned the flashlight off, then turned it back on. The others looked relieved. They even smiled, as if the light amused them. For a moment they didn't move. Then one waved for Remmy and Laila to follow. The three slaves moved away from the garbage chutes.

"McManus, Fry, to me," Remmy called out.

"On our way," Hugo replied.

A moment later, with the group all together, the Marines followed the three slaves. They didn't use the flashlight, but through the beam of his head lamp Remmy could see the girl was treasuring the device. And he couldn't blame her. In the deep dark of the lower levels on their space station, light was valuable.

They went through a small doorway into another room. It was filled with a huge pile of what looked like dirt. Remmy heard rats scurrying and squeaking in the darkness.

"Rats and roaches, even in space," Hugo said.

"Rodents are universal," Tex agreed.

Through their beams of light, they saw the rats running along the corners of the room and bugs crawling on the walls. They also saw traps for the rats and another slave who seemed to be gathering the larger bugs off the walls and putting them into a sack.

"What do you think they do with the bugs?" Hugo asked.

"You don't want to know," Remmy said.

"Protein is protein," Laila said. "Lots of cultures eat bugs."

"Oh, man," Hugo wailed.

They went into another chamber that was much smaller than the others. There a group of six women were sitting on the floor mending clothes. They had small bone needles and balls of yarn that had been spun by hand. It was made from all sorts of materials. Anything flexible enough could be spun in and twisted with the other threads to make the yarn. The women all froze in the blaze of light from the Marine headlamps.

The girl with the flashlight spoke to the women. Remmy only understood a few words that they said. Laila stepped toward the women and introduced herself.

"My name is Laila McPherson," she said. "We are warriors, here to help you escape this place."

It didn't take long for more people to arrive. One of the initial three slaves ran off to find everyone else. Two elderly people were escorted in, and several skinny, weak looking men came into the chamber.

"You are humans," Remmy said. "We come from a star system far away where there are billions of people just like you."

"And we've come on a powerful spaceship," Laila added. "We have space for all of you. We'll take you away from here. You'll be safe. You'll have real food, and clothing."

The elderly woman stepped forward. "How is this?" She asked.

The language device translated her words.

"We learned you were here," Remmy said. "Hiza told us." That got a reaction. The slaves obviously knew who Hiza was. They looked around and murmured when Remmy mentioned Hiza's name. "We came to free you."

"Danger," the old woman said.

"Danger's our business," Tex said.

"And business is good," Hugo added.

The two Marines high-fived. Remmy couldn't help but smile.

"We will keep you safe," he said. "Will you come."

"Danger," the old woman said, pointing up.

Remmy held up his rifle. "We can handle the danger. Come with us, if you want to be free."

By the time they were finished explaining things, there were nearly thirty humans in the small room. They were all in bad shape. Some looked sick. They all looked malnourished and weak.

"Dyka Clan," the older man said. He had no teeth. His lips smacked as he said the strange words in his own language.

"We're prepared," Remmy assured them. "The Dyka clan won't stop us. We'll go up, board our space ship, and leave forever."

"Impossible," the old woman said, shaking her head. "We go, we die."

Remmy didn't think they were really living down in the dark, stinking chambers among the sewage of the space station. But it was obviously all they had ever known.

"We won't force you," Remmy said. "But this is probably your only chance to escape."

"More," the old woman said, before turning to the girl with the flashlight. "Show them."

The girl waved to the Marines. Remmy followed her. Laila stayed behind with Tex. They opened their trauma kits and began to offer aid to those with sores and open wounds. Hugo followed behind Remmy. The girl led them through two more rooms. One had tools; the other had piles of what Remmy guessed were useable materials. He didn't recognize most of it. But in the third room he was shocked to see four women on beds. They were real, raised beds with mattresses and blankets.

"What's this?" Hugo asked.

Remmy felt another cold shiver run down his back as he glanced around the room. The women were all pregnant.

"Breeding program," Remmy said.

"Oh, hell no," Hugo said. "That's... are you serious, Master Sergeant? They're breeding them?"

"Looks that way," Remmy said.

He took his time explaining who he was and why he was there. None of the women got out of their beds except one. Remmy thought he was getting through to them, but she simply squatted down and relieved herself on the floor, then crawled back into the bed.

"They don't want to come?" Hugo said.

"Compared to the others, they probably think they've got it pretty good here," Remmy said.

"Until they can't have more babies," Hugo said. "If I get my hands on these clowns running this place, I'll kill 'em."

"I hope you don't get the chance," Remmy said.

The girl led them to another room. Two older women were watching three toddlers. And there were two more children, a girl around six years old, and a boy who looked to be eight or nine."

"We have to get them off this space station," Hugo said. "It don't matter what they think. They don't know what's good for them."

"Agreed," Remmy said.

They headed back and found the larger group huddled around Laila and Tex.

"Let's go," Remmy said. "I'm not asking any more. Get your people on their feet and ready to move."

"What are you doing?" Laila asked.

"I'm not leaving here without these people," Remmy said.

"But you can't force them to leave," she insisted.

"Yes, we can," Remmy said. "In fact, I think it's the only way to free them."

The aliens were all talking at once. Remmy knew he needed a demonstration of his authority. He caught sight of a rat slinking through the room. He drew his laser pistol, pointed it at the rat and fired. The beam flashed and the rat flipped over. There was a small hole in its side and dark smoke wafted up from it. The entire group of slaves fell silent. Remmy held up the pistol.

"We are here to take you away. Gather the children and pregnant women. You don't need anything else. We are leaving. Now!"

For a second they all stared at him with big eyes. Then a few of the men hurried off. And the old woman started to cry. The old man put a skinny arm around her bony shoulders and nodded at Remmy. He nodded back, then turned to Tex.

"Head back to the ramp and wait for us, Corporal Fry," Remmy ordered.

"Yes, Master Sergeant."

"Hugo, wait here for those children."

"Copy that, Sarge."

Remmy walked over to the old man and took hold of his free arm. Then he gently started to lead him away. The look on Laila's face was total surprise but she didn't argue. That would come later, when they were alone. She was too strong a believer in the chain of command to argue with a superior officer in front of their subordinates. She clearly didn't agree with his decision, but she hadn't seen the breeders or the children. And the one thing Remmy was certain of was the fact that he wouldn't leave anyone behind.

CHAPTER 38

IT TOOK LONGER than Remmy wanted to get the slaves moving. He didn't like thinking of them as slaves, yet that was what they were and would remain, unless he got them off the alien space station. Where they came from or how long they had been on the station would have to wait. It was like a timer had started in his head the moment he gave the order to get the people moving, although he had no reason to think he was in danger. They hadn't seen any of the Dyka clan or any sort of resistance. The alien station appeared to be the type of place where anything goes. Still, he didn't expect to get to walk right out of the station with over forty slaves. A fight was coming and Remmy wanted to meet it head on.

"We should send Tex on ahead," Laila suggested. "I can take point."

Remmy wasn't sure if she was simply supporting him as her superior or if the sight of the pregnant women had changed her mind. Hugo had rounded everyone up. The pregnant women didn't seem happy about it. They wore patchwork dresses and were only slightly healthier than the other slaves. Or maybe it was the children. Several of the toddlers were naked. One had to be carried. There was something infuriating about seeing a child who was starving to death. Hugo had already opened his pack and began sharing his emergency rations with the children.

"Good idea," Remmy said. "When we meet resistance, we have to act hard and fast."

"No mercy," she said.

"None for the animals who would do this to people," Remmy said, waving a hand at the slaves.

Even in the darkness they seemed pathetic. The best most could manage was a slow, limping walk. They moved between the refuse pits slowly. The Marines kept their headlamps on and had passed out their flashlights.

"You were right," she said. "Leaving them behind, even if they didn't want to go, was wrong. I get it now."

She hurried up to the front of the group. The trio of young people who they had first encountered were there. Laila led them on toward the ramp. Hugo was in the rear with the children. He made a quick head count. There were forty-four slaves in total, including the children. Remmy could only hope that was everyone. In the darkness it wasn't a given that they had found the entire group. He remembered the filthy blankets on the engineering level. It was entirely possible that other humans had separated from the group and were living in hiding. But there was no time, and they didn't have the numbers to do a thorough search. It was better to take the group they had found and, if there were more people on the station, they could come back later for them.

Remmy had to keep in mind he only had three Marines on the station with him. That wasn't enough to fight a pitched battle. Speed was their greatest asset.

GIGI, he thought, *can you hear me.*

Yes, Master Sergeant.

I've got forty-four humans from the station, including some children and four women who are pregnant. Pass that along to Captain

Darius. We are making our way back up from the lower levels to the slave ship. Is it docked to the station?

It is. I am currently restoring the breathable air that was vented in order to deal with the thieves who took the ship.

You killed them?

Captain Darius approved the decision.

Remmy had to admit at times Captain Zeke Darius surprised him. The man was passionate about his job. He would do anything for his crew and was dedicated to the mission. At other times he made decisions with heavy consequences. How he managed to deal with that weight of responsibility Remmy didn't know. But he found himself admiring the captain more and more. Klicka-tac had seemed weak and pathetic. Remmy would have never expected him to steal the ship but the spidery alien was an outlaw and slave trader. He should have been a little more cautious with him. It was a lesson learned. No one on the alien space station could be trusted. Not even the humans he was trying to save.

"Let's keep it together," he said, letting the language device translate his words. "Keep moving."

When they reached the ramp, they halted. Remmy moved up beside Laila.

"Staff Sergeant?" He asked.

"Tex is scouting the next level," she said. "He'll signal if it's clear."

A second later a light flashed on and off above them.

"That's it," Laila said.

"Alright, people, let's go. Stay quiet please. Just follow Staff Sergeant McPherson."

Laila led the way up the spiraling ramp. It was only wide enough for two people at a time. The slaves moved up slowly. Remmy could see the fear in their eyes. Some of them were old, some injured or sick. Remmy thought it was a miracle they weren't all dead. They lived on garbage, rodents and insects. How they avoided fatal disease and secured enough food to support over forty people, all in almost total darkness, was hard to comprehend.

Remmy moved forward as soon as he reached the next level. He and Tex led the way through the long hallway and then the room of vats. They were seen there, but Remmy knew that couldn't be avoided. The squid-headed aliens turned, their tentacles waving frantically around them. They had no facial features that Remmy could discern and didn't speak. He was ready to gun them down, but they didn't seem to be a threat.

The slaves had to stop again at the ramp that led up to the engineering section.

"The kids are pretty tired," Hugo said. "A few minutes rest would help."

"That's fine," Remmy said. "In fact, why don't we carry the toddlers up."

He took one, a young boy with no clothes and a ragged cough. The child didn't cling to him. He didn't seem afraid, just exhausted. He lay in Remmy's arms like a rag doll. Remmy couldn't believe how little the child weighed. Laila took the five-year-old girl. Hugo had a child in each arm. They went up to the engineering level and gave the children water from the meager supplies they carried.

"They need more than this," Hugo said.

"They'll get everything they need on board the *Renegade*," Remmy said.

"I'll get the rest of the group moving," Laila said.

A few minutes later they were all together on the engineering level. Remmy got the three young people he had first met and asked them about the dirty blankets among the big mechanical components that lined the room.

"What are these?" He asked.

"Shrouds for the dead," the girl with the flashlight replied.

"You bring the dead up here?" Remmy asked.

The girl shook her head. "The elderly come here to expire in peace."

"It's warm," one of the other slaves said.

Remmy nodded. It made sense. There would be little to no help for a sick person down in the pits. Those who were dying couldn't remain and consume the resources of the healthy. Not that any of the slaves were 'healthy', but it was obvious looking at them that none had enough to eat.

"Where are we going?" The girl with the flashlight asked.

"To our ship," Remmy said. "It's big. You'll be safe there. We have food, clean water, medicine."

"What is medicine?" She asked.

"Help for those who are sick," Remmy said.

At the next ramp the slaves looked up and saw the light above them. They were murmuring in their own language. Some were excited, others seemed afraid. Remmy kept them at the ramp while he and Tex went up to make sure it was safe to pass through the crowds of refugees.

"Only a few more levels," Tex said. "So far so good."

"We'll be a strange sight herding this group through the market-place," Remmy said.

"Been thinking about that, Sarge. It can't be the first time they've seen slaves forced onto slave ships, right? Maybe it won't be a big deal."

"I wish I had your optimism, Corporal," Remmy said.

"Anything is possible," Tex said. "And you have to admit, we're doing the right thing here, Sarge. These people deserve better."

"I can't argue with that," Remmy said.

They went slowly up the last spiral. There was no sign of any resistance. The refugees were still in their hovels. No one paid the pair any attention.

"Go get them," Remmy ordered.

"Copy that," Tex said, hurrying back down the spiraling ramp.

It took nearly twenty minutes to get the forty-four slaves up to the refugee level. They were drawing looks from the wretched souls around them but most stayed down on their pallets or inside their makeshift hovels. The humans were squinting from the overhead lights, which weren't very bright. But after decades in the dark, any light was painful to their eyes. The older people kept their eyes closed.

Laila led the group across the room, with Remmy and Tex just a few paces ahead of her. Hugo brought up the rear. They were all armed, but the slaves were helpless. Remmy felt exposed, yet there was nothing he could do about that. Speed was his friend. The quicker they got off the space station, the better off they would be.

But halfway across the long, low-ceilinged chamber where the refugees squatted, four aliens with well-maintained laser rifles appeared from the spiraling ramp ahead. They were a little taller than Remmy's Marines, and broad chested like Hugo. But that's where the similarities ended.

Remmy had no doubt who they were. The Dyka clan were aliens with two legs, four arms, and long, ropy hair that hung from the back of their head and around the top of their beefy shoulders. They didn't wear shirts. They had fur across their chest and stomach. Their pants were made from some type of animal skin and ended around their calves. Their feet were wide, almost reptilian looking, with three thick toes in front, and a curved claw at the heel.

There was no need to hesitate. Remmy knew there would be no discussion. At a glance, he could see that the Dyka weren't trained soldiers. They had military grade weapons, but that was all. They held them in a clumsy manner and their wide set eyes showed surprise when they spotted Remmy's Marines with the human slaves.

"Go!" Remmy said.

He already had his Nelson LTX tucked against his right shoulder. The safety was off, and the fire indicator was set to three round bursts. Everything happened really fast. He spotted the aliens, noted their demeanor and fired within a second. His rifle bucked against his shoulder. It was loaded with soft metal rounds that tore into the unclothed, furry chests of the Dyka clan and left big bloody holes. Beside him, Tex opened fire at almost the same time. He was carrying a short barreled tactical rifle. They cut down the aliens with impunity.

"Check that stairwell," Remmy said as he turned and looked back.

"On it," Tex replied before jogging forward.

"Everyone okay?" Remmy asked.

The Dyka clan hadn't got off a single shot, but the reports from the human weapons were loud. He had heard the humans screaming and the refugees were all scrambling for cover.

"We're okay," Laila replied.

"Let's keep moving," Remmy ordered. "Go, go, go."

He ran forward and grabbed one of the dead aliens. He pulled the heavy body out of the walkway. Up close he examined the laser rifle. It was similar to those carried by the Ashi, only smaller. Remmy snatched them up. He didn't want the slaves behind him with rifles they couldn't handle, but he didn't want to leave them for the refugees either.

"Ramp is clear, Sarge," Tex called.

"Outstanding! Let's move," Remmy said.

He jogged up the ramp and dumped the laser rifles in the corner. They were on the level with the holding cells. Remmy had just dropped the laser weapons when a second group of Dyka warriors appeared. They were moving fast, but Tex was ready for them. He dropped to one knee and fired a steady barrage into the group. Three died, and two more dashed back up the wide ramp that led to the main level.

"Get to that end of the room," Remmy ordered. "Cover that ramp, Tex."

"You bet," he said, jogging forward.

Remmy turned back to the ramp behind him.

"What's happening?" Laila called up.

"We've got hostiles," Remmy said.

"What should we do?" Laila asked.

"Bring them up," he ordered. "I've got a plan."

Remmy picked up one of the discarded laser rifles and went to the closest holding cell door. He looked inside. There were three aliens inside. They looked a lot like kangaroos, but with longer arms. Their ears drooped and Remmy could see the terror in their eyes.

GIGI, he thought, *what are they?*

They appear to be Hasconians, the alien device replied inside Remmy's head.

He brought the laser rifle up, pointed it point blank at the door lock, and fired. It took several shots to burn through the locking bolt which was substantial. When it did, he swung the door open.

"Come with us and we'll get you off this space station," Remmy said.

The aliens stared at him, blinking their big eyes until the language device he had clipped to this jacket translated his offer. The aliens looked at each other, then nodded. Remmy took that to be a universal gesture and hurried to the next cell.

By that point Laila had seen what he was doing and joined him. They had opened five of the holding cells by the time the humans all made it up the ramp. There were nearly thirty aliens joining the group of humans. They were all scared ... and rightly so.

"We need to move, Master Sergeant," Hugo shouted. "There are enemy troops massing below us."

"How many?" Remmy asked.

"I didn't stick around to find out," Hugo said, handing the children off to the other humans before checking his weapons.

"I've got movement!" Tex shouted.

"Looks like they're trying to box us in," Hugo said.

"Their mistake," Remmy said. "You hold the back ramp, Sergeant."

"Copy that," Hugo said, marching back toward the hatch that led to the spiraling ramp.

Remmy dashed over to where Laila was opening another holding cell door.

"What's the plan?" She asked.

"Keep opening doors," Remmy told her. "The Dyka clan is sending people to both ramps. We can hold them off for a while. Hugo is at the rear, but that ramp is narrow. He should be able to hold it for a while by himself. I'm joining Tex and I'll notify the *Renegade.*"

"There's no telling how many fighters this Dyka clan might have," she warned him.

"I know," Remmy said. "They might even get the other aliens involved."

"Staying here could be a mistake," she said.

"I'm open to ideas."

"If I have any, you'll be the first to know," she said. "Be careful."

"You too," he replied as he reached out and gave her shoulder a squeeze.

"Fire in the hole!" Hugo shouted as he tossed a flash bang grenade over the railing of the spiral ramp. It dropped down the shaft and then exploded. There were screams from the slaves and Hugo opened up with his big gun. It chugged death down onto the Dyka clan climbing up the ramp.

Remmy chuckled. The big man was a ferocious fighter. And they all had something noble to fight for. He saw the looks of desperation on the faces of the slaves as he rushed past them. There was no doubt in Remmy's mind that his team would win the day. None of them would fail the slaves whose lives were in their hands. Even if they had to make the ultimate sacrifice, he knew none of his people would hesitate. He loved them for it.

CHAPTER 39

AGAINST HIS BETTER JUDGEMENT, Lieutenant Micky Colt had loaded his MECH suit into the shuttle and gone with the rest of his platoon to back up Master Sergeant Remmy Steel. They were only a hundred kilometers from the station when word came in that there were over forty human slaves on the space station, including pregnant women and little children.

His comlink crackled in his ear. The signal was distorted by the field of space junk. The shuttle had gone through easily enough, but there were a lot of metal hulls and old components between their ship and the *Renegade*.

"Ronan One, this is Shogun actual," Ensign Bertoli said. "Do you copy? Over."

"I read you, Shogun," Micky Colt said. "What are your orders?"

"We just got word that Alpha team is taking fire. Captain Darius orders you to dock with the station but wait for further orders. I repeat, the shuttle will be docked with the space station, but you are to await orders before moving in. Is that clear, Ronan One?"

"Affirmative, Shogun. We will stand by for further orders," Colt said.

The members of his team were looking at him. Corporal Leigh Ann Poh, Sergeant Dirk Oliver, Corporal Izzy Berry and Corporal Ricky Thompson waited for the update.

"We're going to dock with the station," he said. "Sergeant Steel's team is under attack, but we're to wait for further orders before going in."

"Why?" Ricky asked.

"That's our orders," Micky Colt said. "Master Sergeant Steel is in touch with Captain Darius. We wait on board until called for."

"Forty humans," Dirk Oliver said. "That's the first worthwhile operation we've been called to carry out since we left the Sol system."

"If you say so," Leigh Ann Poh said. "Personally, I'm glad we're doing what we're doing."

"It's historic, really," Izzy added.

Their conversation went on, but Micky Colt didn't follow it. He knew how his platoon felt, but it was his own feelings that he really cared about. He didn't feel strong or much like commanding a platoon of Marines. What he did feel was a strong desire to kill. Never in his life had he been anxious to take another life. He joined the Space Marines because he had a passion for strategy games and the idea of leading men into battle appealed to him. He had a bachelor's degree in history, with an emphasis on military history. He had excelled in Officer Training School but leading Marines into a fight wasn't like a video game. It was dirty, loud, bloody and terrifying. He had killed his first man in a firefight at an outpost on Mars near a mining colony. After the fight he had gone to where the man lay. His eyes were open. The trauma of that battle stayed with him, but he had learned how to deal with it. Micky Colt was not the kind of man who shied away from counseling. He had sought out ways to help deal with the trauma and several strategies had worked. It allowed him to continue to serve and he had done so with distinction. There was talk of promotions and so Micky had volunteered for special forces training, as everyone knew the fastest path to senior leadership was through combat experience.

But in all the missions he had led, and the handful of fights he had been in, never had he longed to kill anyone. Somehow, that had changed. Ever since waking up after the battle on Casasil, Lieutenant Micky Colt wanted to cause harm. He wanted to shoot someone in the face or slash open a throat and watch them bleed to death. Homicidal thoughts and fantasies filled his mind. It was like an itch he needed to scratch. The need to do harm to others simply wouldn't go away. He needed to kill even though he couldn't say why he felt the need. It was just there, like a dangerous beast in his mind that he was having trouble keeping under control.

"The shuttle is docked and ready for you to offload, Lieutenant," the computerized voice of GIGI said.

Micky winced. Not at the message, but at the voice. There was something about the alien artifact that he didn't like. He had never trusted it and he wanted nothing to do with it. But he did heed the fact that the artifact was in control of his shuttle. Every fiber of his being wanted to get away from the ship, just to escape any proximity to the alien device. Micky Colt knew his feelings weren't rational and that frightened him. Yet, his compulsions seemed to make more sense to him with every passing hour.

"Suit up," Micky ordered. "Check your weapons. I want you ready to move on a moment's notice."

"We are suited up," Leigh Ann Poh said.

Micky knew he was talking to himself, giving himself the order to climb back into his MECH. He wasn't afraid of the battle suit, but he was afraid of what he might do once he had the power to wreak havoc at his fingertips.

"Let's get our weapons from the munitions locker," Sergeant Oliver said. "We can take our station at the doorway."

"Good," Micky said, moving toward the MECH which was folded up like a man squatting down near the rear hatch of the ship. "I'm going EVA."

"Sir?" Dirk asked.

"I have to see what I can do to help," he explained. It was a lame excuse, but he knew he had to get out of the ship. He couldn't stay put while there was killing going on. The MECH wouldn't fit through the boarding tube extended from the space station.

"I thought our orders were to wait," Ricky Thompson said.

"Those are your orders!" Lieutenant Colt snapped. "Not mine. Prepare for decompression."

"We're locked in, sir," Dirk said, after checking their harnesses.

Micky opened the panel that gave him access to his MECH. It was a powerful machine. He climbed in and fastened the safety straps across his chest. With one hand, he flipped the activator switch that powered the armor. The pieces of it moved together enclosing him inside the MECH suit. He should have checked his comms and life support. Instead, his hands went right to the weapons control. The suit had been reloaded with missiles and belt-fed high caliber bullets for the rotating multi-barreled machine guns.

"GIGI, open the back hatch," he said.

"Decompression isn't necessary to board the station, Lieutenant Colt," the despicable computer voice said.

"Did I ask or did I give you an order!" Micky shouted. His sudden, almost violent response surprised even himself.

"As you wish, Lieutenant," GIGI said.

He turned off the comlink. He didn't want to hear the alien artifact again. In front of him the rear hatch opened slowly. There was a rush of air, but none of the Marines needed it. Their space armor protected them from hard vacuum and supplied them with air when none was available. Micky Colt got to his feet, or rather, stood the MECH armor upright. He was flooded with a sudden sense of power. He jumped out into space and activated his thrusters. The MECH suit turned. In space there was no one to kill, but that didn't mean he couldn't do damage.

He activated his targeting computer and took aim at the base of the big solar sails. They looked like a series of massive support girders. Without really considering what he was doing, Micky Colt armed a high yield warhead and fired it.

CHAPTER 40

"HE'S DOING WHAT?" Darius asked.

The voice of Sergeant Dirk Oliver was scratchy but clear enough. Darius hadn't misunderstood the Marine; he just couldn't believe what he was hearing.

"He left the ship in his MECH suit, sir. Out the wide hatch in the back, Captain. We questioned him, but he was insistent."

Darius stood up angrily from his chair. There were forty-four slaves on the space station. Forty-four innocent lives, including women and children, and Lieutenant Micky Colt was going rogue.

"Sergeant Oliver, keep your people on that ship until you receive further orders from me. Understood."

"Sir, yes, sir!" Dirk replied.

"What's the Lieutenant going to do?" Pete Best asked.

"Who knows," Henry Nash replied.

Darius turned to Commander Lee. "Get Doctor Lanski up here right away," the captain ordered.

"Aye, Captain," Lori Lee said.

"GIGI, inform Master Sergeant Steel of the situation with the shuttle."

"Of course, Captain Darius," the computerized voice said. "It appears that the Lieutenant has left the shuttle."

"God help us, the man's gone mad," Darius said. "What's the status in the space station?"

"Master Sergeant Steel's commando force is freeing other captives and engaging a group known as the Dyka clan in combat," GIGI reported. "So far, no casualties have been reported."

"Are they close to getting out?" Darius asked.

"The commando team and the human slaves are one level below the main deck on the space station, Captain. It appears they may have to fight their way to safety."

"Lieutenant Best, what's the weapon status?"

"Still off-line Captain," Pete said. "They haven't even begun repairs yet."

It was frustrating to feel like there was nothing he could do to help. Darius turned to Henry Nash.

"Get us as close as you can to that station," he ordered.

"Aye, Captain, but there's too much debris. I doubt we could get more than fifty or sixty thousand kilometers."

"Lieutenant Ramos, plot a course to the closest point and then a course out of the system. Have we determined the best portal to take?"

"Aye, Captain, Nurek has identified several dozen locations. We were going to suggest the Zutek star cluster. It's a crossroads of sorts, sir. Several hyperspace lanes are located there. We could navigate to just about any part of the galaxy from that location."

"Very good. Make it so," Darius said. "But keep tabs on the other slave ships. They'll know we're up to something soon."

As if on cue an alarm sounded. In the distance there was a flash of light.

"What just happened?" Darius said, dropping back into his captain's chair.

"Explosion, sir," Vivian said working the controls on her console. "Something on the space station just blew up."

"It was the solar sails," Nash said, pointing at the plot.

The hologram showed two of the sails crumpling, and third began to drift off away from the space station.

"Lieutenant Colt has fired a high yield missile into the space station," GIGI said in her emotionless, computerized voice.

"What's he doing?" Darius demanded. "He's going to get them all killed."

"According to the space station's computer systems, there is a power failure," GIGI said

"We have to stop Lieutenant Colt," Darius said. "Can you do that GIGI?"

"Negative Captain Darius, the MECH suit is not tied into the ship's computer and Lieutenant Colt has shut down his communications and wireless networking. He is completely isolated and out of communication."

"Get me Sergeant Oliver," Darius ordered.

"He's standing by, Captain," Ensign Bertoli replied.

"Sergeant, I hate to do this to you, but I'm ordering you to go out and stop Lieutenant Colt."

"Sir?" Dirk Oliver asked. "Stop him how?"

"Any way you can, Sergeant," Darius said. "That's an order."

CHAPTER 41

REMMY WAS on the far side of the opening into the shaft with the wide, spiral ramp that led up to the main level. It was twice as big as the ramps below. Normally, controlling the high ground was an advantage in combat, but moving down the ramp left the Dyka clan fighters exposed before they could bring their weapons to bear. Tex had easily turned back the first assault and with Remmy joining him, they held off the attackers.

"How long do we keep this up?" Tex shouted.

"Until Staff Sergeant McPherson gets the captives free, or we have to do something different."

A pair of fighters dropped from the side of the ramp, landing on their feet and firing their laser rifles, but they were off balance, and their aim was high. Tex and Remmy were both kneeling to give themselves a better angle of fire up the ramp. They returned fire and cut the Dyka clan fighters down easily. Remmy glanced over his shoulder. The laser shots had scorched the ceiling but didn't appear to have done any significant damage.

Master Sergeant Steel, be advised that the shuttle has docked and the Marines on board are holding their position, GIGI said.

Remmy was just about to order them out to give him some intel on what was happening on the main level, but GIGI injected more information into his brain before he could.

It also appears that Lieutenant Colt is acting alone. He has left the shuttle into open space using his MECH suit. Captain Darius warns you to be prepared for anything.

"We've got trouble!" Remmy yelled. "Everyone get down. Get on the ground."

He waved his hands and Laila began shouting the warning, too. A few seconds later, there was an explosion that rocked the entire station. Remmy heard metal bending under pressure and suddenly the lights went out. People were screaming. Remmy switched on the night vision on his aiming reticule and charged up the ramp. He had no idea what had happened or what else might happen. All he knew for certain was that as long as it was dark, he had an advantage. He reached the halfway point of the ramp and his enemy came into view. There were almost twenty fighters at the top of the ramp. Fortunately, they had no vision assistance. They were completely blind. Remmy flipped the fire indicator switch on his rifle to full auto and pulled the trigger.

Remmy never felt good about killing. It was part of his job, which was to stop the enemy at all costs. Officers and politicians often made the call about who was a friend or foe. But Remmy had no doubts in his mind as to the culpability of the Dyka clan. They operated a space station that encouraged and profited from human and alien trafficking. They were slave traders and Remmy could think of few crimes as heinous as that. He killed the Dyka fighters indiscriminately. They were between him and getting the humans to freedom. So, he fired straight into the group. A few ran, colliding into walls. One went the wrong way, tripped on the railing around the top of the ramp, and fell down the shaft. The rest were shot. The soft alloy bullets tore through flesh and ripped internal organs to pieces. Blood sprayed in a dark cloud around them. A few managed to squeeze the trigger on their laser rifles. The light flash from the laser blasts were like lightning. None of the laser shots came near to Remmy. He kept moving up the ramp.

When his rifle bucked in his hands, he hit the magazine release. The curved metal dropped to the deck at his feet while Remmy rammed a fresh one into place from the belt inside his coat. He ripped back the charging lever and moved quickly past the dead.

Suddenly, emergency lighting came on. One light panel for every three lit with a dim glow. It left shadows and gloom, but there was enough light to see by. The masses on the main deck were working their way toward the docking arms or other ramps that led to the upper decks of the station. Remmy guessed that the merchants and vendors had quarters on the station. He held his place at the top of the ramp wishing he had a comlink to his companions down below.

GIGI, Remmy thought, *it looks like we've got a chance to escape. I'm going to move the slaves toward the ship now. Inform Captain Darius.*

Acknowledged, Master Sergeant. The captain has been informed. Be advised that the back-up squad was just ordered to go after Lieutenant Colt. Their orders are to stop him any way they can.

That was a surprise. Remmy didn't know what was going on with the Lieutenant or what exactly had happened outside the station, but the timing of the explosion and loss of power had worked in his favor.

Copy that. Stand-by for updates.

Remmy turned and ran back down the ramp.

"Time to go!" He shouted. "Everyone move this way. Quickly, quickly!"

"Where do you want me, Sarge?" Tex asked.

"Fall back, assist Hugo. He can't leave that descending ramp until this level is clear of the slaves. Then the two of you cover one another as you move back and catch up to us."

"Roger that," Tex said. "See you up top."

Remmy led the slaves up the ramp. He had no trouble out pacing them and stopped at the ramp entrance to look around. Anyone thinking about fleeing down the ramp was dissuaded from that notion by the dead members of the Dyka clan.

Suddenly there was another rending sound, a true cacophony that made Remmy drop to one knee and raise his rifle. A second later the lights went out again.

What's happening out there, GIGI? Remmy asked.

It appears one of the slave ships has crashed into the side of the space station. Captain Darius warns you that with the rush to get away from the station, many of the ships are flying erratically. You must move the human slaves to your vessel with all due haste.

Roger that, Remmy thought, then an alarm began to wail. Several laser blasts were heard. Remmy raised his rifle up to peer through the night vision aiming device. There were still several hundred people on the main deck. Some were frozen in the dark, others were running blind.

"What's the situation, Master Sergeant?" Laila asked.

"Chaos," he replied. "A ship just crashed into the station."

"If we lose air pressure, we're all dead," she pointed out, not that Remmy wasn't already thinking of that.

"We have to keep moving," Remmy said. "Get these people to our ship, Laila. The rest of us will fend off anyone who interferes."

"Watch yourself, Master Sergeant," she replied.

"Aye-aye, Staff Sergeant," he responded.

Stepping out toward the chaos, he flicked the fire indicator on his LTX pack to three round burst mode. There were a hundred different species of aliens still in the marketplace, and for the first time, Remmy realized that none of them were combative. Most were terrified. When one came close to him, he could have shot it. The creature was short, with narrow shoulders and a body that resembled a caterpillar. He saw that it had a belt with a small pistol in a makeshift holster, but it didn't have the weapon drawn in one of its many hands. It just shuffled forward; arms outstretched in the hope of not running into anything.

"Not this way!" Remmy shouted.

The alien turned away immediately, even before his language device could translate his words. He decided the alien could discern the danger in his voice and made a good decision.

Across the open expanse many of the vendor carts and booths had been knocked down. There were bodies and debris on the floor, along with the scattered goods that had been for sale. Behind him, Laila led the human slaves along the wall. Unlike most of the beings on the space station, they didn't fear the dark. They kept one hand on the person in front of them and one on the wall. Laila had her head lamp on. It attracted a few frightened alien people. Remmy stayed close enough to warn them off. Once he fired his rifle over the head of a wide bodied, furry alien. The report of the weapon was enough to send it back in the other direction.

Laila reached the corridor to where the slave ship was docked and went down it. Remmy stayed in the market area, guarding the way. He turned on his head lamp but rotated it around so that it shown behind him onto the corridor the humans were hurrying down. He kept watch with his rifle and directed the other former captives where to go.

"Here! This way," he shouted, waving one arm. There was enough reflection off the walls from his headlamp to make him into a shadowy, but visible figure. "Keep moving!"

The aliens undoubtedly couldn't understand him, but they could see the light and were drawn to it. They saw the human slaves and Remmy waving to them.

"Let's go, let's go," he shouted. "There's room for all of you."

Time seemed to creep by as the aliens shuffled toward the corridor where the slave ship waited to carry them to safety. When the last few aliens went past Remmy, he turned and looked for Hugo and Tex. They weren't there.

"Staff Sergeant!" Remmy shouted.

"Here!" Laila called.

"Get these people off the station," he said. "I'm going back to get Hugo and Tex."

"Roger that, Master Sergeant. Good luck!"

Remmy reached up and clicked off the head lamp hoping he didn't need luck. But in combat anything could happen. He set his mind on finding his men and didn't allow himself to consider any other option but total success.

CHAPTER 42

"WE'VE BEEN ORDERED to stop the LT," Dirk Oliver said.

"What?" Ricky Thompson asked.

"He's gone off the reservation," Leigh Ann Poh said. "What do you think that explosion was?"

"He wouldn't have fired without provocation," Ricky said.

"Do you even know what that word means?" Leigh Ann asked.

"Yeah," Ricky said. "I think I do."

"I never knew an officer who did the rational thing all the time," Izzy interjected.

"Listen up!" Dirk snapped. "I don't care what's happening to the lieutenant. He might be having a breakdown or he might be under attack. Our job is to get him back but we are going to be careful."

He pulled out a pair of straps with titanium carabiners on either end. He locked one on each side of his space suit and handed the other ends to Leigh Ann Poh and Ricky Thomson.

"I'm not losing you guys out there," Dirk said. "We stay together, do what we can, but let's be realistic... we don't have the fire power to bring down the LT in that MECH suit. If he won't listen to reason, that's on him. Anyone got a problem with that?"

"No sergeant," Poh said.

Ricky Thompson shook his head.

"What about me, Sergeant?" Izzy asked.

"Stay here and monitor that hatch into the space station."

"Can't GIGI do that?"

"Do you really want to leave it up to a computer if Master Sergeant Steel and the others run into problems? You man that portal until you hear from them."

"Yes, Sergeant," Izzy said, clearly angry about the situation.

Dirk ignored Izzy's attitude as he turned to Poh and Thompson. "Alright, follow my lead. Check your thrusters," he instructed.

They checked the compressed air thrusters that were part of their space suits. Normally, commandos operating in open space used rocket packs, but all the trio had was the air that came as part of the space armor. It wouldn't be enough to fly them far through space. Still, they walked side by side to the edge of the ramp and jumped out into the darkness.

Dirk Oliver turned and looked back toward the space station. Lieutenant Colt was hovering above them and firing his machine guns onto a clusters of alien slave ships that were attempting to escape.

"He's fighting the aliens," Ricky said. "They must have been a threat."

"Or he's lost his marbles," Leigh Ann Poh said.

"Let's maneuver back to the ship. We'll secure ourselves on the roof of the shuttle, then I'll try to reach him."

They used their thrusters to rotate their bodies and send them slowly drifting back toward the drone shuttle they had just left. There was just enough gravity along the top that the trio of Marines could stand and move.

"Lock us in," Dirk told Poh. "You'll be the anchor."

"He's too far out for you to reach alone," Ricky observed.

"Then you'll go with me, Corporal. Leigh Ann can tow us back in once we've got him."

It was a simple plan. Dirk didn't think it would work, but it might get the Lieutenant's attention. He wasn't answering communications, which Dirk thought was a bad sign. That, added to his disobeying a direct order and then firing on the space station, was enough to give the cautious Sergeant a bad feeling about his commanding officer.

As soon as Leigh Ann Poh had locked herself to the surface of the shuttle with another short strap, Dirk and Rick jumped upward. They drifted through space toward the Lieutenant, who fired a series of rockets at a pair of fleeing slave ships. Dirk watched the tether between himself and Leigh Ann. As it neared the end of its reach, he fired his thrusters to slow his ascent. Ricky kept going. Dirk felt stupid. He didn't understand his orders or why three good Marines should risk their lives to stop their lieutenant. Micky Colt had been a good man, might still be a good man, Dirk wasn't sure. But he knew they were taking risks to rescue him from whatever had caused him to go rogue. And Dirk didn't think his life was worth less than an officer's. He was starting to question everything about their mission

"Almost there," Ricky said, which was good because he was nearly at the end of his tether.

"Careful, Corporal," Dirk said.

Ricky reached up and grabbed the wide foot of Micky Colt's MECH suit.

"Got him! Reel us in," Ricky cried.

"Great job, Ricky," Leigh Ann Poh said.

The last thought that went through Dirk Oliver's mind was that Ricky Thompson had made an excellent maneuver to catch onto the lieutenant on his first try. Then, noticing that he was being pulled down, Micky Colt leaned forward and fired a burst from his machine gun mounted just inside the forearm of the MECH suit. The bullets mostly either missed or deflected off the armor plates in Dirk's space suit. But one found a seam and ripped it open. The sudden exposure to sub-freezing temperatures froze flesh and stopped Dirk's beating heart in less than a second. He went limp.

But the kinetic energy from the barrage sent Dirk Oliver's body moving back down. Ricky Thompson lost his grip on his commanding officer's foot. He shouted in concern. From the top of the shuttle Leigh Ann Poh raised her rifle and fired. Her bullets launched into space and sped toward the Lieutenant. Two went wide of his MECH suit, but three hit the missile compartment and set one off. In his designs, Lieutenant Micky Colt hadn't thought of someone below shooting up at him would be a threat. There was no armor on the bottom of the missile compartment since it faced straight down. That oversight allowed Poh's bullets to cause catastrophic damage to the suit. The explosion sent the Lieutenant reeling through space. The damage also wrecked the MECH's computer system, which shut down, leaving Micky Colt completely helpless.

"Shogun, this is Ronan six," Leigh Ann Poh said via her helmet's comlink. "Sergeant Oliver is down. I repeat, Sergeant Dirk Oliver is KIA, requesting orders."

She could hear Ricky Thompson crying.

"Ricky! Are you hurt?"

"No," he said, sniffing loudly on his comlink. "I didn't mean for anything bad to happen."

"It's alright," Leigh Ann said as she pulled the strap that connected her to Dirk Oliver's body and him to Ricky. "Just stay calm. I'm pulling you back in."

Everything was going wrong. She felt a sense of fear and furious anger as she pulled Dirk's body down to the ship. His helmet had protected his head, but the rest of his body was frozen solid. She pushed him down and kept pulling Ricky back by the tether. It wasn't until he was back on top of the shuttle with her that she noticed the bullet holes in the ceiling of the drone ship.

"Izzy, are you okay down there?" Leigh Ann asked.

There was no reply. Ricky Thompson dropped to his knees and bent over the back of the shuttle to get a view inside.

"She's hit!" He cried out.

"Shogun, we have a problem," she declared. "Our drone ship was hit in the fire fight. I repeat, the drone ship was hit by Lieutenant Colt's gun fire."

"What do we do?" Ricky asked.

"We might be in a real mess," she said. "Let's get back in and see what we can do to help Izzy and repair this bird before she has to fly us back to the *Renegade*."

CHAPTER 43

"GIGI, what's the status on that shuttle," Darius demanded.

"Hull is compromised, Captain," the computer aided voice replied. "I am unable to make repairs."

"Can you fly it?"

"Affirmative, Captain Darius. The shuttle is still space worthy, but until the hull is repaired, I cannot seal up the interior and pressurize the ship."

"Meaning, no one not in a space suit can fly in it," the chief engineer said.

"That's a problem," Ramos said.

"What's the status on Lieutenant Colt?"

"Still not responding to hails or communications, Captain," Ensign Bertoli said.

"He's in a tumble through space," Vivian Ramos said. "It doesn't appear that he has any control of his MECH suit."

Do we have any idea if he's alive or dead?" Darius asked.

The crew were quiet. Darius wanted to slam his fist onto his chair, but he couldn't let them see his frustration. He was the captain.

His decisions were life and death to the ship and her crew. They needed to believe he always had the answers. But deep down inside he felt a stab of guilt over sending Sergeant Oliver to bring in Lieutenant Colt. It had cost the Marine his life, and besides the fact that they couldn't afford to lose any more Marines, he felt like he had pulled the trigger that killed Dirk Oliver himself.

He shook off his feelings, shoving them deep down inside himself to be dealt with later. There were still human slaves on the space station to save.

"Sir, we are in position now. I have us forty-five thousand kilometers from the space station," Vivian said. "But this is about to be a busy place. I have fifteen ships leaving the station, and another eighteen in the area making moves for open space."

"Is that a problem for us, Lieutenant?" Darius asked.

"Not us, Captain. But it will be for the slave ship. They can't get away without crashing. Not for a while yet. And who knows what's happening inside."

"GIGI, what's Master Sergeant Steel's status?"

"The last of the captives are boarding the slave ship, Captain. Master Sergeant Steel is returning to help Sergeant Hugo McManus and Corporal Tyler Fry in their retreat."

Suddenly and idea hit Darius like a slap in the face. He turned and looked at Henry Nash.

"Lieutenant, we have power to the artificial gravity, correct?"

"Aye, Captain."

"Does that include the gravity beam generator?" Darius asked.

Nash's face lit up as he realized what Darius was saying.

"Captain, that's brilliant," he said. "Yes, the beam generator works. We can use it to move the debris out of our way."

"Very good, Lieutenant. Make it happen. I want us in close and every other ship out of our way. Can we do that?"

"Aye, Captain, we sure can," Henry declared. "Pete, I'm transferring control of the gravity beam generator to your station."

"I have it, Lieutenant. One moment," Pete Best said. "Can we reverse the beam so that we're pushing things away instead of pulling them in?"

"Affirmative," Henry said.

"Oh, this is going to be fun," Pete said.

"Sir, I'm getting a hail from the slave ship," Ensign Bertoli said.

Before Darius could answer GIGI spoke up. "The slave ship has been impacted, Captain Darius. All systems offline. Emergency power to life support only."

"Put it through," Darius said.

"Shogun Actual, this is Ronan Four, we have a major problem here. We just got hit by something. I've lost power it seems."

"What's your status, Staff Sergeant?" Darius asked.

"We've been ripped away from the space station, Captain. I have the refugees on board and we're okay for the moment, but I can't communicate with GIGI or control the ship. And sir, Master Sergeant Steel, Sergeant McManus, and Corporal Fry are still on the space station."

Darius felt his heart drop into his stomach.

"Very good, Staff Sergeant. We are on our way to help you. Just hang on and keep those refugees as safe as possible. Can you do that?"

"Affirmative, Captain."

"Very good, Staff Sergeant. Darius out."

He felt his face stiffen. Tears stung his eyes.

"Sir, can't they take the shuttle drone back?" Lori Lee asked.

"Not if the hull is compromised," Darius said. "They don't have space armor."

"We can send another ship for them," Vivian suggested.

Before Darius could respond to that suggestion, another explosion went off. Even at a distance, they could see a fiery ejection from the space station, followed by gas and debris. Time was running out for Remmy Steel and his men. And the *Renegade* was still too far away to help. Darius cleared his throat.

"ETA to the station?"

"We're moving as fast as safely possible sir," Vivian said. "One thousand kilometers an hour."

"That's too long," Darius said softly. Then he bowed his head and whispered a prayer for his friend.

CHAPTER 44

REMMY RAN BACK to the spiral ramp but there was no sign of Hugo or Tex. There was a tremor in the floor the station. Remmy knew that was a bad sign.

Any updates? Remmy asked the alien artifact which was his only connection to the *Renegade* and his escape from the space station.

The slave ship is secure with all refugees inside.

And Staff Sergeant McPherson?

Present and accounted for. She is monitoring things from the ship's Bridge.

Remmy felt better knowing she was safe. He didn't think he was treating her any differently than he had before they became romantically involved, but he was relieved that she wasn't on the space station any longer.

It was dark in the shaft leading down to the holding cells. Remmy pulled off his headlamp to make sure it was turned off. He stuffed it in the pocket of his coat and looked down the ramp through the aiming device on top of his rifle. There was no movement, but he remembered well the aliens he had shot and killed who were moving down that same ramp. Still, his men were down there, and he wouldn't let fear keep him from doing whatever he could to help them.

He hurried down the ramp, but moved quietly and kept his rifle ready to fire. When he reached the bottom of the ramp, he swung his rifle back and forth. There were eight enemy fighters with their laser rifles held ready to shoot. Only they couldn't see anything in the darkness. Halfway between them and where Remmy stood, Hugo McManus was bent over Tex's body. The big man no longer had his rifle. In its place he had a pistol in his left hand, and his combat knife in the other. He couldn't see either but was ready for a fight. Remmy felt sorry for the alien who got too close to him.

Moving laterally, Remmy reached the side wall of the hatch that led into the holding cell corridor. He got down on one knee and lined up his targets. As a Marine he had spent thousands of hours on the shooting range taking out targets that were no different than the hairy aliens he faced at that moment and thousands more hours on Fleet ships running simulations against all manner of enemies. He didn't have to think about what to do. With his left thumb he slid the fire control to fully automatic. He lined up the targets to the far left, then with a smooth, sweeping version, he opened fire, moving the rifle from left to right and ending with a turn that moved him behind the wall. During the barrage two aliens had pulled the trigger on their weapons, but they weren't aiming at him. The laser blasts sizzled through empty space and smashed into the metal walls, leaving scorched, smoking metal.

Remmy rolled back out, sweeping the corridor with his rifle again. All the targets were down.

"Sergeant, you hit?"

"Bastards ruined my favorite rifle," McManus said. "I'm a little crispy along the edges, but not hurt, Master Sergeant."

Hugo hadn't moved, not even when the firing started. He was already low to the ground using his body to shield his friend. And he had recognized the human rifle, knowing whoever was firing in the corridor was on his side. But it was still too dark for him to see and he wasn't sure if the danger had passed.

"You have to watch these hairy savages," Hugo continued. "Just because they go down don't mean they're out of the fight."

"Copy that," Remmy said, pulling the head lamp from his pocket. He switched it on and slid it away from his position out into the corridor. None of the aliens moved. They weren't groaning or making noise like the wounded usually did either. His barrage had been enough to take them all down in the darkness.

"How's Tex?" Remmy asked.

"Busted leg," Corporal Fry said in a raspy voice. "I can't walk."

"Don't worry about that," Hugo said.

"I've got you covered, pull him out of there, Sergeant," Remmy ordered.

Hugo sheathed his knife and slipped his pistol back into his belt. Then he bent over and picked the lanky Corporal up and secured him over one shoulder. Tex grunted in pain.

"I think he passed out," Hugo said, moving back toward the light.

"How bad is it?" Remmy asked.

"Bad," Hugo said. "He'll need surgery to repair his knee."

"Bleeding?"

"Cauterized mostly, but I think we should tie it off just to be safe. Can we get to the ship?"

"That's the plan," Remmy said.

Master Sergeant, unfortunately the slave ship was knocked out of its berth by a collision, GIGI said. The words were clear in his mind but caused Remmy's heart to skip a beat. *The passengers are safe, but you cannot leave the space station in the slave ship.*

Alternatives? Remmy said as he led the way up the ramp.

The shuttle is docked but under repairs. I will lead you to the docking berth.

They were almost at the top of the ramp when another explosion rocked the station and parts of the ceiling began to fall. Remmy stopped in the hatch. Hugo was right behind him, one beefy hand on the Master Sergeant's shoulder.

"What the hell was that?" McManus asked.

"Nothing good," he said.

Move to your right, Master Sergeant.

Right? Not left? You sure?

The drone shuttle is in a berth one level above you. Move quickly. There should be another way up.

Remmy had seen other beings running for the ramps that led up higher into the station. Remmy also knew the explosion had come from higher up in the station. He didn't want to get caught in the next blast, but there was no other way out.

"This way," Remmy said.

He moved quickly. Hugo seemed to have no problem keeping up even though he was carrying a full-grown man.

"You good, Sergeant? Need a rest?"

"Negative, I'm good," Hugo said. "Keep going."

They had to navigate around debris. Remmy found another ramp leading down. Discouragement was trying to defeat him, but he pushed himself forward. There were cries for help from the injured who had been in the marketplace. Some had been trampled, others caught under the vendor stalls when they collapsed. Remmy had no doubt that some had probably been attacked when the panic set into the rowdy crowd. They waded through puddles of spilled liquor and around unidentifiable mechanical components that were as big as Remmy was. Eventually they found ramp leading upward.

"Smell that?" Hugo asked.

"Smoke," Remmy said.

"What I wouldn't do for a battle helmet right now," the big man said.

"GIGI, what are we looking for? There's a fire up here. We can't waste time."

Berth twenty-eight. I'll help you interpret the alien numbers, Master Sergeant.

"Come on," Remmy said. "It can't be far."

"Good. Our boy here ain't getting any lighter."

"Need help?"

"Nah, I got this, Sarge. You just get us out of here."

Remmy searched for the first docking slip. There were markings above it. He stared at the lettering for a moment, then realized it said thirty-two.

"We're close," Remmy said. He hurried past the next two corridors without even look. The third said twenty-nine. "Almost there."

They were both coughing. The smoke was getting thick and flickering light was shining down through a hole in the ceiling.

The shuttle has been temporarily repaired, GIGI said.

"Thank God. We're almost there. Let them know we're coming. And once we are on board, notify Captain Darius."

I will do both, Master Sergeant.

Remmy checked the writing above the fourth corridor. It said twenty-eight although he had no idea how he knew that. Doubt cut through him like a hot knife. Maybe he was losing his mind. What if he had led Hugo and Tex to the wrong place? Would they be able to escape? His legs felt weak but at the end of the hallway the hatch opened and Ricky Thompson in full space armor waved them on.

"Come on, hurry," he said.

Remmy stepped aside and let Hugo pass through first. Then he followed. They floated through a connection tunnel, and then had to go one by one through the airlock onto the drone shuttle. When Remmy stepped in, he felt a sense of relief.

. . .

"We're on board, GIGI".

Unlocking the docking clamps, the alien device said. *Please have everyone secured. There is a lot of space traffic and debris around the station.*

Copy that, Remmy thought. "Alright people, strap in. Looks like this is going to be a bumpy ride."

"I hope not," Leigh Ann Poh said. "We filled the holes in the hull with expanding foam. Who knows how that will hold up."

Remmy saw that Tex wasn't the only casualty. Izzy Berry was slumped against the bulkhead, but already strapped in place. There was a hole in the very top of her shoulder, and blood on the deck. Hugo was seeing to Tex and on the floor of the passenger compartment lay Sergeant Dirk Oliver.

"What happened?" Remmy asked.

"Lieutenant Colt went crazy," Ricky Thompson said.

"We were ordered to bring him back and he fired on us," Leigh Ann said, her voice quivering. "Sergeant Oliver was killed, Izzy was wounded."

"And the LT?" Remmy asked.

"We lost contact," Leigh Ann said. "I don't know if he's dead or alive."

Remmy felt his gut tighten. They had lost another good Marine, and two more were wounded. He didn't know what had happened to Lieutenant Colt but he felt a quiet rage building up inside him. He couldn't imagine anything that would cause him to fire on his own people.

"We get them back to the ship and they'll be okay," Hugo said.

"Thanks to you," Remmy said.

"You would have done it for me," he replied.

"Well, you made it look easy."

The joke fell flat. No one felt like laughing. They were trapped in the shuttle with no idea what was going on around them, but with death looking them straight in the eye. Remmy didn't like losing people ever, and yet, he couldn't help but feel like they had accomplished something important.

"We saved forty-four humans from a fate worse than death," Remmy said. "Dirk didn't die in vain."

"I'm not sure I believe that," Leigh Ann said quietly. "The Lieutenant has a lot to answer for."

"No doubt," Ricky Thompson said.

"Then we'll make sure he does," Remmy said. "You have my word."

CHAPTER 45

"ALMOST THERE," Ramos said.

"Can you bring in the slave ship?" Darius asked.

"Aye, Captain," Pete Best replied. "I've got it. Reeling in the slave ship now."

They watched as the crumpled looking ship was pulled into the open mouth of the fish shaped *Renegade*. Darius breathed a little sight of relief knowing the slaves had been saved.

"Captain Darius," GIGI spoke up. "We are approaching the *Renegade*. Please have medical personnel standing by the primary hangar."

"We do," Darius said. "Lieutenant Ramos, as soon as that shuttle is secure take us out of here."

"Captain, I think I see Lieutenant Colt on my screen," Pete Best said.

"Is he moving?"

"Still in an uncontrolled spin, sir," Best said.

"Can we reach him?"

"We will be moving in that direction, Captain," Vivian Ramos said.

"Very well, pull him in, too. He has a lot to answer for."

They ship was surrounded by derelict vessels and slave ships of all kinds trying to escape. The space station was smoking. There had been two more explosions since Master Sergeant Steel had escaped. Darius was glad to have all his people back on the ship, even though some were injured, and one was dead. It infuriated him that Lieutenant Colt had fired on his own people. But while his anger was boiling against the Lieutenant, his personal guilt for having sent the Marines after him was even more potent. He had made a bad a call. Master Sergeant Steel had infiltrated an alien space station, found and rescued over forty humans and twice that number of alien captives. Yet he had only lost one man, who Darius hoped would survive to fight another day. How was it then that Darius, sitting thousands of kilometers away in safety, had made such a terrible decision? He couldn't say. Perhaps he was losing his edge. A fleet captain had to think fast on his feet and make good decisions. But it seemed like Darius was stumbling in his responsibilities to guide the ship and protect his crew.

"Drone ship is secured," Vivian announced.

"Turning to heading two-eight-four," the chief engineer added.

Darius watched as they pushed other ships out of the way. There were collisions around the *Renegade*. Small bits of debris had impacted the sonic screens. But his officers knew their business. They were performing better than their captain, in his opinion.

"I have him!" Pete Best said. "I've got Lieutenant Colt."

"Get him on board," Darius said. "If he's alive, I want him questioned. Commander Lee..."

"Aye, Captain, I'll see to it personally."

"Nurek, get your people down to the slave ship," Darius continued. "There are a lot of captives that will need your assistance."

"Yes, Captain," Nurek said, getting to his feet with a bow. "Thank you for allowing me to help them."

Darius watched the alien go. An hour later they were clear of the debris field and headed toward a portal that would take them to the

Zutek star cluster. Darius looked at the plot which showed the smoking space station. It was dwindling and dark, soon to be just another derelict space vessel, another large piece of junk among many. Darius couldn't help but feel that what he was seeing was a lesson on the nature of life. Nothing lasted forever, he knew. No nation was supreme above others forever, no empires lasted for eternity.

For the moment his people were safe. Remmy and his team had returned. The slaves and captives were free. Even Lieutenant Colt had survived and would be held to account. Everything in his little kingdom was right again.

"Setting course for the transition portal," Vivian Ramos said.

"Main engine is back online, Captain," Nash said. "Not bad for a bunch of bots."

"Not bad indeed," Darius replied. "How far to the jump point?"

"One hundred eighty thousand kilometers, Captain," Ramos replied. "We should make hyperspace in just under three hours."

"Very good," Darius said. "And the plot?"

"Clear Captain. No other ships are in this vector or heading this way."

"Seems a shame to let them go," Pete Best said. "They are all slave traders. I don't think they should be allowed to return to their evil ways."

"That's not our mission," Darius said.

"What is our mission now that we've rescued the human slaves, sir?" Ensign Bertoli asked.

Darius felt tired. He knew what he wanted, but the *Renegade* wasn't his ship. Nor did he have the right to keep the crew from returning home. They had set out to challenge the Imperium and give the galaxy a chance to throw off the chains of bondage. Whether they did that or not was up to them. Darius had come close to losing the ship and the crew. He felt like perhaps it was time to go home.

"We'll take these captives to the free worlds," Darius said. "After that, I'm not sure."

He got to his feet. It had been a few days since he had gotten any real sleep.

"Lieutenant Ramos, how long will we be in hyperspace?"

"Forty-two hours, Captain," she said.

"What about our laser cannons?" Darius asked the chief engineer.

"The bots are working. I'm hoping they can get the external work done before they have to come back inside for the journey through hyperspace."

"Very good. It seems you all have things well in hand. Lieutenant Ramos, you have the con."

"Aye, Captain," she said. "I have the con."

"I'm going to check in with Doctor Lanski in the Med Bay and then I'm going to sleep for the next twelve hours. But you have my permission to wake me in case of an emergency."

"Aye, Captain," Ramos said.

"Sleep well, sir. You've earned it," Best said.

Darius thought about his performance in the Olotimbo system and on the mission to save the human slaves. He didn't think he had earned a rest. More likely, a stern reprimand, which he was certain to face once they went home. Everything would change in the Sol system. Defenses would be built, ships launched, exploratory missions across the galaxy. He was too tired to think much about that.

He drifted slowly down the gravity tube that separated the command section of the ship from the commerce and storage area. When he reached Epsilon deck and stepped back into regular gravity the weight of his own body seemed almost more than he could bear. He moved to the wall and leaned against it.

"Sir, are you okay?"

Darius looked up and saw Master Sergeant Remmy Steel hurrying toward him. There was a genuine look of concern on the Marine's face. It touched Darius that the war hero cared about his well-being.

"Fine, just tired," Darius said. "It's nothing some sleep won't cure."

"You should be headed up to your quarters, Captain," Remmy said. "I can escort you up there if you like."

"No, I'll be alright. Besides, I need to find out what happened with Lieutenant Colt."

"You and me, both, sir," Remmy said.

They were met just inside the Med Bay by Doctor Lanski. He looked harried and the beds were full of people from the space station. The pregnant women were in beds with monitors and IVs, but so were all the other people including the children. Most had trays of food on their bedside tables. The lights in the Med Bay were turned down to a soft glow, and there was some chatter between the rescued slaves. Darius listened to it for a moment.

"Seems like they're getting along just fine," Remmy said.

"They will, in time," Doctor Lanski said. "They're all malnourished. They've got bad teeth, poor vision, weak circulatory systems. I'll be honest, I've only read of such horrible conditions in textbooks."

"But they'll survive," Darius said. "That's the most important thing."

"Yes, I suppose it is," Lanski said. "Your Marines are in surgery, Master Sergeant. And they'll be in recovery for several hours at least. You can get some rest and then see them."

"Good advice," Remmy said. "Captain Darius and I were just talking about that."

"I hope you'll take it."

"We will," Darius said. "But first we need to see Lieutenant Colt."

"Yes, I thought you might," Doctor Lanski said leading the way to a booth at the far end of the medical ward. "I was planning to sedate him, but I waited in case you wanted to see him. I'll warn you, it's not a pretty sight."

Doctor Lanski pressed a panel on the wall and the opaque material became transparent. A hidden speaker was also activated, and they could hear Micky Colt hissing. His neck and face were covered with scratches that had drawn blood. His legs and feet were held to the bed rails with thick straps.

"What happened?" Darius said.

"Insanity, I think," Lanski said. "I'll admit, I made a mistake releasing him from care. Whatever that parasite was, it's had a devastating effect on his mental health."

"Kill, kill, kill you," Colt muttered. "Blood."

"You're sure it's from the parasite?" Darius asked.

"Nothing is certain," Lanski said. "My guess is the time he was trapped in his MECH armor was not good. That could be the source for much of what you're seeing."

"But he fired on his own Marines before that," Remmy said. "He disobeyed orders and then turned on his own platoon."

"That is correct," Lanski said.

"I talked to him just minutes before that happened," Darius said. "He seemed fine. He wasn't exactly his old self, but he wasn't anything like this."

"He fooled all of us," Remmy said. "I knew he was acting strange, but not crazy."

"You're going to sedate him?"

"That's correct, Captain. I want to run scans, get a look at his brain, if possible. We definitely need to get another internal scan of his brain stem and see if we can find the parasite. Also, I think it's a good idea if we keep him away from the rest of the crew. Whatever has gotten into him will eventually shed his body in search of a new host."

"You mean he's contagious?"

"Every parasite is," Doctor Lanski said. "And we certainly can't take any chances on this ship."

"Drink your blood, Steel," Colt said in a harsh grunting voice.

He stuck out his tongue and there was blood on it where he had bitten into it.

"That's enough," Lanski said.

He typed in some orders on the touch pad. Sedatives were pumped into Lieutenant Micky Colt's blood stream, and he seemed to melt into the bed as unconsciousness took over.

"I'm sorry for that," Lanski said. "He's a sick man. Don't give it another thought."

"He wants a piece of me, he's welcome to come and get it," Remmy said. "Dirk Oliver was a good man. And Izzy Berry could have been killed too."

"But she wasn't. The surgical bots will repair her shoulder and patch up her lung. She'll be out of commission for a month or so, but she'll live," Lanski said.

"We should question the captives you freed, Master Sergeant," Darius said as he turned and looked back at the rows of thin, unstable bodies lying in the medical beds.

"Not now," Doctor Lanski said. "Nothing they know is vital. It can wait. You should both rest. Doctor's orders."

"Fine," Darius said. "Just as soon as I check on the other refugees."

"There's no need," Lanski said. "I've seen to them. They aren't sick or injured like those you rescued in the Olotimbo system. And the Dudonus are seeing to their every need."

"Looks like our work here is done," Remmy said.

Darius was slower to agree, but he couldn't think of a reason to argue. The Captain and NCO made their way back to the Command section. Once there, Darius offered Remmy a drink.

"I've got some decent Scotch in my cabin," Darius said. "You probably don't need anything to help you sleep, but I'm having one."

"A drink with the captain, how could I say no," Remmy said.

"You can, of course. You've certainly earned your rest, Master Sergeant. Forty-four slaves rescued. The initial report said there was fighting on the space station. Yet you managed to pull it off without getting yourself or any of your people killed."

"They weren't prepared," Remmy said. "And my people are damn good, Captain."

"Yes, this ship is filled with the best of the best. I fear I'm the one falling short."

They went into his cabin. Remmy took a seat in a comfortable, human size chair that had been produced in the manufacturing plant. It looked like tufted leather and was stuffed with something very soft. As Remmy sat down the seat seemed to wrap around him.

Captain Darius poured up two tumblers with the Scotch. He handed one to Remmy and sat in an identical chair straight across from him.

"To a successful mission," Darius said, holding up his glass.

"Of which this is one," Remmy added.

They both took a sip. The warm liquid had a woody taste as it rolled across Darius' tongue. He felt a wave of warmth waft through his body as it slid down his throat.

"Oh, that's very nice, Captain. Maybe the best I've ever had," Remmy said. He took another sip.

"I'm glad you like it. You're welcome to it any time, Master Sergeant. It seems you'll be the acting lieutenant for the rest of this cruise. You'll have to get used to being an officer."

"Doubt that, sir. And I'm happy to remain Master Sergeant."

Darius leaned forward. "I'm thinking about taking us home once we've delivered the captives you freed, and the volunteers, to the free worlds," he said. "We're taking too many chances, losing too many people."

"Sir, please forgive my candor, but what happened to Sergeant Oliver and Corporal Berry was not your fault."

"I sent them after Colt."

"And they did their duty. Doesn't matter what the order is, we carry it out. That's what we sign up for, sir. We know the risks and the rewards."

"But if I had just let Colt go..."

"We might all be dead," Remmy said. "I don't know why he fired on the space station, but it nearly destroyed the place, sir. If you hadn't stopped him and he had fired another rocket it could have breached the hull or caused an even bigger internal explosion. Your order saved lives, Captain. There's no doubt about that."

Darius took another sip. He appreciated what Remmy was saying, and even thought that maybe the Master Sergeant was right, but he still felt terrible. The weight of his actions was drowning him and he didn't know how to deal with it. Normally, he would go back to face a formal inquiry into his actions. Everything would be looked at, from his decisions to the way his crew responded to orders. When it was all said and done, he would either be exonerated or held to account. He had always felt it was a good system. Accountability was one of the ways he stayed sane.

"I'm sure things will appear differently after I've had some rest."

"No doubt about that, sir," Remmy said, before finishing his tumbler of Scotch. "I appreciate the drink, Captain. That is very generous of you, sir."

"It's nothing," Darius said, as they both stood up. "Master Sergeant, you have to promise me something."

"What's that?"

"It's just, if you think I'm going in the wrong direction, you'll tell me. I'm surrounded by people who don't think independently of my orders. But you can. You're not afraid to tell me the truth."

"I doubt that would ever be necessary," Remmy said.

"But it might. You know, there's something about this ship, Master Sergeant. I don't know if you feel it, but I sometimes feel like I could live here for the rest of my life."

"It's a fine ship, sir," Remmy said.

"Maybe too fine. It's luxurious. And powerful. I almost got us killed in the Olotimbo system because I felt I really could take on the Ashi fleet."

"We didn't have much choice, sir."

"Yeah, we were trapped there, weren't we? Until you found us a way out, Master Sergeant."

"I got lucky, sir."

"No, you've got good instincts, Master Sergeant. If you'd been in the fleet instead of the Marine Corps, you'd have been fast tracked for a ship command. I need you, Remmy. I need a friend who will give it to me straight. Can you do that?"

"If that's what you want," Remmy said.

"It's what I want, and more importantly, it's what we all need. There's a very hostile galaxy out there, Master Sergeant. I'd feel better if we tackled it together."

Darius stuck out his hand. Remmy hesitated for a moment, then shook it.

"Get some rest, Remmy. You've earned it. We've got a few days in hyperspace, then we've got to make some hard decisions."

"Yes, sir, I'll be ready, Captain."

Darius watched him go. He wondered if on his best day he was half the man that Remmy Steel was. They had taken separate career paths and both had success, but Darius felt his confidence starting to slip. The weight of command was getting too heavy. He needed a break.

He walked over to his bed and sat down on it. Sleep was pulling at his eyes. Things would look better with some rest, he knew. But he had to be his best. He couldn't let anything happen to the ship or the crew. Not on his watch. He had to be sure of it. Otherwise, the weight of his guilt would crush him.

As he laid back on the bed and closed his eyes, he wondered for a moment what the future held. He hoped it was good. He hoped they could see a galaxy that was free and prosperous. The thought of that made him smile. Maybe, he hoped, he could be part of it. But there was a threat out there in the darkness. He couldn't see it or even guess what they might do, but he could sense it. There was a terrible reckoning coming ... and Darius would have to face it.

UNTITLED

Author's Note

Thank you for reading *Retribution*. As always, I hope you'll take a moment and leave a rating/review on Amazon or Goodreads. This series has been an incredible journey for me. After writing and publishing over a hundred novels there is still so much to learn about this industry. My hope is to complete the series with the next book, but we'll see how the story unfolds. I do have an outline, but sticking to the outline is hard when a story is as full of twists and surprises as this series has been.

I want to encourage you to join my mailing list. It's the best way to keep up with new book releases. I always send out an email to let my readers know about new books. You can sign up at www.Toby-Neighbors.com

ALSO BY TOBY NEIGHBORS

Joined In Battle

The Abyss Of Savagery

The Vault Of Mysteries

Lords Of Ascension

The Elusive Executioner

Gryphon Warriors

Regulators Revealed

Avondale

Draggah

Balestone

Arcanius

Avondale V

Third Prince

Royal Destiny

The Other Side

The New World

Luck Holds

Zompocalypse

Spartan Company

Spartan Valor

Spartan Guile

Dragon Team Seven

Uncommon Loyalty

Total Allegiance

Kestrel Class

Jump Point

Gravity Flux

Modulus Echo

Zero Friction

Planet Fall

Charter

Jack & Roxie

My Lady Sorceress

The Man With No Hands

ARC Angel

Battle ARC

Broken Crucible

Hidden Kingdom

War INC

Carthage Prime

Cronus Team

Skandia Seven

Mercurial

Magnificus Prime

Incursio

Merlin Appears

Runners

Survivors

Infiltrators

Resistance

Conquest

Occupation

Extraction

The Signal

Battle Orders

Base Of Fire

Hard Site

Recall

Evade

Assault

Space Fever

Staying Alive

Fractal Cut

Blast Zone

Action Zone

Covert Infil

Armor Brigade

Havoc Squad

Thunderbird

Ghost Tactics

Quantum Combat

Infinite Threat

Shadow Threat

Evolving Threat

Lingering Threat

Latent Prowess

Gravity Masters

Gravity Storm

Daughter of the Night

Supernova

Artifact

Blood Moon

Renegade

Juggernaut

With Pete Garcia

Apocalypse One Percenters

www.ingramcontent.com/pod-product-compliance
Lightning Source LLC
Chambersburg PA
CBHW052017240626
47153CB00006B/1843